DEAL WITH THE DEVIL

"Why would Cold Iron's producer make them do something that wasn't good for their career? For that matter, how could he force them, if they really didn't want to?" I asked.

"Mr. Veladora doesn't care about their career," Candy replied. "He cares about power. Especially over elves." She shuddered delicately. "He's a toad. I hate him. But when Jorandel was first starting, he signed this contract, see? With Mr. Veladora as producer. And now he can't get out of it."

"Oh, piffle," I said. "You can always get out of a contract if you can afford a good enough lawyer, which Jorandel certainly can."

She shook her head morosely. "He tried. He went to a whole bunch of lawyers. They all said the same thing. Veladora's contract is unbreakable. It's an elvish thing, 'cause it's a Faerie contract even though it's written in English. It's not magic exactly, but Faerie contracts are more binding, you know. The only way Jorandel can get out of it is by dying. . . ."

COLD IRON

MELISA MICHAELS

A ROC BOOK

ROC
Published by the Penguin Group
Penguin Books USA Inc., 375 Hudson Street,
New York, New York 10014, U.S.A.
Penguin Books Ltd, 27 Wrights Lane,
London W8 5TZ, England
Penguin Books Australia Ltd, Ringwood,
Victoria, Australia
Penguin Books Canada Ltd, 10 Alcorn Avenue,
Toronto, Ontario, Canada M4V 3B2
Penguin Books (N.Z.) Ltd, 182–190 Wairau Road,
Auckland 10, New Zealand

Penguin Books Ltd, Registered Offices:
Harmondsworth, Middlesex, England

First published by Roc, an imprint of Dutton Signet,
a division of Penguin Books USA Inc.

First Printing, August, 1997
10 9 8 7 6 5 4 3 2 1

Printed in the United States of America

For Richard Michaels, our kids, Paul and Melacha Quirke, and my sisters, Ardis Evans and Carla Ellett, without whose love and laughter I would be in deep yogurt; and for Gregory Feely, without whose help this manuscript would still be in my desk drawer.

Special thanks to Poison, Great White, Meatloaf, Bruce Springsteen, Tina Turner, Billy Idol, Guns 'N Roses, Bad Company, Bon Jovi, David Lee Roth, Aerosmith, Huey Lewis and the News, Mozart, and Vivaldi, whose music provided me with hours of harmless pleasure during the writing of this book.

COLD IRON

1

My first sight of Jorandel did nothing to improve my opinion of the kind of elves who abandon Faerie for show business. He was drunk or stoned, I never knew which, and vomiting in the gutter outside one of the most exclusive hotels in San Francisco. Passersby pretended he was invisible. I wished he were. Or I were. I'd been on the job for less than an hour and already I knew it had been a mistake to take it.

Onstage, Jorandel might seem like a god: a long, lean, posturing Adonis with a golden voice and pointed ears and the kind of projected animal magnetism that can make a stadium full of pubescent females turn into a howling, quivering mass of sexual greed and frustration. But that magic dies when the god walks offstage to start guzzling booze, snorting or shooting drugs, groping any females who are still sufficiently dazzled to allow it, and vomiting in the gutter. I'd seen it happen before, back when I still wanted to believe in that kind of magic.

When I found out the kind of elves who go into show business, however much they may look like gods, tend to act like the worst of humans, I walked away. I hadn't willingly listened to elfrock in fifteen years. The last time I'd attended an elfrock concert, I was a preteen runaway in San Francisco's Haight-Ashbury District, trying to recreate the flower-child sixties at a time when the streets were meaner, the drugs were more dangerous, and the naive dream of world peace had long since been battered to an ugly death by reality.

That whole era was a part of my life I had so successfully blocked from my conscious mind that some months earlier, when a halfling told me he had run away from home at the age of nine or ten, I reacted as though I'd never heard of such a thing and couldn't imagine how a mere child could survive alone on the streets. Right. I was almost twelve when I left home. Practically an old woman.

Elfrock concerts and elfrock musicians had seemed the height of romance to a desperate, lonely child of eleven. They did not seem romantic—in fact, they seemed categorically repellent—to the woman I had since become. I no longer felt desperate or lonely, and I no longer believed in romance. I imagined that I was grown-up. I was twenty-seven years old, I had my own house, my own car, and my own half share in a not-quite-failing business. I had a partner who didn't understand me, a client who didn't trust me, and a job I didn't much like anymore. In short, I felt pretty damn sorry for myself, and I didn't even have sense enough to be ashamed of it. And to top it all off, it was the Christmas season: my least favorite of the whole year. Instead of sharing the joyous sense of peace and goodwill rampant all around me, I found myself reverting to sullen childishness, anxiety, obscure resentment, and misery. Not a fun time.

The weather that year was as foul as my mood. After a summer of killing heat, we were now subjected to a winter of driving rains and gray, miserable days when the fog, if it lifted at all, seldom rose much above treetop level. The entire Bay Area seemed permanently encased in damp, dirty cotton wool, the residents permanently affixed to their uniformly drab umbrellas and shapeless raincoats. That morning on the way to work I had bought a new CD of Mozart's *Posthorn Serenade* to play on the office bloodbox, and even listening to that didn't lighten my mood. I suppose I thought that circumstances and/or the gods had conspired to make my life unsatisfactory. I hadn't yet learned that satisfaction is the original do-it-yourself kit: you make your own or you go without. And that was my mental state when I first heard of Jorandel.

Somebody knocked at the office door while the glorious strains of Mozart's serenade floated out the open window, across wet neighboring rooftops, and off toward San Francisco's pastel skyline, invisible somewhere beyond the mist-shrouded bay. I resisted the impulse to shout "Go away!" and, instead, ignored the knock altogether.

My partner had just gone out with her boyfriend to choose their Christmas trees, one large for his mansion in the hills and one small for her apartment on Milky Way. They would, I thought sourly, probably return with some scraggly little branchless twig for the office as well. Or, worse, with a full-scale tree that Shannon would want to set up and decorate even though we had no room for it. Shannon always threw herself wholeheartedly into the holiday spirit. I never did.

The rest of the year we were best of friends, of the lay-down-your-life-for-each-other variety, but not at Christmas. I don't like to admit it, but the fact was that I got so cranky at Christmas that even Shannon had a hard time putting up with me. When we first knew each other she used to try to jolly me out of my holiday megrims, but now she just tried to avoid me as much as possible till the season was past.

This year it was worse than ever. The summer before, I'd had to kill a man—the human father of that halfling I mentioned earlier—and just when I thought I was learning to live with the grief and the guilt and the rage of that, Christmas came around and I began to have bad dreams. I had always had bad dreams at Christmas, confused dreams that left a foul taste in my life, but this year I remembered them. They were about killing Kyriander Stone's father. Only it wasn't his father, it was mine. . . .

Our office had no reception area and no receptionist, so when her knock went unanswered and the dark-eyed little human girl outside tried the door, what she found inside was just Mozart and me, in all my sullen glory. She smiled tentatively and entered, trailing fringe and baubles. I scowled at her from behind the little gray metal desk that faced Shannon's under the window, where I had been counting my petty miseries with a certain grim, unrecognized pride. She said, in a sweet voice barely audible over one of Mozart's grander flights of fancy, "Is it all right if I come in?"

"You already did," I said. "What do you want?" I'd

like to say I'd have been more civil if she had looked more as though she could hire us, but I'm trying to be honest here. I'd have been uncivil if she'd been dripping diamonds. Hell, I'd have been uncivil to God.

She glanced uncertainly at the lettering on the frosted-glass window of the still-open door. It said Arthur & Lavine, Private Investigators, just as it always did. She gestured toward it with one slender, graceful, nail-bitten hand. "I," she said, and cleared her throat, gazing at me with the wide and worried eyes of a fawn. She looked all of sixteen years old, with that look of hopeless vulnerability and sullen pride that marks the battered ones. "I want to hire you, that is, a private investigator, I think, I mean." She said it all in a rush, and left it there with a full stop as though it were a coherent sentence.

"You may as well close the door, now you're in," I said, in a voice made crosser by her vulnerability. I always want to tell people like that to go enroll in an assertiveness training class straightaway. If you act like a victim, you remain a victim. Most people feel like scared kids inside. The trick is to act like you're the exception. Then the ones who get mean when they're scared might leave you alone. But I didn't tell her any of that. I just got meaner, and watched while she put her whole concentration into closing the door and then turned to look at me as though awaiting further instructions. Maybe sixteen was an optimistic estimation of her age.

"Sit down." I waved at the thrift-store couch with its faded chartreuse upholstery and scarred wooden arms that was positioned next to the door for the convenience of clients. "You want some coffee?" It would have seemed more appropriate to offer her milk and cookies, but we didn't have any in stock. We weren't set up for entertaining children.

She sat obediently, thought about my offer, and nodded, anxiously twisting the strap of her beaded shoulder bag. The chewed nails made her hands look oddly, as though she had been trying to claw her way out of some private, personal, suffocating trap. "Yes, please," she said. "I'd like coffee. Black. If that's okay. I mean, if it isn't any trouble. If it's made already, or something. I mean . . ."

"Stop apologizing, for godsake. I wouldn't've offered it if I wasn't willing to give it to you. Just a minute." I went into the alcove, where we kept the coffeepot on top of the miniature refrigerator Shannon's boyfriend had bought us the previous year for Christmas, poured two cups full of stale, bitter coffee, and brought them back into the main room.

The fawn-eyed girl-child watched me, still twisting her shoulder-bag strap with nervous fingers. There were smudges under her eyes, dark against the pale translucence of her skin. Her bones were too prominent under the tender child flesh from which neglect and deprivation had burned away the baby fat, leaving her gawky and frail, like a shrink-wrapped skeleton.

Her costume consisted primarily of artful tatters. Her skirt was short to begin with, and the bottom four inches were unevenly torn in strips, two or three of which were tied in knots. Her T-shirt was cut or torn at shoulder and neckline, and the hem was neatly fringed and beaded, affording very little concealment for her tanned midriff. Around the top of the skirt she wore a decorative strip of leather about three inches wide, wrapped once around her waist and once lower, over her hips, before it was fastened with about twenty pounds of silver buckle that dragged it down almost to crotch level in front. Over all this she had draped a glittery length of fine, cobwebby fabric that hung to knee length in front and back but had no sides or sleeves. Her accessories consisted of the beaded bag, faded with age and missing many of its beads, and an assortment of chains and bangles and baubles that must have weighed more than she did. She looked undernourished and overburdened and likely to cry.

Putting the cups on the Chinese blue Masonite coffee table before her, I sat in the ugly wicker chair across from her. Interior decoration courtesy of our local thrift shop. She stared at me, then at the coffee, saying nothing. Mozart's serenade tumbled through the still morning air like silk. I sighed, not quite audibly. It wasn't this fragile child's fault it was Christmas. Nor was it her fault that startled fawns irritated me almost as much as Christmas did. I said, as gently as I was able, "I'm Rosalynd Lavine. D'you have a name?"

She blushed. It put needed color into her hollowed cheeks, making her look even younger and a lot prettier. "Oh, of course. I'm Candy. Candy Cayne." She spelled it, grinning shyly. "It's really my name. My parents have a terrible sense of humor." The grin exposed a chipped front tooth that must have been recent, because she suddenly remembered it and covered her mouth with one hand, looking almost guilty. "I . . . I fell," she said, though I hadn't asked. "On some stairs. And broke my tooth. I have to get it fixed soon." She gazed vaguely around the room, perhaps in search of a dentist.

"Sure, kid." Parents, or boyfriend? I decided to give her parents the benefit of the doubt. "What's his name?"

She stared. "Who?"

"The guy that broke your tooth."

"I told you, I fell."

"Right, okay." That hadn't told me much. Children protect abusive parents as fiercely as women protect abusive boyfriends and husbands. "Want to tell me what brought you here today?"

"You mean why do I want to hire you? Oh, um." She looked at me, eyes wide, fringe and baubles trembling. Besides several pounds of bangle bracelets and necklaces, she was wearing at least half a dozen mismatched earrings, one of which was a colored piece of faceted glass the size of a small plum that swung at the end of a length of gold chain, catching a stray gleam of watery sunlight from the window and casting prismed rainbows across the office walls whenever she moved her head. Her hair, which was long and permed to a frizz and dyed magenta in streaks, was pulled back behind one ear and pinned with a rhinestoned clip that also glittered, but cast no rainbows.

"If it's your parents, all I can do is direct you to some agencies that handle abused children. If it's your man, I'd suggest you leave him. But we don't do divorces."

"I haven't seen my parents in over a year. Daddy disinherited me when I dropped out of school."

An interesting choice of words. I tried to remember

any Caynes I might have read about in the society pages, but none came to mind.

"I live with a guy," she said, "but we're not married."

"Okay, that was my first guess. Shall I make another, or would you rather just tell me why you're here?"

"I think somebody might be gonna kill Jorie." She spit it out in a hurry, looking scared and defiant, like a startled kitten.

If somebody had already tried to kill her Jorie she would have said so. If nobody had, why did she think someone would? I didn't really care. "Tell the police."

"I can't!" It was almost a wail.

I drank my coffee and wished she would disappear. She didn't. "Okay, tell me about it. First, who's Jorie?"

"Jorandel." She waited for me to react.

It gave me perverse satisfaction to disappoint her: all I could tell from the name was that he was probably an elf. "Should I know him?"

She stared at me for a moment, then said in the tone of one explaining the obvious to an idiot, "He's lead singer for Cold Iron." Her look implied that only the deaf or the dead had a reasonable excuse not to know him.

"And that is, I take it, a musical group of some sort?"

"They're an elfrock band. What country are you from, anyway? They've got three singles in the top ten this week, and their latest album went platinum two weeks after it was released. They're good. They're great. Everybody's heard of Cold Iron." Righteous indignation put fire in those limpid eyes.

"Luckily, I'm not everyone. As you might guess if you listened a minute, I prefer classical music."

"Oh, is that what that is? I thought it was Muzak."

It was my turn to stare. "You mistook Mozart for Muzak?"

She shrugged, rather grandly. "I don't listen to old people's music."

"Right, okay. And I don't listen to children's music. Now that we've established our relative ages, do you want to tell me why you think someone's going to kill your Jorie, or would you rather go find a P.I. who's heard of him?"

"He's not 'my' Jorie."

"Okay. Do you even know him personally?" I couldn't think of a polite way to ask.

"Well, of course I know him!" She glared at me for a fraction of a second, then grinned sheepishly as the realization hit her. "Oh. How could you know, right? Did you think I was just a dumb little groupie with dramatic fantasies? I said I live with a guy. It's the Roach, Jorie's keyboardist."

"You live with a roach," I said, bemused.

She didn't really hear me. "Yeah, so I know all of them. There's Jimmy, that's Jimendan, Jorie's little brother, which some people think they're twins because they look so alike, but they're not. I'm not sure elves even have twins. Anyway, I can always tell them apart. They're just brothers. They really don't even look alike, not if you know them. Jimmy's the lead guitar. In the band. There's Jimmy and Jorie, Blade—he plays bass guitar." She was counting them off on her fingers, as though the list were long and difficult. "And then there's Killer, the drummer. And the Roach."

"The Roach." I was still having trouble with that one.

She nodded impatiently. "Yeah. That's all of them. There's five. Jorie, Jimmy, Blade, Killer, and the Roach."

They sounded like rejects from the Seven Dwarves. "They're all elves?"

"Well, Blade and Killer are halflings."

"And they don't have enough magic among them to protect this Jorie?"

She shook her head, long streak-dyed hair swaying. "Not lately, they haven't."

In that case they were almost certainly drugging or drinking or both. Elves on that path seemed to lose all their elven gifts except the music. I sighed, hating her Jorie sight unseen. "Okay. Why do you think somebody might kill Jorie?"

"I heard them talking."

"Who?"

"I don't know. Somebody. They were sort of quiet, and I was . . . well . . . Look, is this like talking to a lawyer? I mean, are you gonna tell the cops stuff I tell you?"

"Depends on whether they'd be interested."

"But I thought . . ."

People are always thinking. "I'm not a lawyer or a priest. I'm also not a stoolie. I have no legal right to withhold from the police anything a client tells me, but I seldom give them information unless they ask. Sometimes not even then. However, it may have escaped your attention that you're not my client."

She looked earnest. "I know. You want a retainer. Is that the right word?" She was digging for something in the beaded shoulder bag. What she came up with was a wad of bills fat enough to choke a TV evangelist. "Here, I brought this. It's ten thousand dollars, is that enough?"

I accepted the wad cautiously. "Enough for what?"

"To hire you."

"Depends on what you want me to do. It costs more than this to kill somebody, less to take a picture of him. But first things first. Where did you get this?"

"Does it matter?"

I put it down on the table between us. "Yes, it matters. This may seem old-fashioned to you—another peculiarity of the aged—but we try to keep things legal around here. If you stole this, or it's profits from theft or drug dealing or something, I can't accept it. Where did you get it?"

"Oh, hell. I sold one of my earrings." Maybe the one that kept casting rainbows all over the office wasn't faceted glass, after all. "But don't tell the Roach, okay? I'm gonna tell him I lost it, if he notices, which he might not because I never wear them both at once anyway. That'll be bad enough, telling him I lost it, but if he knew I'd sold it and kept the money, he'd kill me. I mean—" She broke off, looking confused. "He wouldn't really kill me. I think he loves me. But . . . you were right, I mean about my tooth, and the thing is he didn't even give me the earrings, Jorie did, but . . . see, they're mine, and what's mine, well, the Roach kind of counts it, you know?"

"What's yours is his."

She said defensively, "Well, that's love, isn't it? I

mean, isn't there something in the marriage vows about that?"

"You aren't married."

She admitted it, frowning.

"And anyway, I think it's supposed to go both ways."

"What do you mean?" She really didn't know.

"I mean it goes both ways. What's yours may be his, but then what's his should be yours."

"Oh. No, the Roach wouldn't like that."

"I didn't suppose he would. Let's get back to the problem at hand. This is a lot of money. What did you hope to buy with it?"

"Well, your services, I mean a private eye," she said in surprise.

"Private investigator," I said automatically. "What did you want me to do to earn this?"

"Keep them from killing Jorie, of course."

"Just that."

She nodded, pleased with my grasp of the situation.

"Candy, look, I'm sorry. I think you should take your money and go get your earring out of hock."

"It isn't enough? I can get more."

"More won't make the job possible. There are too many ways to kill a person. If somebody's determined to do your Jorie in, look at his options: he can shoot him, knife him, poison him, run him over with a car or a truck or a railroad train, electrocute him, drown him, suffocate him, or frame him for a capital crime and let the state do the job, just to name a few. If I lived in your Jorie's pocket I couldn't protect him from half those things. And I don't propose to live in his pocket. I'm really sorry, kid, but we don't do bodyguard, either. I can recommend a couple of P.I.s who do, if you want to try one of them, but you'll be throwing your money away. If somebody really wants your Jorie dead, he's dead."

"Oh, no!" It was a horrified little moan. "You don't mean that, do you? Murder can't be that easy!"

"Murder is the simplest thing in the world. The difficult part is getting away with it."

"Then couldn't you . . . couldn't you sort of find out who it is, and . . . and . . ."

"Yes? And what? Warn him off? All that would do is make him more careful, so he'd be harder to catch after the fact. I really am sorry, but there it is. You're asking the impossible, and I can't do it."

"You could at least listen."

"You're right. I could listen. Put your money away. I listen for free."

"You could get them busted for drugs, couldn't you? If you got them busted for that, they couldn't kill Jorie."

"If there's a crime, tell the police. Catching criminals is their job, and they're pretty good at it. Plus they won't charge you for it, so you wouldn't have to spend your earring."

"I told you, I can't tell the police." She frowned at the floor. "I don't want to get busted, too. For drugs. And I can't tell them what I heard, either, because I was stoned. When I heard them. That's why I'm not sure who it was, or what they said, exactly. The Roach put stardust or something in my orange juice. That's a hallucinogen," she added, translating for the elderly.

"Nice guy."

She ignored that. "So I wasn't exactly sure what I heard."

"Or whether you really heard anything at all?"

"I heard something." She looked up, meeting my gaze with a look of earnest determination to be believed. "I was in the ladies' room, backstage, and somebody stopped outside the window. The thing is that at first I thought it was . . . never mind. I thought I was hallucinating. But then I realized it was real, and I'd missed a bunch of what happened, but it was somebody hitting Jorie, I know that much, and they said if he didn't do something they wanted, but I didn't hear what it was he was supposed to do, they'd kill him. I swear that's what they said. And they said the band could make it without him, but that doesn't make sense, because they couldn't. Jorie *is* the band."

"Okay, I believe you."

"Sorry. Did I sound defensive or something? Anyway, there was something else about he'd threatened to fire somebody and they didn't like that, but then somebody else came in the ladies' room and made a bunch of noise so I guess they realized about the window, that they could maybe be overheard, and they didn't say anymore where I could hear them."

I shook my head. "Aside from the hitting, which you may have imagined, it sounds like somebody just talking. Could have been about anything. People say they'll kill each other all the time, but they seldom actually do it."

"They would." She shuddered. "If you'd heard them, you'd know. And they did hit him. Not in the face, where it would show in a performance, but they hurt him. I saw the bruises, the next day. They meant it. They'll kill him."

"Okay, maybe they meant it, at the time, but they will've thought better of it by now. He made somebody mad, that's all. Somebody who likes to talk big."

"It wasn't just talk. For real, it wasn't."

"Oh, hell, we all say stuff like that. I'll kill him, he'll kill me— You said that yourself, about your Roach, but you didn't mean it."

"If you'd heard them—"

"I'd be saying the same thing."

"You can't know that."

"It's a damn good bet."

She thought about it, studying me pensively. "Okay. You won't take the job, to protect Jorie."

"No."

"How 'bout to just see if I'm right? Would you do that? Would you come with us, and just look around and ask questions and whatever you do, and see if you can find out who it was I heard, and whether you think they really might kill him if he doesn't do whatever it is they want?"

"Maybe you can figure it out for yourself. You must know what employees he's recently threatened to fire."

"He's threatened to fire most of them, one time or another. Prob'ly a lot of them recently."

"Sounds like a lousy employer. Okay, even if it's most of his employees, how many can that be?"

"A hundred, easy." She grinned at my expression. "We're on tour. There's the band, the road crew, drivers, oh, lots of people."

"The band members aren't his employees, surely?"

"Yes, they are."

"Ones he would've threatened to fire?"

"Sure. Anybody but Jimmy. He could get along without any of the others. Without Jimmy, really, too, but I don't think he'd want to. I told you, Jorie is the band. They need him, but he doesn't need them."

"And he lets them know it? Sounds like a lousy setup."

"But I don't think it is one of the band. I don't think it would be. They're best of friends . . . most of the time. They're really close."

"Most of the time."

"Well . . . yeah. I mean, they're like brothers, you know? They have fights like brothers have fights. You know. Kind of squabbles or something, but they aren't really serious. I mean they're serious, but they're not . . . oh, you know. Brothers always make up afterward."

"Ever hear of fratricide?"

"What?"

"Never mind. Let's go back to what you heard. Somebody threatened to kill Jorie if he didn't do something this guy wanted, right? That sounds more like an employer than an employee. Who's an elfrock star's employer?"

"His producer, I suppose. You think it might be Mr. Veladora?" She looked pleased. "I never have liked him."

"At this point I don't know what I think. Hell, maybe your Jorie will do whatever this guy wants, and there'll be no problem at all, had you thought of that?"

"Jorie hardly ever does what he's told."

"I wonder why that doesn't surprise me?"

Shannon and her boyfriend arrived just then, bearing the expected Christmas tree, so much too large for the office that we all had to crowd up against one wall just to get it in the door. And that's how I ended up on tour with an elfrock band. It wasn't so much the nuisance of the tree as it was Shannon's bizarre expectation that I would be pleased with it. If the ensuing argument had been carried to its logical conclusion it would not technically have been sororicide, but I think it would have given Candy the general idea.

However, as soon as she realized there was a potential client present, Shannon turned on the charm and ended the argument. I was left looking sullen and childish for having hurled insults at the Voice of Sweet Reason. I took the job and left the office with Candy, thinking grimly that even an elfrock band couldn't be as hard to live with as the Spirit of Christmas personified.

I was wrong.

2

I put most of Candy's money in the business account and could not talk her into accepting a receipt for it. "The Roach might find it," she said. That was, as far as she was concerned, the ultimate argument. She wouldn't discuss it further, so I gave in and took her home with me to help me pack. We ran into trouble there, too. "Don't you have any decent clothes?" she asked despairingly of a wardrobe I thought quite adequate. "You can't be seen in this stuff!"

"I can and am."

"But not with me," she said. "You're supposed to be a friend of mine, and I don't have any friends who'd dress like this. Come on, don't you have anything trendy?"

"You mean like what you're wearing?"

"Well, yeah."

"I might have a few T-shirts in the rag bag that would suit, but damned if I'm going to ruin a good skirt to match, and I don't have any belts, bangles, or baubles you'd think much of."

"I can see that. Even your earrings match. You know, you'd look a lot better if you'd dress nicer. But there's no time to buy you a proper wardrobe now. Maybe we'll get time to shop in L.A. Do you even have any blue jeans?"

We found blue jeans, a knit shirt she pronounced acceptable, and an old fringed scarf she wrapped artfully around my waist. Standing back to observe the result, she shook her head ruefully and asked to see my jewelry box. It yielded very little that met with her approval. In the end she shared her own trinkets so generously that I felt like a dimestore display rack.

"That's better, anyway," she said dubiously. "Don't pack any of this other stuff. Just get some underwear and, you know, face paint and makeup and toothbrush and stuff. You can wear my clothes till we get time to buy you some things. We'll have to do something about your hair, too, but that can wait."

I did as I was told, feeling crosser than ever. After a moment's hesitation I decided to leave my .38 behind with my wardrobe. I shouldn't need it for this job, and it's too much trouble to carry when traveling. When we left the house to walk to the BART station (I wouldn't be needing my car after we joined up with the band, and saw no sense in leaving it in San Francisco when I could leave it safely at home and take BART almost to the door of the hotel), I had the disturbing sensation that I was a child again, leaving my life behind.

"Don't look so worried," said Candy. "You'll do okay."

"At what? Passing for a teenager?"

"Oh, that part's easy," she said in genuine surprise. "I mean, now that you're not dressed so dowdy, I can see you must not be as old as I thought. What are you, twenty or something? You don't even look as old as Jorie. But of course it's different with elves: he says he's only twenty-eight, but who knows, really? But what I meant, you'll do all right fitting in. Nobody'd guess you're a, well, that you aren't, um. That you never heard of Cold Iron. Just don't say anything stupid about the music, okay?"

"I'll certainly try not to."

"I should've brought a CD, so you could've heard them."

"I'm sure I'll hear them soon enough."

"Course I couldn't know you don't listen to music. I mean elfrock. Most people I wouldn't have to bring a CD." She glanced at me, a shy smile pulling at the corners of her mouth. "You don't have to sound so grim about it, you know. You'll like them. You can't help it, they're so good."

"I'm sure you're right."

"No, you're not. But you'll see."

Maybe I would like their music when I heard it, but I certainly didn't much like Jorandel when I saw him. Candy pointed him out to me as we approached the hotel: a long, knuckly street elf dressed more conservatively than I expected, in ordinary blue jeans and a T-shirt, with streak-dyed shoulder-length hair in blue and green that hid his face from our view. He was sitting on the curb beneath a lamppost festooned with Christmas tinsel, with his bent legs spread, forearms resting on knees, hands dangling, looking more like an exhausted wino than an idolized elfrock star.

"There's Jorie now," said Candy, her voice eager. Then, when he bent forward to vomit between his knees, she said, "Oh, God, poor baby, he's sick," and rushed forward to soothe his fevered brow in the best romantic tradition. The only trouble was, he wasn't interested. He pushed her away, not roughly, but with a muttered curse so unexpectedly foul that I actually took a step backward, away from him, shaken by some buried memory that turned my blood to ice. I was not afraid of him, but I was afraid of something, abjectly afraid, with a child's sharp and unreasoning terror.

The movement seemed to catch his eye. He turned toward me, and the veil of streaked hair parted to reveal the transcendently beautiful, angelic face of a child. "Go 'way," he said blurrily. "No autographs. Lea' me alone." The words were slurred, the voice an unpleasant, throaty whisper with no music in it.

"Come away, Candy," I said more sharply than I intended. "He doesn't need any help."

" 'S right," he said. "Don' need nothin."

"Oh, but," said Candy.

"Look, isn't there somebody with the group who's supposed to take care of this sort of thing?" I asked her. "You'd do more good calling whoever that is, than standing here arguing."

"Oh, Jorie," she said.

"Go 'way," he said.

I thought she would insist on staying with him, but after a moment's agonized hesitation she delegated that responsibility to me. "I'll go get Frank," she said. "Just stay here, don't leave him, and don't let the fans get at him."

I almost laughed. "What fans?"

"Nobody's recognized him yet," she said, "but if they do, there'll be hell to pay. Stay with him." She dashed away toward the hotel entrance, and I was left alone with the boy-faced horror in the gutter.

I thought he had forgotten me, but no such luck. He had let his head drop wearily onto one arm after a racking series of dry heaves, but now he tilted it sideways enough to look at me past a tangled hank of hair that hung between his eyes. To my surprise, there was an irrepressible grin pulling at the corners of his mouth. Without the grin, his generous lips would have looked too soft and pouty to be thought attractive by anyone over the age of eighteen. As it was, quirked upward at the corners like a perfect Cupid's bow, his mouth looked sweet and oddly sheepish, and a lot more innocent than the sultry blue eyes that were studying me blearily. "You aren't a fan," he announced. Then, after an obvious effort to place me, he said, "Friend of Candy's?"

It was my cue to trot out the cover story we'd agreed on. I wasn't sure he was in any condition to remember it, but I had to start somewhere. "That's right. I'm her cousin. She invited me to come along with you guys for a while." I left it there, not asking his permission or approval. I had a feeling that polite formalities were neither expected nor wanted here.

"You wish to rescue her from the clutches of evil?"

"Is she in the clutches of evil?"

He tried to lift his head, to study me more closely, but the effort was too much for him. He let it drop back onto his elbow with a thump and stayed that way for a moment, his face concealed again till he rolled his head sideways to look at me. The eyes were dazed, the Cupid's bow grin faded but still in place, still oddly irrepressible. It took him a moment to gather energy enough to say, "You don't approve."

"Of what? Of getting sick drunk and vomiting in the gutter?" I shrugged. "It's your life."

"Yes." He was silent a moment, watching me. Those sultry eyes were too old, too wise, too weary. "I meant of elves who leave Faerie. You don't approve of that. You're one of those bigots who think all elves should love magic and stick around Faerie to follow the wild hunt whenever they're not strumming harps or munching nuts and berries, right?"

"Is that what they do in Faerie? I wouldn't know."

The eyes narrowed briefly in appreciation. "You're good. You don't give *anything* away. What are you, police?"

That was too close for comfort. I was doing just great. Two minutes' conversation, and he had me pegged already. "There are other people besides cops who keep things to themselves."

"By Mab's grace, what does that mean?"

"It means whatever the hell you want it to mean, I expect. Here comes your nanny." Candy was returning with an enormous, muscle-bound human who didn't even notice me on his way to haul Jorandel up out of the gutter. Sick and dazed as he was, the elfrock star had just about all he could do to stay on his feet while the bodybuilder half dragged him through a side door into the hotel and out of our sight; but he managed another frayed grin at us, deliberately boyish and sweet, before he was gone.

To my surprise, Candy made no effort to follow. "Frank doesn't like anybody around when Jorie's like this," she said when she noticed my look. "Come on, let's go inside and you can meet the rest of the guys."

"Big treat, with this as a sample."

She looked surprised. "He's just drunk. Or stoned. Hey, everybody's gotta let off steam once in a while."

"Right. I suppose it's actually a point in his favor that he turns his destructive impulses on himself."

"Yeah." She thought about it. "Usually he does." That was said in a spirit of simple honestly, I think, because she didn't add anything to it, but just led me solemnly into the hotel without another word.

I followed her through the lobby. At sight of the enormous Christmas tree there, I shied like a nervous colt. My heart thumped against my ribs and I had to clamp my mouth shut hard against a whimpery little moan that tried to claw up out of my throat. For a little while I had forgotten it was the Christmas season.

Candy, fortunately, did not notice my reaction to the recollection. She was walking a little ahead of me, with the self-confident air of one long accustomed to wealth and power. This was an altogether different girl from the startled fawn who had so timidly entered my office this afternoon. She was in her element now, secure and self-assured, planning our method of attack as she led me onto the elevator and used a little key from her purse to tell it to take us to the penthouse. "I'll take you to see Emerson first," she said. "He's head of security. We'll let him know you've joined the tour, and he can make you a tag so you can move around with the crew and all without getting hassled. Then I'll show you around, introduce you to everybody, and you can get started."

"Get started doing what? Don't expect me to start interrogating everybody in sight, Candy. That's not how it's done."

"Then how will you find out who's gonna kill Jorie?"

"I'll watch, and look, and listen, and I'll probably ask some questions, but not so's you'd notice. I'm going to look like exactly what we're telling people I am: a relative of yours who's just come along for the ride."

"Oh. Well, whatever. Here's our floor." There were security guards waiting at the elevator doors to chase us away if we didn't belong. They recognized Candy. She introduced me to them, asked where we could find Emerson, and led me down the corridor in the direction indicated. "It won't be long till they all know you," she said, "but you'll still need an ID for concerts and stuff. Things get pretty confusing there. Even the guys wear ID tags offstage."

We stopped at the door behind which she expected to find Emerson. But before she could knock, the door across the corridor opened and for a fraction of a second I thought the elf who emerged was Jorandel, stumbling and shouting and narrowly avoiding a collision with us. But it was only an imperfect imitation: the same body type, and his face was the same shape as Jorandel's, but the features were less striking. The mouth was thinner, the eyes less sultry and less vividly blue, the cheekbones less prominent. Jorandel was all bones and sinewy meat, as sleek and dangerous as a wounded cat. This one had started just as sleek and just as dangerous, but too much in this life had come too easy for him. He had backed down too readily from too many challenges, fading into drugs and drink and quick, meaningless sex in too many backstage corners on too many empty nights. The bones and the sinews were there, but they were dulled by a layer of girlish fat that rounded and softened and slowed him. The only danger left in him was a sly and ugly danger, deadly and unpredictable and petulant and, ultimately, pathetic.

He was dressed more like my expectation of an elf-rock star than Jorie had been, in sleek black pants studded with rhinestones, a fringed one-sleeved jacket to match, a silk scarf that hung to his knees, and several pounds of gold and silver jewelry around his neck, arms, and fingers. The overall effect was of a younger brother trying too hard to get out from under the older brother's suffocating shadow. I could see why people who saw the two of them separately might not be able to tell which was which: they were as alike as any identical twins. But seen together, the differences would surely be obvious even to the most besotted teenager. This one tried harder to look the part, but he had none of his brother's self-confident style.

"Get off my case, bitch," he said loudly to someone out of sight in the room he had just left. "Fuck off. Just fuck off, you hear me?" The door slammed in his face. He stared at it for a moment, laughed harshly under his breath, and turned away. Noticing us, he did an exaggerated double take, said, "Pardon my English, ladies," in an unpleasant tone that negated whatever courtesy there might otherwise have been in the words, looked me over rather too speculatively, and wandered away down the corridor, still chuckling unpleasantly.

Candy knocked at Emerson's door.

"That was Jimendan, I assume?" I said.

She glanced down the corridor at his retreating back, then at me. "Oh, yeah. Sorry. I could've said that. It didn't seem like the time to introduce you, though."

"No, I think it's as well you didn't."

Emerson, when he answered Candy's knock, was neither as formidable as Frank nor as unpleasant as the elven brothers. He was just a mild-mannered, middle-aged human, a little overweight, with a receding hairline and an uncomplicated smile. But he had the lazy agility, the scarred knuckles, and the watchful eyes of a man who knew his way around a barroom brawl and maybe even knew how to stay out of one when he could. "Candy," he said with obvious pleasure. "What can I do you for?" She introduced me and told him what we wanted. "Your cousin, eh?" he said with a smiling glance at me that was, I felt certain, a complete and competent professional appraisal. There wasn't much those deceptively sleepy brown eyes would miss. I concentrated on looking innocent.

He had in his room all the equipment needed to make a laminated holo ID complete with a swivel clip with which to fasten it to one's clothing. The ID, when it was completed, bore my name, a clear but unflattering hologram of me, the words "Access All Areas," and the name Cold Iron drawn in broken letters on a crumbling gravestone, the whole surrounded by a grotesquely sinister design of thorny vines that sprouted bleeding eyes at intervals. . . . Or perhaps the vines were meant to be sprouting from the eyes. I didn't study it closely. I looked at it and away again, aware I was meant to be shocked, and vexed that I was reacting as intended.

"That's the band's logo," said Candy. I didn't know whether she meant the gravestone or the vine, and I didn't ask.

Emerson was smiling at my distaste. "Not a fan?" The smile didn't hide the shrewd, cop-on-duty look in his eyes.

"Not just yet," I admitted. "Candy tells me I will be, once I've heard them."

"You've never heard them?" He stared. "Where've you been, in a coma?" Now he wasn't even trying to hide that alert look. Amusement still pulled at his lips, but it was a polite social fiction that did not touch his eyes.

"She listens to Mozart," said Candy, with a look that begged him to be kind to the cripple.

"Ah, that explains it." He studied me, still not quite sure what I was or where I fit in. "Mozart, eh? Well, have fun at the concert tonight."

I looked at Candy. "There's a concert tonight?"

She nodded happily. "Come on, let's see if we can find the guys."

We found them in a big, poorly lighted room at the end of the corridor. Jimendan was sitting on the floor in a corner, an acoustic guitar in his lap and a bottle of German beer in his hand. He stared absently out a sliding glass door at the concrete railing of a miniature balcony. From that angle he couldn't see much else but the enfolding closeness of a fog-lowered sky, but he wasn't really looking at the view. He wore the pouty, defiant look of a scolded child nursing his grievances and planning further mischief.

I had decided when I took this job that it wouldn't be either necessary or possible to masquerade as a starstruck teenager awed by meeting a genuine elfrock band, but it was becoming difficult just to hide my disgust. I had not expected much of elfrock musicians, but I had expected something at least outwardly more attractive than I was finding in these self-absorbed, unpleasant young elves. Perhaps they did make good music. What else would explain Candy's and presumably other fans' ability to see something worthwhile in them despite the petulance and the egotism and the ugliness?

Near Jimendan, sprawled in an easy chair with an herbal cigarette in his mouth, a beer at his elbow, and a starry-eyed human girl-child at his feet, was a cadaverous halfling with legs as long and thin as a spider's, huge, bony hands at the end of the tattoo-disfigured goblin arms, and the sick-white skin tone of the terminally ill. He had straight undyed hair that hung like a tangle of silver halfway down his back, pale blue eyes in a saturnine face, and crooked teeth he displayed in an incongruously cheery smile. Ignoring the girl-child, Candy introduced the man as Blade. He waved a negligent hand at me, then closed his eyes and began to strum an imaginary guitar.

That was the closest to a real greeting I got from any of them except the Roach. Jimendan didn't acknowledge the introduction in any way at all. Killer, another halfling, this one a mountain of muscle padded with baby fat and topped by a mare's nest of black tightly curled hair that completely concealed his eyes but not the tips of his pointy ears, turned his broad face toward me and away again without any visible change in expression, and without missing a beat with his drumsticks against the arm of his chair. Maybe he wouldn't have looked so large among humans; but here, among Trueblood elves with their long, frail bones, he seemed enormous. He had a pair of half-naked human females flanking him, both of whom glared at me in wordless challenge, like a pair of dogs guarding a meaty bone. When I made no move toward him, they subsided, dismissing me.

The Roach, when introduced to me, at first barely spared me a glance. He was too busy shoving a stringy-haired girl out of his heavily tattooed arms and pulling Candy into them to worry about formalities. Like the girls with Killer, he behaved toward Candy more like a dog claiming a cherished toy than like a man greeting his beloved. He didn't look like a roach. His face had neither the angelic beauty of Jorandel's nor the petulant charm of Jimendan's, but it had an elegantly chiseled elfin quality that was more classic than theirs and, framed by a mane of shiny-clean green hair, looked positively refreshing in this crowd of scruffy misfits.

When he finished kissing Candy he surprised me by acknowledging my presence. He actually spoke to me, and quite pleasantly. "Welcome to the menagerie," he said as if he meant it. His voice had exactly the sweet, musical quality I had expected to hear in Jorie's, since Jorie was the lead singer. "So you are Candy's cousin." He tightened his arm around her, watching me. His eyes were a curious color more nearly gold than brown, and flecked with green. They were as beautiful as gemstones, and as unhuman. "It seems that beauty runs in your family," he said. "Would you like a beer?"

I wanted gin. "I'd like a beer," I said.

"I'll get it," said Candy.

"I offered, I'll get it." He spoke pleasantly enough, but Candy froze in mid-motion. She did not quite cringe, but her expression said she wanted to. He kissed her gently on the forehead, released her, and crossed the room to a kitchenette area I hadn't noticed before, where he retrieved a bottled beer from the half-size refrigerator, used a built-in opener on the wall, and brought me the smoking bottle with a smile. "Here you are, Cousin." He looked at Candy. "Are the two of you coming to the show tonight?"

"I still have to find her something to wear first," said Candy. "She . . . she couldn't bring all her stuff."

His gaze returned to me, his expression oddly calculating. Suddenly realizing I was studying him in return with a look almost certainly too detached and the wrong kind of self-confident for the role I was supposed to be playing, I tipped up my beer and guzzled half of it in what I hoped would look like innocent, youthful bravado. He let a curiously triumphant smile pull at his lips, but all he said was, "The cars will leave here at seven."

"We'll be ready," Candy said eagerly.

He was still looking at me. "Take her downstairs and buy her something." He raised his voice without turning his head. "Walter?" To Candy, in his normal voice, he added, "That little black-and-silver gown you wanted. It will look well on her. And be sure you get her some shoes to go with it." A small, harassed-looking man entered from a neighboring room and looked at him inquiringly. The Roach said, with barely a glance at him, "Ah, Walter. Candy is going shopping downstairs. Call down and okay it, will you?"

"Right," Walter said agreeably.

"Hey, wait," I said. "I can't—"

"Come on," said Candy.

The Roach grinned at me. "Don't worry about it."

"Come on," said Candy, tugging at my arm.

"But I don't—" I stopped, not knowing what to say. Maybe Candy's cousin would be delighted to let the Roach buy her a dress, but I wasn't. I had a feeling I couldn't afford to owe this elf anything at all.

"Go," said the Roach. His voice was still gentle, still musical, but there was steel in his smile. This was not the time to argue with that. I went.

Outside in the corridor, Candy rushed me along with such eager excitement that I simply followed her, bemused. "First we'll go to my room, you can leave your bag, hey this is great," she said all in one breath. "You'll like the black-and-silver; it's a dress I pointed out to him. He's right, it'll look good on you. And you know what? This means he's gonna let me sit in the house. Us. Out in front. A lot lately he's been making me stay backstage, and you can sort of hear from back there, but you can't really see or anything. Here's my room. You want some soda before we go downstairs?"

I was still clutching the German beer the Roach had given me. "I haven't finished this," I said.

She laughed. "I didn't mean soda to drink!"

"Oh. No, I don't want some soda." It was an insidious drug, similar to cocaine in its effects, but pleasanter and more addictive.

"Well, I do." She got a tiny brown bottle from the drawer of the bedside table, dipped white powder out of it on the tip of a pen clip, inhaled it, and repeated the process with her other nostril before she glanced at me again. "You sure?"

"I'm sure." I took another swallow of beer, but it was bitter even for dark German beer. I wanted gin.

"Okay." She capped the bottle and put it away. "One thing about the Roach, he's stingy sometimes about other stuff, but he usually makes sure I have plenty of soda."

"Nice guy." I put my beer bottle on the bedside table and wiped my hands on the sides of my jeans. They felt strange, almost numb, and the palms were sweaty. Playing teenager for a scuzzy band of elfrock musicians was not as simple as I had expected it to be.

"Yeah." She took my comment at face value, deaf to sarcasm. "He's not as pretty as Jorie, but at least this way I get to see him."

"You get to see who?" My eyes felt scratchy, like I hadn't slept in a week. The beer had left a bad taste in my mouth. I wished I hadn't argued with Shannon.

"Jorie, of course."

I stared. "You mean you live with the Roach because you . . ." I stopped, reluctant to put the thought into words.

She finished it for me, with an eloquent shrug. "Because I can't have Jorie. Sure. It's no secret. They both know it."

"Jesus, Candy!"

"Well? What should I do?" She sounded lost, defensive, desperate. "I s'pose you think I should just leave, right? You think if I want Jorie and I can't have him I should just walk away. Well, I don't. He won't have me, but the Roach will, and if I walk away I'll never see Jorie for real again. I mean, no more than any other fan would. But if I stay with the Roach . . . well, there's always a chance, isn't there?"

"I doubt it."

She might not have heard me. "Come on, leave your stuff here. We'll go get your dress. Hey, it's really neat the Roach decided to get it for you. He must like you. He's not always so generous."

I dropped my bag on the bed and almost lost my balance when I let go of it. It wasn't all that heavy. Putting it down shouldn't have been such a relief. "I can't accept that, you know."

"What? You can't accept what?"

"A gift like that, from an elf I hardly know."

She paused in the doorway, staring at me. "Well, what're you gonna do? We have to get the dress, Rosie. If we don't . . . God, you gotta! He wants you to have it!"

"Okay, okay." There was real alarm in her eyes. "We'll get the dress. But I'll pay for the damn thing myself." I followed her out the door, feeling suddenly old and infinitely weary.

"But why?"

"Let's just say I don't want to owe him for it." One beer shouldn't have made my body feel so unfamiliar to me.

"Oh." She thought about that on the way to the elevator. "So then are you going to tell him he didn't pay for it?" she asked at last.

"Maybe, maybe not. Why?" I reached for the button to call the elevator, and nearly missed it.

"I wish you wouldn't." She looked troubled, like a child uncertain whether it has overstepped the rules.

"Okay, I won't." The guards at either side of the elevator were studiously ignoring our conversation. I didn't have to work at ignoring them. Standing up was suddenly just about all I could handle.

"But the trouble with that, then he won't know you don't owe him."

"I'll know." The elevator arrived. I concentrated on putting one foot in front of the other to follow Candy through the doors. "You know," I said slowly, "I feel kind of funny." My voice sounded distant and blurry. I was having trouble focusing my eyes.

She studied me. "You don't look too good," she said uncertainly. "You should've done some soda, maybe."

"No." I shook my head. That was a mistake; the world tilted dangerously and I had to reach for the elevator's handrail to support myself. "What the hell—?"

"Listen, are you okay?" I saw her punch a button. The elevator doors, which had begun to close behind us, thought better of it and slid obediently open again. "Maybe I better call Frank," she said. "You look kind of sick."

I heard her as from a great distance. "I'm fine," I said absently.

"Sure you are," she said. "Hey! Hey, somebody! Get Frank, will you?" She turned back to me and took my arm, tugging me toward the elevator doors. "Rosie, did you take something, or what? Gee, and I thought prob'ly you didn't do drugs. Come on, we gotta get off the elevator, see? You can do it. It's just a couple of steps." To the guards in the corridor she said, "Help me, will you?"

"I don't do drugs." That seemed an important statement to make at the time.

"Somebody call Frank," she said.

"What's she on?" asked somebody else.

"I don't know," said Candy. "She says she doesn't do drugs, but look at her."

I wondered what was so remarkable about how I looked. Then I realized I was lying on a hotel corridor floor with my nose pressed against the dusty carpet. There had been no sensation of falling, and no pain on landing. Just one minute I was standing, and the next I was lying on the floor. "I don't like drugs," I said. It was hard to speak clearly with my face in the carpet.

People were gathering around me. In the distance I could hear someone laughing. It was a very unpleasant laugh. The sound of it reminded me, incongruously and quite horribly, of the man I'd killed last summer. In the back of my mind some primitive part of me gibbered and screamed, threatening to drag me down out of the sane and sensible world into a region of nightmares and despair. I fought it, struggling against the slow dulling of senses that would leave me trapped in there with myself, and very clearly through the gathering fog I heard Candy say miserably, "Oh, Roach! Why?"

It was the last thing I heard, but it was enough. The revelation followed me down into darkness: the Roach had been oddly intent on serving me that beer himself. The Roach, of whom Candy had earlier said, "He put stardust or something in my orange juice." And I, absorbed in my masquerade as Candy's innocent cousin, had blithely taken the beer from him and drunk it without hesitation. Good thinking, Rosie. Very clever. That'll put them off their guard.

3

As a matter of fact, it did put them off their guard. I never found out what the Roach had put in that beer, or what Frank did to counteract it; at the time I was too uncomfortable to be curious, and later it just didn't seem important. But by late that same afternoon Frank had me on my feet again, a little unsteady and a lot embarrassed, and already ruefully aware that in one way the Roach had done me a service. There was no quicker way I could have gained acceptance in that portable little community of elfrock musicians and their assistants. My "Access All Areas" tag would have let me go where I wanted among them, but it wouldn't have made me welcome. In an odd way, the trick the Roach had pulled on me seemed to do that. When Frank returned me to the group, they received me very much as one of their own.

It could have gone the other way. They could have shut me out, laughed at me, even made me the butt of more "jokes" till I'd have had to resign in self-defense. I couldn't quite see why it didn't go that way. Chronologically, the band members seemed to be my age or older (as Candy said, it's difficult to tell with elves), but as far as I could see, they weren't grown-ups. They were a bunch of spoiled kids who thought they were mature because they'd worked without magic (except that inherent to the music) to get where they were, and they'd had some hard times along the way. But instead of maturing them, their experiences had arrested their development, first because they were too intent on their fight for success to learn any of life's real lessons along the way, and then because success itself had sheltered them. It surrounded them with sycophants and granted their material whims so readily and so lavishly that they could hardly be expected to notice the emotional vacuum of which they had become the greedy center. They had sex, drugs, and elfrock in abundance. It had not yet occurred to them that those three things did not comprise all that is worth having.

They had achieved the only goal they'd ever set. Keeping it would be work, but it was work that would take less energy, less concentration, less total commitment than getting it had taken. They had room in their lives now for something more, and they didn't quite know there *was* anything more. But they were beginning to recognize a lack, an emptiness, and it made them aimlessly angry in the way of children who know they've missed out on something even when they don't know what it is they've missed.

Which was why I'd have thought they would more likely respond to my victimization with ridicule, but it also might have been why they didn't; why the fact that I accepted with reasonable grace the practical joke played on me might have made them accept me as a member of their inner clique. They were obscurely aware that life had played a practical joke on them. They had reached for the brass ring, and caught it, and now it was turning their fingers green.

Whatever the reason, I knew they had accepted me as soon as Frank, who was Jorie's personal bodyguard and general factotum (each of the musicians had one such, and they functioned more as baby-sitters than as bodyguards), delivered me back into their hands with the smugly solicitous pride of a new father. They received me with the casual relief of brothers dubious of their sister's choice in boyfriends and glad to see her home safe from a date.

The afternoon was well advanced, and they looked as though they must have spent a part of it resting. Even Jorie looked relatively healthy. They were gathered, apparently awaiting my entrance, in the room where I had met them before. The women who had been with them were gone, leaving only Candy and the five musicians, all looking surprisingly friendly. I felt a little self-conscious under their concerted gaze, and self-consciousness usually makes me hostile. But I'd had time while I was still alone with Frank to realize that anger would not be the most useful response to this situation, so I forced a grin and tried not to blush.

"Feeling better?" Jorie's voice was gentle. He sounded as though he really cared how I felt.

"Yes, thanks." I sounded frail and prim.

"Will you sit?" said Blade, grinning amiably and gesturing toward the space on the couch beside him.

Killer, reclining on a heap of throw pillows on the floor, silently hurled one of them at the indicated couch. His face was as usual almost completely concealed behind the mass of his hair, so I couldn't tell what his expression was or whether the gesture was a friendly one. It could just as well have been hostile, but I thought I saw the hint of a grin at the corners of his mouth before he turned his head away to continue pounding another pillow with his ever-present drumsticks. I hoped so, because he was by far the most dangerous-looking of them all, the sort of halfling whose presence in a bar makes you decide to try the one down the street instead, unless you're really in the mood for a fight. Maybe it was only the hulking mass of him and the fact that he kept his face perpetually hidden behind that glistening mat of curly ebony hair, but I was as wary of him as if he had been a roomful of Hell's Angels.

Jimendan, looking less sullen and more like his brother because of it, got up and brought me a sealed beer and, with a remarkably angelic, guilty grin, handed me an opener so I could take the cap off myself. I didn't want a beer, but I couldn't resist the gesture. The Roach, seeing me open it, actually blushed. I wondered what they had said to him; I did not think he was easily embarrassed. And Jorandel, looking half angry and half ashamed, said quietly, "We apologize for your discomfort." He glanced at the Roach. "It won't happen again."

That was the closest any of them ever came to referring to what the Roach had done to me. And he didn't give me time to respond if I wanted to. It was as though they had been waiting for my return, and for Jorie to make that little speech. When I was settled and he had said it they seemed to relax, and in moments they looked more as I had first seen them, sprawled around the room absentmindedly playing real or imagined instruments with only Blade, who was nearest, still watching me.

"You really don't want that, do you?" he asked, indicating the beer.

I looked at it. "Not much."

He reached for it. "Let us avoid waste: I'll take it. Is there anything you do want? Coke? Alka Seltzer?"

I grinned ruefully. "Thanks, no."

"Do you have earplugs for the concert tonight?"

I stared. "Earplugs?"

He grinned. "As I suspected: Candy doesn't always remember details. It will be too noisy in the arena. No matter how good the acoustics are, there is always sound bounce and house noise: kids screaming and so on. Good earplugs cut out all that so you can hear the music without going deaf. Ask Candy for some. She'll have extra."

"Thanks, I will."

He studied me a moment. "You expect to dislike the concert, don't you?" When I didn't answer straightaway he nodded, not quite smiling. "We might surprise you."

"You might." I probably sounded as dubious as I felt.

He picked up an acoustic guitar that was leaning against the end of the couch. "Candy says you listen to Mozart." He grinned mischievously and played a recognizable passage from Mozart's Piano Concerto No. 23 in A, K. 488. "Are you surprised yet?"

I admitted it. "That doesn't go well with vines that bleed eyes."

His mouth twisted. "That thing." He shook his head. "It wasn't our idea. Veladora figures we're a magic-metal band, so we have to have an ugly logo." He shrugged. "The kids seem to like it. You see it all the time on T-shirts and whatnot."

"Candy seems to like it."

He shook his head dismissively. "Poor Candy." It sounded as though he meant more than "too bad she likes the logo," but when I looked a question at him he just shook his head again, perhaps remembering I was said to be her cousin, and played more Mozart.

I let it go; it wasn't the time to start pushing for information. A moment later Candy came over and I asked her about earplugs, which she was delighted to find for me. They turned out to be little poison-green cylinders of a magic-impregnated substance that didn't seem to affect my hearing at all.

She grinned at my expression. "They're good, huh? Don't worry, they'll do their job."

I removed them and shook my head, looking at them: they were either useless or strong magic. If the latter, they would filter the sound of an atomic war. Either concerts had changed a lot since the last one I'd been to, or my memory was faultier than I thought. Either was possible. Or both. In those days, groups had been loud, but not deafening. They hadn't sported intentionally disturbing logos. And I had been more disturbed than I knew. "Okay," I said. "I guess you'd know."

"The guys all wear these too," she said. "You gotta, or you'll go deaf, especially elves. Besides not hearing the concert right. The noise is really bad."

"Don't worry: I'll wear them."

She hesitated. "About your dress. For the concert."

"Yeah?"

"Roach bought it," she said. "It's in my room. He called down and told them a size he said would fit you, and had them send it up. With shoes and a bag and everything. You wanta try it on?"

"Later." I found it oddly disturbing that he imagined he knew my size. Hell, I didn't even know my size; I too seldom bought new clothes. Secondhand ones don't always still have their tags. I'd learned to judge by holding them up and guessing. For one brief, too-imaginative moment, I felt rather as though he had done that to me: held me up, looked me over, and guessed what would fit. I didn't like the feel of his hands or of his speculative gaze on me, not even in imagination. Shuddering, I glanced across the room and saw that he was watching me with a knowing smile.

"He meant well, Rosie," said Candy. "I mean, it's sort of an apology, you know?"

"Hush, he'll hear you," I said. Blade had heard her. He was giving us a knowing look too, but friendlier than the Roach's. Bearing in mind that one of these people might want to kill Jorandel, I'd been automatically sifting impressions, looking for a suspect. As I returned

Blade's smile with one of my own that was heavier on bravado than on friendliness, I realized that so far all I'd established was that there wasn't a one of them I'd consider a safe bet not to do murder.

Not that you can really tell by looking, and of course damn near anyone would kill given sufficient provocation, but none of these guys looked like they'd need much provocation. The Roach was clearly vicious for the hell of it, Killer looked like he'd be more at home in a brawl than anywhere else (and likely to start one if somebody looked at him wrong), Blade was all simmering violence coiled like a steel spring inside that lean and deceptively lazy body, and Jim was a textbook example of sullen sibling resentment ready to take out his anger on any convenient target. I wouldn't have wanted to meet any of them alone in a dark alley at night.

And it wasn't just the aversion reaction of an outsider to a cluster of bonded toughs. I'm as ready as the next guy to cross the street to avoid passing too near a batch of young elves, or young humans either, come to that; because they seem to outsiders as dangerous as a tribe of gorillas and just as likely to attack for no reason. But I'm better than most at forcing myself to perceive them as individuals and thus to recognize which groups are looking for trouble and which aren't. My first impression of the Cold Iron musicians was shaded by the recognition that they were one of the groups best avoided on the street. They were trouble waiting to happen, and they would perceive an outsider as fair game.

But I wasn't an outsider anymore. I felt that very strongly: and I still felt their danger just as strongly. They would not attack me as a group, not now that I'd been accepted among them. But as individuals they were still a threat. Even Jorandel and Jimendan, whose faces were as angelically innocent as they were sultry, and who both somehow managed to seem oddly young and dear like huggable cousins or mischievous neighbor boys, held coiled within them that same deadly spring-steel tension I saw in Blade. I had a terrible and terrifying sense that they might, at any moment, explode into violent action for no reason that any mere mortal such as I might understand.

It wasn't until I saw them in concert that night that I began to understand where some of that hidden violence both originated and was vented. Candy and I had seats near the front. The dress Roach had ordered fit me perfectly, as did the shoes that matched it. I was extremely self-conscious in the costume at first, especially after Candy lent me still more of her baubles and bangles to go with it and painted half my face in a complex glitter design. I felt more suitably attired for a masquerade than for an elfrock concert. The dress was too short and too low-cut, and consisted in several surprising places of more lacings than solid fabric. Candy had given me a matching, glittering scarf for a headband that completely obscured my forehead, then arranged my hair in masses of artfully teased and sprayed curls. I had to admit it was attractive, in a bizarre and unexpected way, but I was uncomfortably certain that it looked more suited to performing onstage than to watching a performance.

I was wrong. My dress and hairstyle and even the quantity of paint and bangles I wore were all commonplace in the company in which I found myself in the front rows of the arena. There were people present in ordinary jeans and T-shirts, but the majority of them wore costumes and paint much more bizarre than mine. I was by no means the only person present wearing a broad headband or what I later learned was called "big hair." And the few ounces of silver and jewels that I had accepted from Candy were nothing to the pounds of both that jangled on the fingers, arms, ankles, ears, and necks of the people around me.

When I last saw the band before the concert, they were still a bunch of knuckly boys in battered jeans with only a few too many scarves, bracelets, and rings, and a little too much hair, to distinguish them from any group of young elves anywhere. When they came onstage they were transformed.

Blade still wore battered jeans, but he had added a massive studded belt and a leather vest, as well as bangle bracelets on both arms almost to the elbow, at least one ring on every finger, and half a dozen necklaces. Killer was half-hidden behind his drums when I first noticed him, but he seemed to be wearing skintight bicycling shorts with glittering suspenders and a top hat. The Roach was wearing tight black pants laced up the sides all the way to the waist, leaving lots of pale elven skin showing. His matching sleeveless jacket was open at the front to reveal more skin and several necklaces.

Jim and Jorie were dressed identically in long jackets covered with glitter, tight pants patterned with rhinestones, ruffled lace shirts open to the waist, and a great many wispy scarves tied almost anywhere, including ones worn as headbands. Their arms, like Blade's, were weighted heavily with bangles; they had rings on all their fingers; and somebody had spent more time on their hair than Candy had spent on mine. Killer's hair was always a mass of spiral curls to the end of his nose in front and just past his collar in back, and Blade's was the same straight fall of silver down past his shoulders that it had been before; but the Roach, Jim, and Jorie had all had their hair teased and combed and curled and sprayed and arranged till they looked nothing like their everyday personas.

Jorie and Jim were side by side at one microphone, and Jim still seemed only a washed-out copy of his more charismatic brother. Even dressed alike and standing in the glitter and glory of the stage lights they seemed to be more an elf and his shadow than twins, though obviously they meant to emphasize their likeness.

I had barely registered all that, the transformation from plain street elves to gaudy performers, when Jorandel looked down from the stage, winked at me with a twisted little grin, and they began to play. All that pent-up violence exploded in a maelstrom of sound and feverish activity as instruments screamed and glittering bodies hurled themselves—or were hurled by the force of their music—across the stage, singing and playing and dancing in a mad, joyous tumble of sheer power and glory.

The last band I had seen in concert was Small Silver nearly fifteen years earlier, and while the music had certainly been energetic, the musicians had been calm, aristocratic elven arrogance personified. I had imagined that Cold Iron would be the same, would stand in their assigned places on the stage and absorb themselves in a sort of musical meditation, objectively creating songs as something outside themselves for the enjoyment of the audience.

But there was nothing objective about a Cold Iron performance. They didn't just play the music and then stand back to admire it. It was as though the songs they produced were wrenched by some malign magic from their souls, with their bodies as fierce and yet frail vessels through which the sounds were processed.

And such sounds! My prejudices were all destroyed in the course of the first number they played. There is no way to describe an experience like that. Against my better judgment, my good sense, my musical tastes, and my will, I was profoundly moved by something I had expected to find disgusting or at the very best ridiculous.

It was loud, but it wasn't the volume that mattered. The driving rhythm, as much felt as heard, carried with it something fine and sweet, something so delicate and elusive that reason, had mine been functioning, would have said it could not coexist with the violent intensity of drums and bass and screaming lead guitar. I suppose that was the magic of it, the elvish Gift, to thread that frail perfection through their chaotic snarl of thunder.

Jorie's voice, bellowing lyrics I could not understand over the fury of the instruments, ought to have shattered that brittle thread of loveliness if nothing else did. But it didn't. That pure, clear sensitivity existed not in spite of but as a function of the turbulence the band created. It was the rainbow mist torn by the wind from breaking waves, the halo of St. Elmo's fire on a storm-tossed ship's mast, the diamond sheen of ice in a raging blizzard. Cold Iron committed apparent violence, and out of that violence an incredible beauty was born.

I was as taken with it as if I had come there expecting it. Perhaps more so, because I was caught by surprise. The music and those who made it were far more complex and the elves more talented than I had allowed myself to imagine. Spoiled children they might be, but that was only a small part of what they were. Perhaps the least important part. I would not think of them again, dismissively, as "boys." However immature their actions offstage might be, these were not adolescents caught up in a powerful game they neither understood nor controlled. The brass ring might turn their fingers green, but elves capable of the glorious spectacle I was witnessing would merely accept the color and use it to intensify their palette. They had not thrown away quite all their magic.

Which meant they were also potentially even more dangerous than I had realized—but I didn't think of that then. I didn't think of much of anything then. The music didn't leave room for thought. Most of the people in the front rows stood up and crowded forward in an effort to reach the guys on the stage. I am usually uncomfortable in a crowd scene, but I hardly noticed the press of bodies around me. I stood up, so I could see over their heads, but I didn't move. Neither did Candy: she was smug in the knowledge that she didn't have to resort to such tactics to touch the idols, and it probably didn't much matter to her right then that she would be left with the wrong one when the music ended. Right then there probably wasn't a wrong one.

Jim and Jorie were all over the stage, bounding around with seemingly limitless energy, and with some of the most provocative male antics I had ever seen in public. What Jim didn't imply with his extremely suggestive treatment of his guitar, Jorie did with hip motions that had his fans writhing in sexual fantasies. It might have been repellent if they hadn't been so damned cute. But they were. They both wore that angelic baby-boy look I had first seen when I met Jorie: the transcendent innocence, the sweetly sultry smile, the brilliantly blue summer-sky eyes clear and wide and direct. And they were both clearly having a hell of a lot of fun.

They often came together at center stage, sharing a microphone for effect, so I had ample opportunity to observe how much more effective their attempt at appearing identical was than I had at first thought. Under the glaring lights and caught in the athletics of the performance, Jim didn't look as puffy and Jorie didn't look as gaunt. I thought I could still tell them apart readily enough, till they pulled a neatly choreographed little number designed to confuse, cavorting in complex circles that ended with them—I thought—exactly where they had started. It was a song that Jim sang as much as Jorie did, and they played guitars as perfectly matched as their costumes. I'd been watching for a full five minutes after that before I realized the one I'd taken for Jorie had bangs. Jim wore his hair in bangs. Jorie didn't. So much for my conviction that the unfortunate Jim couldn't hold a candle to his more charismatic brother.

At one point during the evening I removed one of my earplugs, just to see how much difference they really made. The music, heard through them, was so loud I thought they must not be doing any good. They were. Without one, the song I had been enjoying degenerated instantly into a raucous and wholly unmelodic roar of echoes and audience. I put the plug back and kept it there.

The band took about a five-minute break in the middle of the concert. When they came back I thought Blade looked a little dazed, his expression vacuous and his eyes out of focus; but he was off to one side of the stage so far from me, it was hard to tell. He wasn't quite steady on his feet, but by then neither were Jim and Jorie. They were still cavorting all over the stage, but the fun was gone out of it. There was a kind of awkwardness about their actions, especially Jim's: a small, almost human clumsiness that hadn't been there before. The gaiety had become forced, the antics artificial and ungainly. When they came together to share the microphone at center stage, they collided. They'd done that once before as a joke, but this time they hit harder, and Jorie was slow to recover. It didn't look intentional.

Killer was too much concealed by his drums and his hair for me to make a guess at his condition. The Roach looked cool and contained and mildly amused. If the others had used their break time to get stoned or drunk in a hurry, he had either stayed sober or used a stimulant instead of a depressant. Probably the latter. There was a greater tension in his manner than there had been before.

Throughout the concert there had been security guards everywhere on and around the stage, watching the audience. They chased down the ones that climbed, hauled away the ones that fainted, and pushed back the ones that grabbed. Now I noticed that the personal guards, Frank and the other four who were individually responsible for the musicians, were hovering among the amplifiers, keeping nearer the band than they had been earlier. They kept to the shadows as much as possible, so I couldn't see their faces, but their posture said they were ready for trouble, and not from the audience. They were all five bulky fellows, each of them fully capable of picking up his personal charge and carrying him if needed. It looked as though they thought it might be needed.

Three numbers into the second half, someone in the audience threw something—probably a token of affection—that hit Jimendan in the face. He exploded in such a frenzy of rage I thought he would kill the nearest fans before anyone could stop him. He had his guitar half off, either to use as a weapon or to throw aside so his hands would be free, and he was already in the air, leaping straight off the front of the stage into the audience, when Andy, his personal attendant and bodyguard, caught him.

He made it look easy. He caught Jim in both arms and leaned gently backward to haul him back onstage, keeping his feet off the floor, then sedately turned his back on the audience and walked. Jim fought him for a moment, hair flying, legs kicking, the guitar in one hand and the other hand flailing, but he did Andy no harm. It was the directionless, ineffectual tantrum of a resentful child or the emotional paroxysm of a madman, not a reasoned adult's attempt to escape confinement, and it ended as suddenly as it had begun. Just before they reached the drums and started down the stairs at the back of the stage, Jim relaxed.

Andy stopped walking. He stood like that for a moment, still holding Jim's feet up off the floor, and it looked as though he was talking. Jim shook his head. Andy said something else. Jim nodded. Andy set him carefully on his feet. Without a glance at him, Jim returned to Jorie's side and rejoined the performance, which the others had continued without him.

Candy yelled something in my ear, but I couldn't hear what it was. I wondered whether that whole little scene had been choreographed for effect. If somebody hadn't thrown something at him, Jim could have used some other pretense for his display of rage. I studied his face. He was totally engrossed in the music again, as if nothing untoward had happened. There was no way to guess. But I thought it had been real. I had seen his face when he started to go off the front of the stage. If he'd been faking that anger, he was as good an actor as he was musician.

There was no question of design the next time something went wrong. Everything was fine until the end of the last number, but I'd begun to keep an eye on Blade. There was something about the way he moved. The bass never faltered, but he wasn't tracking. He wasn't there: he'd gone off somewhere in his mind, and it wasn't a good place he'd gone to, and I could tell something was going to give. I wasn't altogether surprised when, as the instruments segued into a lingering, howling dissonance at the end of the song, he pulled off the bass guitar and began to batter it against the floor in time to the drumbeat.

By then I'd determined which attendant/bodyguard went with which musician, just by their placement and the way they watched the show, and I looked at Blade's to see whether he would stop the destruction. He was poised for action, but he wasn't moving. I could see his face in a stray reflection off the side of the drums. He looked worried. Candy had told me all their names, but it took me a moment to remember his. I knew it was something geographic, maybe western, and I found myself running feverishly through the names of all the western states and cities I could think of, as though it really mattered. Dakota? Tahoe? The guitar's neck broke in Blade's hands, but the body was still attached. He kept swinging. Cheyenne? Reno. That was his bodyguard's name. Reno. I felt a momentary sense of triumph, as though I had accomplished something useful.

The Roach was watching Blade, and I thought Killer glanced that way a time or two, but Jorie and Jim ignored the whole thing, and the loss of the bass didn't seem to bother anyone. They were involved in one of those wholly atonal but not quite discordant competitions of instruments with which some rock songs' ends are dragged out into a wall of sound that sometimes evolves back into more conventional music, and sometimes simply collides with itself and dies. In that racket, the substitution of guitar bashing for guitar playing was not altogether inappropriate.

Blade lost his footing and went down, hitting the floor hard on knees and forearms. The broken guitar went flying. Reno jolted forward one anxious step and forced himself to a halt again, waiting to see whether Blade could make it up on his own. He couldn't. He crawled awkwardly in a pathetic little circle for a moment, head hanging, limp silver hair dragging the ground, then fell again, face-forward, and for one long moment made no further effort to rise. Reno didn't wait any longer. Cold Iron kept playing while he emerged from the shadows and crouched beside Blade to pull those frail, bony shoulders up off the floor.

When he had Blade sitting with his legs crumpled under him and one long, thin, tattooed arm draped limply around Reno's shoulders, the other still braced on the floor, Reno started to pick him up as one would a child. I thought Blade would let him. I thought he was too far gone to know what was happening, or to care. But his head came up, I saw his lips move, and Reno switched his grip to help him try to stand.

It must have mattered a lot, because Blade made a heroic effort, but his limbs wobbled bonelessly and it was only Reno's combined strength and kindness that made it look as though Blade had anything to do with getting himself offstage. Reno was several inches taller than he and three times as big around, and the mass was all muscle. Even so, it can't have been a simple task to carry a grown elf on one arm and make it look as though they were walking together.

When they came to the stairs, Blade took one blind step into thin air and they would have both gone down if Reno hadn't been ready for it. Blade must have passed out; he went limp, his head lolling back against Reno's shoulder, long strings of wet silver hair bright against Reno's black T-shirt. Reno barely hesitated. He juggled Blade's weight, balancing him, then did something complicated and quick that folded Blade neatly over his shoulder in a fireman's carry. They went down the stairs and out of sight with Blade swinging bonelessly against Reno's back.

Cold Iron brought their dissonance back into the range of music and let it die. They took their bows, the audience screamed and clapped and roared, and the band left the stage. The audience noise increased. When it reached what I thought must be its maximum possible volume, Jorie came bounding back onstage and the volume went up another notch. He took a microphone off its stand, and the volume diminished. Jim and the Roach returned. Killer stayed off, and I don't suppose Blade had any choice in the matter.

The remaining three did a final, quiet, calming number with just the two guitars, keyboard, and Jorie's voice for primary instruments. The other two voices backed him up in the chorus. It was a slow and sad song, a weather-worn and weary song, a song that said with beauty and with grace, "This is all we have left to give you, and when it is gone there will be nothing more. Take it and give us your blessing and let us go," and it said it so well and so clearly and so kindly that the audience heard it, and did it, and the concert was over.

I felt as though I had been wrung out and ought to be hung on a line to dry.

4

It had been a long, hard day. All I wanted to do was go home to bed. But I was living life in the fast lane now: sleeping didn't seem to be on the Cold Iron schedule. Less than an hour after the final number ended, we were whisked to the airport and onto a chartered plane for L.A. The guys had showered and changed at the arena into what they regarded as street clothes. Even Blade seemed to have been hosed down somehow, though instead of street clothes he'd been bundled into a hooded caftan. Reno more or less carried him onto the plane.

Candy assured me she and I could change on the plane. We didn't even return to the hotel for our belongings; they had been packed and loaded for us in our absence. Many of the fans wouldn't be home from the concert—some of them might not have even managed to get out of the arena parking lot yet—when we were already soaring up over the south bay, with the lights of San Francisco winking through the eternal drizzle behind us.

There was Christmas music playing on the plane's PA system. In the course of the day's events I'd managed to forget the season. The reminder was not welcome. Mind you, I had nothing against Christmas, really. The religious aspect seemed innocuous enough if you believed that sort of thing; and I wasn't one of those confused people who, seemingly unaware that they have the option to celebrate a holiday any way they choose but do not have the right to dictate or judge others' choices in the matter, complain bitterly of the season's "commercialism." My objection to the season was nothing so mundane. The plain fact was that it frightened me, and I didn't know why.

In general I would say that I am not a coward. I have a healthy respect for physical peril, but I don't panic and I don't often freeze up. If the situation requires action, and if it is action of which I am capable, I take it. I do what has to be done. I usually get the shakes afterward, when it doesn't matter, when there's time to think about what could have happened and to realize I've made it through another narrow squeak, but that's afterward. When the thing is happening, I deal with it.

The trouble with this fear was that nothing was happening. There was no action to take, no enemy to face, no peril to be overcome, nothing to deal with, and nothing to explain the gibbering terror that twisted my guts and drenched me in cold sweat. It was even worse this time than usual. And I knew that as long as the Christmas music kept playing, it wasn't going to go away. I could beat it back down enough to steady my hands, maybe enough to carry on a rational conversation, but it would still be there: a yammering sense of impending doom that would shadow everything I said and did and thought and felt. If we had been on the ground I could have walked away, but we were already reaching cruising altitude and Candy was unfastening her seat belt to go into the back of the plane to change her clothes. The music would be audible back there, too. I was trapped with it in a steel box with no exits.

"What's the matter, you scared of flying or something?" she said, looking at me oddly.

"No, I—" I caught myself in time. What was I going to say? "No, I'm afraid of Christmas?" Fear of flying might be embarrassing, but at least it wasn't lunatic. "Yeah, I guess I am, a little." It wasn't hard to look sheepish, and that's all it took to convince her. I had said what she expected to hear, and what's more it gave her a minor superiority over me. She was human enough to like that.

"You'll get over it," she said encouragingly. "Try not to think about it. Come on back with me and change clothes and maybe have a little soda or a tranq or something. Or get yourself a drink first, why don't you? There's always beer and whiskey and there might be some vodka or something. Check the bar." There was gin. Not Boodles, but a drinkable brand. I poured a healthy glass of it and told her to lead me to our street clothes. She looked shocked. "Don't you want ice or something in that? You just drink it straight? And warm?"

"That's how I like it," I said, and swallowed some to prove it. It went down smooth and easy and gave me a dangerous sense of my own ability to cope. With enough firewater in my veins, I could take on the world. Even at Christmas.

Candy shuddered delicately and led me to the back of the plane, where her suitcase and my pitiful little tote bag were piled in a latched cupboard in a small curtained alcove. The PA system was playing Bing Crosby's "White Christmas." I swallowed more gin and it didn't help a bit. Someone had neatly folded my blue jeans and sweater and packed them in the tote with my underwear and toothbrush. I dragged them out and began to divest myself of the silver-and-black concert costume. There was a dressing table with an indentation to hold my drink. I needed a distraction from the Christmas music, so I asked her the first thing that came to mind. "Was that for real, what Jimendan did, throwing a fit onstage?"

"What? When somebody threw something at him? Oh, yeah. It happens, sometimes. With him especially. He's got a real short temper."

"He's got a real short career, if his nanny doesn't catch him one time, and he manages to kill somebody." The little room smelled of chemicals and stale cigarettes. Bing Crosby kept singing, clearly audible over the dull roar of the engines.

"Andy's quick," she said. "And he can calm Jimendan down when nobody else can. They been together a long time."

I got the dress off and pulled on my jeans, trying not to hear the lyrics. Candy was quiet, struggling into a pair of colorful leggings that fit her like skin. Topics of conversation didn't come readily to mind, but anything was better than Christmas. I asked another stupid question. "Does Blade smash a lot of guitars? That must get costly."

She shrugged. "He can afford it." She put on a peach-colored smock over the leggings, and sat down to pull on pale blue slouch socks and high-top tennies.

"What's the point? Why would he ruin a perfectly good instrument?"

"I don't know." She picked up a comb and glanced at me. "Maybe it's like that old-timey group that used to break up the whole stage at the end of a concert, all the instruments and everything. You ever hear of them?"

"Yeah." I thought about the phrase "old-timey." The group in question was popular when I was still in diapers, yet I remembered them, and in a way it didn't seem that long ago. To Candy it must have seemed positively prehistoric. I felt about a hundred years old. "I never understood why they did it, either. Conspicuous waste," I said. She was only five or six years younger than I at the most, but they were years that had taken a lot out of me. I'd been old already when I was her age. "I have the idea they did it as some kind of artistic statement. You aren't gonna claim that's what Blade had in mind, are you?"

"I don't guess he had much of anything in mind," she said easily. "He was too stoned to know what he was doing. But the fans like it, you know. When he breaks things."

"Do they like it when he falls down and wallows around on the floor till his nanny picks him up?" There was no reason for me to be that rude about it. I sounded as though his behavior had been a personal affront to me. But it wasn't that, it was Christmas. Bing Crosby segued into a variant of "Silent Night," and I swilled more gin in self-defense. It was a beautiful rendition of a beautiful song and it jangled my nerves like chalk on a blackboard. My glittery headband looked ridiculous with jeans and a sweater. I took it off and glared at myself in the mirror, wondering how to get rid of the face paint: I had neither cold cream nor soap and water.

"They don't dislike it, if that's what you mean," Candy said. I had trouble remembering what the topic had been. "They don't judge him for it." She gave me a look that said I shouldn't judge him, either. "He was stoned, you know? You gotta make allowances. He couldn't help what he did." She handed me a jar of cold cream and a box of tissues.

I smeared cold cream on my face. "He could help getting that stoned."

She glanced at the gin next to me and didn't say anything. She didn't need to.

"Do they have to play this damn Christmas music?" I hadn't meant to say that. It came out too suddenly and too loud, startling us both.

"Don't you like Stevie Nicks?" she asked in surprise.

"I don't know Stevie Nicks. What the hell does he have to do with it? I don't like goddamn Christmas music. I—" It was the look in her eyes that stopped me. She thought I was going to hit her. Maybe I was. I had once hit Shannon at Christmas. Thinking ruefully that I probably ought to be locked up for the duration of the season, I took a deep breath, held it, then let it out slowly, and started rubbing paint off my face again. "I'm sorry," I said. "I don't know what's the matter with me."

"Stevie Nicks is a woman," she said cautiously. "That's who's singing right now."

"Oh." I scrubbed cold cream and scowled, aware that I was being as childishly sullen as Jim or Jorie had ever been. But I didn't know how to stop.

"You're tired," said Candy. "And no wonder, after what the Roach did to you. I'd forgotten about that. And then the concert and everything. You're just tired, that's all. Here, you missed a bit on your chin." She wiped at my chin, examined me for further traces of paint or cream, nodded her satisfaction, and threw away the tissue. "Come on, let's go sit down and maybe you can sleep a little before we get to LAX."

The front of the plane was quiet, except for the unending Christmas music. Stevie Nicks gave way to a forties big-band version of "O Little Town of Bethlehem." Blade was sprawled faceup across two seats with his head propped on a stack of pillows and his long legs dangling into the aisle. His face was serene, the mouth curved in a sweetly mischievous smile. Killer was in much the same position in the opposite two seats, but even sleep didn't make him look either vulnerable or serene. Most of his face was hidden, as always, but the chin jutted defiantly and the generous mouth was compressed in a stern, straight line.

In the seats in front of him, Jim and Jorie were leaning against each other like small boys napping during a long car ride. Jim's head was cradled in the curve of Jorie's neck, and Jorie's rested against the crown of Jim's head. Their bodies, with the adjoining arms linked and legs balanced against each other, the free arms and legs spread out to either side, presented such an exact appearance of mirror image that for one brief moment as I glanced at them, I thought I was looking at one elf reflected in a sheet of mirror where no mirror should be. It took conscious effort to force my mind to understand what I was really seeing.

I had known identical twins, and fraternal twins who were very alike. In all such cases the differences became evident over time, and the similarities decreased with familiarity, till sometimes one wondered why strangers couldn't tell them apart. With Jim and Jorie the reverse was happening. The differences that had seemed so obvious on first meeting were decreasing, the similarities increasing, till I wondered why I had thought it so easy to tell them apart. Candy had said they were not twins, but at that point they seemed more alike to me than any of the identical twins I had known. I wondered whether that indicated something about them, or about me. Maybe I'd had more gin than was good for me. I drank some more.

The Roach was the only band member still awake. He was occupying the two seats across from Jim and Jorie, but he wasn't sprawled out and relaxed the way the others were. He had the overhead light on and a bass guitar in his lap with earphones plugged into it. His fingers flew over the strings, one foot beating time on the foot rest extended from the seat in front of him, all in perfect silence. The beat did not match that of the PA system's persistent Christmas carols. He didn't look up as Candy and I passed him to take our seats. Whatever he was playing, it looked complicated, and he appeared totally engrossed in it.

The personal bodyguards, and a few other crew members whose function I didn't know, were in the next batch of seats. Most of them seemed to be awake, reading or smoking or quietly conversing. A couple of them had drinks, the others coffee. For them, the workday was not yet done. The band and whatever accoutrements had come with it would have to be off-loaded at LAX, transported to a hotel, and safely installed for the night before they could punch their figurative time clock. The personal bodyguards probably couldn't fully relax even than. I imagined they were on twenty-four-hour call, and with this group that might mean they had very few breaks indeed.

As we settled into our seats again and Candy produced pillows and blankets in abundance for my proposed nap, I thought about the many faces of Cold Iron I'd seen so far. First the repellent and dangerous social misfits of the morning, wallowing in the easy offenses so readily available to celebrities in our society, and openly hostile to me as a recognized inferior intruding where I could not hope to belong. Then the sheepish big brothers, relatively well behaved, concerned, and protective of me after the Roach's dangerous practical joke. Then the gaiety, passion, and glory of the performers, the elf-rock stars, the magic makers, the idols who were too powerful to worry about exposing their feet of clay. And now they were just an ordinary bunch of tired young elves on their way to another job in another town. Despite the long hair and pointed ears and the aspects of the bizarre in their attire, they might have been anybody's neighbors or nephews.

Most people wear a lot of different faces according to the company they keep, the jobs they do, the impression they want to make. They adjust themselves in little ways to accommodate the circumstances, so automatically that they are often not even aware of the transition. They produce a friendly smile for the bank teller despite feeling desperate over their account balance, or they treat surly customers in the workplace with patient deference instead of smashing their faces, or they keep quiet about their liberal politics at dinner with their conservative parents-in-law. They say "I like your new dress" when they don't, they say "I'm fine" when they aren't, they say "I'd love to" when they wouldn't. They power dress when they feel powerless. They fawn over ugly babies, caress stinking dogs, and swear they like having cat hairs on their best dry-clean-only clothes. It's all natural, it's often sincere, and it's usually well-meant. And it's all small stuff.

With celebrities, particularly with performers, there are bound to be more faces worn, and bigger differences between them. Few performers can leave all the tricks onstage, and fewer still see any reason to. Living in California, I'd met my share of actors, and acquired the usual mild cultural prejudice against them. I couldn't tell whether I was extending that to include these elfrock musicians. Had they really shown me such an array of different faces? Or was it only my perceptions that had changed?

Certainly they'd been hostile when I first arrived among them, less so after the Roach drugged me. Perhaps I had taken their initial hostility, combined it with my basic prejudices, and turned them into repellent monsters all by myself, then turned them back into normal people when they became more sympathetic. From there it was an easy step to see them as small gods onstage. And I wasn't starstruck enough to let them stay small gods when they came offstage, so I turned them back into ordinary guys.

But they weren't ordinary guys. At least, not decent ordinary guys. That first impression of corruption and menace had not been entirely unfounded. Jimendan had made a sincere effort to attack if not kill someone in the audience, all of them seemed drugged or drunk by the end of the concert, and Blade had become so stoned he had to be carried offstage. Decent ordinary guys don't do that.

Or do they? One had to remember that these elves were spoiled and thoughtless boys in many ways, their development arrested by the pursuit of musical success. Spoiled and thoughtless boys of all ages get drunk when they can, fight pointless battles, and generally indulge in outrageous and self-destructive behavior. So do a lot of other damaged people, and one doesn't necessarily write them off as unredeemably evil and walk away.

That was the bottom line, of course. I wanted to walk away from the corruption, but I was terribly attracted by the music. Which made me want to see its creators as more wholesome than they were. And that frightened me.

Once I had figured that out, I could laugh at myself and relax a little: few things in this life come in clear black and white. It's all shades of gray, and if you don't learn to accept that and cope with it you're in trouble. The Cold Iron musicians weren't agents of the devil, and they weren't candidates for God. They were complex creatures like everybody else I knew. More complex than most, because they were elves, the creatures that some people believed were "fallen angels, not good enough to save nor bad enough to be lost." Nothing about them was likely to be painted in clear black and white.

Having belatedly recognized that simple fact, perhaps I would be better able to deal with them in the future. I still wasn't half sure I liked any of them, but fortunately we don't have to like everyone. It certainly wasn't a job requirement. Not if I expected to discover that one of them was a potential murderer. Of course I didn't know the culprit was a musician, and in fact I thought it likely that if it had been one of them Candy would have recognized his voice no matter how stoned she'd been. But I'd already jumped to too many unfounded conclusions. I was determined from now on to keep an open mind and start using what intelligence I could muster.

As a first step, I finished my glass of gin and relaxed into the bounty of pillows Candy so solicitously provided. I felt much too keyed-up to sleep, but it would be restful to spend the remainder of the flight bundled in pillows and blankets with my eyes closed, reviewing what little evidence I had and planning the strategy of my investigation.

I woke when the plane landed. For a long, dazed moment I could not remember where I was, or why. Vague afterimages of dreams chased themselves sourly through my mind. There was a small, darkened window in front of me and the sound of waking passengers behind me.

I knew I was on a plane, but I could not remember where I was going or where I had been. Then a reflection in the glass resolved itself into Jorandel's face, and the disorientation was transformed instantly into an odd mixture of excitement and unease. At the time, I thought both were in response to the job itself, to the prospect of tracking down a potential murderer.

The gin had left a foul taste in my mouth. I had given up smoking years before, but I wanted a cigarette now. I straightened irritably among my pillows and scowled at the empty glass still in my hand. Candy was no longer beside me. In my sleep I had stretched out to occupy both seats. Had she gone because I invaded her space, or had I invaded her space because she was gone? I didn't much care, but I did look around to see what had become of her.

The Roach had put aside his guitar and accepted her in its place. They were both limp and damp and disheveled and wearing expressions of mildly dazed complacency, and I glanced forward to see whether the crew had, after all, been asleep during the last part of the trip. They clearly had not, but they were just as clearly indifferent to any activities short of life-threatening violence in the seats aft of theirs. The desperate and emotionless couplings of these pathetic young animals held no interest for them.

I heard the judgment in that thought and tried to withdraw it, to tell myself I was being a prude about something that was none of my business. But I could not convince myself there was anything wholesome or healthy about such public sex, and in fact I wondered with an inward shudder whether the Roach's goal might not have been as much the degradation of his partner as the enjoyment of her body. Whether she knew it or not, the act in those circumstances was degrading, if only because it lacked even such dignity as that very undignified exercise can retain when it is performed in privacy and with affection. The two of them had turned it into a circus act. An uninteresting one at that, if the audience-response was any measure. I felt curiously saddened, as though I had witnessed the death of some small, harmless, and pretty thing. In a way, of course, I had. Another small piece of Candy's self-respect was gone forever, and if she didn't know it yet she would feel it in time, just the same.

I shoved pillows and blankets irritably aside and scowled at my feet. Somebody opened a door and the band began filing out past me. They didn't bother to carry anything with them; it would be up to the crew to gather their belongings and bring them along. I wondered rather wildly whether, if I remained where I was, they would gather me up too; and if so, would I be taken to the hotel as luggage, or tossed with the garbage? Between the two, I wasn't sure I had a preference. What was I doing there? I didn't like the client, I didn't like the job, I didn't like the people it put me into contact with, and right then I didn't much like myself. It would have been so much nicer to be home alone in my nice little cottage in Berkeley, listening to the lonely foghorns out on the bay.

Someone paused beside my seat and put a gentle hand on my shoulder. "Come, cousin." It was Jorandel or Jimendan, but I wasn't sure which one. "You will feel much improved when we reach the hotel and you are able to sleep in a real bed the rest of the night."

I glanced up. No bangs: it was Jorandel. Those clear blue eyes looked positively friendly. I forced a smile and hauled myself to my feet. "Thanks, I expect you're right."

"Mine is the voice of experience," he said, and glanced over his shoulder. "Come, little brother, no loitering. Hey, Blade!" He raised his voice. "Blade! Awaken! Collect yourself. It's show time: we have arrived."

"Argh," said Blade.

Killer leaned silently over Blade's seat and hauled him to his feet.

"He will be fine," said Jorandel. He took my hand to lead me off the plane. "If Killer can't manage him, Reno will. Let's get out of here." His hand was firm and strong, as arrogantly self-assured as the rest of him, and I ought to have wanted to pull free of it. I didn't. I let him lead me out into the smog-laden night air, down the stairs, and into the waiting limousine as though I had always followed where he led, and always would.

There was no conversation on the way to the hotel, and no hesitation at the desk; someone had already taken care of the paperwork, and a bellhop led us through heavily carpeted corridors and elevators and deposited us in a vast suite of rooms that I perceived as though in a dream. In fact, the whole time from meeting the band till the present moment had taken on the quality of a dream, and I was having trouble sorting out which bits had really happened and which I might have imagined.

Jorandel deposited me in one of the suite's rooms, planted a brotherly kiss on my forehead, and went away, leaving me adrift in a sea of benign confusion. I stood for a long moment staring at the bed rather as though I wondered what I was supposed to do with it. The door opened and I thought for a moment Jorandel had returned. In my confused state I was not altogether sure I minded. But the moment he put his arms around me I knew it wasn't Jorandel. I don't know why. I couldn't see his face, and there was nothing radically different about their hard, slender bodies. But I knew, and I didn't like it. I had given Jimendan no encouragement. He had no right to assume his attentions would be welcome. I said, "Stop it," and shoved at him, trying to break his grip, but he didn't release me.

"Come on, honey, you know you want it." His voice was disconcertingly like Jorandel's.

"Get out of here," I said, shoving harder. "Jimendan, I don't want to hurt you, but I will if you don't leave me alone."

He laughed softly. "You frighten me." He was tugging at my sweater, trying to pull it up.

"Let go of me, you arrogant ass." I tried to punctuate the suggestion with a solid knee in his crotch, but he blocked me with a dancer's easy agility and laughed at me. I stomped on his foot instead, and used the momentary distraction to try to writhe out of his grip. I refrained from breaking his nose or his eardrums because I was aware of the value of both to his career, and didn't think his offense warranted a crippling response. But the violence of his reaction when I tried to get loose was unexpected and so painful that I cried out involuntarily and forgot my scruples.

At that point he had my arms pinned to my sides in a bruising grip so I couldn't do much against him. I did my damnedest to break his kneecap with one foot, and when he bent to back away from the force of that, I butted my head hard against his, hoping to collide with his nose or at least his mouth, both nicely vulnerable areas. My aim was off. It's always chancy to use your head as a weapon, but it was the best I could do at the time. The point of his chin probably did as much damage to the top of my head as the other way around, but at least the blow connected, and while it dizzied me, it also stunned him enough to loosen his grip on me. I wrenched free and staggered away from him just as the door burst open and Jorandel came charging in.

For one brief second I thought I would have to fight off both of them. I braced myself, but it was Jimendan he attacked, not me. He clearly saw himself in the role of rescuer, a slightly tarnished knight fully prepared to vanquish at least a small fire-breathing dragon. I don't know whether he realized ahead of time that it was his brother in the dragon role. At the time I was in such a foul mood that I really wondered whether the two of them had planned it together to give Jorandel a better chance with me, but I realized almost before the thought was fully formed how silly it was. Both these elves had such physical arrogance, and so many women justifying it by begging for their attention, that it would not occur to either of them to do anything more than announce his selection to the anxiously waiting contestants.

The next few moments are vague in my memory. Jimendan was sent packing in short order by one or both of us, and I was left with Jorandel. I suppose he was at least mildly embarrassed both by his brother's behavior and by his own late arrival. And I was embarrassed both by having been put in such a situation and by having been a little slow to get out of it. Neither of us was in an ideal mood for rational conversation.

I don't know what I said to him, or what he said in response: I only know that the net result was that he slammed his way out of my room even more loudly than he'd burst into it, and I stood there for a long moment afterward feeling as though I'd broken something delicate and precious and utterly irreplaceable. I couldn't forget the look on his face when Jimendan had gone and he'd turned to me to see whether I was all right. No one had ever looked at me like that before, as though I were the delicate and precious and utterly irreplaceable thing that might be broken. I wasn't sure what it meant, if it meant anything, but I knew what I had wanted it to mean, and I thought I could not have more surely destroyed that possibility if I had tried to kick him in the balls instead of his brother.

I told myself I wasn't a trophy hunter anyway. I didn't want to sleep with the celebrity. Hell, who knew where he'd been? A condom might not be adequate protection from things he might have caught. I didn't like elfrock stars. I didn't like *elves.*

I didn't like much of anybody right then. I sure as hell didn't like me. I locked my door, pulled off my clothes, and went to bed, and I did not cry myself to sleep. But I wanted to.

5

I must have managed all of two hours' sleep before I was awakened by the furtive sound of another uninvited guest moving around in the predawn stillness of my room. I'd been dreaming something ugly. Not the standard Christmas nightmare, but something like it, gloomy and full of despair. It took a long moment to understand what had awakened me, and a longer moment to figure out where I was, and why, and whether there ought to be anyone in the same room with me, going over the contents of my purse with a miniature pinpoint flashlight. My mind wasn't tracking very well. It kept drifting back into the dream, confusing it with reality. I stared at the dark, sly intruder and thought it was somebody's father. Somebody's big, strong, ugly, dangerous father.

I'd had to kill Kyriander Stone's father to keep him from slaughtering his children. He was a big man, ugly and mad, and reason hadn't worked with him. In the end I had about two seconds to kill him before he killed me. But I kept thinking there must have been a better way. There should have been a better way. Killing people is not a comfortable solution to any problem. There must always be a better way.

I hadn't found one, and a human being was dead, and now I was trapped in a midnight room with a nightmare. The rage I felt was exactly proportionate to my disorientation. I could have turned on the lamp beside my bed to see who was ransacking my belongings. Or if for some obscure reason I felt violence was essential to the situation, I could have edged out of the bed in silence and tackled the intruder before he knew what hit him. It might have given me enough of an edge to turn that flashlight on his face and find out who he was before he killed me or fled.

I did neither of those things. I was too tired, too cross, too frightened, and too dazed by dreams to behave so rationally. I hurled myself out of the bed in such a clamorous tangle of sheets and curses that the intruder had ample time to drop my purse and flee before I even realized that my haste and confusion had made me so clumsy I wasn't going to land on my feet. When the dim light from the outer room briefly backlighted my intruder as he went through the door, I was too busy trying to save myself from a painful collision with a bureau to see him.

Once untangled from the bedding and the furniture, I stumbled to the door and tried to haul it open, but had to pause to fumble with the lock. When I got it open, there was no one visible in the outer room. Fortunately, I realized, before I dashed out to look farther, that I was stark naked. It didn't seem the proper mode of attire for chasing sneak thieves. I returned to the bed and yanked loose a sheet to wrap around myself, fully aware that by the time I got out of the room there'd be no sign of anyone awake in the whole Cold Iron suite, but determined to look anyway. Maybe there were security guards around somewhere who'd seen something.

Demurely wrapped in the sheet, I clutched its inadequate front closure and was halfway out of the door before I realized how utterly pointless the venture was. Even if a security guard had seen someone coming out of my room, it would have been someone he knew, someone who belonged with the band. He wouldn't know me, and I didn't belong. No matter how carefully or casually I inquired (and it would be hard to look entirely calm and casual, dressed in a sheet), he would know that what it boiled down to was outsider against insider, and I wouldn't learn a damn thing from him. Besides, the door had been locked. It was easy enough to slip the lock with a credit card, but it was also probable that the security guards had the keys. If one of them had admitted my intruder, he wouldn't be likely to tell me so.

Sighing, I stepped back into the room, closed the door,

and turned on the light. The only belongings I had brought with me from the plane were in my purse, which was lying open with its contents scattered on a low bureau near the bed, where the intruder had been standing. Sometime after I'd fallen asleep, someone had deposited my tote bag on a chair by the door, which indicated that the security guards did have keys, and had used them to let in the baggage handler if no one else. The tote's contents, too, had been rifled, presumably before I woke. There had been nothing in it to tell anyone a thing about me, but the ID in my purse was all too revealing. I checked: the wallet had been gone through very thoroughly. My P.I. license was on the top of the stack of cards and papers that had been pulled loose for careful examination. Somebody knew what I was, though he had no way of knowing who had hired me or why. Nor had I any way of knowing who he was or why he hadn't trusted my cover story.

As far as I'd been able to tell, no one but Emerson had even briefly doubted my claim to be Candy's cousin. Of them all, Emerson had struck me as the least likely to be planning Jorandel's murder. Of course there were any number of other things these people might want to hide. They seemed to use as many drugs as the average pharmacy, for example, and they wouldn't want a cop in their midst taking note of that. Maybe Emerson had just been checking to make sure that wasn't what I was. If so, a private cop probably wouldn't worry him. He'd know better than most how little official standing a P.I. really has. But wouldn't Emerson have tried more direct means of learning about me before he raided my room and ransacked my purse while I slept? There were a number of more dignified (and, actually, more effective) ways he could have learned what he wanted to know.

Whoever it had been, it was too late and I was too tired to do anything about it now. I locked my door again—apparently a useless gesture, but I needed a gesture—and went back to bed. At least the adventure had chased the bad dreams from my mind. Maybe I could get some restful sleep before I had to face Cold Iron in all its members' varied roles in the morning.

* * *

It turned out I didn't have to face them the next morning at all. Candy wanted to go shopping, to augment my meager wardrobe. I was just weary enough from the previous day's and night's alarums and excursions to give in to her insistence that it would be a correct and reasonable way to spend some of the money she had paid me. Certainly I couldn't keep wearing the same jeans and sweater forever.

There were no musicians in evidence when we left the suite to begin proceedings with breakfast in the hotel café. Presumably they were all still sleeping; Candy had awakened me earlier than I would really have liked, though it was a good deal later in the morning than I customarily slept. She offered me a line of soda to get me started, but I waited for coffee.

What the café downstairs provided when I asked for coffee was so bad I nearly regretted having disdained the soda. Most restaurants serve boiled cardboard and call it coffee, but this was a very expensive café in a very expensive hotel and I had somehow imagined they might be familiar with the genuine bean in its pure, oily, very darkly roasted form. Silly idea. Places that claim to serve espresso frequently begin with a bean that would not offend the delicate cardboard-judging sensibilities of an instant-coffee aficionado. Why should a place that claimed nothing stronger than coffee do any better? At least it seemed to have some caffeine content, and if I had to drink a gallon of it to get the caffeine I'd have got in a single cup of home brew (at least at my home), what the hell? Doubtless we could find rest rooms during our shopping expedition.

The food was good, and the background Muzak bore no relation to Christmas. I ate a mountain of hotcakes, several eggs, and more bacon than was good for me, and felt a lot better when I finally leaned back from the empty plates. Candy, meantime, picked dispiritedly at a small bowl of cottage cheese topped with chunks of fruit that looked astonishingly fresh and delicious. Soda doesn't do a person's appetite much good. It doesn't do any part of a person much good, but there's no use saying that to someone who considers it a necessary part of her daily routine. It was none of my business anyway.

We all have our little ways of killing ourselves. Some ways are just faster than others. I guzzled my so-called coffee and left it to her to introduce a topic of conversation if she wanted to talk.

"Did Jimendan come on to you last night?" she asked abruptly.

I admitted it.

"He's pretty good in bed."

"I didn't sleep with him."

She stared. "Why not?"

"I didn't want to."

"Oh." She picked at her fruit. "Which one do you want?"

"I don't want any of them, Candy." I think I believed that when I said it. I certainly wanted to believe it.

She looked at me, frowning. "Aren't you . . . You aren't . . . ?"

"I'm heterosexual, if that's what you want to know. But I'm not a trophy hunter. Celebrity doesn't turn me on. I know that's un-American. You're supposed to want a thing more if a lot of other people want it too. But I don't want sex with a thing, with fame. And I don't want it with somebody who thinks of me as a convenience, or as something he just naturally has a right to because of the wonderfulness of himself. Or the famousness of himself. Feet aren't the only parts of idols that tend to be made of clay." *Methinks the lady doth protest o'ermuch.* Besides, I was confusing her. She had no idea what I was trying to say. "Never mind. I just don't want to sleep with anyone in Cold Iron, okay?"

She shook her head in amazement. "Boy, I do. I did, too. Sleep with them, I mean. All of them." She said that with a lifted chin, a defiant little blaze of pride and challenge in her eyes, as though she expected me to refute her claim. Poor little nubbin. She had tossed a ruby into the fire to prove it wasn't the fake kind that fails to explode when heated. She had proved her value to herself if to no one else, but the proof had destroyed her.

The background music segued into the Muzak version of Christmas carols. I stood up. "Let's get out of here."

Candy looked surprised, but followed me obediently.

She hadn't been eating anyway, and she had already signed the check. We caught a cab in front of the hotel and she told its driver where she wanted to go. "Roach gave me some money today if you don't want to pay for cabs and stuff," she said shyly. "I mean, 'cause I know you didn't really want to go shopping anyway, even though you need stuff."

"Don't worry about it." The cabdriver had the car radio on, playing Christmas music. "Why did you ask whether Jimendan tried to, um?" I asked, having a minor fit of discretion in the presence of a stranger.

Discretion was not one of Candy's major talents. "Whether he came on to you?" she said. "Oh, I just thought he would. Usually he's first with most girls. Jorandel could be, if he wanted to, but—I don't know. He's been in a weird mood lately. You know? He used to sleep with everything in sight, but lately he's kinda slowed down or something. He's older than Jimendan," she added, as though in explanation.

"Right," I said. "Twenty-eight, did you say? Practically antique. Probably getting creaky in the joints by now. Elves age so rapidly."

She looked embarrassed. "Well, I'm sorry," she said defensively. "I forgot you're older, too. But you're only Jimendan's age, aren't you? And besides, don't men lose their, you know, so they can't do it when they're older? Even elves? I mean because Jorandel really *doesn't* sleep with the groupies as much as he used to. So I figured that must prob'ly mean—"

"I don't think he's losing his sex drive already," I said. "It doesn't happen in the late twenties. As I understand it, a lot of humans keep going real nicely right into their eighties, and elves prob'ly twice that."

She shuddered involuntarily. "Who'd want to sleep with somebody that old?" she asked with obvious distaste.

"Someone else that old?" I suggested.

"I guess," she said dubiously.

I noticed the taxi driver sneaking glances at us in his rearview mirror, his eyes amused and tolerant. I wanted to ask him to turn off the radio, but I didn't. Instead, I told Candy about the intruder in my room last night, and asked her which of them she thought it might have been.

"Well, nobody!" she said in surprise. "I mean, who would? Why? You mean somebody stole something, or what?"

"No, nothing was missing. I think somebody was trying to find out who I am, where I fit. But I don't know who would."

She shook her head in amazement. "Neither do I. Nobody would. Are you sure you didn't just dream it, or something? I mean, why would anybody want to do that?"

"If one of them really wants to kill Jorandel, and doesn't believe I'm your cousin, that might be reason enough," I said dryly. We had lowered our voices, and the taxi driver had lost interest, but I glanced at the rearview mirror in time to notice that he'd heard enough of that to catch his attention again. I held his gaze impassively until he had to look back at the road for safety's sake. He shrugged and kept his eyes on the road for a while.

"Or what if one of them thought you were a narc?" asked Candy, getting into the spirit of speculation. Her face clouded. "But why would they? Why wouldn't they believe what we told them?"

"Somebody obviously didn't," I said.

"Well, but, who?"

"That's what I want to know."

"Couldn't it have just been one of the hotel maids?"

"In the dead of night? And Cold Iron's security didn't stop her? I don't think so."

"I guess not." She frowned uneasily. "It wasn't the Roach. I was with him. I'd've noticed if he got up anytime. And I don't see how it could've been Blade, because, Jeez, he practically OD'd at the concert and prob'ly hasn't woke up yet."

"That leaves Killer, Jimendan, Jorandel, security, and all the bodyguards. Who else stayed in our hotel? Does everybody, or do the lowly workers stay somewhere else?"

"You mean the roadies?" she asked. "Oh, most of them didn't fly down. There's a truck for the equipment and a bus for the roadies. They're prob'ly here now, but not at the hotel."

"So who was at the hotel?"

"Well, the band," she said thoughtfully, working it out. "The guys' bodyguards, and maybe a couple medical people. Emerson. And some of his people, security people, three or four. I think that's all."

"That seems ample," I said sourly. "We have it narrowed down to only a dozen or so suspects, right?"

She worked on it for a while and couldn't manage the math. "I guess," she said. "But, look—"

We arrived at our destination before she could finish the thought. Some people could manage to get out of a car and continue a train of thought at the same time, but Candy was not one of them, at least not when she'd started the morning with a noseful of soda. Whatever she had been about to say, I did not think it would have been particularly useful, so I didn't pursue it. I paid the taxi driver and watched him nose back into traffic. "Now what?"

We were at a shopping mall full of trendy little shops in which Candy spent a couple of happy hours selecting increasingly complicated costumes for me until I wearied too much of spandex and glitter and fringe to endure more. We had our arms full of shopping bags by then anyway, and the supply of cash that I'd brought with me was nearly exhausted. I hate shopping even for things I want, even in more benign seasons. These were not things I wanted, and the season was not benign. Nearly every store had some kind of Christmas decorations and most of the Muzak was Christmas-oriented. I told her the name of my bank and she found a branch for me with an ATM that accepted my card and spat out money on request. Not as much as we'd spent, but enough to see me through the average emergency. I put it in the trendy new purse that she'd insisted I begin using at once (she had wanted to throw away the old one, but I'd rescued it by hiding it in one of the shopping bags) and told her to find us a source of espresso. It was that kind of mall.

The espresso shop she found surprised me. It wasn't the gilded and mirrored and ivy-jungled horror I'd expected. It was a large, rather barren room with sturdy marble-topped tables and comfortable wooden chairs, a many-handled steamer behind the marble counter, and one large and colorful travel poster on each wall. A *ficus benjamina* in good health beside the front window was the only potted plant in sight. Next to it was a rack of newsmagazines and papers with only a small scattering of tabloids for the thought-free diehards who couldn't handle brute reality (or, okay, for the weary who wanted a laugh).

We placed our order, deposited our shopping bags under one of the tables, and Candy acquired the key to a rest room and disappeared. She came back looking wider of eye and tenser of manner, so it wasn't hard to guess she'd wanted the privacy for other than standard reasons. Leaving her to guard our hard-won possessions, I took the key and went on a more ordinary errand. When I got back, our order had been filled and Candy was happily sipping a café latte and poking incuriously at a sticky bun that had apparently looked better to her at the counter than it did at the table.

"I was thinking," she said when I was seated. It was an announcement, and she didn't seem inclined to follow it up with any additional information. That's a conversational gambit I loathe; I was supposed to prompt her. A polite person would have. I dislike being maneuvered, even in small ways. Perhaps especially in small ways. When people attempt that particular maneuver on me, I don't respond. Sometimes not even when I'm genuinely curious about what it is they want to say. Certainly not when I have no interest. And it was not hard to tell from Candy's tone, which was brisk and vacant and drugged, that her thoughts just now were unlikely to be of interest.

Having given the cue for someone to prompt them, some people will wait quite a while before continuing without the prompt. Some will even give a second cue for a prompt. Others are quick to fill the conversational lacuna in order not to lose points with themselves by admitting the failed maneuver. Candy did none of those things. She was alone in her drug daze, quite oblivious to my response or lack of it. After a hesitation just long enough for me to fill with the expected prompt, she continued exactly as though I had given it. I expect she imagined I had.

"Groupies," she said, as if in answer to a question. "You know, the girls that follow rock bands and try to get picked up so they can sleep with them. Like the ones that were in San Francisco with the guys yesterday. Some of 'em keep score and make notches on their belts for how many they've gone to bed with. You know. Those kind just sort of run through the band and go when they've got all their notches, but some of 'em hang around longer, you know, maybe latch onto one of the guys and travel with us for a while." It didn't seem to occur to her that she might fit in that category herself. "Anyway, you know, Jimendan went out last night after you'd gone to bed and he came back with some groupies for him and Jorandel and Killer. So what I was thinking, you know, prob'ly it was one of them that got into your room last night. You see? Maybe she thought you had some drugs, or she could've wanted to steal your money or something."

"Then why didn't she steal it?"

"What?" She stared at me for a long, uncomprehending moment. I had a feeling that even though she'd been talking to me, she was startled to discover I was still there. "Oh. Oh, you mean why didn't she steal your money? Well, you know, maybe it wasn't the money. What it could've been, she could've been looking for drugs, then. If she wasn't looking for money. Or just a cigarette or something. She could've been looking for a cigarette."

"Right," I said, studying her. "Candy, I think we ought to get you back to the hotel."

"Oh, but there's more shops," she said.

"There'll be more shops another day," I said. "I'm tired of them today. And I think you need to go home."

To my amazed consternation, tears welled in those enormous fawn eyes. "Okay." She nodded obediently and bent to collect shopping bags.

"Jeez, Candy, does it matter to you that much?"

She straightened to stare at me, seemingly unaware of the tears rolling down her face. "Does what matter?"

"Quitting shopping. Is that what you're crying about?"

"I'm not crying." She said it in apparently genuine surprise. A huge tear dripped off the sharp edge of her jaw onto her hand and she stared at it for a long moment without expression, then slowly reached up to wipe her face with both hands. "Oh. Sorry." She was blushing. "I didn't know I was. You must've said that word. That's right, I remember, you did say it. Look, I'm not crazy or anything, it's just that when I hear that word sometimes I kind of cry, you know, without even knowing it, so mostly I ask people not to say it."

"What word?"

"H-o-m-e." She spelled it so quickly, I barely caught it. "It's not real important or anything, I mean I don't exactly mind, and I hope you don't think it's too crazy, I mean there must be other people that can't hear a certain word without crying, or laughing, or something," she said earnestly. "I mean I'm not crazy, really, it's just that one word."

"I understand." I didn't, but I wasn't in a position to criticize her for crying over a word when I was frightened of a season. "I'll try not to say it again." It was a harmless pact between lunatics.

She smiled gratefully. "Thank you, Rosie. You're really nice, you know?"

"Don't count on it," I said, and hesitated. "You don't get much female companionship, do you?"

"Well," she said dubiously, "there's always the groupies."

"Sounds like they're too intent on their score cards to give anybody much companionship. Including the guys."

"Well, yeah, but the guys don't need it. I mean, they've got each other. And their music."

I didn't argue. I had a feeling she would not understand the concept of requiring at least the capacity for companionship in one's sexual partners. Quite possibly, neither would Cold Iron's musicians. The relationship between them and their groupies was symbiotic: they used each other as mechanical sex toys and, in a twisted way, for status. It was ugly, but it wasn't illegal, and it wasn't any of my business.

We caught another taxi and told the driver to take us

to the hotel. On the way I tried to get Candy to talk again about the threat to Jorandel that had prompted her to hire me, but she was too stoned to pursue a train of thought for long, and she seemed indifferent to the whole concept. It occurred to me that she might have invented the threat to Jorandel as an excuse to bring a woman along on the tour for company. It annoyed her that I had interrupted our pleasant shopping trip with talk of violence and intrigue. She seemed happy with things as they were, and not at all interested in seeing me get any work done.

But she had been convincing when she'd come to the office in Berkeley. I decided her lack of interest now was drug-induced, and I would give it a little time before concluding there wasn't a job here for me to do. The band was staying three nights in Los Angeles before moving on. That should be long enough to give me a good idea whether she'd invented the whole thing. If, at the end of that time, it appeared to me that she had, I would return what was left of her money and go home.

Meantime, since I couldn't get her to talk about the threat (if any) to Jorandel, I asked the kind of question she was willing to answer. I learned that she'd been picked up in San Francisco nearly a year ago by Jimendan, worked her way through the band, and ended up with a semipermanent arrangement with the Roach. I learned that Blade's parents were in show business and didn't see much of him. I learned that Killer was the cherished elder son of a successful real estate agent in one of the dusty little towns in California's great inland valley. I learned nothing about the Roach but that she thought he was good in bed.

About Jimendan and Jorandel I learned a number of interesting but useless items. They had left Faerie when they were teenagers and attended a human high school. They had begun the twin act there, substituting for one another successfully in classes and on dates, and had learned to use that success to good advantage in other areas. Each had strengths and weaknesses the other didn't have. In the beginning they were unlike enough to be easily distinguished unless they augmented their efforts with magic, but they worked on it till the switches were automatic and very nearly undetectable to most people. Whenever one of them had to do something at which the other was better, they switched roles and had become so accomplished at it that very few humans could tell them apart, though doubtless another elf could, and Candy maintained she could. I was beginning to realize that I could not; my initial conviction that they were quite different had been based on their very different states of mind and health at the time. But I had mistaken them for one another onstage last night; and when Jimendan first came to my room I thought it was Jorandel till he touched me.

They were certainly successful at fooling others, and they used the twin switch without compunction, even in official situations. When Jorandel became old enough in human years to acquire a driver's license, for example, he wasn't interested but Jimendan was, so Jimendan posed as Jorandel to get one. A year later, so they would each have one, Jorandel got his in Jimendan's name. More recently, Jimendan had made a solo album on which Jorandel had sung in Jimendan's name. Jimendan frequently tricked groupies into sleeping with him twice, once as himself and once as his brother.

Jorandel could play every instrument in the band, but was learning from Jimendan how to play guitar in Jimendan's style. This was apparently a recent endeavor. When Candy had first known them, Jimendan had been the one more likely to instigate a twin switch or to emphasize their likeness when they were together, but in recent months Jorandel had become almost obsessed with the idea of their interchangeability. He even went so far as to change his eating habits, trying to gain weight to match Jimendan; and to try to bully Jimendan into losing weight to match him.

None of this, of course, was public knowledge, and much if not all of it was probably fabricated either by Candy to amaze me or by the brothers to impress Candy. But the telling of it amused us both during an otherwise boring taxi ride, so it served some small purpose.

The guys were awake when we got upstairs, lounging around the main room of the suite with booze and groupies. I had made it past the hotel's Christmas tree and the elevator's Christmas Muzak without incident, but there was a radio blaring Christmas rock in the suite: it seemed there was no escape from the season. When Candy produced a beer and an opener, I accepted them without hesitation. She opened one for herself and led me to my room, where she wanted me to try on all my new purchases again. I let her select a blouse, a belt, and a few baubles to replace my sweater and borrowed baubles, but I was not about to go through the exhausting routine of trying on everything again. She accepted that with minimal argument and, while I was changing into the things she had selected for my afternoon wear, began going through the rest of the stuff looking for the perfect costume for that night's concert.

When she began to complain of the things we hadn't bought, I decided it was time to tell her I wasn't going to stay with them past the L.A. dates. "There's been no sign of any hazard to Jorandel that I can see," I said. "Everybody I talk to says he's one of the most splendid people they ever met, and that the band couldn't exist without him. So who's going to kill such a paragon? I think you must have misunderstood what you heard, Candy."

She stared. "You can't," she said. "Listen, you gotta stay. Please. I swear to God I heard them, Rosie. You gotta help him."

I might have been less firm if I hadn't secretly wanted very much to stay near him. It shocked me to realize how strong that desire was. "No, Candy. I don't think he needs help. I'll refund your money, of course. Minus expenses. And I'll stay till you leave L.A., just to be sure. But nothing's going to happen."

6

Decked out once again in concertgoing finery, I rode in one of the limousines from the hotel to the concert hall that night. But on the way inside I got sidetracked by professional curiosity about backstage security just long enough to get separated from the others. And I wasn't particularly on my guard. Even if I'd thought something was going to happen, I'd have expected it to happen to Jorandel, not to me.

I didn't see where they came from. There were three of them, big meaty biker-type humans with greasy hair and grubby hands. They looked clumsy, but they weren't. They had the pressure points and the arm twists down pat. They walked me right out of the crowd and into the seclusion of shadows beside a huge overflowing trash dumpster with swift and expert ease. Some big guys get awkward when they go up against a woman, but these didn't. And my macho got in my way; I'm not a screamer. By the time I realized I should yell, the chance was gone; one of them had got his broad hand clamped over my mouth and another was waving a glittering knife in my face.

They knew my name and my occupation. They disapproved. Not, they said, a proper job for a woman. I should know my place. And I should stay away from Cold Iron. I should go back to the Bay Area and mind my own business. It was the knife wielder who told me these things. His teeth needed some serious attention. The arm twister leaned in close enough that I became unpleasantly aware of his indifference to the niceties of hygiene, like showers and toothpaste. The third member of the party, who had thus far seemed to be along only to keep the others company, displayed his skills when the knife wielder was through talking. One swift scientific blow expertly gauged for power and placement was all he needed to leave me sick and silly and helpless. While the knife wielder folded his weapon and the arm twister released his hold and the three of them walked away, I landed on my knees in spilled rubbish and very nearly added to it by losing my lunch.

When I could breathe again without gagging, I climbed unsteadily to my feet with the aid of the dumpster at my side and, still clinging to it for support, began very carefully to examine my costume for signs of dirt or damage. It seemed important at the time. I suppose I was embarrassed at having been caught off guard, and wanted to be sure there was no visible evidence. I dusted my knees and inspected every inch of dress fabric I could see without a mirror. It seemed to have come to no harm. After a time, when standing upright seemed less of a chore, I straightened my shoulders, but I did not release my grip on the dumpster. It occurred to me that there was something monumentally silly about a woman in trendy concert attire clinging fondly to a dumpster in dark alley shadows while normal concertgoers were forgathering in the brightly lighted arena behind her, and I heard myself giggle about it. It was a high, thin, hysterical sound, dangerous and sad. I choked it back, braced myself, and released my grip on the dumpster.

They'd been experts, those three. They had hustled me out of the crowd so cleanly that I was sure no one had noticed. My arm ached where it had been twisted, but I knew there would be no lasting damage. The knife had been a nice touch, an effective visual emphasis to the threatening words, and no wasteful spilling of blood for me to use as visual evidence against them. The single body blow that had put me down and given them time to fade into the shadows untraceably had been debilitating, but I thought there would not be so much as a bruise to show for it later. In short, there was nothing to prove I'd been attacked at all. And that was supposed to add to my demoralization. Courage is easier when you can rally companions against a visible threat, a known enemy. Resistance is easier when there is something tangible to resist against. All I had was a wild story of vicious hoodlums who left not a mark on me.

That would be a problem only if I wanted to tell somebody about it. I didn't. I'm as readily demoralized as the next guy, but not by knowing I have to fight my own battles and can't run to some handy authority figure for help. I hadn't expected any help on this one. Of course, I hadn't expected any violence against me, either, but that was pure carelessness. Whether or not anybody wanted to murder Jorandel, there was a potential for violence about this group that was almost tangible. It didn't take much intelligence to figure out some of it might rub off on me. I'd already been drugged and my belongings searched: if that hadn't given me an adequate clue that I ought to be on my guard, I had only myself to blame.

I was more unnerved by the realization of my own carelessness than I was by the hoodlums who'd taken advantage of it. I knew I'd never been in any real danger from them. I recognized the type: rent-a-hoods, cleanly professional at their work. They'd have killed me or crippled me without hesitation if that was the job. But hired only to frighten me, they would rely heavily on their image to do the job for them, especially when the target was a woman. And it was as well I hadn't screamed; they respected macho. That had probably saved me the indignity of being tossed in the dumpster instead of being left to lose my lunch beside it.

But I couldn't count on that kind of luck forever. At the rate I was going, I would make one mistake too many on this job and it would be my last mistake ever. I was not usually this clumsy, even at Christmas. I was good at what I did, and it had been a long time since I had been so easily caught off guard. Shannon would have had a little something to say about that, and it would not have been complimentary. There really wasn't any excuse. I'd worked outside the Bay Area before, I'd worked without Shannon, I'd even worked in conditions almost as alien to me as those surrounding an elfrock band, and I'd never messed up so consistently before. It was time to get my act together.

Somebody had hired those thugs to do what they did

to me. Who? They had known my name and my occupation. Anyone associated with the band might know my name, but only Candy knew my occupation—Candy, and the predawn intruder who had gone through my purse in search of ID. I couldn't see any reason for Candy to hire thugs; if she changed her mind and wanted me to go, she had only to say so, and she knew it. Only hours before, she had been begging me to stay. That left the predawn intruder. which meant I'd narrowed it down to the same list of some dozen people that Candy and I had discussed that morning.

It was almost time for the opening act to make way for Cold Iron. I had regained my breath by then if not my self-respect, and my assailants were long gone. There was nothing I could do about them now. I thought I could walk steadily enough that no one would notice anything wrong, so I went back toward the backstage door the thugs had hustled me away from. There was nobody around but a couple of security guards who glanced at my "Access All Areas" tag and waved me inside. I knew where Candy and I were supposed to be seated, and I assumed I'd find her there, so I headed for the side door into the house. There was some audience noise, but no music, so I figured the opening act was over and Cold Iron would be coming on at any moment. I would find my earplugs and settle in to enjoy the concert. Time enough to worry about murder and mayhem afterward.

I was walking briskly, digging in my purse for the little tube that held my earplugs, not looking where I was going, and I collided full force with Killer coming the other way. For a fraction of a second I thought it was the biker bullies again; the sheer mass of him might have given that impression even without the black leather jacket he was wearing and the fact that he automatically grabbed my shoulders to steady us both. The arm that had been twisted hurt like fury when he gripped it. I was already fighting him before I realized what had happened.

He held me at arm's length, dodged my knees and feet easily, and grinned down at me from behind that permanent half mask of ebony curls. "Hey," he said.

"Hey." His voice was sweet and shy, completely at odds with his fierce appearance.

I subsided, blushing. "Sorry. I—I thought you were someone else."

The amiable grin widened. "Glad I ain't." There was friendly amusement in his tone. "What did he do to deserve all that?" He released my arms watchfully, as though he thought I might attack again the moment I was free. His fingers were already taped for the performance. I had not seen him at such close range before. His face was partially visible through the mass of curls, and it was as sweet and uncomplicated as his voice.

"Never mind," I explained. I resisted the impulse to rub my sore arm. Behind him I could hear the warm-up band's front man saying something into the microphone, but I couldn't hear what he said. They began to play a slow number, heavy on keyboard and bass guitar. "What's going on? Why are they still out there?"

"Not still. Again," he said. The volume of the music made him raise his voice, but it retained that startlingly sweet quality that seemed so at odds with the savage image he cultivated. "Had to send them back out. Caught them before the roadies had their equipment down or we'd have been in deep kim chee."

"Deep what? Why? What's happened?"

"Where you been?" He turned me gently and guided me toward the backstage lounge. "Somebody tried to kill Jorie." He hesitated, then amended it by adding, "So he says. Anyway he fell downstairs. Frank's with him now. And everybody else. In here." He opened the lounge door, and I wasn't all the way in when Candy dived at me to drag me hysterically toward the middle of the room, where Jorandel was sprawled limp on a couch with Frank bending solicitously over him.

"See? See?" she said shrilly. "I said it was real. You gotta do something, Rosie, you gotta stop them, look what they've done, you gotta—"

I slapped her. It was the only way to shut her up before she blew my cover, if she hadn't already. "Calm down," I told her. "I can't understand you. Take a deep breath."

She stared at me with one hand trembling against the

cheek I'd slapped, those great fawn eyes bewildered and hurt. "What? Why did . . . ? What?"

Jimendan was leaning over the couch, looking down at his brother. I couldn't read the expression on his face. Blade was collapsed in a nearby chair with a bottle of whiskey in one hand and a herbal cigarette in the other. The Roach was across the room at a makeup table, coolly arranging his hair. Emerson was in a corner near the door, talking in low tones to a man I didn't know, both of them watching Jorandel instead of each other. None of them appeared to have noticed Candy's outburst, much less heard what she said.

"Save it, Candy," I said. "It'll keep."

"You don't understand," she said, her voice quieter now but still edged with hysteria. "Somebody hurt him. He's hurt bad. Somebody pushed him downstairs. Those awful concrete stairs in the back. He coulda been killed!"

"He wasn't," I said. "Frank will take care of him." I wondered whether that assurance was justified: Jorandel hadn't so much as twitched since I entered the room. "Did someone call an ambulance?"

Candy shook her head tearfully. "He said not to."

"Who said?"

"Jorie. He said he'd be okay in a minute. He doesn't wanta cancel the concert." Her breathing was ragged, but calmer. It seemed to reassure her to report to me, as though I might produce some magical solution to all difficulties.

"Then he must not be hurt badly," I said dubiously, watching him. The lighting in the lounge was garish. Naked hundred-watt bulbs dangled in pairs from the high ceiling, augmented by fluorescent spillover from the makeup tables at the far end. Everything looked ugly and sharp-edged and unnaturally detailed, as in a magnifying mirror. I couldn't judge Jorandel's color. There was a darkening bruise on his forehead, on the right side just below the hairline. His left arm was leaking slow blood onto his chest from a nasty bruised tear near the wrist. As I watched, Frank began to tend to that, cleaning it carefully and laying out gauze to wrap it in.

"He is hurt bad," Candy insisted. I thought she might

just be right. "But he'll go on anyway. If he can walk, he'll go on. He says they've paid for the tickets, standing on line for hours to get them and maybe spending money they've been saving up forever just for this, the kids anyway. They're who he really cares about. He says the older ones could handle it, but it's too hard on the kids if you cancel. You know, the teenagers and them." She said it as though they were an alien breed, quite different and distant from her. "And the schedule's too tight for us to stay an extra night or anything. So he feels like he's gotta go on, you know? For them."

I wondered how much of that was Jorandel, how much her glorified image of him. Surely he wasn't fool enough to risk his health for an elfrock concert. It wasn't the sort of thing for which one made that kind of sacrifice. "The show must go on?" I quoted cynically.

Candy nodded eagerly. "Yeah, that's it," she said.

I stared. "He said that?"

"Oh, no, I mean, that's just what he meant," said Candy, confused. "You know, he said he hadda. He said about the kids. What I mean, that means the same as what you said, right?"

"Sort of," I said. Doubtless he was grandstanding, waiting for somebody to talk him out of it. Or to call an ambulance and carry him safely to a hospital without arguing. Melodrama was all very well, but he wouldn't be idiot enough to go through with it. He might argue and pretend to resist, but he'd let them talk him into taking proper care of himself. You just don't carry macho that far.

But you do carry machismo that far. That Americanism called macho, that empty posturing and preening that leads to so much pointless violence and pain, is entirely self-conscious, composed more of excess pride than of anything else. I know: I'm as guilty of it as anyone. Machismo is something else again. Roughly, it translates as honor. The kind of honor that makes it unthinkable not to fulfill a promise, even when it turns out to be difficult; that makes it obligatory to repay a debt another would ignore; that makes a bruised and bleeding man pry his dazed eyes open, crawl feebly to his feet, and square his shoulders with a wry grin at his own foolishness before he goes out onstage to give the kids what they've paid and waited for.

I didn't know what to think of his doing that. I didn't know whether to admire his dedication or be disgusted by his flair for the melodramatic. If it hadn't been for that rueful grin I'd have dismissed it as the kind of hollow and dangerous bravado human boys of all ages insist on displaying by walking on broken legs, maybe crippling themselves for life rather than admitting to pain. Bigoted elves will do that rather than let a human see their "weakness." But that grin had turned it into something more. Something that didn't fit with the image of Jorandel that I had formulated, of the arrogant and entirely self-involved elfrock idol with feet of clay. I knew that his music was the center of his existence, but I had not thought he had even the smallest concern for his fans.

He accepted their adulation as his just due. Perhaps providing the promised concert even in these circumstances was a kind of noblesse oblige, the condescending generosity of the self-acknowledged "important personage."

And perhaps I had neurotic reasons of my own for insisting on seeing anything he did in a bad light. Humans have an unfortunate tendency to see only what they expect to see, only what they are willing to accept. It is not a useful way to conduct an investigation. I knew better. I knew the importance of keeping an open mind about the people and everything else involved in an investigation, of formulating no hard-and-fast theories until all the evidence was in. Otherwise the tendency would be to force the emerging facts to fit the theory instead of adjusting the theory to fit the facts, and that is not a reasonable way to get at the truth.

Apparently Candy was right, someone did mean to kill Jorandel. I'd told her it was next to impossible to prevent a determined murderer, and it was. But sometimes a tenacious person can do the impossible. It was worth a try. And the first step was to start looking at the evidence with an open mind.

Coincidences do happen, but it didn't seem wise to believe in them too readily, so I assumed the attack on me must be related to the attack on Jorandel. And that meant his potential murderer knew what I was and had guessed why I was there. But so far as I knew, no one else did. I decided to keep it that way. Anything that would differentiate the bad guy from the good guys could trip him up somewhere down the line. If he would only wear a black hat while everybody else wore white, things would be easier, but you take what you can get.

That meant I couldn't go around asking nosy P.I. questions about Jorandel's trip down the stairs. But I could ask dumb groupie questions. I could turn into the wide-eyed country cousin who wanted to gossip about everything. I could become impressed with events and curious about activities and excited about celebrities. And maybe I could find out where they'd all been when Jorandel took that tumble. Maybe I could be curious enough and pushy enough and innocent enough to open them up without their noticing. I wouldn't fool the bad guy, of course, but maybe I could narrow the field. And maybe in the narrowed field I'd be able to tell who wasn't fooled.

I didn't stop to ask myself what I was going to do about it if I did figure out who wanted to kill Jorandel. I had my own kind of arrogance. I was the tenacious person who would do the impossible. I didn't even need a plan. All I had to do was identify the enemy.

Some of the roadies seemed nicely susceptible to wide-eyed innocence. I was terribly impressed with their close relationship with the idols. I asked all manner of idiot questions, slipping the important ones in among the awestruck stupid ones slyly enough that no one seemed to notice. All I learned was that almost anyone in the world could have pushed Jorandel, but that nobody would want to because he was the gods' gift to an otherwise barren universe. The roadies were nearly as arrogant as the musicians, and even more contentious, but the one thing they all agreed on was the wonderfulness of Jorandel. He was the ideal elf, kindness itself, perfect in every way, and he was absolutely essential to the continued success of the band. It was inconceivable that anyone would have any reason to harm him. The only trouble with that was that whether the roadies liked it or not, someone clearly had. I gave up on them and, at the break, made my way to the empty front-row seat beside Candy, earplugs in place, to enjoy what was left of the concert.

When the guys came back onstage I was shocked at Jorandel's appearance. For once it was easy to tell him from Jimendan. He was the one who couldn't stand up without holding onto something. He leaned on the microphone stand, on Jimendan, on Blade, on anyone or anything handy. He held his left arm cradled against his chest, and when he tried to move to the music he favored his right leg, but the really disturbing thing was not strictly physical. He was out of touch with the music. He stumbled over lyrics, so obviously that I could tell even though I still couldn't understand most of them. There was no wild dancing and cavorting; clearly he couldn't handle that, but he tried some painfully limited movements and couldn't even keep time.

The audience must have thought he was remarkably stoned. It was the natural assumption. He wore a wide headband to cover the bruise on his forehead, and his jacket sleeve covered the bandage on his arm. There was nothing to show that his spaced-out clumsiness was due to anything other than drugs. The other musicians covered for him as well as they could: Jimendan even sang lead, taking over whenever Jorandel lost his place or the necessary strength, and perhaps on a CD the transition would not have been obvious. I thought Jimendan's voice was not quite as strong as Jorandel's, but it had much the same quality, and he imitated Jorandel's vocal mannerisms perfectly. Still, in person the transition was obvious each time, if only because we could see Jorandel's increasing disability.

The people crowded at the front of the stage seemed to be reaching and climbing no more or less enthusiastically than people had the night before. I felt more trapped, more conscious of being surrounded by the mass of people, than I had then, perhaps because the distraction of Jorandel's condition prevented my becoming transfixed by the music. I saw Frank hovering between amplifiers, his worried gaze on Jorandel. The other bodyguards were less visible. In this crisis the other musicians would pull together, requiring less care and attention when they had a focal point for their own concern.

There was little of the previous night's joy in this concert. The music was darker and duller, though most of the songs were the same. But there was in place of the joy a sense of cohesiveness, of brotherhood, of dedication to a united cause. Instead of five casually aligned individuals, Cold Iron had become one unit, the violent intensity focused inward, on the single and simple goal of getting safely through the set before Jorandel's determination failed him. It lent a fierce and secretive power to the music and made me more curious than ever about the lyrics, most of which were still unintelligible to me.

I was able to understand more of them tonight than the previous night, and the ones I heard were not promising. One song began, "The only reason we've done what we did is 'cause that's what we do," with many repetitions of the phrase "the only reason." There was one whose chorus was the only part I could make out: "She's so easy, tries to please me, goes down sweet and doesn't tease me, give me more of that." If all the lyrics were on the level of those two songs then I thought it was as well I couldn't understand them. Better to leave Jorandel's voice a bittersweet musical instrument, unintelligible in English, the human counterpart of Jimendan's guitar with its piercing and liquid clarity of meaning without words.

I knew I wouldn't leave it at that, though. Candy had offered me the use of her Diskman and Cold Iron CDs, and if the lyrics were no more comprehensible on CD than in concert, I would probably read them on the CD jackets or find them written somewhere else. Curiosity spoils a lot of good things, and I can never resist it anyway. Fortunately, Cold Iron's music was good enough to enjoy even with bad lyrics.

Jorandel was fading fast. He was clinging to the microphone stand, still trying to sing, but his knees kept buckling. Jimendan was right up against him, sharing the microphone less for effect, this time, than in an effort to help support Jorandel, but he needed both hands for the guitar so there wasn't much he could do. I could see

Frank behind them, edging into the light. If Jorandel gave out, if he couldn't finish the concert, what would happen? It seemed to me the band was doing fine without him already, but would the audience accept that? Everyone I'd talked to insisted that Jorandel was crucial, that the band was nothing without him. Would they even try to carry on, if Frank had to haul him offstage?

If Jimendan and Jorandel had only switched identities at the beginning of the concert, if Jimendan had come on as Jorandel and apologized to the audience for Jimendan's absence, they might have got away with it. The fans would have been satisfied, and Jorandel could have been taken to a hospital. Why hadn't they tried it?

Maybe they thought, because they knew Jorandel wasn't as accomplished a guitar player as Jimendan, that the audience would know that too, and realize they were being tricked. Maybe Jimendan didn't like to suggest it; Candy had said all the band members were Jorandel's employees. It's usually not a good idea to suggest to your boss that you're fully competent to take over his job, even for one night. Not even when your boss is also your brother. And especially not when your boss is as determined as Jorandel had been to go on.

Maybe the possibility just hadn't occurred to anyone. It was irrelevant now. Jorandel wasn't going to make it through another song, and it was too late for Jimendan to switch places with him, since no one would believe it after watching Jorandel's slow disintegration all evening. They would have to either carry on without him or cancel the rest of the concert, and since the conclusion was inevitable I wished they would get it over with. The fans didn't seem to mind watching Jorandel's distress, but I did. Of course, the fans must have assumed he was "feeling no pain," the popular phrase for a condition identical in appearance with that of feeling great pain. There's a clue there, for anyone who hasn't yet figured out that "recreational" drug use is rarely if ever recreational.

The song came to an end, and I thought Jorandel had too; his grip on the microphone stand slipped and Jimendan had to move fast to catch him. I thought Frank would collect him and take him offstage. But he leaned against Jimendan for a moment, getting his breath, then forced himself upright again and stared blindly out over the arena at the thousands of faces staring back at him.

"Sorry." He sounded breathless, as though the effort to stand on his own were as exhausting as his usual acrobatics were. "Little out of it tonight." He grinned that incredible impish grin, all sweet innocence and beauty. "Gonna do you one more number and that'll be it for tonight." There was an audible fuss in the audience and he lifted his hand for silence, wavering dangerously. Jimendan did some fast footwork to brace him till he could hang onto something again.

"No, now," said Jorandel, his voice soothing. "What we're gonna do—" He paused for effect, and I could see the other musicians adjusting themselves, bracing for the next move. They knew what he was doing, if I didn't. "We're gonna—" He broke into a yell: "Take It Hard!" On the final word, the instruments burst into a riotous storm of music, and Jorandel stood there, clinging to that microphone stand, and belted out one last song with all the force and fury he could put into it.

For once I could understand most of the lyrics, and what I didn't catch then I learned later from the CDs. It's a fair sample of the kind of lyrics he wrote: dumb. But the intensity he put into it, and the violent energy of the accompaniment, overrode the banality of the words.

"Take it hard and take it fast/Take it all and make it last, babe, I got mine . . ." Killer did something complicated, almost lyrical, with the drums that Blade picked up on the bass with a deep, driving rhythm that pounded like a fevered heartbeat under the verse. Jorandel was grinning to himself, the broad and foolish grin of a man caught up in a happy fantasy. His hair was pushed back, tucked behind those pointy ears, emphasizing his alienness and at the same time somehow underlining the commonality of humans and elves.

Or maybe it was the banality of the lyrics that had that effect. "I wake up when the sun goes down/And the bus rolls in to another town/I take it easy, take it slow/'Cause first they come and then they go/And if one more shot won't get me through/Then I line 'em up 'cause they're small, take two./Take it hard and take it fast/Take it all and make it last . . ."

The audience sang along with him on the chorus. One-handed, he wrenched the mike off its stand and held it out to get their voices through the amplifiers, and he managed somehow not to fall over in the process. He had his legs braced, and his long frame wavered dangerously, but he didn't fall. That sweet frenzy of drum and bass pulled him back into the verse: "I go to sleep at the break of day/Bus or plane we're on our way/Different girls with the same old faces/Same old songs and go to blazes/All they'll hear is what they see/'Cause they know my name but they don't know me./So take it hard, babe, take it fast . . ."

He'd drawn the mike back to his face for the verse, and braced the hand that held it on the top of the stand as though he meant to hold it out again for the second chorus, but when the time came he just couldn't do it. He tried, but his knees buckled and he had to grab the stand again. With a mildly surprised and rueful look, he forced the mike back into its brace and clung to it, head hanging, only the tips of his ears showing, through the instrumental fill between the second chorus and the third verse. His knees kept folding. I thought he would miss his cue, or collapse.

He did neither. Drum and bass played their complicated trick again, and he lifted his head. His eyes were glazed, his face shiny with sweat, and the arm that held him up by his grip on the microphone was shaking with fatigue, the knuckles white and slippery, but his voice was as clear and powerful as if there were nothing more important to him in the world than that song. Perhaps there wasn't.

"I sleep by day and I work by night/And some folks say I'm a hell of a sight." The song itself seemed to support him, to give him strength instead of using it up. He was grinning again, and his eyes sparkled with amused awareness. "But I'll kick their ass and I'll make 'em smile/And the road runs on for another mile/So drink it up or shoot it down/Babe, we're comin in to another town." The final chorus was a shout of pure triumph: "And I'll take it hard, I'll take it fast/I'll take it all and I'll make it last. Hey! I got mine . . ."

He stayed on his feet long enough to take a bow.

7

Only Frank went with Jorandel to the hospital. The rest of us, including several eager girls the irrepressible Blade had picked up on the way, returned to the hotel. The musicians took the girls with them to shower and change while Candy and I settled in the guitar-littered communal room to wait for news. If she was fond of the Roach, she nonetheless laid no personal claim to him; she seemed utterly indifferent to the fact that one of the girls had happily latched onto him the moment she saw him.

Crew members wandered through, looking distracted. Somebody made a pot of coffee that nobody drank. Jimendan returned from the shower, dressed in faded jeans and a worn T-shirt with a hotel towel wrapped around his hair. He didn't appear to notice us, though the upholstered chair in which he threw himself down faced us across the room. Andy, his bodyguard, entered with the brisk air of a man on an important errand, but paused when he saw Jim and went to crouch next to his chair with a gentle frown of concern. They spoke so quietly I heard only the soft murmur of their voices: Jim's petulant, Andy's soothing.

Nearly all the bodyguards had much closer relationships with their charges than I had at first realized. It wasn't only that they were personal attendants as well as bodyguards. All the pairings except Bob and the Roach seemed more like close friendships than merely employer-employee relationships. I had come to them so deeply prejudiced against elfrock musicians that such a possibility—that they might actually have genuine friends—had simply not occurred to me until I had seen it, and even then I had resisted belief. When Candy had told me that Andy could calm Jim when no one else could, I had rather imagined he must have devised some effective system over the years. Now I could see that his effectiveness stemmed not from calculation, but from his own genuine concern and Jim's response to it. I had seen Jim relate to no one else in the group, not even to Jorandel, with the affectionate respect he showed for Andy.

The same was true with almost all of them. The musicians were bound to each other by their music, and perhaps in the end that was the closest tie; certainly it was the most intense. But perhaps that intensity was, in a way, a disadvantage. Perhaps the focus on the music and on their mutual history in it left them unfulfilled in their basic need for ordinary human friendship. Only the Roach, whose egocentricity rendered him incapable of affection, treated his personal attendant as a servant. The others turned to their attendants as often in emotional need as in physical need.

By the time Killer and Blade emerged from their showers, Andy had Jim cheered to such an extent that he was able to greet them and their giggling girls without a hint of the sullen petulance that seemed to be his most common disposition. One of the girls, a redhead with very long legs, detached herself from Blade and descended upon Jim with an incongruous air of determination. The brunette who came in with Killer moved purposefully toward Blade while Killer sprawled bonelessly on a heap of cushions near Jim's chair.

Candy leaned toward me and said, indicating the redhead now working on Jim, "She's old to be just starting out." The girl looked all of nineteen.

"Starting what?" I asked.

"As a groupie." She paused, studying the redhead judiciously. "Not too many notches on her bedpost yet, at least nobody as important as Cold Iron. You can tell."

"How?" I asked in spite of myself.

She shrugged comfortably, looking smug. "You just can. She'd have more poise. She looks too hungry. I dunno. It's hard to explain."

"Perhaps that's just as well." The redhead took no notice of us whatsoever, but I still found it unnerving to discuss in her presence the ostensible notches on her figurative bedpost. I was fascinated and repelled, however, to observe that it took her less than one full minute to get Jimendan on his feet and headed for the nearest bedroom with her. They both started shedding garments before the door was closed behind them.

Candy had forgotten them already. "Did you see Mr. Veladora?" she asked. "I heard he was at the concert."

"I don't know. Who is he?" Blade sent the brunette to the refrigerator for beers and she brought back one for Killer as well. He accepted it without a word, and without breaking the rhythm he was absently thumping on a pillow he'd drawn into his lap.

"I told you," Candy said impatiently. "When I—I mean, in Berkeley, remember? He's Jorandel's producer. I heard he was pissed Jorandel couldn't finish the set tonight."

I looked away from Blade and the brunette, who were enjoying some touchy-feelie activities with their beers. "Did he know why he couldn't?"

"I don't know." That didn't seem to interest her. "You think he'll come here?" She looked at me as though she seriously expected me to know Jorandel's producer's plans for the evening.

"I don't know," I said helplessly.

"I hate it when he comes to see them," she said. "There's always a fight. Jorie'll be upset for days. I wish he wouldn't."

Blade and the brunette retreated to Blade's bedroom, leaving their beers behind. "Why is there always a fight?"

Candy shrugged ineffably. "Mr. Veladora always wants them to do something Jorie doesn't want to do. Stupid stuff. Like last year he made them play at this wedding reception, you know? Mr. Veladora's daughter's. I mean, it was a big deal kind of wedding reception, but it was still a wedding reception. Cold Iron can fill a stadium. They shouldn't have to play dipshit gigs like that. It's not even good for their career."

"Why would their producer make them do something that wasn't good for their career? For that matter, how could he force them, if they really didn't want to?"

"He doesn't care about their career," she said. "He cares about power. Especially over elves." She shuddered delicately. "He's a toad. I hate him." She said it with innocent, childlike intensity. "But when Jorie was first starting, he signed this contract, see? With Mr. Veladora. And now he can't get out of it."

"Oh, piffle. You can always get out of a contract if you can afford a good enough lawyer. Which Jorandel certainly can."

She shook her head morosely. "He tried. He went to a whole bunch of lawyers. They all said the same thing. Veladora's contract is unbreakable. It's an elvish thing, 'cause it's a Faerie contract even though it's written in English. It's not magic exactly, but Faerie contracts are more binding, you know. The only way Jorie can get out of it is by dying."

"They said that? In those words?"

"Jorie says they did."

"Jeez. Usually I think people should follow their attorneys' advice, but I guess there are exceptions."

"It's not funny," Candy said severely.

"No, I see that. Particularly if Veladora really doesn't care about Cold Iron's career. Why wouldn't he, though? Doesn't he make money if they do?"

"Yeah, but he doesn't need it. He's rich as sin already, both here and in Faerie."

"He's an elf?"

"Yeah, of course," she said impatiently. "That's how he could offer Jorie a Faerie contract in the first place. And he says he'll break Cold Iron if they don't do what he wants, and he could. And would. You ever hear of Phelony?"

"Why? Has he committed one?"

"Not felony: Phelony." She spelled it. "You know. The elfrock group."

"Oh. No."

"Well, it's no wonder. They didn't last long. But they went platinum with *Rape and Murder.*"

"Oh." I must have sounded as confused as I felt.

"The album," she said. "Back in the early eighties." She made the early eighties sound like the dawn of prehistory. "Anyway, they were signed with Veladora. And they didn't do what he said. When they hit it big, they thought they could get out from under, you know? They thought they could say no. So they did. They tried to break the contract. And he killed them."

"Not literally, I assume," I said, wondering whether Veladora would fit the role of First Murderer. If he had been at the concert, he had opportunity, but I couldn't quite see the motive.

"Yeah. Literally," she said, and hesitated. "Well, their careers, I mean. They couldn't buy their way onstage now."

"Why? What did he do?"

"I don't know. He just said, and he can make it true." She shrugged. "Magic, maybe. Or the Faerie contracts."

"But it doesn't make sense that he'd destroy what makes him money."

"It does to him." She frowned at me, clearly debating my intelligence. "I told you, he doesn't need money. He's rich. The only thing he cares about, he likes to know he has power over people. 'Specially elves, or other people that sort of have power over other people, like if they're actors or politicians or elfrock stars or something. He helps them make it mostly so he can push them around when nobody else can."

I assumed I was getting a biased report based more on her sympathy for Jorandel's anger with Veladora than on the reality of the situation. That Veladora would threaten Cold Iron with ruin if they didn't do his bidding was easy enough to believe, but that he would in fact ruin them when there must be so many ways short of ruin that he could get his way, and have the money too, seemed improbable. Even the power-mad usually have sense enough not to kill the goose that lays the golden eggs. I would look into the Phelony thing, but I expected to find that the band had in some way spoiled its own success. Elfrock bands were all too prone to self-destruction.

Veladora did show up at the hotel not long after Candy mentioned him, and there was nothing in his appearance to make me revise my opinion. He looked like what he was, a middle-aged elven businessman, paunchy and self-important. He arrived alone, was let into the suite by one of the bodyguards, and was wholly ignored by everyone else present. After a brief survey of the room, he asked politely whether he could have a cup of coffee, poured it, and sat comfortably at the small dining table to drink it.

Blade had returned from the bedroom and was getting very comfortable with yet another groupie in the middle of the floor. Veladora watched, sipping his coffee, no more disturbed or even interested than if he had been watching a bowl of goldfish. The redhead returned from Jim's room without him, and without most of her clothing, to make a try for Killer. Veladora examined her rather as one might examine a prize cow.

Jim emerged from the bedroom after her, fastening his pants and grinning. I hoped the musicians practiced safe sex, an unlikely thought that led to amusing speculation on the purchase of condoms in adequate bulk to supply an elfrock band's tour needs. Veladora looked startled when he saw Jim, and started to say something; then he subsided with a wry smile and I realized he must briefly have mistaken Jim for his brother. Not surprising. If I hadn't known Jorandel was in the hospital, I might have made the same mistake.

Candy was so studiously ignoring Veladora that she seemed to have lost the ability to converse. Nobody else was saying much, either. Veladora seemed content with his coffee, and only mildly interested in his surroundings. Somebody put a CD on the stereo and turned up the volume. It was the old *Very Special Christmas* album, with the Pointer Sisters singing "Santa Claus is Coming to Town." I stood up abruptly, realized I had nowhere to go, and decided I needed a glass of gin.

Veladora studied me with exactly the same look he had given the redhead, who was now trying to get Killer into the bedroom she had so recently shared with Jim. He hadn't noticed me before, and probably took me for a groupie now that he had. Well, that was what I was pretending to be. But I found myself blushing under that absently speculative gaze. I poured more gin than I'd meant to and gulped a healthy slug of it. Across the room, Killer was rising to allow the redhead to lead him to bed. I wished he wouldn't. I wished they all wouldn't. I had done an about-face: I wanted to think well of them.

But I could understand the musicians more readily than I could the women who wanted sex with them. In their place I would feel far too much as though I had been standing on line. It may be the male's job to bed anything remotely female that comes his way, but it is not my job to acquiesce when I am generously offered my turn.

And yet I might have done, if it had been Jorandel and not Jim who had come first to my room the night before. I gulped more gin. A little self-awareness goes a long way. The Pointer Sisters gave way to the Eurythmics singing "Winter Wonderland" and I thought that if I had the assertive bad manners of an elfrock star I would hurl what was left of my gin at the stereo. It might not have eased my foul temper, but it would have been very satisfying just the same. I didn't do it. Instead, I watched Killer and his busy little redhead.

They had not yet quite disappeared into the bedroom when the suite's outer door banged open and Frank and Jorandel walked in. The redhead tried to convince Killer to ignore the interruption, but he ignored her instead, pausing to watch Jorandel's entrance.

I had not expected Jorandel to return with Frank; after his spectacular collapse onstage I had assumed he would be kept at least one night in the hospital. He looked as though he should have been. His left wrist was heavily bandaged, the bruise on his forehead had already spread to darken one eye, and his right pant leg had been slit up the side to accommodate an elastic bandage on the knee. Frank had one arm around him, and although he tried to look as though he didn't need the support, it was obvious that he did.

Candy leapt to her feet, her face almost as white as Jorandel's. "Jorie! Are you all right?"

He looked at her, his face expressionless, his eyes very dark and hooded. "What the fuck do you think?" His voice was as expressionless as his face, and as savage as his eyes, with no cool elven formality in the words. "Get me a drink."

She obeyed instantly, and without the smallest sign of shock or dismay at his manner. Obviously she had seen him in such a mood before. I hadn't, but I should have expected it. I had known his dark potential from the moment I met him. But I had put it out of my mind after hearing his music, even though it was present in the music, even though it powered the music. I had wanted it to be trapped in the music, to exist only there, and that was another stupid mistake: what existed in the music had to exist in Jorandel as well, because as Candy had said, he *was* the music. Onstage, the others' contributions were focused through him, all their energy processed through him as the center of power, and he had no insulation to protect him from the raging force of that terrible rapture. The dark potential I wanted to deny was the flame-ravaged core of his being.

It's all very well to speak in awe and admiration of great artists and their tormented souls, but it is not well to share a room with one. Pain in our society is like sex and death, unmentionable, a thing to be concealed or ignored or, if absolutely necessary, discussed in quiet tones behind closed doors. It is not polite to call attention to pain except by bleeding. Tormented souls do not bleed. Neither, as a general rule, are their possessors polite. Jorandel scowled at everyone, his sweet boy face made almost ugly by ill temper. And yet he was as attractive as he was repellent. From the moment he entered the room he had become its focal point, the center of power just as he was onstage. It was involuntary and inevitable. People were drawn to him against their will and his. Even when the group made a concerted effort to disregard his presence, his power was implicit in the effort that required.

He ungraciously permitted Frank to help him to a comfortable chair and snarled at Candy when she brought his drink. Everyone else ignored him, but invisible lines of emotional tension tied us to him as surely as if we were all puppets whose strings he held. He gulped down the drink, handed the glass back to Candy with a demand for a refill, and only then affected to notice Veladora. Without any change in expression of either face or voice he said, "What the fuck are you doing here?"

"Waiting to talk to you," said Veladora.

Jorandel laughed unpleasantly. "Keep waiting." He accepted another drink from Candy without thanks.

"Slow down, Jorie," said Frank. "They said no drinking. It won't mix with the medication."

"It'll mix just fine," said Jorandel.

"What happened tonight?" asked Veladora.

"Go fuck yourself," said Jorandel.

"Later, perhaps," Veladora said mildly. "Someone said you were pushed downstairs. By whom?"

"By nobody," said Jorandel. He looked distractedly around the room and said without any interest, "I fell, okay? I got a little stoned and I fell. Will somebody give me a goddamn guitar?"

"You can't play it with that arm," said Frank, nonetheless reaching for an acoustic guitar that was leaning against a nearby chair.

Jorandel accepted it with his good hand and struggled to get it positioned in his lap while everyone else in the room studiously ignored him. Eventually realizing that although he could brace it against his left arm he could not finger the chords, he hurled it against the wall. "Fuck that," he said as it clattered to the floor. "Turn up the goddamn music, then. This place is a fucking tomb. Put on some Aerosmith or Freaks Dancing, why don't you?"

Killer, who was nearest the stereo, silently changed the CD. Everyone else went on pretending Jorandel wasn't there. No one but Frank and Veladora would even look at him directly. It was as odd and as unconvincing as if there had been an elephant in the room that they were all determined not to mention, as if by refusing to recognize it they proved that having an elephant in the room was quite an acceptable state of affairs. But Jorandel in this mood was not as easily ignored as the average elephant. He began crooning obscenities to the redhead next to Killer, describing in graphic and quite unpleasant terms the things he would like to do to her, all the while smiling his shy and innocent, impish smile at her. She seemed mesmerized. When she obediently approached him, he threw his drink in her face and calmly held out the glass for Candy to refill.

"Why don't you cut it out, Jorandel?" asked Veladora.

"Why don't you stuff your head up your ass?" asked Jorandel.

Candy accepted the glass from him and went to fill it. The Roach and the little blonde he'd been with when they first came back from the concert finally emerged from his bedroom just then. The blonde moved eagerly toward Jorandel while the Roach paused, took in the scene at a glance, and grabbed the glass out of Candy's hand to hurl it against a wall. "I've told you not to wait on him," he said evenly, while shards of glass clattered to the floor at her feet. "You're my woman, not his."

"Fuck off," said Jorandel.

"You keep out of this," said the Roach.

"You're fucking fired," said Jorandel.

"I fucking quit," said the Roach. "Come on, Candy."

"You can't," Candy said helplessly, her voice very small and frightened.

"You're all fucking fired," said Jorandel. "Get out, damn you." He surged out of his chair toward the little long-haired blonde, who looked about fourteen years old and frightened in the face of his sudden savagery. He grabbed her by one arm and hauled her toward the nearest window, which he tried to kick open. The glass was too strong for the force he could muster with his injured leg, and he was too drunk to keep his balance. He fell, dragging the blonde down on top of him. Nobody moved. The girl was crying, struggling to extricate herself from Jorandel so she could get up. He wrapped his legs around her, grinning wickedly, and dragged her back down. "Wait, honey, I ain't finished yet," he said.

"You're disgusting," she said, pushing her long yellow hair back from a mascara-streaked face. "Let me go."

"Not till I've had my fun." He seemed to have forgotten they were not alone in the room, or that he had been angry only moments before. "Come on, honey, you know you don't really wanta go, not when you got me all turned on already, now do you?" He pulled her hand toward his crotch. "See what you done, honey? Now, you know what to do about that, don't you?"

To my sickened amazement, she stopped crying, grinned shyly at him, and obediently moved to give him a blow job right there in front of God and everybody.

Nobody else in the room seemed even mildly surprised. I drank my gin. It was bizarre: they were all ignoring the elephant again. With elephant shit up to their ankles, they were pretending it wasn't there. In my bemused, half-drunken state I wondered where I had got that image, mentally tracked it to a book by Janet Woititz called *Adult Children of Alcoholics,* and felt as though I'd accomplished something of value. It was very like my almost frantic effort to recall Reno's name when Blade was falling apart onstage. I seemed to imagine, whenever chaos began to flourish around me, that I could influence it by establishing some small mental unit of order, however pointless.

"Come on, Candy," the Roach said abruptly, pushing her toward the suite door as if there had been no intervening events since he told Jorandel he was quitting.

"Come off it, Roach," said Jim. The Roach stopped, but he didn't turn. "You know you can't quit now," said Jim.

"I was fired," the Roach said obstinately.

"You been fired before," said Blade. "Hey, listen, you got a keyboard in your room? I got this great idea for the ride out of 'One For the Drummer.' " He scrambled to his feet and grabbed the nearest guitar. "C'mon, lemme show you." The two of them disappeared into the Roach's room, immersed in the music.

Candy stood listlessly for a moment where the Roach had left her, then shrugged and went to the refrigerator for a beer. "You want one?" she asked me. I showed her my gin. She said, "Oh, yeah," opened her beer, and came back to the couch to sit with her feet up, facing me, pointedly not looking at Jorandel and the little blonde. They'd begun to make more noise than was easily ignored, but we pretended we could.

Killer was oblivious, happily drumming his pillows. Jim seemed engrossed in the music on the stereo, and Veladora was lost in thought. Nobody paid any attention to us. I questioned Candy, very circumspectly, about everybody's whereabouts when Jorandel fell down the stairs, just to check what I'd learned at the arena. When she realized what I was doing, she said in surprise, "But you heard him: he said he just fell. Nobody pushed him."

I really didn't want to discuss it so openly in front of so many people. "I know," I said. "I'm just not sure I believe it."

"Why would he lie?"

"I can think of half a dozen reasons," I said. "But never mind. We'll talk about it later."

"That was nice, honey," said Jorandel.

"Are you quite finished?" asked Veladora.

"Fuck off," said Jorandel. I glanced at him. The little blonde was sitting up now, grinning like a cat. Jorandel was just zipping his pants.

"You will keep to the schedule," said Veladora. I couldn't tell whether it was a question or a command.

"Yeah, yeah, yeah," said Jorandel. "Honey, get me some whiskey, will you?" the blonde jumped happily to her feet and headed for the bar.

"You'll save yourself effort if you bring him the whole bottle now," said Veladora.

"Good idea," said Jorandel, grinning.

"Have you given any thought to that other little matter?" asked Veladora.

"Fuck off," said Jorandel.

"You know better," said Veladora.

Jorandel stood up carefully. "Fuck off." He walked to the window he had tried to break and unfastened its catch to open it.

"I'll send a limo around tomorrow afternoon for you and your brother," said Veladora. Jim scowled at him.

"Fuck off," said Jorandel. It sounded to me exactly as it had the other times he'd said it, but something in his tone must have alerted Killer, because he was on his feet and diving for the window before I even understood what Jorandel was doing.

He had one foot on the windowsill and was half out already when Killer caught him and wordlessly hauled him back into the room. I wasn't sure whether he really would have jumped or not: it certainly looked as though he would. Candy appeared to think he would. She had screamed just before Killer caught him. The little blonde dropped the whiskey bottle she had been bringing to him. Jim stood up, frowned, and sat back down. Veladora just watched, his long eyes expressionless.

"You okay now?" Killer asked in his sweet, shy voice. He was holding Jorandel by the waist with his feet off the floor, the way Andy had held Jim when he started to go off the stage the night before, and he made it look as easy as Andy had, though he hadn't Andy's bulk.

"Yeah, yeah, I'm okay," said Jorandel, giggling. "And you're fired, you son of a human. Put me down."

Killer put him down and went serenely back to his pillows. Jim glanced at him uneasily and then leaned his head back to stare at the ceiling. The blonde picked up the whiskey bottle and looked uncertainly at the stain of spilled whiskey on the carpet. Blade and the Roach opened their door to see what was going on just as Frank and Andy burst in another door to demand why somebody screamed. Jorandel, grinning happily, headed for the window again. After a fractional hesitation, Frank went after him just as he was lifting his foot to place it drunkenly on the sill again.

"Very showy," said Veladora.

"Fuck off," said Jorandel. It had become an ugly mantra.

Blade and the Roach retreated, closing the door softly behind them. Jim muttered something under his breath. Veladora said very quietly, "We'll talk tomorrow." Jorandel lurched toward the window, but Frank was right there to stop him, and Veladora laughed at him. "Ineffectual," he said. "As are all your histrionics, elfrock star. Perhaps you've forgotten I really don't care what happens to you. You can't hurt me, you know." He smiled pleasantly as he rose to leave, but the inference, "But I can hurt you," was as plain as if he had said it aloud.

Jorandel repeated his mantra tonelessly. The blonde offered him the whiskey bottle and Frank released his arm to let him accept it. He lifted it, drank from it with his eyes on Veladora's departing back, then hurled it with sudden homicidal intent just a fraction of a second too late to catch Veladora before he closed the door. Whiskey and broken glass splattered the door, wall, and carpet. I sipped my gin quietly, ignoring the elephant. Somebody put another Christmas CD on the stereo and I decided maybe I should go home after all.

But I knew I wouldn't. I had a score to settle with whoever hired those thugs to hassle me. I told myself very firmly that that was the only reason I would stay. Myself wasn't fooled. Jorandel was probably psychotic. He was also fascinating. The good sense with which I ordinarily avoided sociopaths and spoiled children simply did not operate in Jorandel's presence. Like it or not, I was as much enthralled by his feral magnetism as any of the groupies competing for his bed.

8

After two days with the band, all I had learned was confirmation of what Candy had told me in the first place: that someone might be planning to kill Jorandel. I was no nearer knowing who that someone might be than I had been in Berkeley. I had drunk a lot of free gin and turned down a lot of free drugs, heard too many Christmas songs, and several times revised my prejudices to accommodate a new perceived reality about elfrock musicians. I was tired, a little drunk, and reluctantly becoming aware that I was out of my element.

I needed Shannon. She had always been my anchor: we were a team. However much I might make fun of the Voice of Sweet Reason, over the years hers had kept me from a number of idiocies I might otherwise have perpetrated. Everyone always thinks that whatever he is doing is reasonable. Shannon had a knack for showing me when what I was doing was not reasonable.

But not at Christmas. I could not handle the level of her bliss at Christmas. I would not call her. Somewhere under the easy alcoholic conviction of my own competence a growing uncertainty struggled for ascendance, but when the automatic response was an impulse to call Shannon, I buried it. There must be another way. If I could not handle the situation alone, there must be someone I could trust among the Cold Iron entourage.

Emerson was the logical choice. Not only was security his responsibility, so that he would be more familiar with the mechanics of investigation (and presumably more open to the idea that it was needed) than the others, but he seemed the least biased of those close to the band. Each of the bodyguards was clearly centered on his own charge, and only Emerson of all the rest of the crew had as close and easy a relationship with the musicians as they had. Best of all, he was not in the same room with the stereo and its damned Christmas music. I poured a fresh glass of gin and went in search of him with the comfortable conviction that what I was doing was reasonable.

Maybe it was, but it wasn't particularly useful. I found him in a room next door to the musicians' suite, and gin-inspired self-assurance made it easy to confide in him. The only problem was that he wasn't impressed. He already knew who I was, which made me wonder whether he had been the one who ransacked my belongings; but he assured me he had checked up on me by more orthodox means and would soon have confronted me with the information if I hadn't disclosed it willingly. Far from concerned with my perhaps disjointed account of the danger to Jorandel, he seemed interested only in the fact that someone had gone over his head to hire me.

"For God's sake," I said, "I'm trying to tell you, it was only Candy."

"Candy hasn't got that much initiative," he said. "Who told her to do it?"

"Nobody," I said. "Maybe she doesn't usually have that much initiative, but she's scared. For Jorandel. She overheard something that scared her, and she wanted to protect him."

"Bull. She'd come to me or Frank," he said.

"Maybe she thought she couldn't trust you or Frank."

"Oh, right, one of us is out to get him, is that it?" There was an odd look in his weary eyes. It didn't occur to me until much later that it was the look of a man dealing not altogether patiently with a tiresome drunk.

I shrugged. "She wasn't sure. I am. About that much, anyway. I don't think it's you or Frank, but I'm telling you, somebody wants to hurt him. Damn it, somebody pushed him downstairs tonight!"

Emerson smiled, but only with his mouth. "Nobody pushed him. He fell."

"That's what he says now, naturally." I had a little trouble with a great big word like 'naturally.' It came out slurred, and I repeated it for clarity. "He's probably scared, you know?" I was careful with my diction, trying to convince us both that I wasn't drunk. "He told the truth when it happened, but they must have threatened him, and he probably realized he'd better not accuse anybody if he couldn't prove it or something."

"So you're saying not only that somebody's after him, but that he knows who it is and isn't telling."

"Yeah." It didn't sound so reasonable when he put it that way. "Well, yeah. Why not?"

"Because Jorandel is the basis of this band," he said. "Honey, why don't you go sleep it off? You'll see things more clearly in the morning."

"I'm not your honey," I said. "And I'm not drunk."

"Right."

"You're not going to do a damn thing about it, are you?"

"About what?" he asked wearily.

"About the threat to Jorandel's life."

"There is no threat to Jorandel's life. Look, Rosalynd, try to understand: without Jorandel, Cold Iron is just another band. You've heard the music now. You've seen how it's produced. Jorandel is the focus of the magic, the one essential key to monumental success. Replace anybody else, and it's still Cold Iron. Replace Jorandel and you just killed a musical phenomenon. All you have left is another elfrock band just like all the other elfrock bands, maybe a little better than most, but no longer great."

"Jimendan could take his place," I said stubbornly. "I bet Jimendan would like to take his place. You think it doesn't bother him to live in Jorandel's shadow?"

"If it does," Emerson said patiently, "he's still got sense enough to know when he's well off. He doesn't have his brother's charisma. He couldn't do it."

"Oh, hell, half the time you can't even tell them apart."

"Physically, maybe," he said. "But creatively, musically . . ." He shook his head. "There's no comparison. Don't you get it, honey? Jorandel's the authentic article, a genuine creative genius. Tell me a crazed fan wants to kill him and I'll believe you. But one of us? One of the musicians, a roadie, a security guard? Huh-uh." He shook his head, smiling distantly. "No way, honey. I can't buy that."

"What about Veladora?" I said. "Candy says—"

"Spare me what Candy says," he said. "Look, get it through your head: I like Candy, but she's a casualty. She's got drugs for brains and she's gone on some kind of paranoia trip that you bought into because you didn't know any better. Get out of it, for your own sake. Candy's wrong. And from what I've seen, this trip's wrong for you." When I started to say something, he gestured me to silence. "I know, I know. I've seen you watching Jorandel, trying to figure him out. You want to get close to him, maybe save him from himself. But it's not a good idea, honey. You can't do it, and you'll get burned if you try. Get out while you can. Jorandel isn't in any danger. But you are: he breaks things. He'll break you."

I think it was a sincere and kindly warning, but I was in no mood to heed it. "I'm not real fragile," I said. "And I think Jorandel is in danger. Doubly so, because you don't think so. If you don't mind, I'll stick around a little while."

"I mind," he said.

"You gonna blow my cover?"

He shrugged. "I don't think I'll have to."

"What the hell does that mean?"

"It means, honey, that I think you're in over your head, but it's none of my business. I'll nursemaid the musicians, but not their groupies. It's your life."

"I'm not your honey, I'm not a groupie, and I don't need your advice with my life."

"Sure, honey."

So much for seeking out fellow professionals. I carried my gin back to the common room, where I found Jorandel settled contentedly in a corner with a bottle and a guitar and a pair of adoring groupies, and Candy pushing a little pile of soda around with a razor blade on a glass-topped table. Everyone else had disappeared. The stereo was blaring a rock song at excessive volume. I felt suddenly, bitterly depressed: too much gin, perhaps. Too much loud music, too many bizarre scenes, too little reality.

"Oh, hi, Rosie," said Candy. "Want a line?"

Why the hell not? Maybe it would counteract the gin and banish my unwarranted despair. I accepted with real gratitude and absolutely no sense whatsoever that what I was doing was in any way unreasonable, inadvisable, illegal, or inappropriate. Emerson had been right, though for the wrong reasons. I was out of my depth, and I didn't even know it. The aura of unreality that isolated these people was so easy to accept. If I hadn't been in such heavy denial of my own pain, I might have been less ready to accept the solutions they had found for theirs. But the fact was that I was in search of easy answers, and I grasped them gladly.

The rush seemed to justify my decision. Everything looked instantly brighter, clearer, easier to cope with. The future seemed less daunting, and the past less stifling, and I thought that with only a little time and determination I should have no difficulty resolving just about any problem I really put my mind to. I was fully aware that my newfound confidence was drug-induced, but that did not in any way diminish its effect. In fact, I realized that this was a much healthier state of mind, and that the anxiety and depression I had been suffering were so abnormal and unhealthy that it was quite correct to take any means available to relieve them.

Fully satisfied with this reasoning, I had another glass of gin. I'd taken too much soda, so I was feeling just a trifle tense and shaky, and I thought the gin would tone that down just right. The stereo had begun to emit very odd sounds. They made me uneasy. I said, "Who the hell is that?" and, at Candy's puzzled look, indicated the stereo. "That weird music. Who is it?"

"Oh, that's Aerosmith. 'Janie's Got A Gun.' Great old song," she said.

I shuddered involuntarily. "You like that?"

She nodded happily. "This stuff at the front, what he does with the vocals, that's great. Compelling. Doesn't it just give you the shivers?"

"That it does." I glared at the stereo. "Why don't you play some of your Cold Iron CDs?"

"Oh, no, Jorie wanted to hear Aerosmith."

I had thought Jorandel was too far out of it to be aware of what music was played, but when I glanced at him he was grinning drunkenly at me. "This song," he said, "was a social statement. Listen to the lyrics." I couldn't understand any lyrics beyond the name Candy had already voiced, and I said so. His grin broadened. It was the calculating smile of a malevolent child about to wring the neck of its brand-new puppy: ageless, unmitigated evil in the eyes of innocence. "Just listen," he said. "It is about a human girl whose father sexually molested her, whereupon she killed him."

It was as though the words were an incantation that turned my bones to ice. I could not move, not even enough to stop staring at him. My face felt stiff and strange, as though it belonged to someone else. I wondered absently what expression it was wearing, and then I wondered somewhat wildly what expression it should be wearing. I thought I ought to say something, but I couldn't remember what we had been talking about. The stereo was too loud, and I didn't like the song it was playing. I thought I might mention that, and decided it was too much trouble. The song would end, and then everything would return to normal. After all, it wasn't Christmas music. I could endure anything but Christmas music.

For one timeless instant I saw not Jorandel and his girls across the room from me but an animal, a blind pink animal, enormous and very near. It was gone as quickly as it came, replaced by the awful image of Kyriander Stone's father dead by my hand. That I knew how to deal with. I had taught myself a little mental trick to banish him, to banish that whole end-of-summer day when he died. Whenever my mind turned to that or to anything else I could not face, I made a small sound in the back of my throat that I had trained myself to respond to by blanking my mind completely. I did not resort to it often, but when I did, it was completely effective self-hypnotism: I could not even remember what it was that had provoked me to use it.

The song on the stereo seemed to have been going on for a very long time. No one said anything. Both Jorandel and Candy were looking at me oddly. I said uncomfortably, "What group did you say that is? The music we're listening to?"

"Aerosmith." Candy studied me sympathetically. "Are you okay, Rosie?"

"Sure, I'm great," I said. "Only I don't think I like Aerosmith, that's all. This song is so unpleasant."

"It's almost over," she said, her tone soothing.

In his corner with his guitar and his bottle and his girls, Jorandel laughed as though she had told a joke.

"Listen, would you guys mind changing the CD?" I said. "I'd really like to hear some Cold Iron CDs."

"Good idea," Jorandel said before Candy could answer. He waved a drunken hand in the direction of the CD case by the stereo. "Candy, get out the *Midnight Son* album, would you?" He looked at me, his eyes curiously shadowed. "You have a good relationship with your parents, Rosie?"

"Sure, okay, I guess," I said. "Why?"

"Just curious," he said. "D'you live with them still?" He grinned and corrected himself with drunken clarity: "When you're not on tour with us, I mean?"

"No. I left home when I was—a long time ago."

"When you were what?" His eyes were heavy and bloodshot, but their gaze was steady."

"What difference does it make?"

He nodded as though I had said something profound. "No difference at all," he said. "Here, you'll like this album. Give her the jewel box, Candy, so she can read the lyrics while she listens. And bring another bottle while you're up, okay?"

"You've had enough, Jorie," she said softly. He didn't say anything, he just looked at her. After a moment she shrugged and tossed the jewel box to me on her way to the bar for another bottle. "Whiskey's all gone," she said.

"Then call fucking room service," he said.

"Jorie—"

He looked at me and spoke as though she didn't exist. "So, cousin. What did you think of the concert tonight?"

Candy dialed room service. I said, not looking at him, "I like your music."

"But?" he said. I looked, but I couldn't read his expression.

"Nothing," I said. "I enjoyed the concert, okay?"

"You thought I shouldn't go on, right?" he said.

I shrugged. "I didn't quite see the point."

He looked impatient, but not quite angry. "The point was an arena full of fans who were there to hear a concert."

"Or to see a freak show." I didn't mean to say that.

To my surprise, he produced one of his most charming impish grins and said carefully, "Well, I guess they got it, if that's what they wanted."

"Jorandel, who pushed you down the stairs?" I didn't mean to say that, either. I guess the grin encouraged me.

He looked sheepish, and for the first time his eyes wandered drunkenly. "No one. I only said that 'cause I didn't want to admit I was so stoned I couldn't walk." He tilted his head and looked at me through a veil of hair. "I was embarrassed." He didn't look embarrassed now, though I thought he meant to. He had a way of watching people to see how they would react to his antics: a calculating, coldly curious look, as though he were forever testing humanity, trying to see just how much we would put up with, just how far he could go. He wore that look now.

I shrugged. "Okay, sure." Clearly I wasn't going to get at the truth by asking for it.

"What do you suppose would happen if I died onstage?" he asked curiously. "That would be an impressive climax to a performance, wouldn't it?"

"Do you always have to talk about dying, Jorie?" Candy had rejoined me on the couch to watch him with sad eyes. "You're not going to die."

"Everyone dies," he said easily. "Even elves, eventually."

"I hate it when you talk about it," she said.

"That's because you're afraid of it," he said, smiling again. "You are afraid to die."

"I don't care about me, I just wish you wouldn't talk about you dying." It didn't occur to her that there was anything wrong with her priorities.

"Silence won't stop it," he said. "Death listens not to silence."

"Don't," she said.

"Death, death, death," he said.

"I hate you." Her voice was completely devoid of feeling.

"You wish," he said.

"I do." She said it almost wonderingly. "I do wish that. I wish I hated you." Huge tears coursed unnoticed down her face. "You like hurting people."

"I only want to wake them up." He had been speaking with the exaggerated diction of the practiced abuser of alcohol, but now his speech slowed even more and he paused between words, clearly searching for exactly the right meaning. "I want them to feel something. Anything. Pain is the easiest feeling to realize, that's all. You are a race of graceforsaken, soulless dead. Humans spend their entire lives trying not to feel anything, and I just like to shake them up. You are such ephemeral creatures, it seems a terrible waste not to get what you can from the little time you have." He shrugged. "I want to make people live a little." He seemed to be making a sincere effort to explain himself to her.

"So you talk about dying," she said sullenly.

"Whatever," he said, losing interest. "Why not talk about it? If all humans want to do is avoid pain, they should kill themselves. Death is the ultimate painkiller."

"Very profound." I am not ordinarily given to sarcasm, but sententious speeches provoke me, and I made no effort to sound as though I meant it.

Whatever response I expected, genuine amusement was last on the list, but that's what I got. He laughed involuntarily, a delighted boyish sound, and said mirthfully, eyes dancing, "I was serious, you know."

"I was afraid you were." I couldn't help grinning.

"You're okay, cousin." His tone was still amused, but the quick pleasure was already gone from his eyes, replaced by that look of malicious curiosity. "But don't you think it's odd how much humans do fear death?" His voice became insistent. "Life hurts more than death. You know that. Don't you." It was a statement, not a question.

What did he see, what had I revealed? In my confusion I gulped more gin before I answered him, which made him smile in perceptive mockery. "The thing about pain," I said, trying to take the topic at face value, "is that you can get over it. You can live past it. You can't get over death." I thought of Kyriander Stone's father, of what I had taken from him. "You lose all your chances when you die."

"You lose all your pain when you die."

Without stopping to think, I said, "Were you really going to jump, before? Out the window? When Veladora was here? Are you in that much pain?" It was an ingenuous question, unintentional and intrusive, and I regretted it before the words were out of my mouth.

He took it seriously. "I don't know," he said, and glanced at Candy with a twisted little smile. "She'd tell you I knew somebody would catch me." His tone was challenging.

"Well, you did," she said defensively. "It was just another of your games. You wanted to scare us."

"And did I scare you?" His eyes were hooded.

"A little," she admitted. "Thing is, Jorie, sometime you're going to miscalculate. When you're acting, it's method acting, and you get so far into it that you forget to check whether there's anybody close enough to save you. Sometime maybe there won't be."

"Out of the mouths of babes." For a fraction of a second as he said it, I thought I saw the real Jorandel, stripped of his masks, and the torment in his eyes was unendurable. It was gone in an instant, veiled by fierce and awful contempt. "That's the turn-on, babe. But don't worry, they will ever and always be there. I am their financial security. They can't afford to let me go."

"You think that's all people care about?" I asked. "Your commercial potential? The money they make with you?"

He shrugged. "What else is there? The image is everything: nobody even knows who I am." The words were indifferent, but the look in his eyes was not.

"Do you let them know?" I knew as soon as I said it that I'd gone too far.

"Well, will you look at that," he said in a slow, cold, easy voice. "Little cousin is a nickel-plated shrink."

Perhaps fortunately, the room-service waiter arrived with the whiskey before Jorandel could say more, and Andy came in on his heels to ask whether anyone had seen Jim. Candy covered the soda on the table with a handy magazine while the waiter was there. When he had gone, she asked quietly over the sound of Jorandel bellowing for Jim, "You wanta do another line before I put the rest of this away?"

We did another line each, and I poured myself another glass of gin to balance it. Jorandel stopped bellowing when Jim appeared at his bedroom door with a naked groupie on his arm. Andy, ignoring the groupie as he would have ignored a bracelet or a bottle, said quietly, "I'm all set, Jim, but . . . You sure you want me to go?"

"Of course: why not?" said Jim. The groupie nuzzled his shoulder and wrapped one leg around his.

"You might need me tomorrow," said Andy.

"Frank can take care of both of us."

Andy nodded reluctantly. "I guess. Look, Jim, I don't need a goddamn Christmas vacation."

Jim shrugged. "Jorandel believes you need it." The groupie, unable to recapture his attention, released him and returned, pouting, to his room. He seemed unaware of the loss. Lowering his voice, he told Andy, "He wants to make up for the other night, Andy. Let him give you this. It will make him feel better. Don't worry: I'll be okay."

Andy hesitated, started to speak, and thought better of it. "Okay," he said. "Okay." He gave Jim a sudden bear hug and turned away, his face impassive.

"Hey!" Jorandel, in his corner, had been watching the exchange. "Andy! You leaving?" When Andy nodded, he said, "You have your tickets and all?"

"Yeah, Jorandel. Thanks."

"It's nothing," said Jorandel. He seemed to think of something. "Hey, wait a minute." He struggled to his feet and staggered toward his room. "Just a minute. I have somethin else for you. Just be a minute." I had almost forgotten how drunk he was. His speech was very little slurred and seemed rational, but he could barely stand.

"Jorandel," said Andy.

"No, really," said Jorandel, rebounding dizzily off the

back of a chair. "I just remembered, it's your Christmas present."

"Jorandel, don't make such a big deal," said Andy. "You already gave me—" But Jorandel disappeared into his room, not listening, and Andy turned helplessly to Jim.

"Let him do it," said Jim. "It is a small price to please him. Whatever it is, you know he can afford it."

"But, hell, Jim. It's not like that was the first time he ever threw something at me," Andy said, bewildered.

Jim grinned. "It was the first time he hit you."

Andy smiled reluctantly. "He'll have people standing in line to get things thrown at 'em if he keeps this up."

"He only wants you to know he's sorry," said Jim.

Jorandel returned with a small, clumsily gift-wrapped package, which he thrust into Andy's hands with a sheepish look. "Don't open it now," he said. "But you needn't wait till Christmas, either. Just—have a good trip, okay?"

"Sure, Jorandel." Andy looked at the gift uncertainly, as though wondering what to do with it. "Thanks," he said. "You didn't have to do any of this."

Jorandel waved a hand negligently. "Don't worry about it," he said. "Only have a good holiday. All right?"

"Sure." Andy glanced at Jim and turned away again.

"See you after Christmas," said Jim.

"Yeah," said Andy, his voice distant and sad.

"Let's go to a party," said Candy as the door closed behind him.

Jim and Jorandel both looked at her. I found myself studying them, forcing myself to see small differences beyond attire and haircut: Jorandel's face was narrower, Jim's eyes paler, Jorandel's mouth broader, but I knew I would see none of that if they weren't standing side by side for comparison. Yet I had known, last night, that it was Jim who came first to my room. I had known when he touched me. Not before.

"By Mab's grace, what party?" said Jim.

"I don't know." Candy gestured expansively. "Just a party. Don't you feel like partying?"

Jim hesitated, waiting for his brother to answer. Jorandel smirked at him, waiting too. At length Jim shrugged and said, looking at Jorandel, "What time is Veladora sending for us tomorrow?"

Jorandel's smirk disappeared. "Fuck Veladora." He tilted his head back to drink from the whiskey bottle in his hand, lost his balance, and collapsed in a great giggling sprawl at Jim's feet. "Lesh pardy," he said, and began to snore.

Jim looked at Candy. "Call Frank," he said wearily, and returned to his room.

"Damn," said Candy. "I guess no party." She went off in search of Frank while the groupies who had been with Jorandel came out of their corner to circle around him like vultures, their expressions as cold and calculating as his ever was. I wasn't sleepy, but I decided it would be a good idea to go to bed just the same. I took the gin bottle with me. Enough alcohol might put me to sleep. It worked for Jorandel.

9

I dreamed of Christmas trees, and blind pink animals, and woke with a strangled scream when I found myself killing my father. The long slanting rays of very early morning sun filtered dustily through my curtains, and I stared at the room in utter bewilderment, unable to recall where I was or why. I'd been dreaming something. Something bad. I thought quite clearly, "Naturally I meant Kyriander Stone's father," and did not even wonder what I meant by that.

This was a hotel room. I was on tour with Cold Iron, looking for a potential murderer. Right. Nothing wrong with my mind. I reached up to push the hair out of my face, and my fingers bumped against each other unsteadily. Scowling, I pretended not to notice. My mouth tasted foul. The room was warm, my body drenched in sweat, and I was shivering. My throat felt uncomfortably as though I might have screamed aloud before I woke. Maybe, if I had, the walls were thick enough that nobody would have heard me.

There was a nearly empty bottle of gin by the bed, and beside it a tiny brown bottle of soda with one white line laid out in readiness on a little mirror next to it. I remembered bringing the gin to bed with me, but not the soda. Perhaps Candy had left it for me. I blinked at it groggily, remembering last night's comforting rush of optimism when I had shared her soda. "There is everything in this life but hope." I couldn't recall who had said that, or even whether I had read it or heard it or made it up, but the words chased each other through my mind with the implacability of truth, and my self-indulgent angst had reached such proportions that I saw nothing absurd in that at all.

Still, I wasn't going to start my day with soda. Nor with gin, either, come to that. I would find coffee somewhere: caffeine was a strong enough drug for any reasonable person. After a shower, clean clothes, and a lot of coffee, I would feel better. It did not for one moment occur to me to try to go back to sleep: I felt punchy and light-headed, but I knew if I slept again I would dream, and I couldn't face that. Swinging my legs over the edge of the bed, I paused, staring blindly at the gin and soda, thinking of nothing.

In a moment I would stand up and make my way to the bathroom. Without thought or intention, I put the tip of my finger on the end of the line of soda and then in my mouth, rubbing my gums and grimacing at the bitter flavor. Why had I done that? It tasted foul. Shuddering, I uncapped the gin and rinsed my mouth, swallowed, and stared at the soda. I must be more rattled than I thought, to have even touched it right after deciding not to. I rubbed my eyes with the heels of my hands, trying to clear my mind. Too much gin last night. Too little sleep, and too many dreams. A little soda would steady me. It wasn't as though I were contemplating a lifetime of drug use: just this once, and just half a line, was no big deal. Unusual circumstances warrant unusual actions, and this was certainly an unusual circumstance.

Without further hesitation I rolled up a sheet from a hotel notepad, bent over the mirror, and inhaled a careful half of the soda laid out. It hurt my nose, but I could feel its artificial confidence banishing my weary morning megrims. Obviously I'd made the right decision: I felt better already. Pleased with this reasoning, I put the rolled-up paper to my other nostril and inhaled the rest, then wiped the mirror with a damp finger and rubbed my gums again. What the hell. No sense leaving the stuff around for the hotel maids to find, and it would have been too much trouble to put it back in a bottle. I polished the mirror on the bedclothes, put it back on the table, had a slug of gin to take the edge off the bitter flavor in the back of my throat, and went to take a shower.

I dressed in designer jeans and a trendy crocheted blouse Candy had selected for me. A number of new bangle bracelets and a mismatched pair of earrings completed my outfit, and my hair was cunningly tousled into the damp spiral curls she had showed me how to coax out of my previously frizzy perm. I stuffed the soda bottle in my pocket so the maid wouldn't find it and took another swig of gin just for the flavor before going in search of coffee.

The suite's main room looked tumbled and dreary in the cold light of morning, with cushions off all the furniture tossed carelessly on the floor, ashtrays overflowing, wet towels discarded on tables and chairs, and empty bottles everywhere underfoot. There were groupies asleep in the corners, but the only musician present was Killer, domestically building a pot of coffee in the tiny kitchenette area. He glanced up when I entered and said good morning in his surprisingly sweet, gentle voice. Only the tips of his ears and nose showed through the hair. "This'll be ready in a couple minutes." He hesitated. "You okay?"

Maybe I had screamed before I woke. "Sure," I said, embarrassed. "You?"

He nodded, turned on the coffeepot, and retired to the table where Veladora had sat the night before. I joined him, watching the coffeepot impatiently. After a long, silent moment he said cautiously, "Bad dreams?"

The image of Kyriander's father obscured my vision for one brief instant, his dead eyes staring into mine. I could feel my face twist in swift revulsion and denial, and I said, "No!" too sharply and then couldn't find anything else to say, and couldn't get the memory out of my mind.

Killer was never talkative. Of them all, he was the least outgoing, the shiest, the quietest. He was also, perhaps, the most empathic. He ducked his head now in recognition of my discomfort and said, with the air of a man determined to make polite conversation, "You up late with the rest of 'em last night?" His sweet, soft voice was uncertain, as though he expected a rebuff.

"Pretty late, I guess." My voice was rough with gratitude. I didn't care what we talked about: anything, anything, just please god no more muddled, miserable, guilt-ridden memories. He must have sensed that, because when I added feebly, "You disappeared early," he accepted the implied query as though I had a right to a report on his movements.

"I don't need the wind-down time the others do," he said. After a moment's awkward silence he added brightly, "Andy get off okay?"

The soda had not cleared my mind as well as I had hoped it would. It took me a moment to remember who Andy was and that he had gone anywhere. "Oh," I said. "Yeah. He didn't seem real thrilled about it, though."

"S'pose he wasn't," said Killer. "Doesn't like to leave Jim when we're on tour. But Jorandel wanted to give him something nice, you know?"

"Whether he wanted it or not," I said sourly.

Killer glanced at me and for a moment those ebony curls parted just enough to show me the vulnerable beauty of his big dark eyes. "Yeah," he said, and his lips twitched in the hint of a smile. "Well, he don't always . . . He's a genius an' all, reads all-kine philosophy and psychology and stuff, knows more about people and what makes them tick than anybody else I'll ever know, but he don't always see what he don't want to." It was a very long speech for Killer.

"Not unreasonable," I said. "Which of us does?"

He seemed to be growing comfortable with the idea of conversation. "Thing is," he said earnestly, "Jorie conked Andy with a bottle the other night, near knocked him out, and he never meant it. When he means to hurt, that's one thing, but damn he's sorry to do it by accident. So he wen give him stuffs. To make up for it." He had just the hint of an accent I couldn't place. It was more in the cadence of his speech than in the pronunciation, but it showed, too, very faintly, in the shape of his vowels and in the occasional odd usage like "wen give" for "gave." I wondered where he had acquired it, but it didn't seem the time to ask. "Wen give him time off," he said, "air tickets, hotel room, li' dat. Makes him feel better, yeah?"

"And to hell with how Andy feels, right?"

"Well, what it is, he don't see it that way."

"People who insist on giving you things you don't want never do," I said somewhat unclearly. "And then they wonder why you're not bowing and scraping in gratitude."

The coffee stopped perking and he poured a cup for each of us. "Cream and sugar?" When I shook my head, he sat back down and studied his cup. "You're awful hard on Jorie." He hesitated. "He hurt you?"

"Not yet." I realized how that sounded and added hastily, "I mean, no. He hasn't."

He lifted his head, but his eyes were hidden in shadow behind his hair. "Somebody did."

"Somebody hurt 'most everybody," I said. "Pain is a universal constant, like death." What was the matter with me this morning? I didn't usually spout grim sophomoric platitudes before breakfast. I lifted my coffee and burned my tongue on its harsh, hot bitterness, then managed a feeble grin. "Sorry. The devil made me say that."

Killer was smiling at me, his head tilted so one of his eyes showed through the hair. "You sounded like Jorandel," he said. "Too much booze last night, or what?"

"Too much of a lot of things," I said wryly. "Emerson thinks I ought to leave the tour. He thinks I'm falling for Jorandel." I seemed to be blurting out whatever thoughts happened to cross my mind. Blushing, I sipped my coffee again, more carefully this time.

"Are you?" He asked it softly, hesitantly, as though afraid he had no right. But I had given him the right by saying what I'd said.

"No!" Again I said it too sharply, and gave myself away to both of us by trying to cover it with a wordier denial: "I'm not attracted to psychotics. He's gross, he's cruel, he's foulmouthed, and he doesn't bathe. Feral elf." I shuddered deliberately. "And a goddamned show-off besides. I don't care for theatrical adolescents no matter what their chronological age, or how physically pretty they are." I subsided, too late for self-respect.

He was silent for a long moment, and I could feel those dark eyes studying me through the veil of hair. "He's hurting," he said at last in a shy, muffled voice.

I made an impatient sound, though we both knew my impatience was as much with myself as with Jorandel. "What is it that hurts him so goddamn much?" I meant to sound derisive, but it came out plaintive. "What's he got to endure that the rest of you don't?" I shook my head. "Hell, he's got it all. What's he got to complain about?"

He shook his head slowly. "You gotta understand," he said softly. "The rest of us, we got what we need. We get to play with the best band goin, we got all the money we need, we're living our fantasies, yeah? There's nothin like making music with Jorie. When we're in sync . . . damn. Don't matter what any of us is like as people, you know? 'Cause when we're jammin, when it's really rollin . . ." He paused, baffled. "I don't know how to say it. It's creation, you know? Creation. The music, making the music, it's like, it's such a high, it's like a little piece of Faerie translated." He ducked his head, embarrassed. "I can't say it. What I mean is, we got that. The rest of us. We got all we want, all we can handle.

"But Jorie's bigger'n that. His soul's bigger. His need's bigger. He's got things he needs to say, places he's gotta go, things he's gotta do. But Veladora owns him, and he puts a lid on that. What it is, he's got Jorandel trapped in this one little band, in this one little aspect of all that he could be, and it don't matter how good we are, how satisfied the rest of us are with it, it ain't enough for Jorandel. He ain't got what he needs. Not all his stars are out, you know what I mean?" It was, surprisingly, a reference from J. D. Salinger, and I did know what he meant. Or at least I had an inkling of it.

"And he really can't break the contract with Veladora?"

"Not except by dyin."

"Is that really what the lawyers said?"

"Close enough," he said. "The only worse case woulda been if Veldora had wanted to seal it with magic. Believe me, if there was a way out, Jorie'd have found it by now."

"Why did he sign a contract like that in the first place? Didn't he have an attorney look at it before he signed it?"

"Nah." He shook his head mournfully. "We'd been to all the record producers, we'd been everywhere. Nobody was interested. We were workin bars, strip joints, whatever, gettin maybe five bucks a night each, maybe not even that. And we couldn't get the attention we needed. We made a demo and sent it around, and one company even signed us for an option, but they dropped us without doin nothing."

"Why, for goodness' sake? You guys are good."

"I know." That wasn't arrogance, just recognition of a fact. "But you know how many good bands there are that you'll never hear of because they can't get that first break?" He shook his head. "We were nobody, and Veladora offered us the moon, and, hey. None of us woulda risked that to call in our own attorney, even if we could've afforded one, which how the hell could we? Sure, Jorie signed. At that point any one of us woulda signed in blood and sold our souls and all. I s'pose we figured if it was a really bad deal, we'd be able to get out of it later. If we thought of it at all. Mostly, we just thought, hey, this is our chance, don't blow it."

"Okay, that makes sense. But if Veladora believed in you—or in Jorandel—enough at that time to take a chance on signing him, why's he limiting him now?"

Killer shrugged heavily. "Money, maybe. We make plenty this way. No tellin what'd happen, if we could do what Jorie wants. The public expects certain things, yeah? They're used to us, they buy a Cold Iron album, and they figure they know what they're gettin'. We can grow a little with each one, but there's a limit to what we can do. It's happened to other bands. You change your focus, and you lose it all."

"And Jorandel's ready to take that risk?"

"We'd all take it, for him," he said. "This way's killin him." It wasn't a dramatic statement, just the truth as he saw it.

"Does Veladora know that?"

"I dunno. Why would he care?"

"No reason, I guess. Especially if Candy was right when she said he's on a power trip, more than money."

He nodded. "Guess he is. Or he wouldn't be willing to break Jorandel for steppin out of line." He shook his head. "I dunno, how'm I gonna understand a guy like Veladora? I dunno what his trip is."

"But he only controls Jorandel, right? The rest of you could do what you want, and he couldn't stop you?"

"Sure. But we're Jorie's band," he said simply.

"Oh. None of you want to break away? I thought some of you did some solo things. Candy said Jim made a record."

"Yeah, but you know what," he said, smiling into his coffee. "That wasn't so much for Jim as it was for Jorandel. Some experimental stuff Jorandel wanted to do. Jim played guitar for him, but Jorandel did the singing." He glanced up, so startled he let his hair swing back, exposing his face. "Shouldn't've said that. Ain't nobody s'posed to know."

"I won't repeat it."

Reassured, he retreated behind his hair again. "Ain't nothin the rest of us want to do, so much as there is what Jorandel wants to do. So it don't matter that we're free, as long as Jorandel ain't. That's the heart of it."

"Is your—" I hesitated, searching for inoffensive words. "Is your contract with Jorandel okay? I mean, he's not in some way doing to you guys what Veladora's doing to him?"

"Nah." He smiled at the idea. "Why would he? Nah, we can do whatever we want, even break up Cold Iron if we want. But why would we?"

"So nobody's got any reason to, well, to want to, um, hurt Jorandel?" I knew even as I spoke that it was a stupid idea. They were an eccentric group, and not one I'd trust as far as I could throw any of them, but the one thing that came out in every conversation with any of them was their unmistakable loyalty to Jorandel.

Killer tilted his head, exposing one eye. "You're still thinkin' what he said last night, that somebody pushed him down those stairs, yeah?" I admitted it. "But he said afterward nobody did," he said, surprised.

"I know," I said. "But—I still wondered."

"Hey," he said. "We get rowdy, sure. We throw things, we punch a wall or shove a cameraman or somethin, we get a little outta hand sometimes, all of us. We'd maybe hit each other, even. What we do, we kind of act out, you know? Like you said, like adolescents, like kids. We feel somethin and we act on it, right there and then.

I ain't sayin it's a good thing, but it's how we do. Spoiled, maybe. We got it all, and we got it early, and you know, when everybody's tryin to please you, when everybody's actin like you're some kinda special, maybe it's hard to keep your balance, yeah? But we don't, we wouldn't, none of us would really hurt nobody. 'Specially not each other."

"Jorandel hit Andy with that bottle, didn't he? Or doesn't that count, since Andy's just a bodyguard?"

He looked stubborn. "Jorandel didn't push him down no stairs."

"But if the stairs had been there?"

He hesitated, giving it careful thought. "Well, I guess I can see that. Maybe. Jorandel loses control, more'n the rest of us. You know, when I break somethin it ain't never nothin I can't get another of, you know what I mean? It might cost a lot, but it's just money. There's that moment when you're pissed and you reach for somethin and right then I still have just enough control that I don't grab nothin that money won't buy. I don't smash nothin there's only one of in the world, you know? Maybe Jorandel don't have that control. It could be. I know he ain't always on top of what he's doin." He frowned. "But, hey, you ain't sayin he pushed hisself downstairs are you?"

"No. I guess I was trying to prove a point. Like, for instance, what about the Roach?" I said. "Nobody can account for where he was when Jorandel fell. And he's not as openly violent as Jorandel, but he's meaner. He's—" I hesitated over the word "evil" and said instead, "He's dangerous."

Surprisingly, Killer grinned. "Jorie calls him a moral retard," he said, and sobered. "But, nah, he wouldn do nothin like that. He's sick, but he ain't that sick. Not to push Jorie downstairs. Besides, Jorandel said nobody did." He looked at me hopefully, like a boy wondering whether he's passed a test . . . or whether he has successfully fooled his parents.

I said ruthlessly, "That's just what he would say, if the Roach did it, isn't it? You guys cover for each other."

"Sure, but . . . Nah, Rosie. Nah. Nobody pushed him." He brightened. "If somebody did, you know, maybe he'd lie to everybody else, but hey, he'd tell us the truth, the band, he'd tell us. For real." He was trying to convince us both.

I couldn't argue with his need to believe, so I changed the subject. "What makes you guys put up with the Roach, anyway? Do you like him?"

"Nah, who could like him?" He hesitated. "Well, there's like and there's like. I mean, he's one of us, yeah? And what he can do with his keyboards, ain't nobody else alive can do what he does." He paused, head down again so all I could see were the tangled curls, the tips of his ears, and the stubborn set of his jaw. "We ain't exactly friends, you know, and it ain't like some bands say, like a marriage. If we were married maybe we would divorce the Roach. If there was somebody else could play like he does. But the thing is, it's more like that song Jorie wrote, you know? That song 'Brothers.' And you don't divorce your brothers."

"It's been done," I said, "but I see what you mean."

"Besides," he said, "He's no problem. What he did to you, he don't go 'round doin that kind of thing all the time." He smiled faintly. "And it ain't as though the rest of us was exactly well behaved."

As though to prove his point, something crashed just then in a nearby room, and I heard an elf voice, either Jim's or Jorie's, furiously yelling something largely incomprehensible except for the curse words. A female voice answered him, shriller and even fouler in her choice of curses. There was the sound of breaking glass, a female shriek, and then silence. While I was wondering nervously whether we ought to do anything about it. Killer calmly poured us both fresh coffee. A door slammed. A moment later Jorandel, identifiable by his bandages, came storming from an inner corridor, still spewing curses. At sight of Killer and me he paused, and it looked as though he were debating whether to attack or ignore us. The face that could look so transcendently beautiful when he wanted was ugly now with petulant, childish rage.

Killer said mildly, "Want some coffee?"

"No. Yes. Fuck," said Jorandel.

Killer didn't say anything. He waited, poised with a

fresh cup in one hand and the coffeepot in the other, for Jorandel to make up his mind.

"Yes, all right, pour it," Jorandel said grudgingly. "Mab's grace." He joined us at the table and scowled at me. "Has anyone thought to order any damn breakfast?"

"Not yet," said Killer.

"Fuck." He got up again and went to the phone. I wondered how room service would react to curses before breakfast, but he spoke quite civilly, put the phone down, and came back to the table. "It will probably take a year to get here," he said. "What are the two of you doing up so early?"

"Just talking," said Killer.

Jorandel glanced at me and away again. The rage was gone from his face, replaced by a curious shyness. "Sorry if I did anything last night to anger you," he said.

When I realized he was talking to me, I said in surprise, "What? I mean, no, you didn't do anything to me."

"Good." He nodded, satisfied. "I suppose you've figured out by now I'm not always a model of propriety, but I do not like to offend you, cousin. I don't remember the sordid details of last night's activities, but I seem to recall feeling moderately peeved with someone, and I was hoping it wasn't you."

"It was Veladora," I said, studying him. This was yet another Jorandel, different from the other faces he had shown me. This one was polite, mildly amused, and about as unlike the volatile elfrock star as a person could get. I had the curious feeling this one was also somehow more authentic, more nearly the Jorandel he might have been if Cold Iron had never happened, and I was curious to know how he would respond to a reminder of the elfrock star's excesses of the night before. "You threatened to jump out a window."

"Oh, yes." He had the grace to look embarrassed. "Well, the problem is, I cannot touch him. Nothing disturbs him, except the possibility that he will lose control of something he owns. I guess I thought I'd test that."

"He didn't believe you," I said.

"No, that's the thing about telling the truth," he said. "Nobody ever believes it."

"You mean you really meant to jump out the window?" I suppose I sounded as dubious about that as I felt.

He looked surprised. "I don't know. Does it matter?" It was an innocent question; he really wanted to know.

At a loss for a sensible answer, I said, "It would matter to your fans."

He shrugged. "It would fit the all-holy image. They'd like it well enough once they were accustomed to the idea. Dead heroes are actually better than live ones in many ways. They are easier to control. They aren't so likely to do anything that will disturb the image."

"You speak of your image as though you resent it. Didn't you create it?" I said.

He smiled innocently. "It's quite possible to resent one's own creation," he said, and shrugged. "Besides, I didn't create what it has become."

"Who did, then?"

"Human expectations." He studied his coffee. When he spoke again it was with the same deliberation he'd used to cover drunkenness last night, but this time he was only very earnestly seeking clarity, as though for some reason it was terribly important to him that I understand. "You set out to create a certain stage persona," he said., "Bizarre, flamboyant, whatever. Elfrock star, in brief. It's as though you're an actor, building a character that you intend to play through every performance. And you plan to take off the character like a costume when you come offstage. You believe you will be yourself, when you're not working; and then you find out the boundaries have shifted. Everyone wants the character, and you keep playing it, till you don't quite know which part is character, and which part is you." He looked at me, his face expressionless. "And then you learn that all the time you thought you were building that character, what happened was that the people around you, the people you have to deal with every day, they've been adding and subtracting character traits while you weren't looking, so that you no longer define the character.

"Humans are a race of observers, a nation of eyes. They don't do things, they create others to do things for them. They invent their own heroes so they may punish them for being heroes. I am not Jorandel anymore, whoever he is. Or was. I am Cold Iron's front man, a cardboard character with a debt to pay. Not dues: I've sure as Earth paid my dues. What I owe now is harder to pay. I owe every human who likes Cold Iron the satisfaction of seeing his own personal longings vicariously fulfilled. Which of course I cannot provide, at least not all of them."

"Elves have no expectations?"

"Not like that."

"Why do you think you owe anything?"

"Honey, I don't think, I know."

"Why? How?"

He sighed heavily. "I don't know why we're having this conversation."

"I don't either, but it'd be way rude to stop now."

He grinned. "Then it would fit the image."

"I wish you'd try to explain," I said. I knew by now that he could if he wanted to.

"Earth defend me," he said. "It's not that hard to understand." He thought about it. "You are a beautiful woman," he said. "Have you never run into other women who thought that meant you'd had it easy all your life because of that, and who wouldn't believe you if you said you hadn't? Or men who think it means you owe them sex, and don't hear you if you say no? Or maybe some people think beautiful women are stupid, and there is no way to convince them otherwise. You never encountered that?" He grinned briefly. "Many men simply believe all women are retards, and you could outthink and outdo them till your Christian hell froze over and they'd still believe you couldn't do it.

"When you deal with that, that's dealing with an image," he said earnestly. "They have an image of 'woman' and they won't interact with the reality no matter how different it is from the image, or how strongly the difference asserts itself. They will not see it. They *cannot* see it. And in fact they will try to punish you for failing to fit their idea of what you should be. Perhaps in subtle ways, because they cannot recognize it openly, but they will try to punish you to get you to conform to what they expect of you. That's all I'm talking about. It's exactly the same thing, only magnified, for a pubic figure. None avoid it. Whatever you do, they will twist it to fit the image or they will punish you for not fitting the image, but either way you are chained for life to the almighty image."

"If you hate it so much, why don't you just quit?"

"Quit making music?" He stared at me as though I had taken leave of my senses. "I can't do that."

"Then, quit recognizing the image. Just be yourself, and to hell with what anyone thinks."

He grimaced. "I might try that—if I hadn't signed with Veladora. Unfortunately I did, so that is not an option."

"How could he stop you?"

"He could kill my career. He could take away the audience. I'm not just masturbating up there onstage, you know. It is a process of communication. However fouled it gets, it remains an interaction. I need the audience, I need the fans, even if they never really see me and they believe they are dealing with some imagined elfrock star image. Music is only noise if no one hears it."

"So there's no way out, as far as you can see."

"Not short of dying."

"Everybody keeps saying that. It seems so . . . I don't know. Melodramatic. How can a contract be that tight?"

"Get it written in Faerie, and it can be," he said. "It is. It's not about your human laws, you know. I could find a way around those. This is about honor and chaos. I cannot explain in English without all the legalese in the contract. Let's just say the lawyers are right."

"I didn't even know Faerie had lawyers and contracts."

He looked surprised. "We haven't. Not the way you mean."

"But you just said—"

"I know. For convenience only, for saying what cannot be said in English. Veladora has some powerful magic behind him. He tricked me, and I signed away my life here. I could get free of him by returning to Faerie, but as far as I'm concerned that's much the same as being dead." He smiled suddenly, innocently, like a child. "A point, though: if I were dead, I wouldn't care about the music anymore. I wouldn't need the audience."

"You wouldn't need anything," I said in what I hoped was a quelling tone. There could be too much dwelling on this idea of dying. I changed the subject. "You speak of so much pain, and yet your music is the most joyous I've ever heard. How can that be?"

He glanced at me sideways with a sly grin that gave the impression, oddly, of embarrassment. "There is a line I read in a human drama once," he said: " 'It's the way I register despair.' "

So much for changing the subject.

10

Veladora sent for Jimendan and Jorandel as promised, just after noon; and they went as directed, though not without sullen grumblings of dissatisfaction. They carried their matched guitars with them. Nobody said where they were going or why, and I didn't ask. Jorandel was sober, for him, but his mood was precarious and I didn't want to provoke one of his fits of unpredictable violence.

While they were gone I did a little genuine investigating, a first for this case. I slipped out of the suite while Candy and the Roach were enjoying a verbal battle in one of the bedrooms, and used the phone in the lobby downstairs to call an old friend who promised to send a car around for me at once.

The phone was altogether too near the enormous hotel Christmas tree. All the time I was standing there I kept hearing my father's voice, of all things, crooning a Christmas carol in the back of my mind. That sounds innocent enough, but the quality of his voice was sly and suggestive and unpleasant: as unnerving, somehow, as that Aerosmith song Jorandel had played on the stereo the night before. When the Christmas carol he was singing began to share the lyrics of "Janie's Got a Gun" and I recalled Kyriander's father's dying face, I retreated to the nearest ladies' room with a vague thought that the music and the memories wouldn't follow me there.

They would. They did. My hands shook so much I could hardly grip the gin bottle I had, with what I considered remarkable foresight, tucked into my purse before leaving the suite. My face in the mirror was ugly, alien, oddly colorless, reduced by the room's harsh lighting to a sour caricature of itself. I resisted the impulse to throw the bottle at the mirror. Instead I escaped into one of the little metal stalls and stood with my back against the locked door, staring blankly into the toilet bowl, noting chips in the porcelain and signs of slipshod cleaning habits and feeling as though such things were in some way indicative of the state of the universe in general. The morning's soda must be wearing off. This was only the downside of that euphoric rush that had got me out of bed. Knowing that didn't make me feel any better.

I had another sip of gin and thought of the soda bottle in my pocket. I should dump it while I was there, get rid of it, forget about it. I had known all along it was a bad plan, that the price of that brief euphoria and clarity of mind would be too high. The ride up had been steep and easy, the heights giddy, the illusion of competence very satisfying. But the ride down was longer and steeper and horribly inevitable, with nothing gained and everything to lose.

I took the bottle from my pocket and stared at it. It was tiny, made of brown glass with a black plastic screw-on cap: an innocent artifact as harmless in itself as any other inanimate object. Even the white powder inside was blameless: a poison, certainly, but in no way responsible for the damage it could do, no more than for the illusory bliss it could provide. It was neither evil nor good, it simply was. Evil—and good, if any—was a function of people, not of things. One had a choice.

The only wise choice in this case, obviously, was to dump the soda, discard the bottle, and forget about it. I had enough trouble already without adding drug abuse to the list. The problem was, I had already started with soda this morning, and had a runny nose and a bad case of jangled nerves bordering on cosmic despair as a result of it. The runny nose would go away, but the despair would take longer, and I had work to do: work I wouldn't do well, to which I wouldn't be able to give my full attention, if I was looking at the world through gloom-colored glasses all day.

Using a little more soda—just enough to see me through my investigations this afternoon—wasn't going to kill me. I would quit when I came back to the hotel, get through tonight's concert without it (the underlying joy of Jorandel's music would surely be enough to lighten the bleakest mood), and a night's sleep would get the last of it out of my system. Tomorrow I would know better than to start with it. But today was already shot without it, and I couldn't afford that.

There was a pen in my purse with a pocket clamp on its cap just the right shape to use for a spoon. I'd spent enough time dithering: my friend's car would be arriving any minute now, and I needed to be at the hotel entrance to meet it. I dipped out a little spoonful of powder, inhaled it, and without a second's hesitation did the same with the other nostril: I had to walk past the hotel's Christmas tree to get out the front door.

It occurred to me, briefly, to wonder what it was with me and Christmas trees; but I shoved the thought to the back of my mind for later consideration. That had nothing to do with Jorandel, and right now the point was to get through one day of seriously investigating his concerns. I could worry about my own aberrations later.

The car was just pulling up to the entrance when I got there. I knew the driver, a statuesque blonde incongruously freckled and pigtailed, wearing a chauffeur's cap and stiff blue uniform modified to accentuate her assets. Her name was Annabelle Eloise Conway, but I had never heard anyone call her anything but "Muffin." She grinned and waved when she saw me, and waited while I ran down the steps to climb into the front seat beside her. "You're looking strikingly trendy," she said, surveying my outfit.

"And you're looking just plain striking," I said. "As you well know."

"Hilly will fire me at the first hint of a wrinkle or a sag," she said, pulling out into traffic. "And with my figure, it'll take the Army Corps of Engineers to prevent some major droops and dips once I hit thirty."

"He'll hire them," I said. Hilly was her employer, an extremely aggressive little man who had made a comfortable and very lucrative niche for himself in the tarnished understructure of Hollywood's tinsel factory. Unlike too many of Hollywood's denizens, he could be as generous as he was aggressive, and Muffin was not just any chauffeur. In fact, she was one of his secret weapons.

She grinned, secure in her pre-thirty magnificence. "Maybe he will, at that. What's up? Anything you can talk about?

Shannon and I had done Hilly a favor once when his daughter was attending U.C. Berkeley and got mixed up with a very wrong crowd. He had been grateful, and besides paying us the going rate for our services had insisted we allow him to return the favor anytime we needed assistance he could offer. At the time it had seemed unlikely we would ever take him up on it, but in fact this wouldn't be the first time one of us had turned to him for information he was in a unique position to provide. I'd had occasion to learn that he didn't keep many secrets from Muffin, so there was no point in refusing to tell her what I wanted to see him about. "You ever hear of a rock group called Cold Iron?" I asked.

Her face hardened. "Oh, my," she said.

"What's that mean?"

She hesitated so fractionally that if I hadn't known her rather well I might not have noticed it. "Veladora is what that means," she said, but I was sure that was not what she had started to say. "You taking him on?"

Whatever it was she was concealing, I wouldn't learn it by asking. "From the tone of your voice, I think I better hope not," I said.

"You'll be more comfortable," she said. "What's your interest in elfrock's bad boys, if it's not their illustrious producer?" The words were mildly jolly, but her expression was not.

"I'm not positive it isn't," I said. "I have reason to believe somebody may want to kill one of them. It could be Veladora."

"Whoever it is, he'll have to stand on line," she said with startling intensity. "You oughta get out of this one if you can, Rosie. Cold Iron is bad news."

"I know that's the image they project," I said, "but they seem pretty okay, really. No worse than most elf-rock musicians, surely?"

She shrugged. "Maybe the others aren't, but Jim and

Jorie themselves are exactly what they appear to be: sociopaths."

"Well, some say that's essentially the definition of fairy folk: that they're fallen angels who possess every charm but conscience."

"Jim and Jorie take it way past that," she said. "I'm talking genuine Jim Morrison piss-in-public and barf-on-your-bagels crazy."

"This sounds like something personal. Did one of them barf on your bagels, by any chance?"

She grinned at the repetition of her alliterative phrase, but there was no humor in her eyes. "You might say that." She glanced at me sideways, keeping most of her attention on the road. "They can charm your socks off when they want to."

I knew it was a question, and I wasn't sure how to answer it. "More than socks, I think," I said, "but so far I'm fully clothed."

She nodded. "So far."

"I'm pretty leery of loony tunes," I said ambiguously.

"In other words, you're falling for them."

I hesitated a long time before I said, "Just the one. Jorandel. And I don't think I'd call it falling, exactly. Let's say I'm less repelled than I ought to be."

"Oh, honey," she said, and sighed. "Well, at least you're trying to be honest with yourself. That's more than most women have the presence of mind to do in their company." She glanced at me again. "Jorandel, you said? You can tell them apart?"

"Yes . . . well, usually."

"That, too, is more than most women have the presence of mind for in their company. There's hope for you yet."

"What did they do to you, Muffin?"

She didn't answer for so long I thought she wasn't going to. "Tell you what," she said finally. "Talk to Hilly. If you still want to know more when I drive you back, we'll talk about it then."

She was right: I didn't want to know more than Hilly told me. I didn't want to know everything he told me. The words from one of Jorandel's songs kept chasing themselves through my mind: "Somebody save me. . . ."

I'd gone to Hilly for information on the people around Jorandel, and I'd got it. But he wouldn't let me go till I'd heard what he knew about Jorandel, as well. He was a perceptive little man. He knew, I think, how close I was to the edge, and he wanted to make sure that if I fell, it wouldn't be for Jorandel. He did his best. And I knew damn well that all the information I got from him was reliable. He had always been honest with me, and he wouldn't have changed that even if there hadn't been enough ugly truth about Jorandel to do the job without lies. Which there was.

Jorandel was not just a charming rogue, but as Muffin had said, genuine Jim Morrison piss-in-public and barf-on-your-bagels psychotic. Item: he tried to kill a man for offering him a beer. His justification afterward was that he hadn't liked the brand. Item: he urinated and then deliberately vomited on the automobile and person of a fan who neither pressed charges nor would offer even a guess as to the reason for Jorandel's behavior. Jorandel was forcibly prevented from smashing the car's windshield (and perhaps its owner) with a baseball bat, and the bewildered fan departed in some haste. Item: he was prevented, by the fortuitous arrival of a friend, from his evident intention to knife a woman to death (and he subsequently spent the night with her, which in my opinion cast some doubt on either the intended knifing or her intelligence, but there was no knowing which).

Items: he defecated in a hotel bedroom, he broke all the mirrors in a different hotel suite and had started on the windows before anyone could stop him, he urinated and vomited in a number of inappropriate places (and on a number of people), he had been narrowly prevented from jumping out of any number of windows at varying heights from the ground, he had been narrowly prevented from inflicting serious physical harm on any number of innocent individuals, he had been narrowly prevented from killing himself by drug overdose on any number of occasions that had frequently resulted in ambulance trips to and overnight stays in the hospital. . . . The list went on and on.

The hell of it was that it didn't quite do the job. Oh, I was repelled. I was disgusted, I was primly horrified, and I had (thank the gods) sense enough not to feel a maternal yearning to heal the poor misunderstood elven urchin genius. I understood it was no hurt boy I was dealing with, but a seriously damaged and dangerous man. And I fully understood that any healing of that damage would have to be instigated and implemented by him, not by some well-intentioned, lovesick maternal type with delusions of competence.

Besides, delusions of competence I might have, but I was not then nor had I ever been maternal. I admit to the occasional good intention, but I reject the very idea that I was lovesick over Jorandel. I was not even attracted to him in the ordinary sense. His physical beauty was overshadowed, for me, by his mental impairedness. That powerfully charismatic personality that seemed to mesmerize the groupies only put me on my guard, instinctively and completely. But . . .

Moonshadows wake the dancing land
The stars have stung the laughing man
My footsteps echo on the sea
Somebody save me. . . .
Somebody save me. . . .

Maybe it was the music. I found myself looking for loopholes. Maybe it was Jim who did all those things; it really was difficult to tell them apart. Maybe Jim was the psychotic, and Jorandel was just an overgrown adolescent who could, with time, turn into a human being.

But I'd seen him hurl a bottle at Veladora, try to climb out a window, and casually have sex with a stranger in a relatively public situation. I'd heard him fighting with a groupie this morning, I'd seen him vomiting in a gutter, I'd observed his alcohol intake and inferred his drug intake. Maybe I hadn't seen any certifiably sociopathic behavior, but close enough. And Hilly had been very convincing in his documentation. It just wasn't rationally possible to pretend Jorandel was really a perfectly nice guy. He wasn't. Not even close.

Death is a singing promise
Life is a loaded gun

Strangers are people, people are strange
When you're the Midnight Son. . . .

The last soda I'd done (furtively, in Hilly's bathroom, and I was afraid he'd guessed why I had such frequent need of his bathroom) was wearing off. My nose was runny and the world was ugly. There were Christmas decorations on every lamppost. I felt like crying. I wished Muffin would say something, but she'd been silent since we left Hilly's estate, and I couldn't think of anything to say to her. Except to ask her the question I didn't want to ask: "Okay, I give up. What'd they do to you?"

Somebody save me . . .

She gave me an odd, measuring look, and said slowly, "Not 'they': Jorandel. And not to me: to my sister." She hesitated. "You've heard Hilly's stories. You sure you want to hear more?"

"No." We were almost at the hotel. "But I think you'd better tell me."

She looked straight ahead, her face expressionless. "He got her hooked on drugs, and pregnant, and he abandoned her. She killed herself."

If she had told it with more convincing detail, in an effort to paint her sister innocent and Jorandel evil, it would in fact have been less effective. Perhaps she knew that. I think she simply couldn't bring herself to relate the details. There was no need: my imagination supplied them readily enough. And there was nothing I could say.

She pulled the limo neatly up to the hotel door and looked at me, her face stiff and pale, her eyes cold. "Be careful, Rosie.

"I'm always careful," I said. "Thanks for the ride."

I made a quick stop in the ladies room before I went up to the suite. The last of the soda to wake me up, and the last of the gin to take the edge off, and I made it past the Christmas tree to the elevator without disgracing myself. Maybe I walked a little stiffly, and maybe my eyes were too carefully averted from the signs of seasonal joy, but I didn't feel like crying anymore, and nobody was likely to notice how my fingers bumped together when I pushed the button for the elevator. That was just an effect of the soda, not a sign of irrational fear. I had everything under perfect control.

I spent the time in the elevator running quickly through the information Hilly had given me about the people around Jorandel. Veladora for starters: a powerful elf who lusted for more power, but Hilly was convinced he would never kill anyone or have anyone killed who was in his power. It would be more satisfying to him to keep Jorandel alive and aware of Veladora's control. He could document a number of Veladora's more vicious behaviors, including verification of Candy's story of the group Phelony's destroyed career. There was even some physical violence involved in some of the cases. But it was all bruises and threats, never even a broken bone, much less a murder. Veladora was a villain, but a very unlikely prospect for the role of First Murderer. Hilly told me to be careful of him, but that was fatherly advice on the order of "look both ways before you cross the street," not really anything to do with the case.

The band's manager, Alec Reich, was just as unlikely. I hadn't yet met him, but Hilly assured me he was a frail, awkward, silly fellow whose only talent was the expert management of elfrock bands. He had his work cut out for him, managing Cold Iron. Not that he minded their unruliness: he was accustomed to that sort of thing in a magic-metal band. What made his job difficult was Veladora. "If Alec wished to execute anyone," said Hilly, "it would be Veladora himself, not one of Alec's musicians. Them, he can handle. Veladora he cannot. But dismiss Alec, anyway. He had his fill and more of death in the war. He won't even go hunting anymore. He won't go to shoot-em-up movies, won't read murder mysteries. Nothing. Says it nauseates. He's not your suspect."

That left the roadies, about whom Hilly knew nothing, and the band members themselves, about whom he knew seemingly everything. He said he thought Killer the least likely suspect, but he wouldn't rule out any of them. "These are not just wild elven adolescents, Rosie," he said. "Possibly at the start they were performing for the stage only, but it's an intractable and intricate life they've selected. Sex, drugs, and elfrock ain't what their fans imagine it is. It's laborious for an individual to maintain a solid connection with reality in that life, and it takes a remarkable personality to keep his balance. By now I'd lay you odds that what you see is what you get, with them. You lie down in a pig sty long enough and in all probability you'll rise up smelling quite whiffy."

He gave me their histories, adding considerable detail to what Candy had already told me, but none of it seemed particularly relevant to the case. In fact, the only thing I had learned that seemed to be of any real use at all was more daunting than helpful: it seemed that the potential for crime in the recording industry was much more varied than I had imagined.

I had assumed that drug abuse and related crimes were the main ones to look for, but it turned out there were varieties of piracy that could run into millions of dollars (millions of dollars can be excellent motives for murder), forms of double-dealing that the record companies themselves not infrequently performed at considerable profit to themselves and expense to the artists, and concert-related scams that people had in the past considered worth killing for. Recordings were stolen, copied, over- or under-pressed, and their sales over- or under-reported. There were inaccurate accountings, early and late and faulty releases, lies, and advertising fiascoes. There were oversold concerts, overbooked schedules, illegal tapings. . . . In short, the music business was indeed a business, and like any business it was a potential breeding ground for shady dealings. And where a lot of money is involved, as in the music business, shady dealings do seem to proliferate, humans being what they are.

Innocent that I was, I had always just bought the tapes or CDs or tickets I wanted and never once considered whether the artists involved would receive a fair percentage of the purchase price. I never guessed in how many complex ways they might be cheated. Hilly assured me that I needn't begin to worry about it now: that although crime and double-dealing was prevalent, legal and honest deals were still the rule rather than the exception. But I felt as though I had just picked up a gorgeous art nouveau sculpture and found its underside thickly stuck with used chewing gum. The sculpture wasn't ruined, but my opinion of the people who'd handled it before me was.

People, I decided, were scum. In light of which, Jorandel's adolescent posturing and posing and wallowing in all the more childishly dramatic grievances of life seemed less offensive than they might have. By the time the elevator deposited me at the Cold Iron suite I was almost in sympathy with him. His actions were frequently repellent, but perhaps not psychotic after all. Perhaps he was only that overworked hero of song and story, the misunderstood genius driven by visions mere mortals could not understand.

I had believed that even a genius might find time and sense enough to attain some maturity by the time he'd reached Jorandel's age, and that any genius worth his salt ought to have intelligence and decency enough to learn a little self-control; but I'd always known that was an unpopular opinion, and I was beginning to see why. Maybe the rules of polite society were beneath the notice of true genius. Maybe Jorandel wasn't so much a spoiled brat as he was a genuinely superior creature as bewildered by humanity's social requirements as I'd have been by the social requirements of a pack of dogs.

After the day I'd spent with booze and soda and Hilly's fatherly, unintentional condescension, I wasn't feeling much above a pack of dogs myself. The last of the soda hadn't brought back the morning's euphoria. I knew that if I had any sense I'd give the rest of Candy's money back to her and get the hell out of an ugly situation while I still could. Maybe I would even have done it, if Jim and Jorie hadn't got back to the hotel before I did. But they had, and I walked in just as they were trying to kill each other, and by the time they'd been dissuaded I'd forgotten all about leaving.

It took three of the baby-sitter/bodyguards to separate them. I was surprised to realize that it was Jim doing most of the fighting. Jorie defended himself, and struck at Jim a time or two, but when they were pulled apart he relaxed and even looked relieved, while Jim kept trying to break loose to get at him again.

I was also surprised to see that Jim was crying. He

didn't seem to know it. He didn't make any effort to wipe away the tears that streamed down his face. From the time I came in neither he nor Jorie had said anything articulate enough for me to guess what they were fighting about, but both of them looked more stricken than angry, and it didn't take long for the bodyguards to calm Jim enough to lead him away to another room.

The rest of the band members and Candy were all present, as well as several groupies who watched the scene with detached interest and promptly returned their attention to the remaining band members as soon as Jim was led away. Jorie went to the bar and got a bottle of whiskey. Blade, after a moment's hesitation, succumbed to a groupie's urgent insistence and led her to his bedroom. Killer was settled with two groupies on the couch and I couldn't tell whether he had even noticed the battle. The Roach had noticed, and seemed mildly amused, but was easily distracted by a groupie who provoked him to shed Candy as though she were a bracelet he had tired of wearing and follow the groupie out of the room.

Candy was crying, too, as unconsciously as Jim had been. She started toward Jorandel, thought better of it, and looked blindly around the room as though quite lost and uncertain what to do. When she saw me her face twisted in grief like a child who has scraped her knee and managed not to cry till she found her mother. "Oh, Rosie," she said, and hurled herself at me in woeful relief. "Oh, it's so awful! Can we go to your room? We can't talk here. Oh, it's so awful!" She sobbed audibly, dragging at my arm. "Please, let's go to your room."

We obviously couldn't go to hers, since that was where the Roach had taken his groupie. I let her pull me toward mine, wondering what it was that was so awful. She was not quick to enlighten me. By the time we got to my room with the door closed behind us, she was so overcome with audible grief that she could barely speak.

"Candy, for godsake, what is it?" I asked impatiently.

"It's awful!" she wailed.

"What is? Candy, tell me what's going on! Why were they fighting? Come on, calm down, you can do it."

"It's Andy," she said.

"What about Andy? What's he done?"

"He's dead!" she sobbed. "He died, he OD'd, all by himself in a motel somewhere, it's so awful!"

"Andy died?" I grappled with the wholly unexpected. "For godsake, you're saying he took a drug overdose?" I'd assumed, I don't know why, that the bodyguards were health types who wouldn't use drugs at all. The concept that one of them had overdosed was so far outside the image I had of them that I could barely understand it. "When? Why? How do you know?"

"Jim just got the call," she said. "They found him this morning." Satisfied with my stunned reaction, she was bringing her tears enough under control to allow her to speak coherently. "Jim was already mad at Jorie because they had to go to some private party today, him and Jorie, to play for Veladora, and then when they got back he got the call about Andy and I swear to God I thought he was going to kill Jorie, I really did, because he said it was all Jorie's fault."

I thought of Andy's reluctant parting from them last night, with trip tickets and even a little ill-wrapped gift package, all Jorandel's awkward efforts to make up for a fit of violence. "You mean because he sent Andy away? That's why Jim thinks it was Jorie's fault?"

She nodded. "And because of the drugs. He says Andy wouldn't have OD'd on purpose, so whatever Jorie gave him must've been too pure and he didn't warn him. At least, that's what I think he meant. He wasn't talking very clearly. He hardly even put the phone down before he started trying to kill Jorie, and everything he said was while they were fighting, so it got a little mixed up."

"I expect it did." I thought of that little ill-wrapped package again, and wondered bleakly whether it had contained some drug. If so, and if the drug was indeed more pure than Andy might have expected, had Jorie known it? "That's ridiculous," I said, as much to myself as to Candy. "Why would Jorie want to kill Andy? He wouldn't have any reason to. It doesn't make sense."

"No, I think Jimmy was just upset, and he was already mad at Jorie so he fought with him. I mean, Andy was his best friend."

"But if Jorie did give him the drugs," I said, "and

they were more pure than usual, or there was something else wrong with them . . . maybe they were meant for Jorie. Maybe whoever he got them from meant to kill him, not knowing he was going to give them to Andy."

"You mean somebody tried to kill Jorie," she said.

"And Andy got in the way."

She absorbed that. "Then you got to find out where Jorie got whatever it was," she said firmly, and then her face crumpled into tears again. "Poor Andy. Oh, Rosie, it's so sad, I can hardly believe he's dead. He was such a good person, and now he's dead!" She was working herself up for a nice fit of hysterics, and I really hadn't the patience for it.

"Stop that," I said in my most quelling tone. When she stared at me in startled surprise, I said, "I'm sure he was a very nice person, and I'm sorry if he's dead, but it's not going to do him any good for you to go all dramatically bereaved about it. You've been hanging out with these guys too long. You've lost track of your own genuine emotions."

After a long, staring moment she said crossly, but with the surprising hint of a sheepish smile, "You're such a goddammed grown-up. Don't you ever get tired of yourself?"

"Frequently," I said truthfully. "Do you have any soda? I sure as hell could use a little some about now."

"Oh, sure, is that all?" she said, and reached in her pocket for a soda bottle while I listened to the echoes of my own voice asking for it and wondered with a shock of horror what the hell I thought I was doing.

Neither shock nor horror prevented me from accepting the line she laid out for me, nor the refill she subsequently provided for the little brown bottle she said the Roach had told her to leave by my bed last night. Not even knowledge of the source slowed me down. I accepted it with gratitude and with the vague thought that the Roach must not be all bad, after all. Which shows exactly how clearly I was thinking by then.

11

The concert that night was pathetic. Jimendan, having been discouraged from assaulting his brother physically, was still hostile toward him in every way short of that, and apparently saw no reason to modify his behavior onstage. And Jorandel, who responded with childish petulance and sullenly outrageous misbehavior to the ordinary tribulations of his life, was for once sincerely enough hurt that he dropped all pretense and simply endured. He had done his best all afternoon to mollify Jim. At last, having resigned himself to failure, he had withdrawn into a whiskey bottle, which he had brought onstage with him, and from which he refreshed himself all too frequently. I had not been able to speak to him about the drugs that killed Andy; he was in no mood to speak rationally about anything.

Killer, Blade, and the Roach were all relatively sober. As they had done the night before, when Jorandel was injured, they were making a real effort to hold things together, but neither of the brothers was helping this time. Perhaps neither of them could. Jimendan's malice was only a desperate defense against a grief he was not prepared to face, and Jorandel was for once bereft of any defense at all.

Too much had happened too fast: even Jorandel's consummate skill at posturing and posing couldn't withstand this reality. It was evident in the way he moved that he was still in some pain from yesterday's physical injuries. The afternoon with Veladora, from what I understood of it, must have been humiliating, if only because Veladora so clearly enjoyed displaying his power. And even though Jorandel hadn't been as close to Andy as Jimendan had been, the shock of his sudden death must have grieved him. Now of all times he needed the automatic, unthinking intimacy of his brother's friendship, and it was gone.

I had seen Jorandel in all stages of boyish anguish even to the point of threatened suicide, and nothing had touched me as this did. He was no longer a petulant adolescent wallowing in cherished, romantic inequities and dreaming the childish poetry of finding surcease in death. He was a man, devastated, broken, alone. I had never felt the smallest inclination to comfort the surly child, but I longed to soothe the tormented adult.

He was also, however, a performer, with a concert to get through before anyone could soothe him, and then I suspected he would choose either defiant solitude or the easy, meaningless sex of the nearest groupie, and perhaps that was as well for me. I was committed to finding his proposed murderer if any, but I had enough problems without letting him any further into my life than that.

By the end of the concert he was stumbling drunk, and I thought more than once that Frank would have to rescue him from an on-stage collapse as Reno had rescued Blade in San Francisco. But although Jimendan stood away from him in spiteful and obvious disdain, Blade and the Roach managed time and again to be in just the right place at just the right time to keep him on his feet and to cover the worst of his lapses. There wasn't much Killer could do but fill in with the drums when the music would otherwise have degenerated while they were occupied with Jorandel; but that he could and did do with such perfect skill that I doubt the audience was even aware it wasn't a planned part of the act.

Frank hauled Jorandel offstage while the lights were down after the last number, and that night it was Jimendan who sang the encore. He chose a song I hadn't heard before, which was clearly meant to be sweet and gentle and filled with love: the accompanying guitar was tranquil and tender, the bass a smooth riffle of deep water song, the keyboard lyrical, and the drums a papery rustle like autumn leaves in a wind, but there was an edge to Jimendan's voice that transformed the whole from dream to nightmare, like a bloody razor dropped carelessly among fragrant rose petals.

We caught the wind together
We danced on the demon's grave
We spent our lives in little ways
We thought it was all so brave
But where's the wind now, who's the demon,
What of the life we didn't save?

His voice broke at the end of the verse. The drums deepened, the bass quickened, pulling him into the chorus. He screamed in real agony, tears visible even in the sheen of sweat on his face, and I couldn't understand one word in five from then on. There was much about brotherhood and honor and loyalty and blood, and doubtless in the ordinary way it would have been one of those naively virtuous "brotherhood" songs rife with nobility and righteousness. But this wasn't, not the way Jimendan sang it.

His voice was like jagged glass, tearing away the pretentious nobility, shattering the naïveté, shredding the solemn righteousness to a bloody pulp. He made a mockery of the unkeepable promises that kind of song is always swearing to, yet somehow not a mockery of the song itself. That remained not only intact, but probably improved. I had not heard it as Jorandel would have done it, but I thought it would not have been this candid. Jimendan's version was heartfelt, and searingly honest in a way elfrock's "brotherhood" songs seldom are. It did not promise anything it could not deliver. It reflected the real world, with the romantic artifice torn from it, and all the savage compulsion of love and hate exposed.

I thought fleetingly of the sly, pathetic elf I had met in San Francisco, that slowed and softened image of the knuckly brother, and of how I had thought him dulled by excesses and ease. I had been wrong. I would not see him that way again. And I wondered whether, if I had met them in reverse order, I would have thought Jimendan the sleek and dangerous one, Jorandel the one whose power had been transformed to petulance. When he was in one of his fits of adolescent rage, Jorandel actually appeared physically less angular, softened by self-indulgence. And when Jimendan, as now, was caught up enough in passion that he acquired the self-confidence to forget his brother's suffocating shadow, he seemed as much all bones and supple, sinewy meat as Jorandel had when I met him. There was sleek danger in both of them, and baby-fat petulance, too. I had accepted, in each of them, the first image I was presented, but the fact was that either image would fit either man.

Candy had told me, when she first spoke of them in my office, that they were easy to tell apart once one knew them, and apparently for her it was true. But not for me. They were by no means interchangeable, and yet . . . even this song, which Jimendan stripped bare of the easy lies of elfrock romance, must have had that powerful twist of genius in it or Jimendan's savage interpretation would have done no more than to rob it of any meaning. Jorandel's vision had created the potential that Jimendan, in his wrath, had revealed. Even in conflict they were united by a deeper congruence than either of them recognized.

The song ended, the lights went out, the band fled the stage, and the houselights came back up to reveal what I had come to expect at the end of a Cold Iron concert: an audience battered by exaltation, satiated, their eyes dazed and their faces tranquil with exhaustion. I felt the way they looked. For a long time, while people filed slowly out till the front rows were clear enough for Candy and me to wend our way backstage, we just sat there, silent and appeased. I don't know what Candy was thinking. The echoes of that final song were still ringing in my mind, a wordless paean to the awful ecstasy of brutal truth.

"We better go," she said finally, almost uncertainly.

"I guess so," I said. Neither of us moved. The sound of my own voice had dragged me down out of the music at last, but another kind of brutal truth held me motionless: the last soda I'd had at the break was quite worn off, and the mere thought of hauling my leaden body out of that uncomfortable chair and off into the fatiguing realm of feuding elves was more than I could face.

I became aware that Candy was watching me, smiling a little in perceptive sympathy. "You're crashing, aren't you?" she said. "Did you bring your soda with you? Nobody'd notice if you kind of duck down like you're looking in your purse for something while you snort a little. Go ahead, you'll feel better."

She was right about that part, anyway, but I had a morbid fear of being caught at it. Still, I really could not bear the thought of human interactions or even the mild exertion required to walk backstage, and when I glanced around I saw that nobody was paying the smallest attention to us. Bending forward as she had suggested, I found the soda bottle and my pen clip and furtively inhaled white powder, humiliated by the necessity even as I felt my weary outlook respond to the drug's restorative powers.

"See?" she said. "Nobody noticed. You didn't, when I had some while Jim was singing."

"That was different," I said, putting away my accoutrements. "I think everybody must have been transfixed by that performance. Nobody saw anything but him."

"Well, they didn't notice you doing it, anyway," she said. "Jim was good, wasn't he? That wasn't at all the way Jorie does 'Brothers,' but I liked it."

"Yes," I said. "I wouldn't've guessed he had it in him to do that."

"To do what? Sing?" she asked, confused.

"Not exactly just sing," I said. "Never mind. We'd better go, I think, before we get left behind."

"They wouldn't," she said, rising. "They better not: we're off to Hawaii tonight."

"What, not even another night in L.A.?"

She shrugged. "Why would we? They don't have to work tomorrow night, but why not spend our free time someplace nice? Have you been to Hawaii? You won't believe the shopping. And we'll be there over a week, so there'll be time to get a tan."

I suppose it was another example of wrong priorities due to advanced age: I had always wanted to visit Hawaii, but neither shopping nor suntan had been anywhere near the top of my list of reasons. I had dreamed, instead, of the deserted tropical beaches and mysterious green mountains whose jungled slopes, streaked with glorious waterfalls, adorned the postcards and travel books I had seen.

I also imagined, I'm not sure why, that there would be no Christmas trees in the tropics. I was wrong about that. True, they don't grow in Hawaii, but the residents in their infinite wisdom import shiploads of cut trees every year, and they have as much access to tinsel, fake trees, colored lights, and Santa suits as anyone anywhere.

Fortunately I didn't know that at the time, and I didn't really give it a lot of thought beyond the fleeting expectation of escape from seasonal reminders. As before, the musicians showered and changed at the arena. While we were waiting for them I found a bottle of gin to take the rough edges off the soda that was keeping me going. Tomorrow I would quit drugs and drink both, but I wouldn't even make it to the plane if I tried to stop now.

Jorie was still unsteady on his feet, but Frank had got him sobered enough to shower and change on his own. He looked worn and frail, and at every subtle viciousness from Jim he seemed to collapse a little more into himself, but bravely: a fractured thing held together by will alone. More than once I saw him make some automatic little gesture toward his brother, some unthinking corollary of affection that he would stop almost before it was begun, and every time the look of bewildered desolation that crossed his face was heartbreaking, though he covered it as quickly as he did the abortive gestures. I'm not half sure anyone else even noticed.

The ride to the airport was interminable. Somehow I ended up in the same limousine with both Jim and Jorie, and the brittle silence between them was devastating, worse even than the Christmas carols from the radio that were the only sound inside the car all the way. On the plane, the PA system was playing Christmas carols, too. While Blade settled in with his inevitable groupies, Killer composed himself for sleep, the Roach and Candy curled together in a pair of seats, and the rest of the crew scattered into the forward area in various attitudes of repose or resignation. Jim installed himself and his belongings over adjoining seats without a glance at Jorie.

Jorie hesitated only a fraction of a second in the aisle

next to Jim, then moved several rows forward to the next pair of empty seats. I was behind him, so I couldn't see his face, but I saw him square his shoulders and lift his chin and I thought of the two of them sleeping together on the plane from San Francisco in perfectly paired mirror image, and my throat hurt. When, in my own search for an empty seat, I started to pass Jorie's and he caught my hand to pull me down beside him, I didn't even try to resist.

He didn't say anything. He just looked at me, those summer-sky eyes shadowed, the generous lips pulled into a wry little smile. There was no smell of alcohol about him, and no look of drunkenness in his eyes. Either he still had some magic outside his music, or Frank had access to healing magic: there was no other way Jorie could have got that sober that fast. I met his gaze, and I don't know what my expression looked like, but after a moment he pulled me toward him, tucked me gently against his chest, and said into my hair, "Poor little cousin. Who hurt you so?"

It was the last thing I expected. The words were artless, the tone of his voice ingenuous, his arms around me utterly sexless and gentle, the way you would hold a frightened child. If it was a trick to make me drop my guard it was flawlessly performed, but I don't think it was a trick. I think it was a side of him I had neither seen nor looked for: a perceptive empathy beyond any mere human ability, and at the same time alien to an elf. Maybe that was why he had left Faerie. Empathy is not a highly regarded trait among them. Nor was it one I'd ever have looked for in Jorie. One would not expect it of the sulky boy, and the man was so nearly broken it seemed impossible that he could see past his own pain. But Jorie was in no way ordinary.

Moonshadows wake the dancing land
The stars have stung the laughing man
My footsteps echo on the sea
Somebody save me . . .

I said, my voice muffled against his shirt and the clean

male scent of him dizzy in my brain, "Nobody hurt me. I don't know what you mean."

His arm tightened around me, a reassuring gesture, brotherly and dear. But the Christmas carols persisted, and I could not relax. After a moment he said gently, "Can you sleep? Or have you had too much of the Roach's nose candy?"

"It's not that," I said, my voice a small and startled sound. I had not meant to say anything.

"Oh," he said, "I forgot. Candy mentioned you're afraid of flying."

I felt warm and dangerously safe in his arms. "No," I said, and was not sure myself whether I meant it as a response to his comment or to the situation. "I," I said, and cleared my throat, and moved my head against his chest. His shirt was soft against my cheek. "I don't," I said, and closed my eyes hard. "It's the music," I said. "I don't like Christmas carols." My voice sounded wild and frightened, almost a cry of pain, and I wished I hadn't spoken. But he only held me closer and raised his voice to call someone to him. I kept my eyes closed, my face pressed against him, pretending I was invisible.

Someone paused beside our seats and he said curtly, "Get the music changed. Not Christmas music, okay? I don't care what else. Give them one of our CDs if they've nothing better."

I felt three years old and coddled. "I'm sorry," I said when the unseen other had gone to do his bidding. "I know it's stupid. I mean, to be afraid of Christmas music."

"You're afraid of it?"

I had revealed more than I intended. I stiffened against him, wondering how he would use it.

"It's okay," he said, jostling me encouragingly in the way one might an anxious child. "Everyone is afraid of something foolish." He laughed a little, almost soundlessly. "I, for example, am afraid of the dark; how's that for a grown-up? I can't sleep without a light on." It was a generous gesture: a trade, his vulnerability for mine. The Christmas carols ended abruptly, cut off in mid-note, and after a moment the Cold Iron *Midnight Son* album began to play. "It seems they could find nothing better," he said.

Death is a singing promise
Life is a loaded gun
Strangers are people, people are strange
When you're the Midnight Son. . .

"I like this album." I said it almost defensively, as though he had attacked it.

"Thank you." He sounded genuinely surprised. "That's quite a compliment, coming from our little Mozart lover."

"Does everybody know everything about me?" I felt betrayed, though why or by whom I couldn't have said. I had not exactly made a secret of my fondness for Mozart.

"Rosie, in this group everybody knows everything about everybody."

"I don't," I said, because I felt oddly isolated and ignorant, exactly like a child in a crowd of adults. My emotional equilibrium, always unstable at this season, had been perilously overbalanced by drugs and drink.

"Give it time," he said. "It isn't important, is it? You're still not relaxing. Hey. Come on, let go. Everything's fine."

But everything wasn't fine. I'd had the worst fight ever with my partner, over a Christmas tree of all things, and I didn't know whether we could patch it up when I went back. I'd fled to a job that should have been simplicity itself, and after nearly four days on it I had learned nothing I couldn't have learned with one phone call to Hilly from the Bay Area. I had been drugged, threatened, and beaten for no discernible reason; I'd drunk too much and used soda; I'd developed a taste for a kind of music for which any sensible adult had no respect at all; and now I was enveloped cozily, comfortably, in the arms of an elf I knew to be sociopathic. Hot tears of confused self-pity welled behind my closed eyelids.

"Everything's fine," he said again. He didn't act like a sociopath. "It's fine. Cry if you want to." How the hell did he know so much? "Just relax, you're fine."

"I never cry," I said, and resisted the impulse to sniffle.

"There's your mistake," he said, and tightened his arm around me again in a brotherly hug. "Poor little cousin. What did they do to hurt you so bad?"

That did it. It was the primal question, phrased in the universal "me/they" dichotomy that struck right to the heart of every unresolved wrong in my life, every injustice, every rejection, every denial. I was too near the edge already to accept it with equanimity. All the hard-won layers of adult defenses over all the tender scar tissue of a lifetime disappeared, and in an instant I reverted to the pure, pitiless rage of utter terror. I tried to kill him. I wanted to kill everything. In the grip of that brief, shattering anguish I would have reached out to destroy the world if I could. I did my best to destroy as much of it as I could reach. Which was, primarily, Jorandel.

I must have hurt him, though he gave no sign of it. I may be small, but I am strong; and even in the aimless grip of hysteria, I doubt I forgot all I knew of efficient fight techniques. He was injured already, and I certainly made no effort to spare his prior bruises. But he restrained me as much as he could with real gentleness, silently endured the blows he could not avoid, and patiently waited it out. It didn't last long. I was too drugged, too drunk, too bone-weary, and too close to the edge of despair to maintain that level of intensity for long. When it was over and I collapsed into helpless, shuddering sobs, he folded me tenderly in his arms again and whispered soothing, half-meant love words till I fell asleep with my head resting trustfully in the curve of his shoulder.

And when I woke again sometime in the middle of the flight, with a strangled scream of protest at the sound of my father's oily voice echoing in my ears and the image of a dead face staring accusingly into mine, he was still there, his head rested comfortably on the crown of mine and his arms still curled protectively around me. He murmured something soothing and smoothed my hair back from my face and lifted his head to smile at me, a sweet, warm, sleepy smile that banished demons and let me sleep again, secure and incongruously content. I did not wake again until the plane came down in Honolulu and we all trooped drowsily out through the moist, fragrant, tropical night to the waiting limousines to be whisked to the hotel.

Not even the brightly lighted hotel lobby and corridors through which we were led to reach our rooms disturbed the slumberous contentment of my mood, or the easy conviction of the innate rightness of his casual, protective embrace. When we were shown into our suite, it seemed the most natural thing in the world to accompany him to his room. He was careful to let it be my choice, and to be sure I was shown a room of my own to which I could flee if I changed my mind at any time. It seemed almost absurdly courteous of him.

We were both worn-out, emotionally and physically, too exhausted for either modesty or awkwardness. It was a major, unself-conscious effort, performed with fumbling, lethargic fingers, to shed our clothing before tumbling into the big, clean bed. He dragged the covers up snug over our shoulders and we curled against each other in sleepy serenity. His body was lean and hard and warm, his furry chest soft against mine, his breath a warm whisper on my neck. A lock of his hair tickled my nose. We fit each other's curves and hollows exactly, legs tangled, silken skin against velvet, the heavy warmth of his thigh a welcome pressure against my hip, the protective bend of his elbow over my ribs a vast and reassuring comfort. He ran one hand along the curve of my spine in an idle, unthinking caress, and I kissed his ear in drowsy contentment, and we fell asleep clinging to one another like children lost in a storm.

If I had given it any thought at all I would have assumed that the awkwardness we were both too drained to feel that night would be doubly strong in the morning when we woke still tangled in unconscious need, strangers trapped in accidental intimacy. It was not. I woke to the warmth of his kisses, and not even the dazed lethargy of a gin-and-soda hangover could diminish the pleasure of my response.

Sex had always been an uncertain thing with me, most especially during the Christmas season when my emotions were at their flightiest. My partner said I was unnecessarily choosy: my ex-husband had said I was cold. I was never a cuddly person. I liked solitude, liked to wake alone in the morning, and disliked the intrusiveness of another person's body next to mine. Sex seemed too often a sweaty exercise in mutual masturbation, and I knew how to do that better by myself. I admired men, I liked the look of their bodies and the workings of their strange and alien minds. I even wished sometimes for the easy physical familiarity I saw between them and other women. But when it came down to it I could seldom be enough at ease with a man to experience anything but an embarrassing execution of practiced artifice that seemed to satisfy them but left me desperately uneasy and alone. Sex ought, I thought, to have something to do with friendship, and that was a word that seemed to mean something quite different to me than it did to most men.

Jorie was not most men. And in our mutual desperation last night we had, quite without thought or intention, moved effortlessly past barriers and restrictions that might in ordinary circumstances have stopped us somewhere along the line far short of sex. It wasn't only that we had become comfortable with proximity: That had happened to me before, with other men both human and elf, over longer periods of time, and still I had found when they tried to take it to what they saw as the logical next step, sex, I felt used and tricked and isolated. I felt the relationship had been established not as a basis for or as a result of friendship, but only as a first step toward sex. And the usual line if I said so, "Do you think you're so damned irresistible that I'd go to all that trouble just to get in your pants?" only increased my discomfort. I knew I wasn't that irresistible. I also knew that men habitually, instinctively, and constantly went to a lot of trouble to get into a lot of perfectly resistible pants. That contemptuous line only meant that they didn't really care whether or not they were wanted in the pants, as long as they got there.

Which is to say, I suppose, that even with men with whom I had formed some modicum of asexual friendship, I felt quite strongly that they, as men, could really see me only as an object. I was, in other words, either a militant and paranoid feminist or a female chauvinist pig, maybe both. But that was the heart of what was different with Jorie. That careful courtesy last night, showing me my escape route by making sure I knew which room was mine before I went with him into his, was indicative. He saw me as a person, with thoughts and feelings that might be different from his, and he recognized my right to them. He recognized me, separate from my sex. And when he began to make love to me, he was making love to me, not just to my body.

He was a practiced lover, naturally enough. But contrary to my expectations that did not make me feel as though I had been standing on line for the privilege. It just banished first-time awkwardness. He took his time, slow and sweet and attentive, learning the little idiosyncrasies of my body and giving me all the time in the world to learn his. I had just presence of mind enough to insist on a condom, the ugly necessity of modern sex. He was experienced in that, too: he had one handy.

The hard pressure of his bones and lean, lanky muscles against mine was hungry, but not demanding until my need matched his, so that when we came together at last it was a consummation, a completion. Not two units joined, but one unit mended after a lifetime of imperfection, separation, and despair. There was a look of fierce, wild exaltation in his eyes then, and I suppose it was matched in mine. We were united by more than the physical.

And in that look of his, under it, through it, there was a sweetness, a gentleness, a perfect awareness of our individuality, even a hint of laughter at the cosmic oneness that we both really knew was illusory even as we exalted in it. It was another of the endearing and heartbreaking traits of him, that he could stand outside himself even in a moment of shining bliss like that, and see the silliness of the animal, elf or human, and honor it.

He smiled at me, a wry, almost uncertain little upward tug at the corners of that perfect mouth. I forgot philosophy and gave myself up to the wonder and the glory and the passion of my dangerous, empathic feral elf.

12

It was nearly noon when I woke again, still tangled in his arms. His shadowed eyes were open, watching me, sleepy and content. When he knew I was awake he smiled drowsily and murmured, "I feel like a child on Christmas morning." My face must have betrayed me, because his hands were suddenly soothing, his expression remorseful. "I'm sorry, cousin," he said. "I forgot." He kissed the tip of my nose, and the gentleness of it let me relax against him, secure again. "What troubles you so about Christmas?" he asked.

I shook my head, trying desperately not to think. "I don't know," I said. "Don't ask." Unspeakable terror gibbered in the back of my mind. "Please. I'd forgotten it was Christmas. Don't talk about it."

He was watching me steadily, and there was something cold, almost calculating in the deep blue of his eyes. "Did you know you talk in your sleep?" he said.

"Please," I said.

"You said—"

"Stop it!" I said, before he could repeat whatever I'd said in my sleep. I didn't want to know. I was afraid to know. "Stop it, damn you!" I pulled myself free of his embrace. He didn't resist. I sat up, unconscious of my nakedness, looking down at him in rage and dismay. "Is this your insurance, for godsake? Is this the way you keep people from getting too close to you? What is it with you and intimacy? Are you afraid if you don't push people away they'll find out what you're really like and go on their own? Is that it? Because if it is, believe me, you don't have to give me a push. I know what you are. I came into your bed with my eyes wide open and I'll leave it the same way, and gladly. You don't have to pull your psychotic tricks on me. I had a good time. If it's over, fine, I'm going. Save your petty little cruelties for somebody who'll be surprised by them, okay?"

"Hey," he said. "Hey." I was half out of bed when he caught my arm, not to pull me back, just to stop me, so he could study my face.

"Let me go," I said dully. I knew I had revealed more than I meant to. The reminder of the season had shaken me, his threat to reveal what I said in my sleep had frightened me, and in trying to hide that I had only emphasized it. And let him know how much I cared about him. Sometimes I just talk too damn much. I wished he would let me go. Last night was gone, we couldn't get it back, and I did know all along exactly what he was: Hilly's stories were still fresh in my mind. I hadn't kidded myself that the side of Jorandel I saw for the first time last night was the "real" Jorandel, and the psychotic episodes only an act. He was more complicated than that. He was all the contradictory things he seemed, and dangerous as all Faerie, and I should have had sense enough to stay out of his bed.

"Hey," he said again, tugging at my hand. "I apologize, cousin."

"It's not that easy, Jorie."

"Nothing is easy," he said with a wry little grin that tore at my heart. "I don't ask easy. But I do apologize."

"Damn you." I said it without force of conviction, wearily, because I knew he had won. Dangerous or not, I loved him.

He sat up suddenly, a sleek and graceful dancer's motion, and put his arms around me, pulling my head down against his shoulder. "Poor little cousin," he said, "Hey. I don't want to hurt you. I like you. I hink I might trust you if I knew how." That was quite an admission. And a calculated, sulky-child reminder of his own pain, as well. Very few of the things he did had one simple motivation. There were layers on layers of meaning in every move he made. "I just, I don't know," he said. "It's as though I'm an alien. As though I'm watching, learning how people do it, how they, you know, how to be decent with each other. And sometimes I get caught up in the fascination of the study and I forget . . . I suppose I forget it's not just an exercise, you understand? I forget it's real."

I let my forehead rest against his neck, breathing the sweet shampoo-and-sweat scent of his hair, and thought that I ought to get up and walk away while I still could. "Oh, Jorandel," I said. "Spare me the cute, earnest little games, okay? I told you I know what you are."

He caught his hand in my hair and pulled my head back, not roughly, but hard enough that it would have hurt if I'd resisted. I didn't. He studied my face for a long moment, his own expressionless, his eyes deeper and darker than I had seen them before, an eternity of ghosts and shadows swimming in their curiously emotionless depths. I knew then, without any sense of fear or even surprise, that last night or no last night he would kill me now without hesitation if he happened to feel like it. And that it was not beyond the realm of possibility that he would happen to feel like it. I waited, passive, not even wondering at my own indifference to clear and present danger.

"Christmas," he said suddenly, still expressionless. "Christmas, Christmas, Christmas."

I laughed at him. "You can't hurt me, Jorandel. Not that way." For some reason, unexpectedly, it was true. A moment ago he could have, but not now.

He studied me a moment longer, still holding my head at an awkward angle so he could see into my eyes. "Your father fucked you, didn't he?"

Something dark and deadly stirred in the back of my mind, but I pushed it down into silence and smiled at him and said quite calmly, "Not that I recall." And that was true, too. But only because I refused to recall what I could not bear to know.

"I saw the way you reacted to 'Janie's Got A Gun,' " he said. "Your father fucked you." The shock of that repeated phrase finally tore a gaping hole in my defenses. Hell yawned cavernously, a black pit of horror and despair peopled by dead fathers with staring eyes. "And you," he said. "How did you respond? Did you run away? Did *you* get a gun, like 'Janie'?" Something in my expression alerted him. "Is that it? Did you kill your father? What? Tell Cousin Jorie, sweetheart. What did you do?"

I was still smiling. My face felt frozen, stiff, as if I would smile for the rest of my life, blindly, empty of emotion, forever smiling. One can smile, and smile, and be a villain. Was that how it went? The line from *Hamlet*? I thought of Kyriander Stone's father, or my father, or someone's father, dead and deadly, monstrous, horrible, hurting me, haunting me, hiding under a Christmas tree, and I smiled at Jorandel and I said very sweetly, "Fuck you, Jorandel. You've made me love you." Because it was still true: I did. "Isn't that enough hurt for one day's work?"

To my utter astonishment, huge tears welled in those summer-sky eyes and spilled down his cheeks before he could blink them away or even turn his head to hide them. He made an abortive little gesture, furtive and frightened, as though he would have hidden his face if he could. But it was too late, and I saw him decide to brazen it out, to pretend it was another of his tricks and poses. He released my hair, wiped his face with the back of one hand, and said in a small, defiant voice, "I'm hungry. I'm gonna find something to eat. You want anything?"

I realized with mild surprise that I couldn't remember the last time I had eaten anything. "Yes," I said, "I do. But I want a shower, first."

He had regained his composure and, with it, his fey sense of humor. "Me, too. You're welcome to share—but your clean clothes will be in your own room, you know."

I looked at the rumpled concert finery I had dropped on his floor last night. It wasn't fit to put on again after a shower. It wasn't even fit to be put on before a shower. "Thanks, I'll just borrow a towel," I said. "Or a robe, if you have an extra. Just to get to my room."

He produced a robe, grinning. "You don't need this," he said. "We're not so formal here."

"I am," I said. "Thanks." Suddenly shy, I wrapped myself in overlapping folds of voluminous velveteen and looked up at him, oddly at a loss.

As usual, he knew too much. "Would you like to act

like a tourist after breakfast? We could rent mopeds or something."

That "we" was exactly the reassurance I needed. He knew it, which should have irritated me, but it didn't. I had always been the sort of person who positively bristled with false pride, but I realized in that moment that I had no pride with him. I had lost it, somewhere between the childlike innocence of last night's cuddled sleep and the deadly adult battle of this morning. Maybe later that would bother me, but right now I didn't even care. I said, "Yes, please," in simple gratitude, and fled, blushing, from the gentle mockery in his eyes. I might have been sixteen years old and deep in the throes of my first infatuation for all the poise I showed.

There was no sign of the others in the common room. My belongings were in my room, more neatly packed than I would have done: I wondered fleetingly whose job it was to pick up after us all, pack our possessions, see they were brought along, and distribute them in each new hotel. And, being accustomed to living on a thrift-store budget, I thought of the cost of providing a room of her own for Candy's "cousin"; a hanger-on's hanger-on, as it were, yet no one had even mentioned it. A room had simply been provided from the first, booked already when we arrived in L.A., no questions asked. I was one step up from a groupie, anyway. They didn't always even get to share a bed.

Would the ones who had come here from L.A. with Blade be given plane fare back? Or when they had worked their way through the group would they be abandoned as readily as they were forgotten once they'd served their purpose? I supposed they could attach themselves to another elfrock group on its way back to the mainland. Maybe they toured the world that way, just another form of musicians' accoutrements, hitchhiking from one impersonal sexual encounter to another, a new breed of homeless, working a very cosmopolitan angle on the oldest profession in the world.

They would wear out fast, the succulent eighteen-year-olds leathered to middle-aged bone and gristle before they were out of their twenties. The ugly little compromises and ignorances and abuses would take a heavy toll of those tender bodies, coarsening them, cheapening them, cheating them of the glories of the youth they exploited beyond redemption. Their eyes were always old. It was one of the first things I had noticed about them, that their faces and their bodies might still be baby fresh and brilliant, but their eyes were old. Whatever thrills they were buying with youth and beauty, they would pay for all the rest of their lives.

It wasn't the act of prostitution that would exact such a price, but the groupies' own emptiness, and their belief in the thing as an end, not a means. I'd known a number of women who'd spent a few years as working prostitutes and come away no more harmed by the experience than the average professional artist is by painting commercial calendar scenes to cover the rent, or a novelist by turning out porno books or any other potboilers when the market turns bad and the bills need paid. The evil is not in prostitution itself, but in human degradation; and while there's plenty of potential for that in any form of prostitution, it isn't always realized. Unfortunately, with these groupies, it seemed always to be part of the bargain.

Or maybe I was just trying to establish my superiority by believing that was what was happening to them. I was certainly having some qualms about my own recent activities. How superior could I really feel to a teenager collecting elfrock stars when I was old enough to know better, and was nonetheless hurrying through my morning ablutions because I was afraid that by the time I got back to him, Jorandel with his quicksilver moods would have forgotten his offer to spend the afternoon with me?

I was in such haste that I didn't even think of drugs or drink. I hadn't needed them to get me out of bed that morning. Jorandel was a better antidote to both lethargy and my tedious seasonal angst. There was still soda in the bottle in my purse, but when I performed my morning ritual of dumping the purse in a handy drawer and replacing only the items I expected to need during the day, the soda bottle stayed in the drawer. I suppose I would have come back for it soon enough if Jorandel had forgotten his offer of an afternoon with me. But I needn't have worried. He didn't forget.

Jimendan was with him when I returned to the common room, and the two of them had obviously made up. Jimendan was still subdued, and given to fits of petulance over any obstacle to his most aimless intention, but his anger over Andy's death was directed now at the world, not at his brother. By blaming Jorandel, he had lost him as well as Andy for a time. Having a direction for his rage must have been sustaining, but the loss of his "twin" had been a high price to pay. Now they seemed closer even than before, anticipating each other's moves and moods as if by desperately close attention they could eliminate even the memory of their temporary emotional separation. Jorandel was almost giddy with relief, and I thought, when I saw what had happened, that he would choose if possible to spend the day with his brother. But he bustled happily into plans with me as though freed not just of an emotional burden but of some painful physical constraint. It was almost as though he could not bear the intensity of his own delight in Jimendan's renewed affection.

My first sight of Oahu when we left the hotel was disappointing. Having expected wide, empty beaches and jungled mountain slopes, I was unprepared for the concrete and chaos of busy city streets. If I'd given it a moment's thought I'd have realized one could hardly expect to find unpeopled tropical wilderness directly outside the hotel's front door, but I hadn't really given it any thought beyond vague, dreamy expectations. The only one that was fulfilled was the weather. It was hot and brilliantly sunny, and the moist air smelled of sweet tropical blossoms, not smog.

Jorandel had obviously been there before. He had, rented and waiting for us when we went downstairs, not the mopeds he had suggested earlier but a Karmann Ghia. He whisked me through the city streets as if it were his hometown, onto a freeway that seemed to me only slightly less crowded than a Bay Area freeway, and from there onto a smaller highway that curled gently between steep green subdivided mountains. Finally he took a turnoff that brought us into the jungled green gloom I had expected at the outset.

"This is the Old Pali Highway," he said. "There is little enough of it remaining, but it's a pretty drive."

"Who's Paulie?" I asked.

He grinned, and spelled it. "It means cliff, I think," he said. "Anyway something to do with mountains. Ask Killer: he speaks local."

We were passing a steep ravine full of fading ginger blossoms. The trees on either side of the road trailed vines the size of sturdy ropes, and there was a deep forest of bamboo beyond the ravine. The air through the car window smelled of rich, moist loam and ginger blossoms.

"This is what you expected of Hawaii, right?" he asked.

I admitted it. "I guess I hadn't thought it through: Oahu must be incredibly overpopulated, and I was expecting a lush tropical garden with hardly any people at all."

"There are still pockets of unravaged Earth remaining." We passed a walled estate, its stucco mansion huddled in the chill gloom under brooding banyans. "But not a great many, anymore. You humans breed carelessly." That ought to have sounded insulting, but in context I could only agree.

He took me to Pali Lookout, where we leaned against the wind to stare out over the emerald mountains and meadows of the windward side of the island. He showed me how one could scavenge empty beer cans from the tall grass beside a wall of naked rock, and hurl them at the mountainside. The violent wind would catch them and blow them up toward the peaks above us before they chanced into some protected pocket between the rocks and, prey to gravity once more, rattled back down to be thrown again. He laughed into the wind with the uncomplicated joy of a child and raced me back to the car. We landed tousled and giggling against it moments apart, and he caught me in his arms for a breathless and wholly unexpected kiss.

From there we swooped down the mountain, past the needle-sharp peak of Mt. Olomana, turned onto another highway at a traffic light in the middle of steep green nowhere, and fled between rolling emerald mountain flanks to the Valley of the Temples, where we stopped at the peacock-guarded Byodo-In Temple nestled in under the Koolau Mountains in perfect koi-stream-moated duplication of a temple in Japan. We lit sticks of sandalwood incense to the enormous Buddha, and Jorandel bowed gravely, his expression brooding and earnest. Then he stuck his incense in the provided box of sand and, with a mischievous grin that banished all solemnity, caught my hand to lead me off to a corner of the garden from which one could admire to best advantage a perfect arrangement of moss-covered stones and falling water.

Later, at a secluded and unpeopled beach, he showed me how to open immature coconuts to drink the sweet, almost effervescent water inside; how to snorkel; and where to look among the coral heads for the serpentine, colorful eels that looked so fierce and fled in swift silence among the broken coral and seaweed at the bottom of the bay where we swam. We found and followed a clumsy-looking sea turtle for minutes before it wearied of the game and bolted, suddenly as gracefully swift and sinuous as it had seemed ponderous the moment before. We fell in with a school of what he later told me were *manini,* hundreds of striped fragments of sunlight dancing their brilliantly choreographed ballet in the salty depths. We saw coral in every color from iridescent living purple to sad, dead gray where boats or pollution or incautious swimmers had destroyed in moments the colonies that had taken centuries to grow.

And we emerged at last, with me sunburned despite the supposedly waterproof, factor twenty-five sunscreen we had so diligently applied to all my exposed skin (elves don't sunburn), our faces marked by the pressure of our snorkel masks, our hair wild salty masses of tangles, our skin sensitive from too-long immersion. Both of us were exhausted and self-satisfied in the long, slanting rays of hot afternoon sun. We had talked of going out to dinner. I suppose we could have, even looking as we did; money and fame are a heady combination with which one can attain some remarkable freedoms, and Jorandel had both. But in the end we decided against it. Home, a soothing shower, a change of clothes, and room service or the hotel restaurant sounded much more appealing—though it might not have, had I remembered that "home" included all the other Cold Iron musicians and their entourage.

We drove back by way of the South Shore, a windy rush through gathering shadows between the mountains and the sea as the sun set on the other side of the island and the swift tropical darkness settled gently over the Earth. I felt as though we had been together forever, belonged together, as though there were no world outside the blessed independence we'd shared that day. We had learned each other's unthinking ways: learned to interpret unconscious signals, to respond to unspoken comments and questions, to move together in as perfect harmony as the schools of fish we had followed.

When we left the hotel we had been strangers, awkward and a little shy. We returned to it united by more than just the hours we'd spent together. There was a bond between us, forged perhaps in last night's intimacy but tempered to exquisite intensity by this afternoon's quiet joy. Anything could happen between us now, and that would remain. By tomorrow we could be mortal enemies, but that bond would hold through anything. Burden or blessing, it was an inalienable part of who we were, of what we had become together, of what we would always be. And even in the thrall of that enchanted afternoon I was aware of the daunting aspects of that; but not enough to regret it.

The spell broke the moment we entered Cold Iron's hotel suite. All afternoon there had been no drugs, no drink, no drama, nothing to mar the benign sorcery of sunlight and jungle and sea and our own sweet awareness of each other. Jorandel didn't have the door all the way open when a hurled bottle hit it so hard we were both splattered with shards of broken glass and a fine spray of whiskey. The sound of its breaking, and of Jorandel's inarticulate, enraged response, was drowned by a sustained shriek of female curses and the simultaneous bellow of Jimendan's equally obscene replies. The idyll was clearly over.

Jorandel kicked the door open with such force that it bounced back and nearly hit him on his way in. It did hit me, but luckily I saw it coming and had my arm up to catch it, so it did me no harm. The scene inside was not very startling to one who had been with this group for long. There were several nearly naked women scattered about the room in various attitudes of repose on and around fully clothed musicians. A few of the women were incuriously watching Jimendan and the redheaded woman he appeared to be trying to strangle, but only one or two looked at all troubled by what was going on. Some looked amused. Candy, alone on a loveseat in a far corner of the room, seemed wholly oblivious.

All three of the musicians were watching Jimedan and the redhead: Blade with indifference, the Roach with a certain avid amusement, and Killer with his face concealed behind his hair so that one could not tell what he might be thinking. At first glance he seemed relaxed, but his hands were still. With him, that was a dead giveaway: he was forever drumming, with or without his sticks, on anything handy. I had sometimes thought with amusement that he must incorporate it even into the sex act. Certainly I had seen him drumming in his sleep. If his hands were still now, it was because his body was poised for action, however relaxed he might look.

Perhaps he had meant to save the redhead from Jimendan if he must. But Jorandel's entry prevented the necessity by distracting Jimendan long enough that the girl broke free of him and snatched up another bottle to hurl. She was naked except for the tumble of carrot-red curls to her waist and a dainty, lace-topped sock on one foot. Her entire body was mottled with freckles, her face twisted with rage, and her throwing arm was strong and steady. Jorandel reached her just too late to prevent the throw, and Jimendan ducked the bottle barely in time.

Without a word, Jorandel lifted her off her feet, carried her to the door I had closed behind me, and waited while I opened it again at a glance from him. He deposited her in the corridor outside quite gently, disentangled himself from the clawlike fingers that tried to rake his face with vividly orange-painted nails, and closed the door firmly in her face.

"You'd better find her clothes and put them out with her," I said. "Even you might not be immune to the trouble she could cause otherwise." She was beating on the door and screaming, but no one paid that any heed.

Jorandel looked at Jimendan. "Get her clothes."

Jimendan scowled, but did as he was bid, returning from a bedroom moments later with a bundle of cotton and lace in his arms, a pair of orange sandals clutched in one hand, and an eelskin purse dangling from the other. The redhead's curses had abated, but her pounding on the door had not. "This will be interesting," said Jorandel. " 'Ware the broken glass." Jimendan was barefoot. "I'll open it, you put the clothes out. And be quick, so I don't catch you when I close it again."

The move was performed with practiced dexterity. The appearance of her clothes silenced the redhead, and while she (I assumed) hastened to cover herself on one side of the door, the two brothers collapsed against the other in a fit of uncontrollable giggles.

"For godsake don't sit down there," I said. "There's broken glass all over." That sent them into new paroxysms of merriment, but they did move away from the doorway.

Killer was drumming again, with open hands on the lean hip of a swim-suited groupie who seemed to find the experience arousing. Everyone else who had taken any interest in the incident had turned away now, bored by its conclusion. The area near the doorway stank of spilled whiskey. The other bottle the redhead had thrown had collided with something softer and failed to break.

"Someone ought to call housekeeping," said Candy. I stared at her in surprise, having quite forgotten she was there. "About the glass, I mean," she said defensively.

"I expect you're right," I said absently. She was studying Jorandel and Jimendan with a curiously cold look in her eyes, and I wondered in sudden guilt whether she resented the time I had spent with Jorandel.

"They won't." She gestured with childish irritation at the brothers. "But somebody should."

"What was that fight about?" I asked her, wondering whether it was the reason for her odd mood.

"Oh, I don't know. Who cares?" she said. "It's always

the same thing, one way or another. You want some soda?"

"Not right now, thanks." After such a day I certainly didn't need cheering. But that seemed to clear up the question of resentment: I didn't think she'd be offering me soda if she were cross with me. Maybe she thought the time I spent with him was devoted at least in part to the matter for which she had hired me.

As indeed it should have been. It occurred to me for the first time that in all the afternoon's adventures, I had not so much as considered the possible danger Jorandel was in, much less done anything useful like pumping him for information, telling him my suspicion about the drug that had killed Andy, warning him in case he had kept any of it for his own use, or trying to find out where he had got it. Some detective. This was clearly not the moment to try to rectify matters, so I headed for my room and a soothing shower, wondering whether I was really fit to pursue my life's work or whether I should perhaps take up some occupation better suited to my talents, like maybe truck driving.

To my surprise, Candy was waiting in my bedroom when I emerged from the shower, damp and sweetly scented from the hotel's surprisingly expensive French soap. She was sitting on my bed with her back against the headboard, examining her painted toenails, and she barely glanced up when I entered. "We're going to Killer's family's place for a luau tomorrow," she said. "Have you ever been to a luau?"

"No. I thought Killer's family lived in California."

"They do," she said. "Do you think gold would be better than green for my toenails?"

"Depends what else you're wearing, I suppose," I said, less patiently than might have been quite nice. "If Killer's family lives in California, and we're going there for a luau—"

She laughed suddenly. "Oh, I'm sorry. Sometimes I'm a real airhead, aren't I? I meant, his mother lives in California. All the rest of his family lives here. On Oahu. Somewhere on the windward side, but I never can remember all the names. I think it's a place that starts with a 'K' and goes on forever, but they all do. I don't know why they don't name anything in English."

"I suppose the Japanese wonder why they don't name anything in Japanese," I said dryly. "And the Germans would doubtless appreciate some German, and so on."

"Yes, but this isn't Japan or Germany," she said defensively.

"It isn't England, either."

"No, but it's part of the United States. It ought to be named in American words like everyplace else."

"Los Angeles, San Francisco, Ojai, La Jolla . . . ?"

"Exactly." She nodded, pleased with my grasp of the concept.

"Well, I suppose they'd already named a lot of things in their own language before we came along," I said, trying to sound sympathetic. I found the Hawaiian place names as confusing as she did, and perhaps I'd have resented them if I had imagined they'd been created just to be cute. "Tell me about Killer's family. Have you met them before?"

"Yes, the last time we were here. They're not all white." She said it with such comic trepidation that I imagined a multicolored family of pastel bug-eyed monsters.

Since it might have hurt her feelings if I showed my amusement, I turned away abruptly to search my luggage for something suitable to wear that evening, and asked in a strangled voice, "No? What color are they?"

"All different," she said. "Besides elves, there's Japanese, and Black, and some I don't even know what are."

"Well, I suppose they do," I said reassuringly.

"I guess," she said dubiously. "Killer calls some of them 'poi dogs.' He says that's what he is, too."

"A poi dog?" I said.

"Yeah. I guess it's what they call a human that isn't all white," she said. "His dad's only a halfling, you know, so Killer's only one-quarter elf. As far as elves are concerned that's human, even though he has pointy ears and all."

"Oh." I really couldn't think of anything more intelligent to say. Last I heard, Trueblood elves considered even halflings human; a minor point that seemed to have escaped her attention.

"Listen, why don't you do some soda with me?" she said. "Or let's smoke a joint or something. It's so damn boring when the guys aren't working. You wanta go shopping?"

"Good God, no!" I said it without thinking, and promptly regretted it. "I mean—I'm sorry, Candy, I'm just awfully tired, and the fact is I really hate shopping anyway."

"Oh. You do?" She stared as though I had suddenly sprouted extra limbs or horns. "You hate shopping?"

"I'm afraid so."

"Oh." She absorbed that. "Well, but you haven't been shopping here. You haven't been to the International Market Place, for instance, or Duke's Lane. How can you know you hate that if you haven't done it? It's open at night. We could just go for a little while, and if you really still hate it we could quit." Her tone was pathetically hopeful.

"Oh, God," I said, and turned to look at her. Those big fawn eyes were staring at me with such a pitiable and earnest desire to please that I wanted to kick her. "All right," I said crossly. "But not till I've eaten. I'm ravenous."

"Jorie ordered a whole bunch of good food while you were having your shower," she said encouragingly. "It oughta be here by now. C'mon, come eat so we can go, okay?"

"I'd kind of like to finish dressing first," I said.

"Oh. Oh, yeah." She leapt to my assistance. "Here, this blouse'll go better with that skirt. This little one. No, don't wear a bra, it'll spoil the lines. Boy, you got a little burned today, didn't you? You better bring a shawl or something when we go out. It gets chilly if there's any wind at all, and sunburn'll make you get cold easier. Here, not those shoes. These. Gosh, you hardly know anything! Wait, you don't have any earrings. And what about bracelets and stuff. Here, these, and these, and don't you have any rings? We better get you some while we're out. There." She surveyed me. "Oh, Rosie! You forgot your face paint!"

"I thought maybe I could get by with just mascara and eyeliner since we're not doing anything special."

"You ought to at least have eye shadow," she said accusingly. "Here, hold still, I'll do it." She didn't stop at eye shadow, but I was able to prevent her from going much beyond cheek glitter by suggesting that the food was probably getting cold. Maybe it had been, but if so it didn't matter. We never tasted it.

13

The scene that met us when we left my room was ordinary enough, much as it had been when Jorandel and I returned from our afternoon except that the bodyguards and a couple of people I didn't know had now joined the crowd, and several tables piled high with food had been wheeled in. Frank was fussing over Jorandel, insisting that he shouldn't have gone swimming with his injuries. Jorandel was sullen and unrepentant, mostly ignoring him while Frank replaced the bandage on Jorandel's arm that I had clumsily renewed when we came out of the water.

Candy identified one of the newcomers as Alec Reich, the band's manger (Hilly's description of Alec as a "frail, awkward, silly fellow" was remarkably apt). She didn't know the other, and dismissed him without interest as "probably a friend of Alec's." Nobody was paying any attention to the tables full of food. Alec was talking earnestly to Jorandel, who ignored him as he ignored Frank. The Roach was curled with two groupies in a corner and ignored everyone else. Blade was for once without a groupie, and seemed to be doing five-finger exercises on the edge of an occasional table near the windows. The bodyguards were gathered around Killer in the suite's miniature kitchen, discussing something in quiet tones with occasional outbursts of hilarity. Jimendan was nowhere to be seen.

"Isn't anybody going to eat any of this stuff?" demanded Candy, approaching the food tables. "I'm hungry."

No one gave any evidence of having heard her. After a quick survey of the room I decided I was much too hungry to stand on ceremony, so I joined her at the tables. They were loaded with succulent edibles of every sort from fowl in a thick, rich sauce to fresh-sliced fruit in its own juices. But before I could do more than reach for an empty plate to fill, the suite door burst open and Jimendan fell, bruised and bleeding, into the room.

Jorandel was on his feet so fast Frank barely had time to get out of his way. The Roach never moved, and although Blade stood up to see what had happened, he stayed where he was. Everyone else except Candy and I descended upon Jimendan in a chaotic horde. While two of the bodyguards dragged him inside and closed the door behind him, another bent to take his pulse, and the fourth began to examine his wounds. Jorandel got in their way as much as possible, his face white and strained, his eyes dark and wild with emotions I couldn't read. Not just anxiety for his brother, not just anger at whatever had harmed him, but something deadlier than that. Something murkier, obscure, ugly.

Candy stood frozen with an empty plate in her hand, staring. Alec Reich and his friend returned to the comfort of the couch, wearily annoyed. Blade sat back down to his soundless keyboard exercises. Killer, who had gone with the bodyguards to the door, stood back for a moment to survey the situation and then, with a resigned sigh and a determined squaring of his shoulders, waded in to draw Jorandel out of the way. Properly speaking, that was Frank's job, but as no one had yet been hired to take Andy's place he was responsible for Jimendan as well and couldn't be expected to pull them apart. The other bodyguards never made any effort to subdue each other's charges, though they were quick to assist as needed in the case of an injury or collapse. Since the other musicians were indifferent and their manager clearly incapable, that left only Killer to try to control Jorandel.

He had his hands full. I couldn't see how severely Jim was injured, but when Killer hauled Jorie out of the way, he reacted as though he were being dragged from Jim's deathbed. He kicked and fought and bellowed frenzied curses, his face contorted and his stormy eyes shadowed by disproportionate grief or guilt. I doubt Killer could have held him if Frank hadn't, just in time, come to his aid.

"He's all right, Jorandel," he said firmly. "Come on, you're no help in this state." One of the other bodyguards rose and went to the phone while Frank helped Killer subdue Jorie and the other two carried Jim to a couch. I got a look at Jim when they carried him past me. The gods, I thought, had an odd sense of humor. The brothers liked to switch identities, and since Jorie fell or was pushed downstairs his bruises and bandages had been a dead giveaway. But now the two would match again. It was almost uncanny: there was a swelling bruise on Jim's forehead exactly where Jorie had knocked his on the stairs, and an abraded and bleeding injury to his left forearm almost identical to that on Jorie's that Frank had earlier been fussing over. I wondered rather hysterically whether his right leg would prove to be injured as well, since Jorie still limped on stairs or when he was very tired, as this evening after our exhausting day. But that was silly: of course his injuries wouldn't be identical to that extend.

. . . Unless someone meant them to be, to make the brothers match again. The fleeting thought seemed nonsensical; who but the brothers themselves cared whether they matched? I pushed the idea to the back of my mind for later consideration.

When the two bodyguards placed Jimendan gently on the couch he added to the general confusion by opening leaden eyes and demanding in a frail and petulant voice to know what had happened. Since that was exactly what we had all hoped he would tell us, the result was a mystified chorus and, from Jorandel, another fit of aimless and inarticulate rage. I thought I saw a flicker of relief in his eyes when Jim spoke, but if he was glad to see his brother regain consciousness, it wasn't enough to wipe away his fury at what had happened to him. White-faced and wild-eyed as a small boy crossed, he attacked the room as if it were his personal enemy.

Killer wasn't watching for it, and Frank had turned to Jim when he woke, so there was no one to stop Jorandel from hurling furniture indiscriminately at walls, windows, and people. He was muttering to himself as he did it, but the only words I caught were a fierce and furious phrase, the words carefully spaced and clearly enunciated and heavily emphasized, and ambiguous at best: "Nothing, else, matters!" The tables full of food, being handiest, were the first to go. Candy and I were still ducking flying crockery and sauces when he turned away to fling a convenient guitar at a window, throw a wooden chair at a nearby groupie, and grab at a heavy lamp that, fortunately, turned out to be firmly affixed to a still heavier table. That gave Frank and Killer time to catch him.

Candy seemed oblivious to the struggle as the two of them wrestled him to the ground in the midst of scattered rice and sliced fruit. She was frowning blankly at her empty plate, a look of innocent disappointment in her eyes. "I was hungry," she said plaintively.

Jorandel relaxed the moment they got him down. All the anger seemed to go out of him at once and for a moment I thought he was going to cry. But he only drew a long, unsteady breath, said, "Sorry," quietly, and glanced up at Jimendan, who was watching with dazed interest from the couch. "I'm fine now," he told Frank. "Tend to my brother."

After only a moment's hesitation Frank nodded shortly, released him, and returned to Jim's side. Killer sat up and absently brushed sticky rice from his elbows. Jorandel lay perfectly still where he had fallen, breathing hard, his face pure white and his eyes unreadable. I could not understand the intensity of his emotion, and I could not get over the feeling that he was as guilty as he was aggrieved. Guilty of what? He certainly hadn't done this to Jimendan; he'd been in the suite with the rest of us when it had happened. Was that it? Just standard big-brother guilt at not having been there when his little brother needed him? Maybe it was. It seemed that everything Jorandel did, he did to excess. Maybe that applied to his sense of responsibility as to everything else.

Candy startled me abruptly out of my reflections by heaving her empty plate across the room with force and fury quite worthy of Jorandel at his worst. "Dammit, I was really hungry!" she said.

I couldn't help it: I laughed. She glared at me, but I caught Jorie's eye and underneath the grim self-loathing, I thought I saw a flicker of amusement. Even in his most earnest tantrums he was always prey to an incongruous appreciation of the absurd.

It was only a flicker, gone as quickly as it had come. "Then get something to eat," he told her sourly, and picked himself up off the floor, scowling at the scattered remnants of the meal he had ordered. "And call housekeeping to get this cleaned up." He said it as though housekeeping, and not he, were responsible for the mess.

"Yes, Jorie," she said meekly, and glanced anxiously at the Roach to see whether he had heard her accept an order from Jorandel. If he had, he chose to ignore it this time. That was as well. Jorie's mood was still precarious. If the Roach had, as he sometimes did, challenged Jorie's right to tell her what to do or hers to obey him, things could have got uglier than they already were. But the Roach was involved with his groupies, and none of them seemed even mildly interested in what went on in the rest of the room.

While Candy was making the phone call, emergency paramedics arrived to carry Jimendan away to the hospital. Rather to my surprise, Jorie made no effort to accompany them. Frank, after a moment's anguished hesitation, went with Jim, and Jorie retreated in sulky silence to his room, carrying an electric guitar and earphones. I thought he would soothe himself with music, as nothing else really could. When Candy suggested we continue our interrupted plans to go shopping, with dinner out as the first stop on the agenda, it seemed as sensible a plan as any. I was hungry. And I did not much want to be there when the maids arrived and saw what they'd been called to clean up.

I'd like to say I had qualms about leaving Jorandel alone, but I hadn't. And while I certainly knew he was upset, the bond between us didn't extend to telepathy. If what he later did was intentional, he didn't telegraph it. Maybe he hadn't decided yet. Maybe he never did decide. He liked to set up situations and leave the final outcome to calculated chance. When Candy said, for instance, that he knew someone would keep him from jumping out a window, she was only half right. He knew someone *could* keep him from jumping out the window. If someone happened to be looking, if someone moved quickly enough, if someone didn't decide it was a bluff and try to call it. It wasn't a bluff. He would jump. So far, he'd been lucky—or had calculated the chances correctly.

He was lucky again that night. It wasn't a window, it was a drug overdose. And I've often wondered since whether it was a genuine accident or one of his calculated risks. If the latter, was I part of his calculations, or the stroke of luck that upset them? There's no knowing. He naturally insisted afterward that the overdose was entirely unintentional. Maybe it was.

He always spoke of his own death with a peculiar mixture of humor, curiosity, and childlike defiance; and although he was quite young for an elf and could look forward to probably twice my life span on Earth before he even felt inclined to return to Faerie as most older elves did, he liked to pretend that he was ready for death now. He liked to tempt it, to play with the possibility. But I never knew whether he was really courting it. If he was, he almost won it that night. When Candy and I returned to the hotel, I had no intention to seek him out. To my own surprise I'd had a good time with Candy in the lanes full of tourist trinkets in Waikiki, and I was feeling much too contentedly weary to face any more of Jorandel's tantrums.

The common room was deserted when we came in. Candy, her arms full of packages and drooping like a small child at the end of a long day of play, said good night to me at the door of her room. I went on to mine with my much smaller collection of packages. I meant to lock the door and fall directly into bed, but something stopped me. I don't know what. Maybe the unnatural quiet of the empty suite after all the fuss and bother earlier. Maybe some premonition, some urgent sense of danger through that intangible bond between us. I thought at the time that it was only a bleak realization that, weary of him though I was, I was also in love with him.

That took me as far as the common room, where I belatedly realized that he might not be alone in his room. When there were no groupies in sight, it usually meant they were present but with the musicians somewhere out of sight. After the initial stab of jealousy I realized I had no claims on him, not even the right to jealousy. We'd had a good time together, and that was all. Neither of us had made any promises. Neither of us could.

I turned back toward my room, trying not to feel desolate. After all, I didn't know he was with someone else. I just knew it would be too embarrassing to find out by knocking on his door. And if I weren't willing to face that chance, then I would have to wait for him to come to me. Which he might never do. I paused again, irresolute, dissatisfied. Was he with someone else? Was he alone? Would he want me to come to him if he were alone? Did he, asked the eternal girlish voice in my mind, really care for me?

Do any of us ever really grow up?

I don't know how long I stood there, undecided. And I don't know what finally broke the spell. I just know that after a long time I finally straightened, and lifted the hand that I had let fall on the back of a chair for support, squared my shoulders, and went to knock on Jorandel's door.

No answer. I started to turn away, desolate again, and again I don't know what stopped me. Maybe just the need to know he was there, and safe, even if it was in someone else's arms. I was aware of a growing anxiety, groundless but insistent. I tried the knob cautiously. He hadn't locked it. The bedside lamp was on: I remembered he had said he couldn't sleep without it, and indeed the night before he had left it on while we slept.

There was a bent spoon, a half-burned book of matches, a syringe, and a wad of cotton in the yellow glow on the table beneath the lamp. Jorandel was alone on the bed, fully clothed except for his shirt, lying as though he had been seated on the edge of the bed and had fallen backward with his feet still on the floor. His face was turned away from me, his long hair fanned in a shining blue-and-green-streaked halo around his head, one pointed ear showing. One hand lay across his naked chest, the other flung out away from him, palm-upward, the fingers marble-white and gently curled.

He was asleep. It was late: of course he was asleep. Nothing could be more natural. And if he had not bothered to get undressed, or to get fully into bed, well, he must have been very tired. He had only fallen asleep.

My mind told soothing lies, but I did not shut the door and walk away. I waited, staring, hardly daring to breathe myself, until I saw the smallest hint of breath in his body. The rib cage moved, the chest lifted and fell under the limp white hand. Scarcely, but it moved, and that barely perceived motion freed me to move and breathe and live again.

I've said I'm not a screamer. I truly cannot seem to manage a scream, even when it might be wise. I heard myself moan, just audibly, but I could not draw breath enough even to raise my voice. I ought to have screamed for Frank, for anyone who knew how to deal with this. I knew what it was, well enough that I did not even go to him: the evidence was there in yellow lamplight beside the bed. There was no time to waste in establishing what the arctic void in my heart had already told me. Trembling with fear and remorse (I should have told him my theory about the drugs) I backed out of the room, looked frantically around the common room for some magical solution to disaster, and ran to Candy's room. It was locked. I banged on the door, kicked it, and finally managed a strangled scream. "Candy! Damn it! Help me, it's Jorandel. I don't know what to do!"

That brought her out in a rush. She was dressed only in a flimsy nightgown, but she headed straight for the suite's outer door, saying cryptically as she went, "OD'd?"

"Yes, I think so, what shall I do?"

"I'll get Frank." She was as quick and competent in this crisis as any grown-up could have been. "You see if you can get Jorie up. Hit him, pour water on him, anything. Get him awake. That's the main thing." The suite door slammed on her final words.

I returned to Jorandel's room, reluctant, terrified, feeling much less competent than Candy seemed. He lay exactly as I had left him, pale and still as death. At least, now that I knew what to do, I was no longer paralyzed. The worst of the terror had been in not knowing what to do. He was heavy, a dead-weight, but I hauled him by main force into a sitting position, talking to him, slapping him, trying anything I could think of to get some reaction from him.

His head lolled backward, lifeless, mouth open and eyes only half shut but with no awareness in them. I could not tell whether he breathed again. He was too heavy for me to lift him onto his feet, or even to shake him very forcefully without losing my grip on his shoulders and letting him fall back again. His arms dangled uselessly at his sides. I balanced him against my shoulder and grabbed a handful of his hair to pull his head upright. His face was lax, but I thought the eyelids flickered. And suddenly all my apprehension was replaced by irritation.

"Damn you!" I used my grip on his hair to shake him, hard. "Wake up, damn it! You stupid, thoughtless, arrogant Trueblood, wake up!" No reaction. I let go of his hair to slap him. "Damn you, wake up, or I'll—"

"You'll what?" asked Frank, distantly amused. I hadn't heard him come in. "No, it's all right, you're doing fine. Candy's calling the paramedics. They won't be long." He caught up one of Jorandel's wrists, felt for a pulse, nodded to himself, and calmly edged in past me to haul him onto his feet. "Here, steady him. But it's no good if he won't do some of the work himself." He had got one of Jorie's arms over his shoulders and was holding him upright by that alone, balancing the dead-weight of Jorie's limp body against his hip. I got under Jorie's other arm. I was too short to take any of the weight, but at least I could keep him from flopping slackly against Frank's chest.

"Don't you have any magic for this?" I said anxiously.

"I'm afraid not," said Frank. "If there's anything for OD'ing he's never told me." He raised his voice, suddenly harsh and insistent. "Jorandel. Walk, Jorandel." He said it exactly as one might to a disobedient dog. To me he said, "Hang on: I'm gonna try to get him to walk.

It's a reflex; if he's conscious at all, he'll do it. You just balance him, okay?"

Since he seemed to be waiting for an answer, I said unsteadily, "Okay."

He bounced Jorie a time or two, as if to get his attention, then took a step forward. "Walk, Jorandel," he said again, in exactly the same stern, commanding voice. But Jorie's legs were as limp as the rest of him, dragging behind as we pulled him forward. "Jorandel," he said. "Walk," and he took another step.

"Oh, please," I said. My voice startled me; it was thin and small and frightened, like a child's.

"You're doing fine," Frank said encouragingly. "Keep him balanced." And to Jorie he said, commanding again, "Walk!" He took another step. Jorie's legs dragged. But then, slowly, clumsily, and quite uselessly, he tried to draw one foot forward to get it under him. "Good," Frank said heartily. "Come on, Jorandel. Do it again. Another step." He took one. Jorie didn't.

"They'll be here in a minute," said Candy, bustling into the room, still wearing only her delicate little nightgown. "What shall I do with his outfit?"

"Just get it out of sight," said Frank. "We'll deal with that later. Jorandel! I said walk, damn you!" Jorie obediently dragged one foot two inches forward.

Candy swept the spoon, syringe, and other evidence into the drawer of the bedside table, beside the Gideon Bible already there. "Front room's clean," she said, returning to Jorie's bedroom door and holding it open for us as we made our painful way toward it. "Is Jim back from the hospital?"

"Yeah," said Frank. "You better get him."

She went away, leaving the door open. We proceeded toward it at a snail's pace, with Jorie making only an occasional effort to help us. I realized Frank was looking past him at me with a curiously compassionate expression on his big, square, ugly face. I tried to smile at him, but I could tell it wasn't much of a smile.

"I've seen him worse," he said encouragingly. "You found him in time. He's got a good chance."

"Only a chance," I said dully, absorbing it.

"A good chance," he repeated. And added, in his

commanding voice, "Walk, Jorandel," because Jorie had stopped trying.

We dragged him through the doorway into the common room, and I reached automatically behind me to close the bedroom door, as if it mattered. At just that moment I wasn't quite sure what mattered, beyond Jorie's spiritless efforts to drag his feet by inches across the resisting carpet. There was no question of him supporting his own weight: he never even got his feet under him. But at least he did, when urged strongly enough, make an effort to move them. His head didn't loll quite so lifelessly against Frank's shoulder. And I distinctly saw him blink, twice, as though trying to focus his eyes, before closing them with a weary sigh that was almost as reassuring as his feeble movements, because it proved he was still breathing.

It felt very like trying to force a corpse to walk. His skin was cold, his muscles utterly relaxed, his body so flaccid it seemed almost boneless, like a cat's. But Frank never relented, and Jorie tried increasingly, if mindlessly, to obey him.

Jim had been asleep. While we dragged Jorie into the common room, I had been distantly aware of Candy's voice raised to wake him, and of his responding in surly irritation. When she got through to him what it was she wanted, he came limping out of his room in sleep-dazed apprehension, saw Frank and me walking Jorie, and promptly tried to displace me. I'd have been willing enough, since I felt worse than useless and my knees had begun to tremble with exhaustion and despair, but Frank waved him away.

"Let her be," he said. "You're not strong enough yet."

"Am too," he said pettishly, and sat down abruptly on the nearest chair, head in his hands. "Damn."

Frank scowled at him. "You're drunk," he said. "I wouldn't've woke you, only I knew damn well you'd have my ass if I didn't. There's nothing you can do for him. I'll go with him to the hospital, and I'll call you as soon as I know anything. He'll be okay; he's not in a coma yet, and he won't be if I have anything to say about it. Now, go back to bed, will you?"

"No," said Jimendan. He lifted his head to stare helplessly at his brother. The bruise on his forehead was already spreading, like Jorandel's, to blacken one eye. "Damn it, I will go with him."

"No, you won't," said Frank.

"You really shouldn't," Candy said timidly. She was hugging herself, looking cold and small and frightened now that there was nothing for her to do.

Jim didn't look at her. "Fuck off," he told Frank.

To my utter amazement, Frank grinned at him. "Good try," he said, "but you haven't quite got it yet. You put too much feeling into it."

Jim bristled and I thought for a moment he would fly into a petulant rage, but after one tense moment he matched Frank's grin, sheepishly, and said again, "Fuck off." This time it was a perfect imitation of Jorandel, utterly toneless, indifferent, deadly.

"That's more like it," said Frank, joggling Jorie on his arm. "Come on, son, walk," he commanded.

Jorie's head dropped bonelessly forward against his chest, and I felt the breath go out of him in a long sigh, hopelessly final.

Frank shook him. "Oh, no, boy," he said. "No you don't. You get a grip on yourself, you hear? Walk."

No response. I felt as though the light were going out of the universe. For a moment my vision actually faltered.

"Damn it," said Frank. There was a note of desperation in his voice. "Damn it, Jorandel!" He shook him again, hard, and I felt Jorandel draw a faint, shuddering breath, but that was the only response he got.

"Oh, God," said Candy. "Oh, God."

The paramedics arrived at just that moment, like the cavalry to the rescue when the last settler had already fallen under the hostile Indians' arrows, but everyone behaved as though there were still a chance. At least he was still alive. I now knew that whatever bound the two of us, it was strong enough that I could not be mistaken about that much: I would feel it if he died. There would be a howling void in the universe that would drag me down with him, if it could. I was put gently aside by someone, possibly one of the paramedics, and when my trembling knees nearly gave way someone else caught me and placed me with dispassionate care on the nearest seat, which happened to be the arm of the chair Jimendan was occupying. I was scarcely aware of it when he put a steadying hand on my arm. Nothing seemed quite real. When Jorandel and Frank and the paramedics had gone, and Candy and Jim and I were left alone in the silent room, none of us spoke for a very long moment.

"Better clean house, I guess," Jim said at last. "Did you tell Emerson, Candy?"

She was standing next to us, still hugging herself and staring at the door through which Jorandel had been hustled so efficiently. "No," she said. "I guess I better."

"He might be able to keep them out of here," said Jim.

I became aware of his hand on my arm, and stood up suddenly, moving away from him. But there was nowhere to go. "Keep who out of here?" I said.

"The police," said Jim.

"Oh," I said.

"Looking for drugs," said Candy.

"Yes," I said.

"It's better when there's time for us to take him in ourselves," she said. "Something about probable cause, or something." She shrugged. "I don't know. Besides, this is Hawaii."

Jimendan emitted a sound that may have been meant for laughter. "What does that have to do with it?"

"Well?" she said defensively. "I don't know how cops act in Hawaii."

"Probably much as they do elsewhere," said Jim. "And I don't think we'll have any trouble with them. But it still might be a good idea to clean house."

I almost asked what it mattered whether the suite was tidy. That's how clearly I was thinking. Of course they were talking about getting rid of whatever drugs they had on the premises. And I sincerely doubted the necessity, but what did I know about either Hawaii's laws or the interactions of police with elfrock stars anywhere?

"I'll go tell Emerson," said Candy, not moving.

"You do that," said Jim.

"Frank told you to go back to bed," she said suddenly.

"I know," he said.

"You should," she said.

"Fuck off," he said.

She studied him for a long moment, shrugged, and left the suite, presumably in search of Emerson. I wished I had told her to get a robe first, since she hadn't thought of it herself. Jimendan didn't move. I made my way unsteadily to a chair facing his and collapsed in it, wondering absently why my legs felt so wobbly.

"Reaction," he said.

I stared. "What?"

"Reaction," he said, smiling blandly. Exactly like his brother. How the hell did he know what I was thinking?

"Don't do that," I said.

"Okay," he said agreeably.

"What the hell is it with you guys, anyway?"

He gave me a look of boyish innocence, only slightly marred by the blackening eye. "What?"

"Oh, hell." I scowled at him, trying not to think of Jorandel's lifeless face in a pool of lamplight, with the accoutrements of his self-destruction laid out on the table beside him. "What happened to you this afternoon?"

"When?"

"You know damn well what I mean. Did you get shoved downstairs too, or what?"

He shrugged, magnificently unconcerned. "Maybe. I don't remember."

"You don't remember at all?"

"No. The last thing I remember, I was getting into a rental car in the garage downstairs. Next thing I was getting off the elevator up here with the worst headache I have ever endured." He grinned, boyish again. "But I was somewhat stoned at the time, and you know how it is. Shit happens. I probably did fall downstairs. There are some in the parking garage."

"And you just happened to get exactly the same injuries Jorie did when he fell downstairs."

"I didn't plan it that way." He stared. "By Mab's grace, cousin, you don't think I did it on purpose, do you?"

I shuddered involuntarily. "Don't call me that."

He grinned unpleasantly. "Cousin, cousin, cousin."

"And you're surprised I think you'd go to some considerable length to be able to be mistaken for your brother?"

"Hey, it's Jorandel who's into the twin-switch business. Naturally I mimic him: why not? But Earth defend me if I chance the breaking of my skull to match his bruises!"

It did sound ridiculous, put that bluntly. "It still seems a weird coincidence," I said feebly.

He studied me dispassionately. "You know, you are fully as freaky as my brother," he said.

But I wasn't really listening. Damn it, it was a weird coincidence. In fact, too weird to be a coincidence. It hadn't escaped my attention when he had come limping out of his bedroom that Jim's right leg was, indeed, injured in apparently the same way Jorie's was. The gods may have an odd sense of humor, but that really was pushing the boundaries of likelihood a little far. Yet I believed him when he said he hadn't done it on purpose. Besides, why would he?

But if he hadn't done it on purpose and it wasn't a coincidence, that meant somebody else did it on purpose. Who? Why? Surely not Jorandel. Surely even though he was, as Jim said, "into the twin-switch business," he wouldn't physically injure his brother in its pursuit. Besides, he couldn't have; he was here in the common room with the rest of us when Jim came in.

But he could have hired it done. And it would certainly explain that terrible undertone of guilt and self-loathing in his tantrum afterward. It might even explain the overdose tonight, if the overdose was deliberate, and not the result of over-pure drugs I should have warned him about. Suppose he'd hired someone to give Jim injuries that matched his, not really thinking what it meant, and been faced with the reality when Jim came bleeding into the room?

"No. It's absurd." I didn't realize I'd said it aloud till I saw Jim watching me.

"What is absurd?" he asked. "The idea that you are as freaky as my brother? That seems obvious to me."

"Oh, God," I said, "I hope you're right."

He laughed. "That proves it," he said.

"Rosie, you look terrible," said Candy. She was standing between us, and I hadn't even seen her come back into the suite. "You better go to bed, maybe," she said.

I shook my head. "I can't. Not till I know . . ." I couldn't finish the sentence. "I should've warned him," I said instead.

"Of what?" asked Jim.

"Never mind," I said, thinking again of Jim's injuries. If Jorandel had hired that done, then the overdose must have been deliberate, and no warnings from me needed.

"He'll be all right," Candy said doubtfully.

"But he couldn't have done that," I said wildly. "It doesn't make sense. Surely it isn't that important to him." But I remembered him saying over and over again, when Jim was brought in, "Nothing else matters," as though trying to convince himself it was true. It didn't sound quite like what he might say about their ability to switch places, but what else could he have meant?

"Who couldn't have done what?" asked Candy.

"Don't ask," said Jim, eyeing me mockingly.

Candy nodded in sudden, indulgent comprehension. "You're all upset," she said. "And no wonder. Listen, what you need, if you can't sleep yet, you need a little soda, that's all. I'll go get some."

"I don't want—" But she was gone. And I found I did want, really. I wanted very much. I wanted the impossible. I wanted the world to be a sensible place full of easy answers. Soda wouldn't give me that. But it would give me the illusion, and that was better than nothing.

14

Whatever else the soda may have done for or to me, it did at least provoke some more rational thought. Instead of wallowing in guilt over having failed to warn Jorandel, or recoiling in horror from the thought that he might have had Jimendan deliberately injured, I was able to be at least moderately objective about both possibilities.

First, the drugs: street drugs, I knew, were not to be relied on for consistent purity, or even content. If the drugs Jorandel had given Andy had been too strong, that still didn't necessarily mean that either Andy or Jorandel was the victim of our hypothetical murderer. It could have been an accident. True, I should have warned Jorandel of my suspicions, but it was not safe to assume that all I had to do now was track down his source and I'd have our murderer.

Nor was it necessarily true that Jorandel had overdosed from the same batch of drugs. I had no idea in what quantity he purchased or was given them. What he used tonight could easily have been from a different batch, or even a different drug, so that even if Andy had fallen victim to the murderer, Jorandel's overdose was either intentional or a miscalculation.

If it was intentional, it might be due to guilt over Jimendan's injuries. But the more I thought about it, the more improbable that seemed. True, it seemed to fit Jorandel's reaction when Jim came in. But everything he'd done and seemed to feel could as easily and much more reasonably be explained by other means. The rage because his brother was hurt, the guilt because he hadn't been there to protect him . . . and the phrase, "nothing else matters"? It could mean anything. Or nothing.

It was surely an extravagant phrase for even Jorandel

to apply to the notion of their twin switches. There were a lot of things that mattered more to him than that. His music, for instance. If someone had just quoted that isolated phrase and asked me what Jorandel might have said it about, his music would have been my first guess. I didn't quite see how that could apply in the present situation, but neither could I see how he could possibly have meant the twin switch.

If he hadn't overdosed out of guilt over what he'd had done to his brother, which he surely had not, then I was back to the question of accident or attempted murder. If the latter, was it necessarily connected with Andy's death? I couldn't know for certain without knowing where and in what quantities Jorandel got his drugs, and whether he'd used drugs from the same batch he gave to Andy. Jimendan might know that, but in my guise as Candy's cousin I couldn't ask him.

Besides, there were other and uglier possibilities. Suppose Andy's death had been an accident. Suppose Jimendan had believed otherwise. Suppose he did to his brother what he believed his brother had done to Andy. He had certainly been angry enough with Jorandel, yesterday, to conceive of such a plan, and maybe he thought he would be achieving poetic justice. That would explain, too, why he'd been so friendly and forgiving this morning. Once he had doctored Jorandel's drugs he might consider Andy already avenged and be quite content to make up with Jorandel while he still lived.

That scenario left a number of things unexplained. Who had Candy overheard threatening Jorandel? Who had searched my room to find my ID? Who had knocked Jorandel downstairs, and why? Andy wasn't dead then, so presumably Jimendan had no motive, if Andy's death was his motive now. Who had hired hoodlums to mug me that same night? If I were about to push someone downstairs I might warn away a detective beforehand, but not at the same time. Had Jorandel's assailant imagined I might somehow have prevented the stairs-pushing if I hadn't been got out of the way while it was being done? That seemed unlikely at best. Better to get Frank out of the way: bodyguard was his job.

I didn't know where Frank had been at the time The

bodyguards, being more baby-sitter than bodyguard, didn't tend to follow their charges around as closely as they would if they expected serious attempts on their lives at any moment, but at the concert locations they did stick pretty close as a rule. A lethally disordered fan would not be exactly unique. In these unpleasant times he would hardly even be a novelty. The bodyguards kept their eyes open. Where had Frank been when Jorandel was attacked? Was his absence mere chance, or had he been deliberately got out of the way as I had?

He would certainly have said so if he'd been as clumsily dealt with as I was. But he might easily have been drawn away by someone he trusted, on some errand so apparently authentic and harmless that it still hadn't occurred to him to question it. It was a thought worth looking into, anyway.

But it didn't get me anywhere right now. Frank wasn't here to question, even if I could think of an innocuous reason for asking where he'd been that night. Was I seriously considering Jimendan for the role of First Murderer anyway? I wasn't sure. A lot hinged on the drug question, on whether Jorandel had overdosed on the same batch from which he'd given Andy his Christmas gift, and I didn't see how I could find that out till I could talk to Jorandel. Candy might know, but I couldn't ask her in front of Jimendan, and he showed no sign of going back to bed.

It was just too damned coincidental that his injuries should so perfectly match Jorandel's. I didn't believe Jorandel had hired it done just to further the twin switches, but what other reason could he have? And who else would do it for that reason? Who else wanted them to be able to pass for each other? No one, as far as I knew, except Jimendan. And he seemed convincing in his denial. Besides, why would he go to such incredible lengths to make it possible for him to pass for Jorandel? Unless—

Unless he intended to pass for Jorandel forever. I stared at him, shaken, as my fertile imagination filled in that scenario. Suppose Jorandel's overdose was, in fact, an accident. Suppose the people Candy overheard threatening Jorandel were either Jimendan and cohorts, or at least people hired by Jimendan. Suppose it was Jimendan who, alone of all the band and retinue, imagined Cold Iron could get along quite well without Jorandel—because he intended to take Jorandel's place. He could kill Jorandel during a twin switch, and in such a way that it would look like an accident. He could take Jorandel's place as front man for the band, and be out from under his big brother's shadow forever. Except of course that he wouldn't be out from under Jorandel's shadow, he'd be more suffocated by it than ever. But he wouldn't see that until too late. Neither of them was really much good at thinking things through.

But Jim couldn't take Jorie's place even if he wanted to. Surely it was impossible. There must be proof of some kind as to which of them was which. Fingerprints . . . but no, their driver's licenses had each other's fingerprints, if Candy was right, and being singularly untraveled myself, I didn't know whether fingerprints were required for passports. I could easily enough imagine that if they were, the brothers would have gotten their passports in each other's names as they had their driver's licenses, to avoid having to explain the erroneous licenses.

Dental records? Surely dental records would prove which was which. But not unless, should one of them die, someone questioned the identity of the corpse. In which case, the survivor could prove himself to be his brother by means of the erroneously fingerprinted driver's licenses. Which would establish by elimination the identity of the corpse, and that would be that. As long as no one accused the survivor of murdering his brother so he could switch places with him, he'd be fine. And to make things a little more certain, he could kill Jorandel in some way that would destroy any identifying factors other than fingerprints. If he were willing to kill his brother in the first place, he was unlikely to have qualms over the messiness of the method.

Could he seriously expect to get away with it? Would the other musicians be fooled? Surely they wouldn't knowingly go along with it. It was Jorandel whose devotion to the music was supposed to be so obsessive that he'd risk anything for it, not any of the others. Besides, they were all excellent musicians, and Cold Iron was not their only way to stay in the business. No, I was sure they wouldn't risk complicity in a murder charge just to keep the band together.

Could Jim fool them, then? He and Jorie both had, on occasion, as they had fooled everyone else. But for how long? Candy could always tell them apart. Could he hope to fool her? And if he could not fool a fawn-eyed little idiot like her, how could he fool the others?

But if he couldn't fool her, maybe he could, in a way, buy her. Maybe if he was the closest thing to Jorandel left alive, and he offered her himself as Jorie never had, she would switch her allegiance without hesitation. It was hard to know whether she would hate him for killing Jorie, or be grateful to have won at last an approximation of her dream. If she was either fooled or willing to go along with the thing for the sake of being "Jorandel's" girl, would that help fool the others? Would they buy it? Or could it actually make them suspicious where they otherwise might not be, because "Jorandel" suddenly capitulated to the girl-child's charms?

If he couldn't fool her, and he couldn't buy her, would he kill her? It was that thought that led me, at last, to the realization that he must already have killed one of the people who could certainly not be fooled, and be planning the death of the other. Andy and Frank, the brothers' closest friends, would not mistake them for each other. I'd have thought Andy might even go along with the whole ugly plan for Jim's sake, but maybe he had refused. Maybe that was why he had to be got out of the way first.

Which meant Frank and Candy were both in terrible danger now, as well as Jorandel—if he survived this night. It also meant this night must have been either an accident or Jorandel's own intention, since an overdose when he was clearly in his own persona would not serve Jim's purpose.

That thought drew me up short. I had no real reason in the world to imagine Jim a murderer. Particularly not a sly and wily plotter of his own brother's death. I had just absolved Jorandel of injuring his brother simply on the basis of my belief that neither of them could intentionally cause the other serious harm: could I reasonably go from that to accusing Jim of intending Jorie's murder?

The two of them were successful at the twin-switch not so much because they were alike as because they were the same: two parts of one whole. Neither would be complete without the other. Poor as they were at thinking things through, I couldn't believe they didn't know that. And the love that I had seen between them, the automatic gestures of affection, the instinctive drawing together against the world, surely proved that neither of them could seriously wish the other dead. How could he? It would be like killing your Siamese twin. It would be like tearing out your own heart. It was impossible . . . wasn't it?

"You are quiet," said Jim.

I realized suddenly that I had been staring at him for several minutes, and that he had been returning my look with increasing amusement. "Oh," I said stupidly. "I was, um."

"You were wondering whether I had deliberately given my brother an overdose," he said.

"What?" said Candy. She was bundled in a warm robe now, but she still looked cold.

"No," I said, not quite steadily enough. Both brothers' habit of knowing or at least guessing one's thoughts was unnerving. "Why, did you?"

"No." He grinned. "But if I had, would I admit it?"

"But why would you?" asked Candy, staring.

"What, OD Jorie?" he asked, and shrugged ineffably. "I can't think. Ask Cousin Rosie. It was her idea."

"No, it wasn't," Candy said ingenuously. "It was you who said it."

"Ah, but it was Cousin Rosie who thought it."

"You can't tell what she thinks."

"Oh, for God's sake," I said.

Those wide fawn eyes turned to me, all innocence. "What? He can't tell, can he?" she asked.

"Of course not." I sounded a good deal more sure than I felt. His guess had been just a little too damn close for comfort. "He just thinks he can read my expression." I looked at him. "In fact, you were pretty close. Only I wasn't thinking you'd done it, I was wondering whether someone had. Because you said someone did it to Andy. Someone could just as easily do it to Jorandel, couldn't they?"

His expression turned ugly for just a fraction of a second; but he controlled it, and his voice remained mild and apparently indifferent. "I was just talking when I accused Jorie of that," he said.

"But he could have done it?" I said.

"Probably." He hesitated, studying me, then produced a rueful smile. "I was angry with Jorandel for sending Andy away. But he couldn't know Andy was depressed already. He did give Andy drugs for Christmas, you know, but I doubt if he gave him anything Andy couldn't have handled if he wanted to. The problem was, Andy wasn't really experienced with drugs, and he was probably feeling lonely, in the way you humans have." He shrugged wearily. "Shit happens."

"You think he just did it on purpose? Andy?"

"More or less, perhaps," he said ambiguously.

"Jorie does it all the time," said Candy.

"Does he?" I asked.

"Well, yes," she said impatiently. "Look at tonight."

"He does, you know," said Jim. "That is, he overdoses fairly often. I don't know whether it's entirely by accident or not. You know Jorandel. He plays dangerous games."

"So does somebody else around here, by the look of things," I said.

"What do you mean?" asked Candy.

Jim just looked at me. After a moment's hesitation I decided it wouldn't be entirely out of character to show a little intelligence. "Look what's happened just since I came along with you," I said, answering Candy. "Jorie fell or was pushed downstairs, Andy overdosed, Jim got beat up—" I glanced at him and added in clear disbelief, "Or maybe fell downstairs. And now Jorie's overdosed. Even if you say the overdoses are part of the natural order of life in an elfrock band—which I suppose they may well be, come to that—surely you don't claim that two people falling downstairs within two days of each other is also a common occurrence."

"It is not beyond the realm of possibility," said Jim, grinning indulgently. "Springs from the same source, you know. Or haven't you noticed that drugs and drink can make even Truebloods clumsy?"

This was getting us nowhere. "Where do you guys get your drugs?" I asked abruptly.

"I get mine from the Roach," Candy said innocently.

"Yes, but where does he get them?"

"You still believe that someone gave Jorandel a hot shot?" asked Jim.

"If you mean do I think somebody made him overdose," I said, and paused. I didn't know what to think, anymore. He probably hadn't been made to overdose, if Jim meant to kill him and take his place, and at this point that was the only theory that fit all the facts. Still, I could hardly say that. "I did wonder," I said, "whether he used the same drugs he gave Andy. I mean from the same batch, you know? If it was too pure and killed Andy, the same thing could've happened to Jorie."

Jim shrugged. "It is possible. Street drugs are notoriously unreliable, as you may know," he said. "It seems late to worry about that now."

"I wish Frank would call," said Candy.

Jim glanced at his watch. "It's soon yet." He looked at her with something very like sympathy. "Don't worry, urchin. He'll be fine."

"I just wish Frank would call," she said stubbornly.

I did, too, but it seemed pointless to say so. "Where's everybody else?" I asked Jim, thinking a change of subject might distract Candy from her worry. "Surely they're not all demurely in bed already like good little boys?"

"Killer is," he said. "Not alone, of course, but probably asleep by now. Blade and the Roach went in search of a party, or so I'm told. They were gone already when I got back from the hospital." He picked up a handy guitar, tried idly to finger a chord, and hurled it away when his injured arm hurt him.

Candy watched it collide with the back of a couch and clatter to the floor. "I wish Jorie had gone with them," she said wistfully.

I lost patience with her suddenly. "And I wish I had

a million dollars," I said crossly. "Hell of a lot of good wishing does anybody."

"I just meant," she said meekly, and let her voice trail off uncertainly.

"Oh, hell," I said. "I know what you meant. I'm sorry. I'm worried, too. It makes me cranky."

"Have some more soda," she said brightly. "It'll help. Really." She took some herself.

"Oh, God," I said, watching her.

Jim grinned knowingly. "Clutches of evil, cousin."

Jorie's voice. Jorie's words, from before I knew him. Jorie's name for me, now that I did know him. "Damn you," I said bitterly.

"That's been seen to," he said mildly.

I stared. "What?"

There were shadows in his eyes again, belying the impudent grin with which he mocked me. "Just do the soda and shut up, cousin," he said.

I did the soda. Don't ask me why. It was there, it was offered, I did it. It was going to be a long night.

Blade and the Roach came in, drunk and rowdy, with giggling women hanging on their arms, about two in the morning. Jim, who hadn't been doing any soda, was beginning to fade by then, but Candy and I were preposterously wide-eyed and alert. Frank hadn't called yet. Candy had been solicitously trying to get Jim to go to bed, telling him she'd wake him when Frank called, but she stopped when Blade and the Roach came in, and watched their progress across the common room with expressionless interest.

"You guys still up?" the Roach asked blearily.

"As you see," said Jim.

"Where's the party?" said Blade.

"Wherever you left it," said Candy.

The Roach and his woman found that hilarious. Blade, perhaps slightly less drunk than the Roach, perceived that no one else was amused, and scowled in ponderous thought for a moment. "Something wrong," he said at last, with the air of a man having solved a meaty problem. "Whass happen?"

"Jorie's overdosed," Candy said in the vibrant tones of a tragedy queen.

"What, dead?" said the Roach, alarmed.

" 'Course not," said Blade, before any of us could answer. "Killer's luau tomorrow. Wouldn miss that."

This reasoning seemed to satisfy the Roach.

"He might be dead," Candy said accusingly, as though the two of them were responsible.

"Fact," said the Roach, much struck. "Don't know he isn't. Haven't seen him."

"Ought to see him," said Blade, looking owlishly around the room for him.

"Well, you can't," said Candy. "He's in the hospital, and we're waiting for Frank to call to say how he is."

"Who's Jorie?" the blonde on Blade's arm asked contentiously. She seemed to need Blade's support to stay on her feet.

"You know, Jorandel," said the brunette on the Roach's arm, with a conspiratorial shushing motion.

The blonde looked startled. "Jorandel?"

"Yeah," said the brunette, nodding.

"Oh," said the blonde, her eyes wide with awe. The two of them tried to look serious and sober, and failed rather spectacularly, since neither of them could stand steadily upright even with assistance.

"Frank's with him," Blade told the Roach.

The Roach thought about it. "That's all right, then." Clearly, if Frank were with him, nothing would go amiss.

"Yes," said Blade. "All taken care of, right as rain." He grinned suddenly, remembering the blonde clinging to his arm. How he could have forgotten her for even a moment, when her clinging presence was dragging him heavily to one side the whole time they stood there, I don't know, but he clearly had, and was delighted to discover her. "Going to bed," he announced decisively, struggling for balance.

"Good." She giggled.

"Nothing else to do," said the Roach, nodding wisely. The four of them trooped unsteadily across the room and, with some brief confusion, down the short corridor toward the men's two rooms. I thought I heard one of the women announce that she was going to be sick, just before the doors slammed behind them.

"Ugh," said Candy, shuddering delicately.

Jim glanced at her. "You're quite the little hypocrite."

"I'm not!" she said, offended.

"Oh, stop it, both of you," I said.

"Yes, Mama," said Jim, grinning derisively.

"I wish Frank would just call," Candy said plaintively.

But it was another hour and a half before he called; and then the news he gave us, while encouraging, was not the satisfactory resolution we'd hoped for. Jim took the call, responded in monosyllables, looked moderately cheered when he rang off, and told us, "He says he's not in a coma, but his recovery is not yet assured. He means to stay at the hospital with him, and he suggests we go to bed. There will be no more news till morning."

I untangled his pronouns with weary deliberation while Candy, more accustomed to him, said uncertainly, "If he's not in a coma then he'll be all right, won't he?"

Jim shrugged, his eyes unreadable. "Probably. Go to bed, urchin. Would you like a downer to put you to sleep?"

"I couldn't sleep," she said. "Not till we know."

He limped back to his chair and sat in it heavily, watching her. "Have you forgotten Killer's luau tomorrow?"

"I won't go," she said.

"Not even if Jorandel does?"

"Oh, if he does," she said.

"Then you ought to get some sleep, or you'll be in no fit condition for it," he said. I was surprised at the gentleness in his voice. "He'll be okay, urchin, and ten to one he'll go to the luau. Let me get you a downer, okay?"

"I've got some," she said doubtfully.

"Then take one, and go to sleep." He glanced at me. "You, too, cousin," he said firmly.

He was right. There was no sense staying up, but the last thing in the world I felt like doing was going to sleep. "Yeah," I said, sounding as dubious as Candy. "Okay. I will."

He grinned. "Candy'll give you a downer."

"Jeez, I've taken enough drugs already," I said.

"Not if you want to sleep tonight, you haven't," he said. "Don't be a prig. One downer won't hurt you."

That wasn't necessarily true, and we both knew it, but I was dazed enough at that point by drugs and exhaustion that I responded automatically to his tone of authority, obeyed him, and went to bed.

The hangover from mixed soda and sleeping pills was not as uncomfortable as one from soda and too much booze, but it wasn't a jolly experience, either. I didn't wake till nearly noon, and didn't want to get up then. My whole body felt leaden, my head stuffy, my mind stupefied, and I'd had bad dreams. I wanted to turn over and go back to sleep, but fear of further dreams kept me from that. I lay for a long time staring at the ceiling, wondering whether I could possibly summon the energy to go take a shower; and whether, if I did, it would clear my head at all.

Then I remembered the soda. I still had the bottle Candy had given me, refilled again last night. That would clear my head. "Don't be stupid," I told myself. Myself didn't listen. And it did clear my head.

I knew better than to use drugs recreationally, and yet I had been doing it almost since I joined Cold Iron's entourage. I had accepted Candy's money, and her drugs, and her friendship, and repaid her by falling in love with the man she loved. By, in fact, sleeping with him. And letting him be pushed downstairs and overdose himself on drugs, instead of figuring out who wanted to kill him.

Unless last night's wild fancies about Jim were correct; but in sober daylight I couldn't believe them. Neither of the brothers could possibly want to harm the other. That had been a ridiculous, drugged fantasy, as useless as anything else I'd done since leaving the Bay Area. If I had any decency I'd resign, return Candy's money, and go home.

Yes, crawl home to Shannon and her damn Christmas tree, and admit I'd been an ass to fight with her over it. Right. Exactly what I was most eager to do. Damn it, I hadn't been an ass to fight with her over the tree, she'd been an ass to insist on bringing it to the office when she knew I didn't want it.

Besides, if I went home now, I'd never see Jorandel again. I wasn't ready for that. Maybe—probably—there was no place in his life for me, at least not on a long-term basis. I wasn't even sure I wanted a place in his life, really. But I knew I couldn't walk away yet. I'd be leaving too much unfinished business behind me.

And I might be leaving his murderer an open field. I hadn't talked to Emerson since Jim was attacked. Maybe he would believe me now. More likely he would point out, as Jim had, that drugs make people clumsy, and that if it was an attack it was Jim not Jorie who had suffered it. If Jorie had been attacked again he might have believed me. But he hadn't been. Unless whoever attacked Jim had thought he was attacking Jorie.

Of course. God, I was slow. My whole construction against Jim last night had been based on the idea that they could pass for one another, and it hadn't occurred to me that they could also, even when they didn't intend it, be *mistaken* for one another. That would explain everything. It was a much more rational idea than that Jim was plotting his brother's murder. Someone, meaning to attack and maybe even this time to kill Jorie, had got Jim instead, and had either realized his mistake in time, or perhaps been frightened away before he could complete the job. The fact that Jim's injuries happened to match Jorie's was pure coincidence, after all. It wasn't all that improbable. Curious, but not impossible.

Heartened by this apparent revelation, I hauled myself out of bed. I wanted to find out how Jorie was doing, and to talk to Emerson, and to get together with Candy to make her go over her story one more time. Maybe there was some clue in it that I had missed on the first telling. At that time I hadn't even believed in the idea of a potential murderer. Now I did. It was time to do some real digging to find the culprit and to prevent him from accomplishing his goal. No more wild flights of fantasy for me: it was time to act like a real detective for a change.

The real detective, sanguine after a strong dose of soda, sang in the shower, dressed afterward in a trendy teenager costume, and returned to the common room in time to witness another Cold Iron battle.

15

It was only Jim and Jorie expressing heartfelt dissatisfaction with each other. Their hotel bills must have been prodigious. You have to pay quite a lot to be allowed to stay in a place you tend to destroy on a daily basis. And I thought someone in the entourage must be quite a diplomat, because money alone could not be enough to placate a hotel staff confronted with as much breakage and willful damage as Cold Iron tended to provide.

No one was making the smallest effort to stop them. There were three bodyguards present (although not Frank, whose responsibility they both were), two musicians besides them, four groupies, and Candy, and they were all just watching, as at a freak show. Which, in a sense, it was. A perfectly matched pair of elfrock stars hurling furniture and curses at each other like distempered children was a sight that people at a carnival would have paid good money to see.

When I had to duck an airborne stereo speaker I lost my cool. I suppose an appropriate reaction would have been anger, or even fear; they were both of them enraged, and probably psychotic, and certainly dangerous. But it was just too silly, the pair of them imagining they were such serious grown-ups, arrogant and important and earnest about their all-important image, and behaving like spoiled infants. I burst out laughing.

It stopped the fight, anyway. The moment they realized what they were hearing they both froze for a long second of startled incredulity, then turned on me in such a perfectly synchronized movement, identically outraged, that I laughed even harder. Since both were still gripping objects they'd meant to hurl at each other, though, I did have sense enough to assume as defensive a posture as

I could manage. "I'm sorry," I said helplessly. "You just look so damned silly!"

It wasn't a remark perfectly contrived to soothe their possibly wounded egos, but for a wonder it worked. They looked at me, looked at each other, made a last and rather obvious effort to retain their fury, and finally succumbed to the lively sense of the ridiculous that was their saving grace. I don't know which of them was the first to give way, but in a moment we were all three laughing.

Everyone else in the room continued to stare as at a freak show. Only now I was part of it. Well, I'd spent time in worse company. "You looked less than dignified yourself, cousin," said a brother. I hadn't yet sorted them out, so I didn't know which.

"With your arms up to defend your head," said the other, finishing his brother's sentence. "You looked as though you didn't know whether to laugh or run."

"And you looked like a pair of bad-tempered brats," I said. "What is it with you two, anyway? Has either of you ever got through a single day without flinging furniture at someone?"

"Only by flinging other objects instead," said one of them, eyes dancing. I decided that was Jorie: his bruises looked older, and now that I'd had a chance to study them, he seemed the leaner of the two. But their hair was in such disarray that I couldn't tell which had bangs, and in their mutual amusement they looked more alike than ever. I had never seen Jim laugh at himself before. It improved my opinion of him to know him capable of it.

"It wouldn't hurt either of you to exercise a little self-control," I said severely.

"Yes, Mama," said Jim. But he was smiling.

We were beginning to lose our audience, all of them but Candy turning to other interests. She went unerringly to Jorie and said with shy solicitude, "Are you all right? Shouldn't you sit down?" To me she added confidingly, "He shouldn't even be out of the hospital, only he wouldn't stay no matter what they said."

"I'm fine," he said impatiently, and glanced at Jim with a question in his eyes.

Jim smiled ruefully. "Don't ask," he said, and backed suddenly into the nearest chair with one hand pressed cautiously over the bruise on his forehead.

"Me, too," said Jorie. He sat down more carefully than Jim, and pressed both hands to his head. "Earth defend us."

"You're both idiots," I said. "What the hell were you fighting over, anyway?"

"Oh, nothing," said both of them.

"Whether Jorie should've left the hospital," said Candy.

"Oh." I looked at Jim. "You thought if he wouldn't stay in the hospital, maybe you should break a bone or two that would put him back in, is that it?"

Jorie laughed. "Hey, it could have worked."

Jim looked belligerent for a moment, then grinned. "Not quite that, cousin," he said, "but my brother is right. It could have worked."

"If I hadn't put you in the hospital instead," said Jorie.

"Do you truly believe you could?" said Jim.

"Cut it out," I said, "while there's still some furniture left fit to use."

That made them both grin. "Okay, cousin," said Jorie. "Just to spare your sensibilities, we'll call a truce. That is, if my little brother is prepared to agree to it?"

"Fuck off," said Jim. But he was still smiling, and although Jorie looked at him quite steadily as if in expectation of a clearer capitulation, Candy seemed ready to assume their dispute was resolved.

"Can I get you anything, Jorie?" she asked.

"No, go away," he said, not unkindly. "I need to talk to Alec. Where is he?"

"I'll get him," she said eagerly.

"Fine," he said, and watched her departure with a weary shake of his head. Confident that he found me at least as superfluous as he had found her, I turned to leave, but he stopped me. "Where do you go, cousin?" he asked, reaching for my hand.

"To find some coffee," I said, but I let him catch my hand, and waited to see what he wanted.

"I have a new song to show you," he said. "I wrote it last night."

"In the hospital?"

"Before that," he said impatiently. "Here, Jim, hand me that guitar." He gestured toward an acoustic guitar leaning against Jim's chair. Jim lifted it with his good hand and dutifully held it out toward Jorie. I took it from him, and Jorie released my hand to take it from me. "Thanks," he said shortly. It took him a moment to find a position in which he could play it despite his injured arm.

"Don't you guys have a concert tomorrow night?" I asked suddenly.

"Yeah, why?" He strummed a minor chord.

"Jim's arm," I said, looking at Jim. "Will you be able to play?"

"Of course," said Jim.

Jorie, clearly not having considered this, frowned at him. "Are you sure, little brother?"

"Yes, yes," said Jim, as though we'd been nagging for hours. "Show us your song, Jorandel."

Shrugging, Jorandel strummed another chord, found a rhythm, and began very quietly to sing. I suppose I shouldn't have been surprised at the lyrics. The mockery in Jorandel's eyes should have warned me. The subject was the same as in "Janie's Got a Gun."

I decided what I needed was not coffee but gin. And breakfast. I needed breakfast, too. Not in the suite. I would go downstairs to the restaurant. I wasn't hungry, but I had to get away from there. I didn't really even understand why, only that I could not stay. This was worse than Christmas music. Worse than "Janie's Got a Gun." It was worse than anything.

I put down the gin and looked at Jorandel, trying to control a suffocating panic that said this was the end of the world, impending doom, nuclear weapons about to immolate the universe. Jorandel smiled as he sang, sweet and innocent and deadly. Jimendan had found another guitar and was trying to pick out an accompaniment, but his injured arm hampered him. Jorandel didn't seem to notice. He was watching me: I could feel his gaze even when I turned away.

He knew exactly how to get through a person's defenses. The lyrics of "Papa's Little Girl," Cold Iron's last double-platinum single, were not in their final form that morning, and even the melody changed somewhat before it was finally released, but it had that disturbing quality already that seems to be what people admire most about it. I can listen to it now. I can even admire the genius of its musical composition, if not its lyrics. At the time, it literally made me nauseous. I think Jorandel knew perfectly well that it would. I know he intended it to upset me.

I don't know why. I mean, it was one of his pastimes, of course, testing people, upsetting them, seeing how far he could push them and what would happen when he found their limits. But that wasn't all there was to it. When he first played the song for me he had the same look in his eyes that he'd had when he told me, the previous morning, "Your father fucked you." He meant to be provocative, he meant to upset me, he may even have meant to push me away from him, but there was a hint of something more in it. A look not just of curiosity, but also of a kind of sympathy, and a certain trepidation as well. I wondered, even then, whether he might not be trying, in his twisted and rather brutal way, to do me a kindness.

Some kindness. I escaped the suite before my heaving stomach betrayed me, but when I'd gone a few steps down the corridor and quite out of range of the music I had to stop with one hand on the wall for support while I waited for the panic to subside. I hated Jorandel. I hated Cold Iron, I hated elfrock music, I hated myself. I wanted to cry. Or throw up. Or die. I wanted to run, and keep on running, till I found the end of the world or at least the end of civilization—some peaceful place where there were no people, no holidays, no singers, no songs.

But in fact I couldn't go anywhere at all. I couldn't even go to the restaurant downstairs. I hadn't brought my purse with me. I hadn't brought anything with me, because the trendy costume I'd selected didn't have pockets, and in my panic I hadn't thought to bring anything I wasn't wearing. I could go exactly as far as I could walk.

If we'd still been in L.A. I think I would have started walking for the Bay Area and damn the consequences. Some five hundred miles is a good long walk, but it sounded preferable right then to going back into the Cold Iron suite. Perhaps it was as well that we were more like two thousand miles from my home, and that most of those miles were across water. I might have tried walking, but I knew quite well I couldn't swim that far.

Reality can be so damned trying. I stood there, with my stomach feeling a little steadier but my knees still wobbly, staring blindly at the hotel's ugly gold carpet, and considering my options. I could, of course, go for a walk on the glorious tropical beach outside, only it was bound to be thick with tourists, and I wanted to be alone. But that was about all I could do without first going back into the suite to get my purse. I was afraid to go back for my purse. They might still be playing that song. They probably were. I didn't want to hear it.

Your father fucked you.

What do you say to a line like that? "Yes, and I killed him?" Oh, God. What was I thinking?

"Rosie? Are you all right?" It was Candy, bringing Alec Reich to Jorandel as requested. I stared at her, just able to comprehend that I knew her, that she had spoken to me, that I ought to answer her. I couldn't remember what the question was. "Alec," she said, "you better go on in." She pushed him toward the suite. "He wants you now."

"He wants everything now," he said sourly, but he went, a busy little businessman, fussy and ridiculous.

Candy waited till the suite door closed behind him before she said, "You need some soda or something?"

"Oh, God," I said, still clinging to the wall for support.

"What happened?" she said. "What did they do to you?"

I shook my head. "Nothing. I—I'm all right. I just . . ." But there wasn't an end to that sentence, and my legs were going to give way at any second. Something dark and deadly scrabbled at the back of my mind. I would not think about it.

"You better come back inside, anyway," she said. "You don't look too good."

"No." I wanted to sit down, but this was a public corridor, and I had just enough presence of mind to remember rather primly, like a well-taught child, that one doesn't sit on the floor in a hotel's public corridor. It's not done. What would people think? I thought I heard my father singing Christmas carols.

"Then sit down, before you fall down," said Candy, and sat beside me with her back to the wall. "Come on, sit," she said. "You don't have to talk about it if you don't want to, but you might feel better."

"No." I stared down at her, trying to comprehend an altered universe. Something had happened. Something had shaken the foundations of my world, and I didn't want to know what it was, and I was afraid I did know. "I don't have to talk about what?" I said stupidly.

"Whatever upset you," she said patiently. "Rosie, sit down, okay?"

I sat. I remembered that one ought not to, but it didn't seem important. I didn't really have a lot of choice in the matter: my legs gave way and it was all I could do to complete the maneuver with reasonable grace instead of just crashing down beside her all angles and bones. "Nothing upset me," I said, blinking. There was a curious roaring sound in my ears, and I wondered dizzily why I couldn't seem to focus my eyes.

"Right," she said skeptically.

I leaned my head against the wall. "I didn't kill my father," I said. I sounded defensive, as though she had accused me. I didn't know why I'd said that.

She looked at me. "Did somebody say you did?"

That was it. "Yes." I nodded heavily, pleased with her comprehension. "Mama."

"Your mother said you killed your father?"

I nodded again, feeling sick and stupid, thinking of Christmas trees. Ridiculous to have forgotten. How could I have forgotten half my childhood? How could I have never noticed there was a blank space in my mind at least six years long? *Your father fucked you,* said Jorandel's voice. Was this what he meant to do to me? Make me remember? Make me know what I was running from? Make me understand why I was afraid of Christmas?

"Why?" asked Candy. "Why would she say that?"

"Because she wanted to believe it," I said. "God knows, I wanted to kill him. He f—" But I couldn't quite say it, not that bluntly. I swallowed hard, thought about it, and said, "He molested me," instead. That wasn't much better: I still felt dirty and defensive and used. "It scared me," I said. "It hurt me. I didn't want it. I didn't!" I sounded like a defiant child.

"I know," she said, but I hardly heard her.

"I didn't ask for it," I said. "I didn't. But how could I stop him? He was too big, too strong. He was my father!" It came out in a wail of desolation, of betrayed trust, of the awful lostness and littleness of the battered child. Tears spilled unnoticed down my cheeks. I knew now what the blind pink animal was that haunted my dreams. I remembered him thrusting it in my face, in my mouth. I had been so young when it started, I hadn't even understood it was a part of him.

And I knew now, too, why Kyriander Stone's father kept turning into mine, in my dreams. I had wished my father dead a hundred times, a thousand times, with every breath, with every waking thought, with every desperate and hopeless prayer to a god that did not save small children from despair. "The last time," I said, and swallowed again, eyes closed, remembering, wanting to forget. "Oh, God. It was, he pretended to make a game of it, he hid under or maybe behind the Christmas tree, I don't remember exactly, only that he—" My voice broke and I wondered dully whether I was going to be sick.

"You don't have to talk about it if you don't want to," Candy said, her voice almost as thin and small as mine. "I understand," she said.

I looked at her. When she had first come to the office, I wondered whether it was her boyfriend or her parents who had battered the poor fawn-eyed girl-child. I should have known it might very well be both. "You do, don't you?"

She nodded. "Daddy wouldn't leave me alone."

"So you ran away?"

She shrugged. "All the time. But he kept getting me back, till I hooked up with Cold Iron, and he knew I'd slept with all of them, and he said he washed his hands of me. He said I was a dirty little slut like he'd always said, and he wouldn't have anything more to do with me, and he wasn't my father anymore. And I was glad." She smiled crookedly. "I read in this book once that it happens to like one girl in five, or something. That's supposed to make you feel better. To know you're not alone. The book kept saying it wasn't my fault. But Daddy said it was."

"I know. My father said that, too. That he couldn't help himself because I was so cute and sexy." Intellect said it had been sick of him to believe that about an infant. But infants look at the world through the same eyes they'll use when they grow up. They don't see themselves as children, but as human beings, burdened by responsibility and an awful mixture of elusive power and hopeless vulnerability. I didn't remember my father with a child. I remembered him with me. "Oh, God." I shuddered and hugged myself, suddenly cold and lonely and desperately afraid, though I couldn't have said of what. "I'd forgotten. You know? I'd forgotten the whole thing. I'd forgotten why I left. Why Papa died. Why I hated Christmas, everything."

"He did it to you at Christmas?"

"The last time," I said, and realized there were tears dripping off my chin onto the front of my trendy blouse. I wiped them away with the back of my hand. "In front of the Christmas tree. I was eleven. I was as tall as I am now, but not as strong. I was all bone and baby fat, clumsy as a folding chair, and too scared of him to fight dirty even if I'd known how. There was loud Christmas music playing on the radio, so Mama wouldn't hear us. She was in the next room. I kept hoping she'd come in and stop him, but she didn't. I think she guessed what he was doing. I think she was careful not to find out for sure. So she didn't save me, and I couldn't get away from him till he was finished. Then I ran away, and . . . when I got in touch again, years later, Mama said he'd died. A heart attack, but she said it was because I ran away."

"Did you tell her then? What he'd done to you?"

"She didn't believe me."

She nodded. "I tried to tell my mom, but she wouldn't listen. She doesn't want to know."

"All this time, I never remembered any of it till now," I said, bewildered. "How is that possible? How could I have forgotten? How could I not notice such a big blank place in my past?"

"That book said a lot of people forget," she said. "It's a way of coping. What made you remember?"

"Jorandel wrote a song," I said, and shuddered again. "He saw I didn't like that Aerosmith song. He knew it made me uncomfortable."

" 'Janie's Got a Gun'?"

"Yeah. He guessed why I didn't like it. And I guess he—You know how he is. He wanted to—I don't know. To hurt me, maybe. Or just to see what would happen."

"He kind of can't help himself," she said. "He has to push the limits. His, everybody's. He has to know what's beyond."

"Is that what he told you?" I wiped my face with the heels of my hands. My chin wasn't dripping anymore, but my hands came away wet.

"Yes," she said innocently.

Well, I suppose it was as true as any other thing he might have told her to explain himself. He might even have believed it. Clearly, she did. "He's such an ass," I said.

"Oh, no," she said seriously., "He's really not, Rosie. It's just that he's a genius, and—"

"Save it. I've heard that one before."

"Well, he is," she said, "and—"

"And a sociopath," I said. "And there's somebody coming." The carpet muffled footsteps, but I could clearly hear voices approaching around a corner in the corridor, and I didn't want to be found sprawled on the floor like a child.

"So?" she said.

"So I expect we ought to get up," I said wearily.

"Why?" She really didn't know.

"You don't sit on the floor in public hotel corridors."

She giggled. "You do if you want to," she said. "What can they do? Arrest us?"

She was right, of course. The worst anyone could do to us was disapprove, and what was a little disapproval to a slut who'd had sex with her father? "I'm embarrassed," I said. *I didn't want it, I didn't ask for it, I didn't do it! It's not my fault!*

"Why?"

"I don't know. Because it's undignified, I guess." But it was too late to do anything about it; the voices had manifested themselves as the speakers came around the corner and into sight. At first glance I thought they were all strangers, and speaking a foreign language. Then I realized Killer was among them, and that what they were speaking was mostly English, but with that odd intonation of his intensified, and a smattering of unfamiliar words thrown in. They were all male, and all of much the same size and coloring as Killer, though he was the only one who wore his hair in his face. He wasn't the only one with pointy ears.

They were so engrossed in their conversation that they hadn't noticed us yet. "Oh," said Candy, "look, it's Killer!" She scrambled happily to her feet. "Killer, hi! Is everything ready? Did they dig the *imu* already? How soon will we go?" She plunged joyously toward them, all seriousness forgotten. "Hi, guys. I'm Candy. I'm with the band." She said that with clear pride.

While Killer introduced his friends to her I climbed to my feet more slowly, feeling old and very much in awe of her resilience. But then, she'd had longer than I to accustom herself to knowledge of the past. Maybe when I'd had time I would be reconciled. Now it was still new and newly repellent to me, as vivid and humiliating as if it had happened moments instead of years ago. *Your father fucked you.* I felt as though some stain of it must be visible to anyone who looked at me. I wanted a shower, and thought I would never feel clean again. It was all I could do to lift my head and greet Killer and his friends with equanimity, as though I were a decent, ordinary human to whom nothing filthy and degrading had ever been done.

If it showed, they were polite about it. It seemed to

me that Killer studied my face a moment when I first came up to them, but I couldn't be sure, since his hair hid his eyes. If he did, it was not in censure, and whatever he saw made him put a shyly impulsive arm around me during the introductions. I was absurdly grateful for such unexpected kindness. There was something infinitely reassuring about the warm bulk of his body against me, and the brotherly pressure of his big hand on my shoulder, and the unthinking kiss he bestowed on the top of my head. I shivered involuntarily and leaned, childlike, into the comfort of his embrace.

"Ho, da cold, eh, you?" he said, his accent thickened by association with his friends.

"A little," I said. "It's the air-conditioning, I expect." I made polite noises at the half-dozen strangers whose names I promptly forgot once I had acknowledged their introduction, and let him guide me with them back into the suite. It was warmer there. Jim and Jorie had abandoned their guitars and reassembled the stereo to play an elfrock CD I didn't recognize. I couldn't face either of them just then. But I didn't have to: once inside the door Killer gave my shoulder a final encouraging squeeze and released me, and in the ensuing bustle of introductions it was easy for me to escape to my room unnoticed. I grabbed a bottle of gin from the liquor cabinet on the way. Killer's friendship had warmed me, but there was still an icy core of horror within me that even gin might not dispel.

I thought Candy was engrossed, childlike, in the excitement of new arrivals, but I had hardly closed the door behind me when she knocked and then timidly opened it to peer in at me, those enormous fawn eyes shy and smiling. "Is it okay if I come in?" she said, her voice uncertain, but friendly.

"I'm okay, Candy," I said. "You don't have to leave the party."

"Oh, I know." She entered, closing the door behind her. "Let's do a little soda and both go back out, okay?" She settled on the edge of my bed to lay out lines of soda on a little mirror without waiting for my agreement. What the hell. I swallowed gin and watched her. When she had the lines laid out she glanced up at me like a child hoping for approval. "It might make you feel better," she said.

I did the soda. And it did make me feel better, at least marginally. I was still offended by the existence of my own body, tool of my father's repellent pleasures, an obscene object I was obliged by unkind gods to live within. But maybe if I took enough soda, I would begin to believe it possible to live with my body, and the memory of what had been done to it.

"When I was little," she said thoughtfully, "I used to imagine how much nicer it would be if people didn't have to have bodies, just heads." I stared: like Jorie, she knew too well what I was thinking. But I shouldn't have been surprised. She had been through this before me. "I thought that was all we really needed," she said. "Just heads to think and talk with." She sighed, smiling at past foolishness. "But then I figured out you need lungs to breathe so you can talk, and a heart to get blood to your brain, and legs to walk around on to get to food and that, and arms to feed yourself. I had to justify every body part, piece by piece like that, and I still felt like there should've been an easier way. A cleaner way. So that we could have just decent parts, and not hurt each other."

"No reproductive parts, you mean."

She nodded soberly. "Yeah. But then we couldn't reproduce, and there'd be just one generation of us and no more. So then I wished we would be like ferns or something. You know, have spores, and not have to touch each other." She grinned crookedly. "Only I do like touching. I felt so isolated, and you keep going to bed with people hoping you can get closer to them, you know?" She shrugged. "And it didn't matter, since Daddy said I was a slut already. But it's so hard. Sometimes it seems like even when you're having sex you're not really close to anybody."

"I know." I looked at her and after a moment's hesitation said, "You know I went to bed with Jorie."

"Oh, sure," she said lightly.

"You don't mind?"

"Nah," she said, not looking at me.

"Candy, I'm sorry." It wasn't an apology for going to bed with him. I didn't know quite what it was for.

She looked up, and those urchin eyes met mine steadily, the hurt in them a deep thing, isolated, uncritical, accepting. "I know," she said. "It's all right." She was silent for a moment, gazing past me at nothing. "He likes you," she said. "I think he likes you a lot." Another moment of silence, and her gaze met mine again. "I'm glad."

"Oh, Candy." But there was no doubting the honesty of that open gaze. She was much more complicated and in many ways more mature than I had guessed. "I'm sorry," I said again, helplessly. "Hell of a lot of good I've done you. I haven't protected him from anything. I haven't found out who wants to kill him. All I've done is spend your money and end up in bed with him."

"And make him happy," she said.

"Right," I said. "That's why he overdosed last night."

"Oh, that," she said, dismissing it with a wave of one nail-bitten hand.

"About that conversation you overheard," I said. "The one that made you hire me." She looked at me, waiting. "I had the feeling there was more about it you would've told me, only you didn't quite trust me then."

"Oh," she said, thinking. "Well . . . it wasn't that I didn't trust you, really, only that it was kind of silly."

"What was?"

"Just that when I first heard the voices," she said sheepishly, "I thought Jim and Jorie were both there. But when you think what they said, and hitting Jorie . . . well, that can't be right."

I wished it couldn't. But it fit too well. If true, it made it an ugly certainty that Jim had not been mistaken for Jorie last night: he had caused his own injuries, so that he could more easily pass for Jorie. He must, in that long-ago encounter in San Francisco, have tried to get Jorie to go along with his little masquerade, on a temporary basis, and then decided to kill him and make it permanent only because Jorie refused. It must have been he who searched my room, who hired thugs to keep me busy while he pushed his brother down a flight of stairs, who found some way to lure Frank away at the same time, and who later provoked Andy's overdose. He had motive, and opportunity, and I did not want to believe he had done it.

"I don't suppose you've remembered who Jorie had recently threatened to fire when you overheard this fight?" I asked.

"It could've been anybody," she said helplessly. "Or everybody. You've seen how he is."

"Yes." Although the musicians chose their own bodyguards, Jorie hired them all, so it could have been Andy he'd threatened to fire. But if that had angered Jim enough to attack Jorie when Candy overheard them, would he then have killed Andy himself when Andy wouldn't go along with the proposed murder of Jorandel?

Probably. If he was willing to kill his brother, what was a mere bodyguard beside that? Anyway, Andy's death might have been an accident. Still, the question provided a minor barrier against the grotesque probability of fratricide.

"You suspect somebody, don't you?" said Candy.

"Don't ask," I said.

"Okay," she said, willingly enough. "Let's do some more soda and go see what the guys are doing."

I was about to accept the offer when I finally came to my senses. I didn't want soda. I wanted the courage, the hope, the illusion of euphoria soda would give me, but that was the problem: it was an illusion. I'd been living with too many illusions for far too long. "Let's just go see what the guys are doing and forget the soda," I said. It wasn't an easy decision, and I wasn't half sure I could stick to it, but it was the first smart thing I'd done since joining the Cold Iron entourage. If I did stick to it, who knew? Maybe I'd even be able to do what I'd been hired to do.

16

Before we went back to the common room, I asked Candy where Jorie got his drugs. There was still at least a distant chance that Andy's death and Jorandel's overdose were the result of Jorie having been given dope that was too strong; that someone other than Jim was plotting Jorie's death. But she didn't know Jorie's source. The Roach got his soda from Veladora, and she thought Jim got his downers from one of the roadies, but Jorie might get his anywhere. People, she said, were always giving them drugs, besides what they bought, so there was really no way to know where a particular batch came from, unless Jorie happened to remember.

I wasn't sure I could ask him. I wasn't sure I could talk to him at all. My self-image was of a person who could handle anything—even an involuntary, incomprehensible, and unbreakable bond with a cold-blooded and psychotic elfrock star who deliberately made me remember things I didn't want to know—but I carried my gin with me when we went back into the common room. I wasn't quite ready to handle anything wholly unaided. My knees were still weak, my hands shook, and I had a disconcerting tendency to cry.

It wasn't until we came into the common room to find Christmas music playing on the stereo that I realized the deepest emotion I felt was not humiliation, or pain, or anguish, or even guilt. It was outrage. Sheer, unadulterated fury: at Jorandel, for having deliberately made me remember; at my father for having done what I remembered; and at my mother for having known, and never saved me. The hot tears that prickled the back of my eyes were of rage, not of pain or self-pity.

Jorie smiled when he saw me: his sweet boy smile,

artless and beguiling and utterly ingenuous. "Hi, cousin," he said. "Are you well?"

"I'm fine, Jorie," I said, though I wasn't. That was perhaps his greatest talent besides the music, that ability to disarm and bewitch when he didn't want conflict. It was almost certainly magic of a sort, elven glamour, and if there was any defense against it I never knew what it was. The odd thing was that as skilled as he was at manipulating people, he didn't seem to realize the power of that one apparently involuntary trick. He never used it as he might have, to deliberately set people up for the kill. Maybe that's why it worked so well.

Candy had gone directly to Killer and his group of friends and was chatting with them excitedly. Jorie watched her for a moment and then looked at me. "You use too much soda," he said abruptly.

I stared. "Jeez, any is too much, Jorie, but I sure didn't expect to hear that from you."

"I don't like to see you get started." His eyes were shadowed, unreadable. "You were clean when we met you. I wouldn't be surprised to hear you didn't even drink, then."

"Not as much," I said. "But why the sudden concern? What's this about?" I felt curiously as though he were trying to shut me out, to make me an outsider again.

He seemed to consider the question quite seriously. "I don't know," he said, sounding surprised. "I suppose . . . I know what an easy pit it is to fall into," he said. "It was for me. I'm always in control, you see." He didn't have to tell me that; I'd seen it. He could not relinquish control no matter how he tried. He could lose his temper, lose interest, lose patience, but he couldn't lose control. "That is probably a large part of why I do drugs," he said. "Trying to let go, you know? Trying to let life happen instead of making it happen, trying to find out what it's like not to have to hang on so hard all the time. But there's a part of me that is ever watching, judging, deciding how I'll act and seeing how other people react, and it's the last part of me to go. I have to be half dead before that lets go, before I can really do anything totally unconsidered, spontaneous, unintentional." His lips pulled upward at the corners in a wry smile. "And that's not much use when you're half dead. There's little enough you can do in that condition."

"I know all this, Jorandel," I said. "What's it got to do with me?"

"Only that I don't think you're that kind of person, I think you are the kind that can let things happen, and when you do all this soda, you might be letting something happen that you don't want. That's all."

"You think I haven't thought about it?"

"I think you haven't thought enough, or you'd stop."

He was dead serious. I almost laughed. "Jorie, for God's sake. A temperance lecture from you is just plain ludicrous."

He nodded. "Because I do drugs."

"That, and because you damn well don't do them only for the reasons you've just said. You do them to kill the pain. You've said so."

"I have also said it doesn't work."

"I could've told you that before you started. So? Does that stop you? Does it stop anybody? Hell, why should it? You can't kill it, but you can step outside it for a little while, make it just a weight you carry, a goddamn parasite, and that's worth it, isn't it?"

"Is it?" he said. "When you know that as soon as the drugs and drink wear off it will creep back inside, bigger and stronger and deadlier than ever?"

"I don't believe we're having this conversation." I shrugged. "I don't know whether it's worth it. A week ago I'd have said certainly not. Now I can only say I doubt it. But it's hard to make an intelligent choice when you're frightened and hurt and you've got chemical courage and painkiller, effective or not, at your fingertips. You tend to grasp at straws, however frail or foolish. Okay?" He had goaded me into admissions I had not thought I would make, and the realization angered me. "Damn it, what do you want from me? I know you: you don't do a damn thing at random, and you don't do very damn much out of unadulterated kindness or concern for your fellow creatures either, so what is this? What do you care whether I drink or do drugs?"

"I like you," he said in apparently genuine confusion. "I am concerned for you."

I didn't suppose it was true, but it was flattering, and I knew I wasn't going to get a straighter answer out of him, so I let it go. "Well, if it's any comfort to you, I am concerned for me, too. And I'd already figured it out, about the soda. I haven't done much today, and I don't plan to do more. The ride up is good, but you come back down too hard, too fast, and too damn far. From now on I'm sticking to gin. It's more manageable. You can avoid the downside a lot easier. I don't like downsides."

He produced an odd little smile, diffident, almost sly. "I know," he said.

The smile didn't register: I'd just realized this was the opening I needed, to ask, "Jorie, where do you get your drugs?"

"From various sources; why?"

"Because I was thinking about what Jim said about Andy," I said. "About you giving him something too pure, and that's why he overdosed." He was scowling, but I ignored it. "When you overdosed last night I thought what if it was the same batch? What if it really was too pure, and you didn't know it? So then I wondered where you got the stuff, that's all."

"It is of no importance where I got it," he said. "What I did last night was my doing, no one else's. And nothing to do with Andy." He had stopped scowling, but there was something dark and deadly in the shadows of his eyes. "I should not have given Andy drugs. He was inexperienced with them. And I didn't know he was depressed. Jim ought to have told me."

"But last night," I said.

"Last night I just OD'd, child. A simple miscalculation. It wasn't the first time and likely it won't be the last. It happens. You ought to know that." That diffident smile again, not sly this time. "It's one of the reasons I worry about you and the Roach's nose candy. Soda is the easiest thing to miscalculate."

"Then shouldn't you be worried about Candy and the Roach, too?"

He shrugged ineffably. "They are none of my concern."

"Oh, and I am?"

He studied me seriously, those incredible eyes so vividly blue I thought a person could drown in them. "I hope so," he said.

He was trying to sucker me, and I didn't know why. "Yeah?" I meant to sound skeptical, but it came out too light. "And is the reverse true, then?"

That startled him. I was supposed to have been so flattered by his interest that I wouldn't ask conditions. "The reverse?" he said, and his eyes danced with sudden merriment. "That I am your concern?"

"Because if you are, maybe it's my turn to give a temperance lecture," I said.

"You would only waste your time."

"I know."

"Cousin," he said, "I think I love you."

"I know you do," I said. "As much as you're able. But that's not much, is it?"

He was easy to startle. Arrogance does that to a person. But he covered it well. "You think so ill of me?" he said, trying to make it a joke.

"Yes. But I love you anyway. You'll just have to make do with that."

His lips twitched. "You are a hard woman."

"Yeah."

"Oh, cousin." He let the smile out, and then a slow, reluctant chuckle to go with it. "I have never come closer to a proposal of marriage in my life."

"You'd only waste your time," I said, straight-faced.

"Would I?" That made him laugh again. "You know, I believe I might at that." He sobered abruptly. "You are wiser than you know, cousin."

"I know exactly how wise I am, elfrock star," I said. He was putting on his "famous elf" face, petulant and self-important. "Now don't go all grim and earnest and start talking about death and pain and drugs again. I bet if you worked at it you could enjoy yourself for minutes at a time without that or flinging furniture either."

I think he'd been about to throw something. The petulant glower had been darkening, but when I mentioned flinging furniture it startled a bark of helpless laughter from him, and the danger was past. When he had his mirth under control he said solemnly and with great dignity, "I must speak to the roadies about the arrangements for tonight. I hope you can endure the strain of losing my company for a while." Every time I started to think I'd seen all his faces, he surprised me with a new one.

"I'm devastated, of course," I said, "but I can handle it. I'm tough."

"Yes," he said. "I know."

For some time now, security people and roadies had been showing up to chat with Killer and his friends. Jorie crossed the room to join the group of them, to discuss the transportation of people and equipment to the other side of the island for Killer's luau. I stayed where I was, on a couch in a corner of the room, watching and listening. Blade came in, having acquired half a dozen groupies from somewhere that he wanted to bring along to the luau, and argued with Jorie at some length about whether they were really necessary.

"We'll need another limo," said Jorie. "This is become a fucking parade."

"That's okay," said Killer.

"It's not okay," said Jorie.

"Hey, the more, the merrier," said Blade. "The Roach'll want them, won't he, Candy?"

"Yes." She said it without bitterness or regret, clearly regarding it entirely as a practical matter, like which guitars and how many chairs will we need. "And Jim might, mightn't he, Jorie?"

"Fuck Jim," said Jorie.

"That's the point," said Blade.

In the end, the groupies were included, along with a surprising number of guitars and, hauled in a truck behind the limos, seemingly all the amplifiers and equipment needed to produce a full-scale concert. I didn't know what a luau was, but I had thought it was more to do with eating than with music. Clearly, at least when Cold Iron was involved, I had been wrong.

Killer later explained to me that strictly speaking, the word "luau" just meant a feast, but that when locals had a luau it usually did include some kind of music as well as food cooked in a pit in the ground called an *imu*. And when Cold Iron attended a luau, it was an opportunity for Jorandel to play with music he wasn't allowed to do in concert or on record. Thus the equipment: Cold Iron was going to do some serious jamming with local musicians, and no limits.

We left for the windward side of the island late in the afternoon, in a string of rented limousines with the equipment truck trundling along behind. Killer's family had a big ranch back up under those steep green jagged mountains in a valley all their own, with a spectacular waterfall like a ribbon of silver down the cliffs that formed a backdrop for the ranch like an emerald curtain across the sky. To reach it we passed through towns with names like Kaneohe and Kahaluu, along a highway named Kamehameha; and that's all I can say about where it was, because that's all I know. For much of the drive there was vivid turquoise ocean on one side of the road and jungled mountains on the other, so that I hardly knew which way to look. Even Jim and Jorie, who were in the car with me, took time out from their absentminded squabbling to stare at some of the more spectacular vistas.

Eventually we turned off the main highway onto a long, narrow road graveled with crushed white coral. Brooding banyans dappled the hot, slanting sunlight that shimmered on the white bodies of our limousines nosing their technological way through primeval green jungle. Vines as thick as my arm brushed the rooftops, dangling variegated leaves as big as a car door. And when we came out from under the trees it was into a broad sun-drenched meadow of tall grass strewn with wild orchids that nodded their purple heads sedately in the wind. This was truly how I had thought Hawaii would look: tropical splendor even more glorious than the travel books had promised.

It was while we were passing through that meadow, headed toward another thick stand of vine-shrouded trees, that I became aware of the suppressed tension in the car. I thought Jim and Jorie must have escalated their squabble while I was entranced by the view, but when I looked at them they were leaning against each other in perfect accord, like little boys again, the way they had been on the plane from San Francisco. Only they weren't asleep. They were wide awake and as wound up as I had ever seen them, almost rigid with excitement, impishly expectant grins tugging at the corners of their mouths.

I thought they were plotting a prank. I said, "What are you guys up to?" and they looked at me in bewilderment. "You both look like kids about to raid the cookie jar."

Jim just looked at me blankly. Jorie said, "We get to play," in a voice that made it sound like they were seldom allowed to.

"You mean music?" I said, confused. "You play almost all the time."

"Not like this," he said. "Tonight we play no Cold Iron trash. We're gonna *jam*."

"You do that all the time, in the hotel and stuff. What's so exciting about doing it at a luau?"

"Audience," he said. "Other musicians." When I still looked puzzled he shrugged indifferently and said, "Only wait. You'll see."

We had slid through forest shadows and out into another sunlit meadow with a huge house in the center of it. It was a rambling construction with as much open air as closed rooms under its sprawling shingled roof. Such walls as it had were painted brilliant white, glowing in the sun, with the dark mystery of the emerald mountains behind it. A towering waterfall misted the whole upper end of the valley behind the house. It was a fairy-tale setting, with cascades of vibrant bougainvillea blossoms in every color spilling over low, tumbled lava rock walls encrusted with lichen, wild orchids nodding in the sun by the roadside, mossy rocks glistening at the edge of a sparkling little pebbled streambed that ran under the road and away into the forest, and one sleek ginger tomcat distrustfully watching our arrival from its place of partial concealment behind potted anthuriums on the porch stairs.

The limousines pulled up in a row in front of the house. The tomcat, confirmed in its low opinion of us, poured itself off the stairs and streaked away. People spilled out of the house to greet us with flower leis as we climbed out of the limousines: women in brightly patterned muumuus, barefoot men in garish aloha shirts and tattered shorts, children in all stages of undress including one little dark-eyed, pointy-eared, thumb-sucking imp who wore nothing at all. They were all laughing, smiling, putting flower leis over people's heads and hugging, enveloping the entire band and its entourage in kindness.

I wanted to hang back and watch from the fringes, because I felt suddenly extraneous and uncertain in the face of such a lavish welcome, but I was inexorably gathered into the group with the others, given a fragrant flower lei and a hug, and bustled up onto the porch. Everyone wearing shoes removed them, the locals with an automatic and unthinking dexterity, and the rest of us with a certain embarrassed awkwardness. Leaving our shoes behind us, the whole laughing and chattering mass of us proceeded through an open and windy corridor to the backyard, where tables had been set up for the luau.

At a similar function on the mainland, there would have been chairs at the tables. Here there were pillows, straw mats, blankets, towels, squares of cardboard or carpet, anything to keep out the damp of the grass; and the tables were boards supported by cinder blocks, low enough to the ground that a person seated on a square of cardboard would be at exactly the right level to eat from them. At first glance I thought it would be uncomfortable, but actually the informality of it was very pleasant.

At one end of the tables there was a sort of bandstand, built of plywood sheets and forklift pallets, at the back of which a drum kit had been set out in the arrangement Killer preferred. They were not the drums he used in concert. I wondered whether they were his, kept here for visits perhaps, or left from some earlier time when he might have spent his holidays here with his relatives. It was silly, really; they could just as easily have been someone else's drums loaned for the occasion, or even a spare set of Killer's sent, for some reason, ahead of the truck that brought the rest of the equipment. But I thought they were his, and that they lived here, and for some reason that did more to make me feel at home here than any number of flower leis and hugs from strangers could have done.

Jorie was everywhere, greeting old friends and getting introduced to new ones, bouncing with excitement and grinning from ear to pointed ear. He had a guitar in one hand and fully half a dozen flower leis around his neck and, in his flowered shirt, tattered jeans, and bare feet, looked quite at home with Killer's friends and relatives. The only things that set him apart were the Trueblood pallor of his skin and the summer-blue of his eyes.

I had no idea which of these people were Killer's family and which were friends invited along for the occasion, but as far as I could tell, the Cold Iron elves and their entourage were the palest people there, and just about the only ones with blue eyes. The Trueblood musicians especially looked shockingly white in this crowd; and the halflings were paler than they might have been if they lived ordinary lives, awake in the daytime and occasionally in the sun. Even Killer looked almost unhealthy beside these golden-tanned folk, and he had the darkest complexion of any of us.

He brought his mother to meet me, introducing her simply as Vyla. She was a beautiful black woman, tall and stately with merry eyes. "It's a little overwhelming, isn't it?" she said sympathetically. "When I first came to Maunalani Ranch with my brand-new halfling husband in nineteen sixty-four I didn't know whether I was more in awe of this beautiful valley, or of the sheer number of his relatives." She smiled fondly at a pair of infants chasing a fat calico cat beneath our feet. "I miss them equally when I'm in California." She laughed and hugged Killer impulsively. "So I embarrass my son by popping up at Maunalani just when his band is passing through."

Killer returned her hug with no sign of embarrassment. "Ma says she'll come to the show tomorrow night," he said. "I figured maybe you and Candy could take care of her."

"Mom-sitting detail," grinned Vyla. "He thinks I need somebody to hold my hand."

"Maybe he thinks Candy and I need parental supervision," I said.

Killer grinned. "You'll be good for each other."

"Aren't you afraid I'll reveal your secrets?" asked Vyla. To me she added, "I didn't name him 'Killer,' you know."

"Ma," said Killer, grinning.

"We'll be just fine," I told him, and looked at Vyla. "Is this gonna be like Indiana Jones turning out to be named Henry?"

She laughed. "No, it's not that bad. It's only that I named him Kimo, which is the Hawaiian pronunciation of Jim and absolutely the most common fake name the beachboys adopt to impress the tourists, so when he was growing up here nobody ever believed him when he told them his name. My brother used to call him 'Killer' and when he was ten Killer decided that was his name. He wouldn't answer to Kimo anymore."

"Well, it works for an elfrock musician," I said, "but he might have run into difficulty if he'd decided to become a neurosurgeon."

She chuckled, looking across the yard at her son and his band mates as they fussed with instruments and amplifiers. "Oh, he was a drummer already," she said. "He used to drive us crazy with drumming on things, even when he was no bigger than this little guy here." She indicated the thumb-sucking naked imp I had seen at the front of the house, who was squatting nearby staring up at us in fascination. "We got him his first drum kit when he was five. He gave us no peace till we bought it—and no quiet afterward!" Her laugh was a delighted gurgle of mirth. "But that was one thing about living out here; at least there were no neighbors to complain."

Somebody began to play slack-key guitar. I glanced up in time to see Jorandel join her with an amplified acoustic guitar. Killer climbed up behind the drums, an enormous stranger with a tiny ukulele in his arms sat on the edge of the band platform to pick out an accompaniment to Jorie and the slack-key player, Jim plugged in an electric guitar, and the music began. Blade came bounding out of the house with an electric bass on one arm and a groupie on the other, hauled her onto the bandstand with him, and plugged in the bass. Another slack-key player sat down beside the groupie and casually leaned against her while he played. The Roach came out of the house with another groupie, shook her off before he got to the bandstand, and leapt up to his keyboard.

There had been no planning, no one spoke, and I saw no visible signaling, but as each new instrument joined in, there was no confusion, no fumbling, not one wrong note or beat. They might all have been playing together for years, the piece rehearsed a thousand times: each seemed to know instinctively how best to support and complement the others, where to make room for whose impulsive flights of fancy, when to step forward and when to step back.

I was so taken with their creation that it was several moments before I noticed that here, as onstage with Cold Iron, Jorandel had somehow become the focal point, the core of the music, the living instrument through which all the power and glory of the others' inspiration was funneled to produce this perfect musical unity. Without a word or a sign or even, perhaps, any intention, he had taken the lead in this, gathered them all under his spell, and was leading them to play as none of them might ever have played before. This was nothing like Cold Iron music, and I had a feeling it was just as unlike what the other musicians present were accustomed to. It was a distillation of all their varied potential, augmented by his magic. If someone had told me such a thing could be done, even by an elf, I would have denied it. I would have been wrong.

I had heard much about Jorandel's sense of confinement under Veladora's contract, but until that moment I had not come close to understanding what was being stifled. I had seen that Jorandel was the core of the band and that music was the core of his being, but Cold Iron was a good band that made excellent music, the best of its genre. Without really thinking about it, I had been dismissing as mere arrogance the complaints that Jorie could do better. Now I saw how much better he could do.

Veladora was right, something like this might not sell. It might ruin Cold Iron as a platinum-record-producing machine, knock them off the charts, destroy their massive popularity. But to deny an artist the right to build such beauty simply because there might be no market was sinful. And this was only what he could do with Cold Iron and half a dozen random amateurs thrown in. What could he do if he could choose the instruments, the arrangements? What would he create if he were given complete autonomy?

The improvisation segued into the Cold Iron song "Brothers," and Jorie began, very quietly at first, to sing. Not the easy romance Cold Iron had recorded, and not the savage interpretation Jim had sung on our last night in L.A.: this was something between the two, and greater than either. The romance was there, but it wasn't lies. The savagery was there too, but without anger. Somehow, with that impromptu band and the power of his voice and his vision, he turned that trashy little song into a thing of clarity and truth and radiance, a grown-up song, simple and profoundly moving. There was love in it without naïveté, nobility without pretentiousness, promises that were no less valuable for the fact that they could not be kept. There was life in it, real life and real people—all of Jorandel's wild, laughing exaltation in the shining glory of the silly, frail, beloved creatures that we are.

17

They never quit. That whole long evening and late into the night they kept playing, and every piece seemed more magical than the last. There were sparkling little jazz instrumentals, driving elfrock songs with their roots in rhythm and blues, slow country songs with the sweet slack-key twang of the islands, hard rock, New Age, pop songs: every variety of popular music, and odd mixtures of varieties. The only thing they all had in common was excellence of execution.

The number of musicians playing at any one time varied from fully a dozen on some really powerful elfrock numbers to Jorandel alone singing a gentle ballad with just an acoustic guitar for accompaniment. There was a great deal of food eaten that night, but I'm not sure Jorandel had any. While the rest of us ate such mere mortal dishes as *kalua* pig, *laulau,* chicken long rice, *haupia, lomilomi* salmon, sticky rice, sashimi, poi, and macaroni salad, Jorandel fed on the music. After hours of playing and singing, he seemed fresher than when he began, and reluctant to quit when everyone else was exhausted and ready to go home.

That lush tropical valley was as beautiful by moonlight as by daylight. There were lights strung all around the luau area, but after the moon came up I slipped away for a while to see what the countryside looked like by its light, and what Jorandel's music sounded like at a distance and in solitude. The waterfall at the end of the valley was a colorless ribbon of fairy gold, with "moonbows"—rainbows cast by moonlight—at its base, not quite colorless, like dew-strung spider webs in morning sun. The meadow in which the house was set lay drenched in moonlight, surrounded by mysterious forests of darkness and towered over by those imposing mountains so near and so steep they were like a giant's wall, with wisps of white, misty clouds tucked into the shadowed hollows near their peaks.

Jorandel's music belonged there. It was a thing of myth and magic, the sound of a mystical moonlit field under a silent waterfall down enchanted mountains where unicorns might dwell. Even the heavy metal songs had that sorcery in them, that bewitching shimmer like blue sky reflected in still water, a radiance of freedom and joy that belonged in a wild tropical garden under a full moon so bright it spun rainbows in waterfall mist and drowned all but the most brilliant stars in the black depth of eternity.

I wondered briefly whether, if Veladora could hear this, he might relent and let Jorandel do it onstage and on record; but I knew he would not. This was a spectacular sound, entrancing, delightful, but not commercial. I thought it would sell, perhaps even better than the Cold Iron music Veladora was selling now, but not right away, and there would be defections by fans who wanted the sounds they were accustomed to. Cold Iron would have to build a new audience, and businessmen do not like to risk an established clientele in the hope of building a new one.

After a time I went back to the luau and ate more exotic foods while I watched the music makers. They changed places, switched roles, joined and departed the jam session with the casual ease of Cold Iron jamming in a hotel room. There was none of the frenzied energy expenditure of a concert, no athletics, no bounding around and bumping into each other, and yet they were never quite still, either. Jorandel in particular never really relaxed; his body was the instrument through which the enchantment was funneled, and he seemed almost to vibrate with the splendor and the strength of it. But he never tired of it. I think he'd have played all night if he'd been allowed.

Indifferent as he was to social niceties, however, even Jorandel wouldn't impose on Killer's family when all the other guests had gone home and the Maunalani residents had begun to yawn and gather up the debris of the party.

Or at least, he wouldn't when all the other musicians had wearied to the point of exhaustion, failing voices, and stumbling fingers. In a last flurry of hugs and smiles and soft-voiced alohas, we tumbled into the limousines for the long ride back to town. It was then that I first realized the other major difference between this and any other Cold Iron event I had attended: not one of the musicians was drunk or stoned. They had all been drinking, and they were staggering and bleary-eyed with exhaustion, but they were sober.

Candy wasn't. She ended up in the same car with me and the two brothers, perhaps because the Roach had a groupie on each arm when he entered the car behind us. Jimendan was falling asleep on his feet during the prolonged good-byes, and although Jorandel seemed wide awake then, he leaned against his brother in the car and was asleep before we'd left the driveway. I was just barely awake, but Candy was absolutely wired. She talked a mile a minute about anything that crossed her mind, most of it incoherent. She tried three times in the space of five minutes to convince me to have a line of soda with her. She told me everything she'd done all evening, in excruciating detail but with major gaps in the telling, so that even if I had wanted to follow the story I'd have got lost in minutes.

"You've done too much soda," I told her.

"I know," she said, "but I drank a lot of booze too, and that kind of balances it, you know what I mean? Well, of course you do, that's what you do, isn't it, only tonight you wouldn't do any soda, why was that? Did you feel like you shouldn't do it in front of strangers or what? I feel like Killer's family isn't even strangers anymore because we were here just six or eight months ago and I met them all and you know they even remembered me, isn't that neat? When they don't have any way to know whether I'm just another groupie and won't be around again or anything? I mean I thought that was really nice, they treat everybody like people, I just think they're the nicest people I've met in such a long time, and you meet a lot of people that aren't very nice when you're traveling with an elfrock band, but they're really nice people, I wish my family were like that, so nice I mean."

She went on like that, all run-on sentences and very little punctuation, talking just as fast as her mouth could move, most of the way to town. Eventually I quit making the effort to follow. She didn't seem to require any responses, but some demon of politeness kept me awake and mumbling noncommittal remarks whenever she paused long enough to give the impression she might hear them. She didn't, I think. She might not even have heard their absence had I stopped, or noticed had I fallen asleep, but I couldn't bear the thought of her chattering brightly all the way to town to a carful of sleeping people. She seemed so lonely, so desolately lonely, I thought the least I could do was pretend to listen.

Jim and Jorie woke when we got to the hotel, and for some reason put their arms around us when we all got out of the car. We went inside like that, a united foursome with the brothers on the outside and Candy and me in the middle. As it happened, it was Jim who had his arm around me, and I felt no fonder of him than I had the night he'd tried to rape me; but one glance at Candy's face kept me from objecting. She wore an expression of transcendent awe. Wired or not, she was conscious enough of her surroundings to know it was Jorandel who had his arm around her. She hardly dared even to look at him. She moved as though she were walking on spun glass, terrified of breaking the spell, of losing even the illusion of his attention. When we had started walking, she and I had automatically put our arms around each other, and I could feel the singing tension in her body. However much I disliked Jim, I couldn't do anything to endanger such happiness.

It made me think about the essential difference between Jim and Jorie. Hypothetical murder plots aside, what was it, really? Jorie's musical genius was hardly evident in a walk through a hotel lobby; neither, for that matter, were Jim's fratricidal tendencies, if any. I had not observed any other major differences in character. True, Hilly had catalogued extensive psychotic behavior for Jorie and none for Jim; but at this point I thought it likely that was because when one of them was seen doing something psychotic he was assumed to be Jorandel. I'd seen them in action: they both threw fits, furniture, and groupies. They took turns at sullen and petulant (or did it together). They both drank too much, did too many drugs, and thought very little of anyone's comfort but their own.

And yet the feel of Jimendan's arm on my shoulder was repellent, and I was in love with Jorandel. Was it because Jorie had surprised me with so many faces Jim had not shown me? I did not know whether Jim was as capable of unexpected gentleness or as perceptive or well-read as his brother, because I'd had less contact with him. But I thought he was, or nearly so. He'd certainly seemed to read my mind a time or two last night, and shown some comprehension of basic psychology if not philosophy.

Like everyone else except Candy and Frank, I couldn't always tell them apart on sight. But I could always tell them apart the instant one of them touched me. What was the essential difference between them that made that possible, and made me love the one and dislike the other? What, I wondered blearily, was the essence of an elf, that could be recognized so surely by touch but was invisible or at least obscure to the other senses? It was very late, and I was very tired. I was starting to consider ambiguous words like "soul" and "spirit" and "aura." Luckily the elevator arrived at our floor before I'd gone much more metaphysical than that. It was a relief to know that in minutes I would be safely in my room, asleep at last.

Only it didn't work quite that way. I really was so nearly asleep on my feet that I don't know exactly what happened, except that Jimendan removed his arm from my shoulder and I think he may have put it around Candy's instead. Certainly Jorandel released Candy and took my hand; and I, dazed with weariness and the aftermath of musical magic, followed him without hesitation or even a backward glance. It was the most natural thing in the world to follow him: I had known that even before I knew I loved him. The first time I had followed him off a plane I had thought something of the sort, something about following him "as though I always had and always would." It seemed now as though I always had, and it didn't matter in the least that the "always would" part was entirely fantasy. This elf, this musical wonder, this psychotic genius, was my love.

As before, we were so weary that the process of disrobing and falling into bed had no sexual overtones whatsoever. This time, however, we were neither stoned nor emotionally overwrought. Physical weariness was instantly overcome by physical proximity. When we curled into each other's arms, it was not as children. The pressure of his body burned against mine. There was no time for gentleness, for the sweet attentions to which we had devoted ourselves before. Our bodies fit together so well that there was no need to learn again what they already knew by memory and instinct.

There was less a sense of joyous union this time than of brutal urgency, of shared and terrible need, as though whatever it was that bound us had been drawn too taut by time and circumstance till separation was an exquisite pain, and sex only the readiest available path to the fusion that might bring surcease. And yet on another level it was every bit as sweet and even as gentle as it had been before. In a way it was like his most powerful music, fierce and exultant, the beauty and the glory of it a direct consequence of the savagery, a function of it.

I fell asleep afterward secure in the shelter of his arms, and woke in the morning still caught in their protective hold. He was watching me with a drowsy little smile of contentment. I felt cherished, treasured, almost beloved, and I snuggled sleepily deeper into the warm, bony tangle of our embrace. But the sound that woke me repeated itself: someone knocking at his door and calling his name. Frowning almost absently, he called an answer.

The door opened, and Emerson looked in. Ignoring me as completely and coldly as if I had been a groupie or some unlovely piece of furniture, he said abruptly, almost brutally, "Get up, Jorandel. Candy's dead."

"She's what?" I sat up, staring, so startled I forgot to pull the covers up with me.

Emerson's ice-colored eyes glanced at me briefly, indifferent, and returned to Jorandel. "Get dressed," he said. "I'll try to deal with 'em, but there may be cops."

I swallowed hard and pulled a sheet up over my breasts in an absent, automatic gesture meant more to protect myself from reality than from his eyes. "How did she die?"

This time that steady gaze met mine and he hesitated, judging, then gave a grudging little nod and said, "OD'd. Soda, it looks like. You better get dressed, too. I'm kicking the groupies out, but I guess you can stay if Jorandel wants you."

My status had clearly changed with Candy's death, but I didn't quite take that in at the time. Jorandel wrapped a possessive arm around my waist in much the way a dog will put a paw on a bone another dog wants: an automatic gesture unrelated to desire. "She stays," he said, and I felt absurdly grateful, as if I had been given a reprieve from a mortal threat.

Emerson nodded without interest and backed out of the doorway, closing the door softly behind him. I stayed where I was, staring after him. "Damn," I said. "Damn." I could see her face again the way it had been last night when Jorandel had his arm around her: the tremulous smile of transcendent awe, the way she had moved in fear of shattering the spell and losing his proximity. And when he had released her and taken me to bed instead, I had not even looked back once. I had not given a moment's thought to her needs. I had not considered how that smile might have crumpled at his rejection, his indifference, his desertion.

Had she gone directly to her room and overdosed at once, on purpose? Could I have saved her if I had looked back, if I had recognized her desolation, if I had given just a moment's thought to any needs beyond my own?

"Come, cousin," said Jorandel. "It would seem we must arise to meet the day." He was annoyed: not at me, but at the situation, at Candy's death.

In that moment I hated him, but it was at least as much because I knew I had failed her as because he cared for her no more in death than he had in life. I'd have hated him just as much if he'd shown some hypocritical fondness for her now. I hated him mostly because I did not want to recognize how much I hated myself.

"Yes, all right," I said, and clambered unsteadily out of bed. "I need a shower. Loan me a robe?"

He loaned me the same robe I'd borrowed after our last night together. I went through the common room, past the uncritical stares of musicians and security people, into my room. With numb, blind fingers I selected one of the outfits Candy had helped me purchase and carried it with me into the bathroom, where I scrubbed under a steaming shower till my skin was uniformly pink, and I still didn't feel clean. Not because I had slept with Jorandel when she wanted to, not because I had failed her, not even because I was alive and she was dead and I could see no reason for it. I think I felt unclean because I knew, really for the first time in my life, that I could do the best I could till hell froze over and it wouldn't always be good enough. If you're human, you make mistakes: it's the nature of the beast.

I didn't want to know that. It didn't do any good to tell myself I was suffering from a God complex, that I couldn't have saved her, that people are responsible for their own lives, that I wasn't the only person who could and should have seen her distress, that it was perfectly reasonable to have been so put off by the obnoxiousness of her soda high that I couldn't care enough to make sure she was okay when Jorandel released her, and all the other things you tell yourself at a time like that. The fact remained that last night the best I could do was to walk away from Candy without a backward glance, and this morning she was dead.

When I had dressed in a costume she would have approved, and put on as many bangles and baubles as she would have thought needful, and applied almost as much makeup as she would have liked, I went to see her. Emerson didn't like that. I didn't give a damn what Emerson liked. When he saw that, he stood aside with a shrug that managed, despite the stony stillness of his face, to imply a sneer.

She was on the bed, her hands folded on her chest, her hair smoothed back from her narrow little face, the huge fawn eyes half open and seemingly even larger and sadder than in life. Her mascara was smeared. Her unpainted lips were parted, showing the broken tooth that had embarrassed her the day I met her. She still had on the dress she had worn to the luau last night, its crumpled ruffles pulled neatly down to cover the smooth curve of her thighs. Her shoes were off, and there was still a film of dirt on the soles of her feet from walking barefoot at the luau.

Emerson was standing in the doorway. I said, "Is this how you found her?" and he nodded watchfully. I looked at her again. She had asked for so little, and been granted so much less. I wondered whether Jorandel had even bothered to come to say good-bye to her while I was showering. I said, "Maybe the police will believe it. They didn't know her."

"What's that supposed to mean?" said Emerson.

"You want it to look like suicide, right?"

"Far as I know, it was suicide."

"No." She hadn't done it on purpose. I knew that the moment I saw her: she hadn't dressed for it, or made up her face, or arranged her hair, and she would have done all that and more before committing suicide. Even in the grip of terminal despair she would have prepared her body as carefully for that final journey as she had for any in life. "She hadn't even washed her feet," I said. My voice sounded thin and plaintive.

Emerson looked at her feet, looked at me, and shrugged.

I swallowed hard, concentrating on facts. "She'd have showered," I said. "And changed her clothes. And fixed her hair and her makeup."

"She was stoned already," he said.

"She'd have thought Jorandel would see her. She was never too stoned to care what he saw when he looked at her." Poor little nubbin. "He hasn't looked, has he?" I said.

It wasn't really a question, but he answered it anyway. "No," he said.

Something in his voice made me look at him in surprise. "You liked her, too, didn't you?"

The flash of hatred in his eyes was as brief as it was deadly. "Too besides whom?" he asked, his voice controlled.

"Besides me," I said, and knew I sounded too certain

no one else had, and knew also that I was too probably right.

"Sure, you really liked her." His voice was bitter, his eyes cold. "You liked her so much you took her money, and her drugs, and the only man she wanted, and couldn't be bothered to give her the time of day in return."

It was close enough to my own estimation that I didn't know what to say. "Emerson . . ."

"Get out of here," he said. "Leave her alone. She's earned that, hasn't she?"

She had earned that. There was nothing I could do for her now. The urchin smile was gone, the generous heart forever stilled that had been so uncritically glad for the man she loved when he found happiness in someone else's arms. It would do her no good for Emerson and me to argue over her like two dogs over a stale bone neither of them had wanted when it was fresh. I turned away from her for the last time and walked past him out of her bedroom, but the image of that starved little pixie face went with me. I had a feeling it was going to be with me for a long time.

Roach, Blade, Jim, Jorie, and several bodyguards were gathered in the common room. Killer had stayed the night at Maunalani and wasn't expected back till afternoon. Frank was fussing quietly over the brothers, both of whom looked cross. Blade and the Roach both looked indifferent to their surroundings; Blade was absently strumming a bass guitar, and the Roach had a pair of Killer's drumsticks with which he was beating time to unheard music on the arm of a chair. Their bodyguards sat far from their charges and sipped coffee in silence, their expressions bland and watchful.

Clearly, Candy made no more impact on any of them dead than she had alive. The only concession they had made to her death was the removal of the groupies, and I wasn't sure why they had bothered with that. I should go home, I thought, and glanced involuntarily at Jim and Jorie. They wore matching terry robes and I couldn't tell which was Jorie. Neither of them looked at me.

I should go home. But Candy had depended on me to find Jorandel's potential murderer, and I hadn't done that yet. Unless my wild speculation about Jimendan was correct. In which case, Candy was certainly one of the two most dangerous people to him; she could always tell the brothers apart on sight and without hesitation. I had thought she and Frank would be in danger from him, and now she was dead. And Jim had been with her when I left them last night.

"Soda is the easiest thing to miscalculate," Jorie had said yesterday. It didn't have to be anyone's fault. Drug overdoses seemed to be the expected state of affairs with an elfrock band, or at least with this elfrock band. Blade had overdosed, or close to it, the first night I met them, and had collapsed onstage. Andy had overdosed on his vacation, and died. Jorandel had overdosed the night before last, and nearly died, and it hadn't been the first time he'd done it, only the first time I'd seen him do it. With such a high incidence of accidental overdoses, it was ridiculous to insist that Candy's was murder, just because murder would fit my theory. Unless one of those others had not been an accident. If Andy's overdose was murder, then Candy's was murder.

There was no way to know whether Andy's was murder. And I wasn't going home till I had at least attempted to find out whether Candy's was. It wouldn't matter to her now, but I owed her the effort anyway. I owed her more than I had power or possibility to pay even when she was alive. At the very least she had saved my sanity.

I thought of that sweet, small voice telling me what her father had done to her, and that it wasn't her fault, and I wondered how anyone could have imagined that it was. It wasn't hard to imagine her as a child, pixie-faced and innocent; she hadn't been much more than a child when she died. Certainly she would have been an attractive child, but even if one postulated that some men would perceive that as sexual attraction, it was impossible to understand how they could seriously convince themselves she was culpable if they acted on the impulse. The mere idea enraged me.

It also, unexpected and unasked, freed me of the burden of complicity I had carried since I remembered what my father had done to me. Unbidden, the memory of my own appearance as a child popped into my mind, recalled from photographs as clearly as if my child-self stood before me now in all her vulnerable innocence. I had been every bit as blameless as Candy. Having seen her innocence, I could for the first time really see my own. A pretty child is not a sexual invitation. No child has the capacity to give informed consent to sex. And no healthy adult is incapable of resisting his or her sexual urges.

It was a revelation. I had known right along that I hadn't really killed my father. Now I knew that neither had I invited his abuse of me. Even if I had been deliberately provocative, a healthy adult would have recognized my innocence, my ignorance, and controlled his response if any. I truly was not to blame for what had been done to me. I nearly laughed aloud at the giddy sense of freedom that made me feel literally as light as air, as though I could spread my arms and lift my feet and float across the room on pure joy.

It was Candy's last gift to me. She had tried to give it to me when she was alive, but I hadn't been able to accept it then. I hadn't really been able to see it then. I had been able to see her lack of complicity, but not mine. I didn't fully understand why I could see it now, but I could, and I knew it was her doing, and the impulse to laughter changed to tears. I wanted to hug her, to thank her, to share the wonder of the revelation with her, and she was not there. She would not ever be there again. Only her ghost remained, fawn-eyed and innocent, standing fierce and formless guard over those she had loved, perhaps smiling a little at how slow I had been to understand the obvious, and doubtless as uncritical now as she had been in life. My own irritation at everyone's apparent indifference to her death would draw from her only a wide-eyed and questioning glance: surely I would not rather see them distressed. Didn't I want them to be happy?

No, damn it, I did not want them to be happy. Not in the face of this. I wanted them to know what they'd lost. I wanted them to remember her love, her generosity, her urchin smile, even her nonstop soda-induced chatter that had always been so artless, so ingenuous, and so damned good-hearted. She had been the best of them, and she was gone. I wanted them, by God, to notice, even if they were too self-involved and too damned dense to care. I did not want that sweet smile so soon forgotten, the little pixie face confined only to my memory, the selfless good nature dismissed as though it had never been.

The quality of my love for Jorandel was not as generous as hers had been. I wanted him in particular to care that she was gone, even if none of the others did or could. She had loved him, as faithfully as she knew how, as uncritical and undemanding in her adoration as any human being could possibly have been, and all he had given her in return were thoughtless orders to fetch and carry for him, or an occasional gift or gesture that cost him money at most, but never anything he cared about, not even time.

Prolonged exposure to the behavior of psychotics does odd things to one's concept of self-control. I felt a certain pride in having selected a light, acoustic guitar to throw at Jorandel instead of the heavy hotel lamp that was nearer to hand. I could tell which one he was because Jim had run a hand through his hair that dragged his bangs down across his forehead. That was as well for him, because there were two acoustic guitars within my reach.

As it happened, I nearly used them both anyway, because the first one missed Jorandel. It was Killer who stopped me. Someone had called him to let him know about Candy's death, and he had come home early. I hadn't heard him come in. The others were just staring at me in startled confusion. Even Emerson, standing in Candy's bedroom door and scowling, only looked at me. The outer doorway was behind me. Killer must have come through it, seen what I was doing, and moved straight to me. He caught my arm as I reached for the second guitar. Very gently he turned me toward him and enveloped me in an enormous, compassionate hug. "Hey," he said. "Hey, Rosie. Hey."

I struggled urgently against him, my brief rage forgotten, aware now only of the need to save the tattered remnants of my pride. Candy's amiable ghost smiled her urchin smile at me in fond acceptance from some metaphysical dimension of memory or grief. "Let me go," I said frantically. "Let me go, Killer, or I'll cry."

He didn't let me go.

18

Killer had brought Vyla along "because he thought you might need me," she said when I had calmed enough to notice her. "Where's your room, honey? You need to fix your face." She had looked elegant in a muumuu. She looked even more elegant in a short cotton print sundress, pale against the smooth dark of her skin. Her eyes, so mirthful last night, were warmly sympathetic today.

I led her to my room. "They don't even care," I said dully. "She's dead, and none of them even care."

"Oh, they care," she said, dampening a washcloth to wipe my face as if I were a child. "They just don't know what to do with it. They're only boys, don't forget. They haven't learned how to react to tragedy."

"You don't have to learn. You just react." I held my face up dutifully for her ministrations, feeling about five years old.

"That's what *you* do," she said, smiling faintly. "For boys it's different."

"I don't know about the others, but Jorandel's nearly thirty," I said crossly. "Maybe that's young for an elf, but it's still grown-up."

"Thirty may be, but he's not," she said. "There, that's better." She stood back to survey my appearance. "You might want to put on some fresh eye shadow. And cheek gloss, if you have any; you're looking much too pale, even for a person of the white persuasion."

I grinned reluctantly at the expression, then frowned at myself in the mirror. Candy would have thought it essential that I mend my makeup before anything else. "What difference does it make?" I said listlessly.

"Not much, really," said Vyla, "only it might make you feel better to know you look your best."

"My best," I said sourly, "was about ten years ago."

She chuckled. "Ten years ago you were a baby."

I grinned at her reflection behind mine. "Ah, but I was a beautiful baby," I said, and to my own surprise I began to cry again. "Damn," I said. "Damn it." She gave me a handkerchief and, when I stopped crying, helped me mend my face.

Candy's body was hustled quietly out of the hotel by service elevators and back stairs; dying is frowned on by one's fellow guests. The hotel wanted the whole affair hushed up as quickly as possible. I think they'd have kicked out the rest of Cold Iron and entourage if they hadn't realized that might cause more fuss than letting us stay on. They worked wonders keeping the press away from us, and their influence probably helped with the police as well. It wasn't as though there were any question of how Candy died, and while the police may not have accepted the suicide theory, there was no reason for them to suspect foul play. By early afternoon they were finished with us. Candy was relegated to an obscure paragraph on a back page of the evening edition of the local newspaper, and Cold Iron began to prepare for that night's concert at Blaisdell Arena.

When the last of the officials had gone and it was clear that there was nothing left to do in the suite, Vyla announced that she and I were going out to lunch. "You could call room service, Ma," said Killer, while behind him Jim and Jorie indulged in what was for them a very quiet argument over song lyrics, the Roach pounded out an unfamiliar melody on a portable keyboard, and Blade unexpectedly hurled a guitar against the wall with an inarticulate shout of rage that seemed to be a complaint against strings that willfully broke themselves.

"No," she said. "We need to get out. At least, I do; I'm too old to be amused by the preconcert antics of a bunch of overgrown adolescents."

Killer's lips twitched. I wished I could see his eyes. "Meaning us, eh?" he said.

"Meaning you," said his mother.

"Okay, Ma," he said. He turned his face toward me.

I thought for a moment he was going to say something, but he only nodded expressionlessly and turned away.

"Chatty lad, my son," said Vyla, "isn't he?"

"Has he always been so quiet?" I asked.

"Except on the drums," she said with a wry little smile. "Come on, let's find us a restaurant. How do you feel about Korean food?"

"I don't know, I've never had it."

"Time you did, then," she said.

I didn't feel hungry, but neither did I feel inclined to stay in the suite and watch Cold Iron behave as though nothing untoward had occurred that morning. Emerson was in Candy's room, visible through the doorway as he carefully packed her trendy little dresses, and I wondered whether he would send her belongings to her parents. It didn't matter. She wouldn't care what happened to the things she had left behind. And no one in the suite besides Emerson seemed aware that she had ever existed. I got my purse and followed Vyla out of there.

The Christmas tree in the lobby gave me a brief start, no more. The Christmas decorations on lampposts and leafy trees outside seemed tawdry and vaguely ludicrous, but not alarming. Christmas carols emanating from various shops we passed annoyed me only in the way that any music would if broadcast onto the street like that without regard for the involuntary listeners' preferences. I thought of my father, but only fleetingly, and more with distaste than with even the remnants of fear. Candy's ghost smiled at me. "You see?" she said. "You shouldn't be mad at Jorie for showing you that song. He was trying to help you." I reserved judgment. My view of Jorandel was, I hoped, more objective than hers had been.

Korean food was very tasty. We ate in a little garden restaurant with a tinkling fountain at our side, and Vyla kept the conversation neutral by relating anecdotes about Killer's childhood that I thought would embarrass the hell out of him if he knew she was repeating them to me. Mothers are like that, I guess. Anyway it kept my mind off current events, and did me good to laugh with her over Killer's youthful escapades.

But reality wouldn't stay safely at a distance. When

our plates had been taken away and our cups filled again, we both fell silent, listening to the fountain at our side. I tried to keep my mind on the adolescent Killer she had so clearly pictured for me, admitting to forbidden ventures into town at night to listen to drummers at the local clubs, but Candy's pixie-faced ghost was always there at the back of my mind. Vyla leaned her chin on her hand and looked across the table at me. "Okay," she said, "Give. What's really bothering you? It's not just Candy's death, is it?"

"Not exactly," I said, wondering how much I ought to tell her.

"What, then?" she said.

"I'm not sure," I said. "I mean . . ."

She waited, serious and patient, giving me time to find my own way into it.

"I'm not sure it was an accident," I said. "And I know it wasn't suicide." I told her why.

"I see that," she said slowly. "But why not an accident? What are you saying? That someone killed her?"

"Oh, hell," I said. "I don't know. I suppose that sounds as dramatic as all hell, and yet . . . You know, I didn't believe her when she suggested it, but that's what she hired me for: to find a murderer."

"She hired you?"

What the hell. You have to trust somebody. "I'm a P.I.," I said. "A private investigator. In California. She hired me because she thought somebody was going to kill Jorandel." I sighed, studying my tea. "I told her I couldn't prevent it if somebody really wanted to."

"But nobody has killed Jorandel," she said.

"No. Not yet." I looked at her. "I don't know how this will sound," I said.

"I don't know either," she said with the flicker of a smile. "Try it."

I drew my breath, hesitated one last time, and then blurted it out in a rush: "I'm afraid Jim means to kill Jorandel."

She took it calmly enough. "Why?"

"You mean why would he, or why do I think it?"

She shrugged. "Either would do for starters." At least she wasn't dismissing the idea out of hand.

"I don't quite know why he would," I said. "Because he's jealous, because he hasn't thought it through, because he wants to be Jorandel and thinks he can and doesn't understand what it will do to him if he kills his brother." My voice trailed off uncertainly.

"Okay, let's skip why he would, for now. Why do you think he's going to? I mean, what makes you think he's planning . . . murder?"

"I think he's already done murder," I said. "I think he killed Andy because Andy could tell the brothers apart and wouldn't go along with Jim's plans. I think he killed Candy because she could tell them apart, and I'm afraid he'll kill Frank for the same reason."

"You're saying he's actually planning to take Jorandel's place? To pretend to be Jorandel?"

"I'm afraid so." I said it almost apologetically.

"Goodness," she said. "You'd better tell me all of it. You have some reason for your suspicions, I assume?"

I told her. She was dubious at first, and wanted to be dubious when I was finished, but I could tell it didn't come easy. "I can't believe it," she said.

"I can't either, when I think about them, about how much they love each other," I said. "But I can't quite disbelieve it, either."

She sipped her tea, staring at nothing. "No," she said. "Not quite." She sighed. "They're such damned, spoiled brats, even for Truebloods," she said. "You can't tell what they might take it into their heads to do."

"No," I said.

After a long moment she said uncertainly, "You'll have to tell Jorandel. If you really think there's anything to it."

"I suppose I will. I kept thinking I'd catch Jimendan at something, find some hard evidence, something. I don't like to go to Jorandel with wild accusations against his brother and nothing more than circumstantial evidence to back them up."

"He won't believe you."

"No." We were silent again. "But it might make him think," I said finally. "It might give him a chance, at least, when Jimendan does . . . whatever he's going to do."

"I wish I really thought it would," she said.

So did I. After another long silence I said wearily, "Well, it's all I can do. I do think there's something to it, so I guess I have to tell him. Whatever happens after that, I'll have done my best for him, anyway." And we've seen how good my best is, I thought wearily, remembering Candy's white, dead face.

"One thing that will happen, almost certainly, is that he'll kick you out," she said.

"I know." My voice sounded as desolate as I felt. I cleared my throat. "I think I've been unconsciously using that as an excuse not to tell him." That was too revealing. I tried to correct it: "Once he's kicked me out there'll be no chance I can stop Jimendan." Neither of us believed that was my primary reason to stay. "I'm not doing much good at stopping him, as it is." I watched the sparkle of sunlight on the water in the fountain. "I guess I'll wait till after tonight's concert, anyway."

She hesitated, watching me. "You do know, don't you, that—" She broke off, at a loss for words.

"That there's no room in his life for me anyway, in the long run? Yes, I know," I said. "Come to that, there's no room for him in my life." I was a little surprised to realize that was quite true, regardless of how much I loved him. My life wouldn't accommodate an elfrock star, and I couldn't imagine loving anyone enough to change my ways to the extent that would require. "It still hurts to think of ending it this way."

She nodded soberly. After a moment she said, "You know, you could be wrong. About Jim."

"I hope I am. And that's one of the reasons I'll wait till after the concert: I'm going to ask around, about last night. Maybe I'll find out Jim was actually seen handling her soda. Or that somebody else had as good a chance as he did to doctor it."

"And if nobody did? Couldn't it have been an accident?"

"It could have been," I said. "Maybe it even was."

"But you don't think so."

"I don't know what to think. Except that I've been holding off, waiting for evidence, while people around Cold Iron have been dying like flies, and if the only thing I can do that has a chance of stopping that will also get me kicked out of the group—well, I wasn't thinking of making them my life's work, anyway."

"There aren't any other options? Have you talked to Emerson? Maybe he could think of a way to get evidence."

"I talked to him. He didn't believe me. I don't blame him. Hell, I don't know why you believe me."

She smiled faintly. "I imagine I'm more objective about elves than Emerson is," she said. "And maybe about female detectives, too."

I didn't really hear her. "And as to getting evidence—I don't think there's any evidence to get. He's been too damn careful, too sly, too cagey. Now we'll probably never know who it was that Candy overheard. There's no way to prove who searched my belongings, and as long as Jorandel isn't talking, there's no way to know who pushed him downstairs. Anybody could have hired those thugs to scare me off, and anybody could have doctored Andy's drugs. Or that could even have been a genuine accident. Or suicide. And as to Jim and Jorie getting injured in exactly the same way—well, that's the one that keeps stopping me. I can't believe in a coincidence like that. And I can't think of anybody but them who'd care whether they're identical. Jorandel surely wouldn't do that to Jimendan just for the sake of casual switches. And if Jimendan did it to himself for the sake of a permanent switch, he's not going to admit it."

She looked excited. "That's it!" she said. "He couldn't have done it to himself. I mean, could you really hit yourself over the head that hard? Somebody must have done it to him. All you have to do is find out who, and ask who hired him. Or them."

"Simplicity itself," I said.

"Oh," she said, crestfallen. "I guess not, is it?"

"If I had the resources the police have, maybe I could find whoever did it. But by myself? No way."

"No, I see that." She finished her tea and put the cup down as carefully as if the universe depended on its placement. "Well, that's that, then." I didn't know whether she meant the tea, or the case. After a long moment she searched in her purse, found a business card and a pencil, and scrawled a phone number on the back of the card. "If you need help, you know, a place to go, or—or whatever, here's the number at Maunalani. I'll be going back there after the show tonight." She handed me the card. "Let's get out of here. Feel like going for a walk?"

"I sure don't feel like going back to the hotel yet."

"Good. Beach, or park?"

"I don't care."

"Beach, then," she said. "I think better with my feet in the water."

If she imagined she was going to come up with an alternate interpretation of recent events that didn't include potential fratricide, more power to her. I seemed to have lost the capacity to think. We left the restaurant in silence, and she led me straight to the nearest beach access, where we paused to take off our shoes before stepping into the sand. I thought with a pang how intent Candy had been, before we left the mainland, on getting a suntan while she was in Hawaii. She'd never found time for it. Now she never would.

I didn't realize Vyla was watching me till she said, "You liked her a lot, didn't you?"

"Candy?" I said, surprised. "Yeah. She was a peculiar little thing, but she—We shared some things. We had similar histories, I guess you'd say. She helped me in a lot of ways."

"I didn't know her well, but she seemed a very caring girl," said Vyla.

I thought of the look in her eyes when she told me she was glad Jorandel was happy with me. "Caring" seemed wholly inadequate, but I could think of no better word. "Yes," I said. "She was."

We walked in silence for a time at the water's edge, slowing when the waves washed up around our ankles. The water was chilly, but not frigid like California water. The sand beneath our feet was so fine it packed hard where there was any moisture in it, so that walking was not the strenuous task it can be in deep beach sand. With the hot weight of the sun on my shoulders and the cool, salt-sticky water alternately washing around my feet and rushing away again I fell into a dreamy, summery daze. The oppression of both past and future faded into an infinite, ethereal *now* in which there was no pain, no fear, no regret, no hope: only brute existence, mildly pleasurable, mindless, remote.

Vyla asked unexpectedly, "What made you decide to become a private investigator?"

I blinked at her, struggling dumbly with vast philosophical concepts, and giggled when I hit on the exact truth: "I wanted to be a cop, but I failed the dummy test."

She lifted one eyebrow. "The dummy test?"

"Yeah. You have to pass some written tests, and then do all this physical stuff: running flat, and up and down some stairs, and along a balance beam, and over a couple of six-foot fences, stuff like that. And press some fake arms together for thirty seconds, and then drag a hundred-sixty-pound dummy I forget how far. All with a weighted belt that's supposed to simulate a policeman's equipment. It's all timed, and they didn't have a belt small enough for me, so they said if it fell off they'd stop the clock while I put it back on. But it didn't. The dummy's the last thing, and I had a lot of time when I got to it, so I thought I had it made. I knew I could drag a hundred sixty pounds as far as I had to, easy.

"Trouble was, the dummy wasn't stuffed good, you know? I mean, the man-shaped bag was a lot bigger than the sand they filled it with. A taller person could've handled it, even if she wasn't any stronger than I am, because it's all physics. If you can take the weight on your hips, you can do it. But even when I folded the dummy in half, half the sand in his feet and half in his head, there was so much empty cloth in between that I couldn't haul the weight any higher than my knees. I saw afterward that I should've tried putting my shoulder under all that extra cloth at his middle, just to get the weight up off the ground, but at the time I was busy resenting the fact that the test was deliberately—or maybe ignorantly, I don't know—biased for tall people. I figured it was a way out for them because they had to pretend they had no height requirement, but they didn't really want short people.

"Thing is, I knew damn well I could haul an unconscious, hundred-sixty-pound person to safety: I'd done it. With a hundred-eighty-pound person. You put him on his back, fold his arms on his chest, reach under his shoulders, get a grip on his elbows, and his own arm bones give you the leverage to get his weight up off the ground, onto your hips, so you can drag him as far as you want. But this dummy didn't have any bones. Hell, if I came across a person that squashy, I wouldn't waste time trying to save him. He'd had it."

"You're still angry, aren't you?"

"I guess I am." I shook my head, remembering. "Damn, they were smug about it. When I complained, they told me if I'd really dragged a person like I said I had, he must've unconsciously helped me. Unconsciously was the word: the guy had a goddamn head injury, didn't wake up till three days later. And they think he helped me—" I broke off, grinning sheepishly. "Jeez. I guess I am still pissed."

"With good reason, it sounds like," she said.

"Maybe," I said. "But if I'd been really determined, I could've tried their damn test again. Or tried in a different town, maybe, where the dummy might've been better made or the test different. Some places you have to fireman's-carry the dummy down a flight of stairs without bumping it on anything. They gotta use a better dummy for that one, or even the tall folks'd fail it."

"But you didn't try again?"

"No. Sour grapes, you know. I figured if that was the kind of cop shop they ran, I didn't want any part of it. And if I couldn't be a cop in my chosen town then I didn't want to be a cop at all. So I went for my P.I. license instead." I shrugged. "It was a better choice. I like being my own boss. I'd make more money as a cop, but if I were in it for the money I'd have taken up something really lucrative, like construction or garbage collection or plumbing."

"What made you want to be a cop?" she asked curiously.

"I thought of it as a service profession," I said, embarrassed. "You know, 'To Protect and To Serve,' like it says on the doors of their cars. I s'pose I had visions of myself righting the wrongs of the universe, or at least rescuing the frail from the foul. I was pretty young and naive at the time."

"If more of the people who become cops thought of it as a service profession," she said, "maybe it would be a service profession."

"Or maybe they'd just burn out from dealing with scum all day every day, and lose track of who it was they wanted to protect and to serve. That's what happens to the best of 'em now."

"What happens to private investigators?" she asked, smiling just enough to take any possible sting out of it.

"They end up on tour with elfrock bands, chasing possibly imaginary murderers," I said. "Seriously, or maybe I should say more usually, we repossess a lot of cars for the Bank of America. It's a living."

"No burnout?" she said.

"Not from repossessing cars," I said. "Elfrock bands are another matter."

She smiled, acknowledging sour humor. "But you must do more than repossess cars and follow elfrock bands."

"Actually, this is my first elfrock band." I thought about it. "And my last, if I've anything to say about it. But yeah, we get interesting cases once in a while. Too interesting, sometimes. As in the ancient Chinese curse, 'May you live in interesting times.' "

"Who's 'we'?"

"Oh, my partner and me. Didn't I say I have a partner? Shannon Arthur. She's why I ended up with Cold Iron, actually. I was gonna turn Candy down, but then Shannon came in with this giant Christmas tree—It's a long story, but the thing is, we had this stupid fight, and I took Candy's case mostly because I was pissed at Shannon." I kicked at a pebble in the sand. "One thing, if Jorandel does send me packing . . . I'm kind of anxious to tell Shannon I'm sorry."

"I take it you feel the fight was your fault?"

"I know it was my fault." A wave came up, washed over my ankles, and slid away in a glittering whirl of sunlight. "I had this thing about Christmas. That's another long story, and maybe not worth telling. Except . . . hell." I stared across the water, toward the thin Prussian-blue line where sea met sky. "I don't want to make it a dirty secret I can't tell anyone. It wasn't my fault. I didn't do anything wrong. My father molested me."

"Oh, honey!" She reached for me instinctively, a quick motherly hug and a wordless, encouraging look of such compassion it brought tears to my eyes.

I swallowed hard and looked at the sand at our feet. "The last time it was at Christmas. I ran away, and I blocked the whole thing out of my mind for years, but I was always afraid of Christmas. Always in a bad mood during the holidays. Shannon put up with it as well as she could, but I didn't make it easy." I looked at her, wanting to explain what I didn't fully understand myself. "See, I didn't know why I felt so weird about Christmas. I didn't remember. So how could I tell her? I mean, I didn't even know there was anything to tell."

"And now you remember?"

"Yeah. Jorandel wrote a song. He did it just to get at me, I think. To hurt me. And if Candy hadn't been there, maybe that's all it would've done. But she was. And she knew . . . as well as anyone could, anyway, she knew what to do. Because she'd been there: it happened to her, too." I was having trouble with words; I didn't want to say what happened to her. "Her father molested her." It came out too fast and frail. I remembered her inability to say the word "home," or to hear it without tears. "Poor little pixie. I wish . . ." But I couldn't say what I wished. I didn't know. Just that things were different, that the world were a pleasanter place, that people wouldn't hurt each other, that Candy could have had a better life. "Oh, hell."

"I know," said Vyla. "Honey, I know. I'm so sorry."

"It's not about me," I said.

"I know. You want to give her all the things she never had, and take away the things that hurt her." She said it with such understanding certainty that I stared in surprise, but she was looking into the distance ahead of us and I couldn't read her expression. "The hardest lesson I think I ever learned," she said, "is that you can't ever do that for someone. All you can do is give him what you've got to give, and hope it's enough. And sometimes it won't be."

I looked at the sand again. "It's too late to give Candy anything."

"I think you gave her what you could, didn't you?"

"I don't know. She gave me so much more."

She chuckled. "Life isn't a comparison study," she said, "and what she gave you doesn't lessen what you gave her. I think you did your best, and I think that's all any of us can ever do."

"My best wasn't good enough."

"It often isn't," she said. "That's what you've got to learn to live with, honey. That it won't always be good enough, but all you can do is learn from your mistakes and keep trying."

"Jeez." I grinned. "You sound like me at my most infuriatingly facile philosophical."

She looked at me, eyes dancing with irrepressible merriment. "It's a universal truth, girl, what can I say?"

"You've said enough," I said severely. "And I thank you very kindly for it. No wonder Killer's the best-adjusted elfrock musician, under all that hair, that a person could hope to meet. You'd keep anybody's feet on the ground."

"I think I'll thank you for that and not look at it too closely," she said, smiling.

"And I think we'd better get out of the sun before we both burn to a crisp," I said. "Unless you're working on your tan?"

"Oh, lord, I wasn't thinking!" She looked at her bare arms and legs in comical dismay. "One thing I do not need is a suntan." We fled the beach in giggling haste, all my problems blessedly, if temporarily, forgotten.

19

Cold Iron went to Blaisdell that afternoon for a sound check. Vyla said she had some shopping to do in town, but I went along with the band. It seemed a good opportunity to question people about Jimendan's activities the previous night. I thought I might have some difficulty getting them to talk without making them suspicious, but in the end all I had to do was wax sentimental about Candy, an emotion not entirely feigned, and say I was trying to get a picture of her last hours. I said I wanted to believe that her death was an accident, not suicide.

I didn't talk to Emerson; he'd have seen through my ruse too readily. But the others were politely willing to spend a little time answering Candy's cousin's dumb questions. They had no reason to imagine I was anything but what I pretended to be. They'd seen me stoned, drunk, and stupid right along with Candy. They treated me as they had treated her: with patient forbearance. I wasn't one of them, but I wasn't an outsider either, and of course they knew I was in Jorandel's favor at the moment. They told me what I asked.

Most of it was wasted time. Everyone had been tired after the luau and most of them had gone straight to bed when we got back to the hotel. One security guard, on duty during the night, had heard Candy and Jimendan laughing together shortly after Jorandel and I had gone to bed. Another had seen them raid the liquor cabinet half an hour or so later, and said she'd seemed happy enough then. that established that Jim had stayed with her, at least for a while, but it didn't prove he'd had anything to do with her death.

I was down to frail hopes, roadies who didn't stay in the suite and had no reason to pass through it last night, when I finally found what I was looking for. "Nah, I didn't see them after the luau," said the last roadie I asked. "But I figured they'd be together, you know?" He was a tall, skinny, long-haired halfling with pale blue eyes and a cautious smile.

"Why?" I asked, surprised. Jim and Candy had not exactly been an item while I'd been with the band.

"Well, he brought her a bottle of soda before the luau." He sounded surprised at my ignorance. "He wouldn't do that if he wasn't going to spend some time with her."

"Soda? You're sure?"

"Sure," he said. "In a little brown bottle." He grinned at me, a knowing look. "You've seen 'em."

"Yes." This was what I wanted, wasn't it? So why was my stomach tying itself in knots? "How d'you know he brought her one? I mean, they're small little bottles. And he wouldn't exactly hold it up on display, would he?"

He studied me incuriously. "No, but he wasn't making much effort to hide it, either," he said. "Why would he? He was among friends. He was kind of playing with it while he walked, you know? Tossing it and catching it."

"And he gave it to Candy?"

"Well, he took it to her room. I don't know whether she was in there. I think maybe she was in the living room with Killer and the guys, now you mention it. But I was getting ready for the luau and I didn't pay much attention. Why? What's it matter now? If she didn't get it from Jimendan, she got it from the Roach, and she did too much and OD'd, and that's that, right?"

"Right." I had what I wanted, and now I was looking for an out, and there wasn't one. I stared at him, realizing with a sinking dread that here, perhaps, was another potential victim. How many would Jim kill for his macabre masquerade? "Can you always tell them apart?" I asked.

"Jim and Jorandel?" he said. "Nah." He was safe, then. "But it hadda be Jim, didn't it? Jorie was spending the night with you."

"You knew that before the luau?" I said, surprised. "I didn't."

"Well, no, I didn't know it then," he said. "But he did, didn't he?"

It didn't matter. "Yes," I said absently. "He did." There was a certain logic to that: circular, but it made sense. And the point was that now I had evidence, of a sort, to bring to Jorandel. I'd thought that would make the job of telling him easier. But it wouldn't.

The roadie was looking at me with a patient smile. "I got work to do," he said. "anything else you wanta know before I get back to it?"

"Just your name," I said.

"Mitch," he said, surprised. "Mitch Adams."

I attempted a smile, but it didn't work very well. "Thanks, Mitch," I said.

"Any time," he said cheerfully.

I watched him walk away. Jorandel, your brother was seen bringing Candy the soda that killed her. Would this make him believe me, when I told him what I thought Jim was planning, and what he had done? It convinced me, horribly and finally, but it wasn't exactly irrefutable proof. In fact it was easily refuted: if the soda Jim brought Candy was meant to kill her, would he have carried it so openly, tossing it in the air for anyone to see, when he could have hidden it in his hand or in a pocket so no one would know he'd given it to her?

I thought he would have. In fact, I was sure he had. He was arrogant enough to play with that sort of risk, and clever enough to know that openness was really less of a risk than sneakiness. The very fact that he'd been unafraid of being seen robbed his action of any apparent evil. I knew Jorandel wouldn't believe my accusations. Perhaps, in his place, neither would I. But I had to tell him. And after that the near future mired in bleak inevitability: Jorandel would send me away in anger; and I would go in anger, and in relief, and in sorrow. Jimendan would persist in his plans; and Jorandel, forewarned but fiercely, defiantly blind, would make no effort to stop him until it was too late.

Maybe he wouldn't try to stop him, even then. Maybe he wouldn't believe, even if he saw the blow falling. I thought of the pair of them asleep in the car last night with their heads together and their arms intertwined, and for a moment I didn't believe it, either.

"He brought her a bottle of soda before the luau." No, that was too telling: I had to believe it. Why else would Jim bring Candy a bottle of soda? She got her soda from the Roach. She'd told me so. And I didn't believe Mitch's interpretation that he brought her soda because he was going to spend time with her. If that was the case, he'd have waited till after the luau, wouldn't he? The implication was that they were going to share it, and he certainly hadn't used any during the luau, or he wouldn't have fallen asleep so readily on the way home.

But if he wanted to poison her, what better way than to put the deadly drug in her room, perhaps mix it with her own supply, or replace her supply, in her absence? The soda she had used at the luau hadn't killed her. It wasn't till we got home, and she had perhaps dipped into the supply she kept in her room, that she died.

Had he been with her still? Had he watched her inhale the fatal dose, and walked away, leaving her dead or dying? Probably not: that was a risk he didn't need to take. All he had to do was stay with her long enough to be sure she used up the supply she was carrying, so that the next bit she used would kill her. He probably left her then. In fact I was surprised he hadn't made some kind of fuss about it, to be sure there were witnesses to show he'd left her alive.

But of course he had no reason to think anyone would suspect foul play. Murderers often give themselves away by their very efforts to provide themselves with alibis and the appearance of guiltlessness, but Jimendan wouldn't make that sort of mistake. He'd already proved himself too sly, too cold-blooded, too arrogant for that. He would not be caught out in an excessive display of innocence, at least not before he was accused. And probably not then. Probably he would laugh off an accusation with disdainful confidence that no mere mortal could catch him out. Perhaps, if Jorandel accused him, it would startle him into some betraying response. . . .

But Jorandel wouldn't accuse him. I knew that as surely as I knew that I could delay in telling Jorandel no longer. I had to present him with my theory, and with my evidence such as it was, and accept the consequences. Sighing, I left the backstage area and found a seat in the arena from which I could watch Cold Iron and their roadies at work. But all I really watched was Jorandel. I found myself studying him, trying to memorize the lines of his face, the movements of his body, the sound of his voice. One last afternoon, one last concert, one last confrontation, and I would almost certainly never see him in person again.

I would be able to follow his career, if I chose to, through teenybopper magazines and MTV news. The thought of that was numbing. I could not imagine knowing him only through glossy photos, printed interviews, and audio CDS. I did not know what would happen to that strange bond between us when my only contact with him was through the media, and he had none with me. Would it bother him? Would he feel the bond stretched taut, as it had been last night, till separation was an almost physical pain? Had he felt it, last night? Or was the whole thing only a demented fantasy of mine, nothing to do with him?

Fantasy or real, it was something I would have to deal with, and wondering forlornly whether it would bother him was not a sound way to begin. What bothered him was his problem. And yes, it would bother me, but it wasn't going to be a life-threatening problem. I'd have had to leave him sooner or later, anyway. I'd told Vyla there was no room in my life for an elfrock star, and I'd meant it. Even if he wanted me to, I couldn't be jauntering about the world on tour with him—or waiting patiently at home, either, come to that. I had a business to run, work to do, cases to solve. Or at least cars to repossess.

The only kind of man with whom I could possibly share my life on a long-term basis would be one as strong and as independent as I, who didn't begrudge me my strength and my independence, and I had decided a long time ago that there was no such man in the universe. Certainly, Jorandel wasn't he. If Jorandel ever did want a long-term relationship with a woman, it wouldn't be a woman who had a life of her own. He needed a person's whole attention, all the time. Candy would have been perfect for him. But not I.

I had just reached that comfortable plateau in my cogitations when a heavy microphone stand came sailing off the stage to clatter among the seats some distance to my right. I'd been staring absently at a man clambering among the lights overhead. I sat up abruptly to stare at the guys onstage. Killer was absent. Blade and the Roach were watching without interest as Jim tried to throttle his brother. Jorie was hurling anything he could get his hands on, anywhere but at Jim. Frank was doing his best to separate them. Mitch Adams appeared to be trying to trip them; I realized later he had been trying to save a battery pack that had got under their feet.

Frank got Jim loose and pulled him aside. Jim fought him. Jorie just stood there, breathing hard. Frank held Jim back and I could see them talking, but I couldn't hear what was said beyond the occasional curse Jim shouted loud enough to reach me. He calmed slowly, and finally shut up. Frank kept talking to him. Jim kept shaking his head and scowling at Jorie, but he finally threw up his hands in a gesture of defeat, pulled free of Frank, and stalked offstage.

Frank said something to Jorie. Jorie nodded, said something, and they both started looking for something on the nearby floor. Mitch Adams, who had backed off with his rescued battery pack clutched lovingly to his breast when Frank got the brothers separated, was staring at Jorie with an odd expression on his face. Frank said something that made him start, look away sheepishly, and turn to leave the stage. Frank said something else. Mitch stopped, thought, went to an amplifier, picked up a small object, and handed it to Frank. Frank handed it to Jorie.

Jorie put it to his mouth and said, suddenly audible throughout the arena, "Okay, fine. I believe that's it for the sound check." His voice was not quite steady. "If you have any problems . . . solve them." He put down the microphone and walked away.

I sat there for a long moment, considering events, before I suddenly realized that had probably been my cue if I wanted a ride back to the hotel with the musicians.

Luckily they hadn't all been ready, either. I caught up with them just as they were leaving the arena, and tumbled into the limousine with them before I realized I might have preferred to struggle with the city bus system than to ride in the same car with Jim and Jorie just now.

It wasn't as bad as I feared; they didn't indulge in open warfare again. They were behaving very much as they had after Andy died. They didn't speak to each other. They barely looked at each other. Jim was hostile, Jorie was hurt, and both of them were taut with pent-up violence waiting to explode. But the presence of the other musicians helped balance that. The Roach was completely indifferent to those around him, as always. Blade seemed aware of the strained atmosphere, but uninterested. Killer's face was concealed, but he was as relaxed as the brothers were tense. He seemed to regard them with tolerant amusement. Once when Jim's leg accidentally touched Jorie's and then jerked away as though burned, I thought I saw Killer's lips twitch with irrepressible mirth just like his mother's.

If you didn't know that one of them was a murderer, intent on killing the other, their childish squabbling would be amusing. It nearly was, anyway. It was certainly a very strange thing to watch, because the bond between them was so strong that even in anger they couldn't just turn away and ignore each other. Even after we returned to the hotel suite where they could move physically apart, their whole attention remained centered on each other. It was the way I would always remember them: identical, at odds, and inescapably interconnected. I was still half consciously trying to memorize Jorandel, in painful anticipation of separation, but when I studied the lines and planes of his face I saw the reflection of Jimendan in his eyes. When I studied the lanky grace of his body I saw the yearning in it, almost literally leaning toward his brother. And inevitably I saw his brother. They were a unit, joined by the invisible force of affection, their movements as surely interlocked as if puppet strings ran between them so that when one stirred the other responded, and it was not possible to look at one without seeing the other.

When Vyla returned from her shopping expedition we

ordered an early dinner from room service and ate it on the broad lanai outside the common room, overlooking the ocean. By then the brothers had calmed somewhat, and Jorie at least made a real effort to be polite and sociable to Vyla. He and Killer joined us for dinner. Jim ordered separately and ate in his room, Blade went out, and the Roach was too wired to eat. He sprawled on the couch with an electric guitar and earphones, fingers flying inaudibly over the frets.

With Jim out of sight, Jorie was better able to function. He was visibly on edge; but for once, perhaps because Vyla was there, he made a genuine effort to keep his behavior socially correct, and for the most part he was successful. There were lapses: a dish that offended him, for example, was unthinkingly hurled to the floor before anyone could take it from him. But when Vyla broke the startled silence afterward with a mirthful chuckle and said, "That certainly won't trouble us any longer," it pulled him back from the brink of a raging tantrum to laugh with her.

"I apologize," he said.

She shrugged. "Luckily for you, it wasn't my dish."

He grinned at the implications and went on eating. "What would you have done if it were your dish?"

"Spanked you and sent you to your room," she said without hesitation.

His eyes flashed. I thought he was going to take offense. But instead, after only a fractional hesitation, he burst into laughter and glanced at Killer. "Did you spend much of your childhood in your room?" he asked.

Killer nodded lugubriously. "She's a hard woman," he said.

The phone rang. Jorie glanced in through the open door, saw that no one was making a move to answer it, and yelled at the Roach to get it. The Roach, if he heard, ignored him. "I'll get it," said Killer, rising.

"Fuck it," said Jorie.

"Did you know," Vyla said unexpectedly while her son went to answer the telephone, "that 'fuck' is the only word in the English language that can be used as almost any part of speech?" Jorie and I stared at her. She was wholly engrossed in the delicate task of separating a bit of lobster meat from its shell. Without looking up at us, she went on placidly, "You can make a whole sentence with just 'fuck' and one other word."

"What sentence?" I said, diverted.

"This fucking fucker's fucked." She looked up in triumph and, noting Jorie's fascinated stare, added almost apologetically, "My father was a military man."

"That explains it," I said solemnly. Her eyes met mine, and we both snickered.

"It's for you, Jorandel," said Killer, coming back through the doorway. "Sorry, but it's Veladora." He sat down and picked up his chopsticks while Jorie hurled his fork to the floor and rose, scowling. "I told him you weren't here," said Killer, "but he didn't believe me."

Jorie cursed fluently, knocked his chair over backward, and stalked inside to the telephone, brushing so hard against the sliding glass door on his way that it rattled in its frame for several seconds after he was past it. Nobody said anything. Vyla put the lobster aside and transferred her attention to a plate of sashimi. Killer, whose chair faced into the room, appeared to be watching Jorie. I stared at the sunset-stained horizon, thinking of nothing. I could hear Jorie's voice in the background, but I couldn't hear what he said. Distant traffic sounds competed with the faraway hush of the surf that rose on the still evening air scented of exotic flowers and the sea. The setting sun cast a ribbon of gold across the water. Jorie's voice was rising, some of the words becoming distinguishable, but mostly only the curse words. I ignored them.

"Damn it," said Killer. I couldn't ignore that; he said it with considerable force, at the same time rising so suddenly his chair joined Jorie's on its back on the floor.

"What—?" I said, but he was already gone. My eyes were dazzled by the sunset. There were few lights on in the suite, and for a moment I could not understand what was happening. It was like coming in on the middle of a very bad print of a very old movie: it took time for the images to resolve themselves into something I could comprehend.

Jorandel was doing his window trick again. There was one window in the common room that opened not onto the lanai but directly onto the many-story drop to the ground below. Killer got there just in time to stop him. The Roach watched, unconcerned, as Killer made a flying tackle that caught Jorie around the legs and jerked him back into the room just as he released his grip on the window frame and flexed his knees in readiness to jump out. They landed in a tangle of arms and legs against the wall and for a long moment neither of them moved. The Roach straightened a little on the couch so he could see them better, but that was the only sign he made that he had even noticed what was going on. I rose uncertainly. Vyla, also watching, put a hand on my arm, and I sat back down.

Killer extricated himself from Jorandel and climbed unsteadily to his feet, pressing one hand protectively against the side of his head. Jorie sat up, rubbing one shoulder, and scowled up at Killer. He said something that Killer answered with a shrug, and then he put out a hand for Killer to help him up. They spoke briefly, and Jorie laughed, and Killer picked up the phone Jorie had thrown on the floor. He put it on its table, said something to Jorie, and Jorie laughed again, happy as the proverbial clam. In a moment they joined us again on the lanai, picked up their chairs, and resumed eating as though nothing had happened.

Ignore the elephant. I stared at my food for a moment, then put my fork down very carefully beside my plate and stared at it instead. Killer had only just got there in time. Jorandel had no way of knowing whether he would make it. Or even whether he would try. When Jorandel stepped up onto that windowsill he was alone in a room with the Roach, and he must have known damn well the Roach wouldn't make a move to save him. Calculated risk, hell.

"Is something wrong, cousin?" asked Jorie.

I looked at him. His expression was all innocence, his smile concerned and interested. I looked past him at the dazzling colors of the fading sunset. The ocean was a solid mass now, mysteriously joined to the sky in a darkening distance starred by the lights of dinner cruise boats slowly wending their way through soft shadows under the purpling sky. Aware that I had been asked a question, I said vaguely, "No," and could not remember whether that was the correct response. Ignore the elephant. I glanced at Jorie, saw that he was satisfied, and ignored the elephant: I asked some inconsequential question, and he answered me, and conversation was restored.

After dinner there was time only to dress for the concert, tumble into the cars, and go. At the arena, Vyla and I found our seats and settled into them with a minimum of confusion while the opening act's equipment was being cleared from the stage. It was odd to be attending a Cold Iron concert without Candy. Vyla was a very comfortable companion, but Candy's absence made it a new experience, strange and a little daunting. Or perhaps it was Jorie's latest showy little trick with the window that did that.

But I didn't want to think of that. I didn't know how to think of it. I had convinced myself he only did those things to impress; that, as Candy had said, he knew someone would stop him. This time he couldn't have known that. He couldn't have known whether Killer could even see him. And he had been ready to jump anyway. He very nearly had jumped.

And where would Jimendan's plans fit with that? Maybe, I thought sourly, instead of being angry with me for accusing Jim, Jorie would thank me kindly and ask Jim whether he could help him in any way.

"You okay, honey?" asked Vyla. She had to raise her voice over the growing clamor of the impatient audience waiting for Cold Iron to come on.

"I don't know." I said it without thinking, and stared at her, and tried to muster a smile. "I mean, of course I am. Jeez, I don't know. I guess I am."

"He didn't mean it, you know."

"You don't think so? That's what I've always said before, but this time . . ."

"He knew Killer'd be watching," she said comfortably.

"Well, he cut it damned close." I sounded resentful, as though I imagined he had done it solely to irritate me.

"Killer says he often does," she said. "And I suppose someday he may cut it too close. But there's nothing to do but hope he gets some sense before that happens."

"He won't, you know. It's not sense he's lacking."

"I know," she said, looking at me. "They're not quite stable, those two."

I laughed involuntarily. "Understatement," I said. "They're psychotic, is what they are."

"Yes," she said seriously. "But Jorandel, at least, is also a musical genius. I understand that's not uncommon."

"What isn't? That genius is accompanied by madness?" I said. "I never quite believed it, before."

She smiled, but without her usual merriment. "Seeing is believing, eh?" She studied me gravely. "I wish I could help you."

"I'll be all right," I said, embarrassed.

"Yes," she said, considering it. "Yes, I think you will. You're a survivor."

Cold Iron came onstage before I had a chance to respond to that. Which was as well, since I had no idea what to say. Vyla and I inserted our earplugs in unison as the roar of the crowd became a thunderous bellow. Jorie and Jim came to the front of the stage, identical and graceful and grinning. The Roach touched his keyboard, and a sparkling little melody fell out of the amplifiers, stilling the crowd. Blade slid a deep bass lick in under it. Killer picked up the beat with a brush on cymbals, almost inaudible, building tension. Jim's guitar moaned, and whispered, and sobbed, and drifted almost imperceptibly into a swift, lyrical melody that rose and fell and faded like sunlight on clear river water. Blade's bass held the rhythm steady while Killer's drums picked up an urgent counterpoint. Jorie braced himself against the microphone stand and screamed: a long, drawn-out wail that began in painful dissonance and ended in perfect harmony with the melody that Jim and the Roach had built.

With that opening he created serenity in a maelstrom, order in chaos, fire in ice: it was Jorie's particular, gut-wrenching gift to produce frail, intense beauty that was an intrinsic function of savage turbulence. It occurred to me that a Cold Iron concert was in a way a parable of Jorie's personality told in music: psychotic and sensitive, repellent and compelling, invincible and vulnerable; opposites weirdly and improbably apposite, alluring, enchanting, dangerous. And I gave myself up to the glory of it as I had given myself to the glory of him, with the bittersweet awareness that I need not dread the annihilation of my self in the radiant vitality of his awful power. After tonight I would not again be near enough the flames to get burned.

20

It should, perhaps, have occurred to me that Jorandel might be too stoned or drunk for rational conversation by the time the concert was over. On some level I must have been aware of the possibility. Perhaps I hoped for it, as for a stay of execution, keeping the thought from my conscious mind out of superstitious fear of jinxing the chance. It was certainly not a far-fetched hope, and not only because it was common Cold Iron practice to drink or drug themselves silly during a concert. Only the visually impaired could have failed to notice that Jorandel was drinking onstage throughout the performance that night.

But when the bodyguards herded us into the cars after the guys' showers for the swift, silent rush through deserted night streets to the hotel, he was sober enough to chat amiably with Vyla all the way. He put a proprietary arm around me when we got in, and I leaned comfortably against him and tried not to think what I would say when we were alone.

Vyla said good-bye to us in the hotel lobby, with a swift hug and an encouraging smile for me, and we trooped to the elevators in a weary and no doubt bizarre-looking cluster. The musicians hadn't bothered to put on street clothes after their showers. Instead, they were bundled in floor-length, hooded caftans, like the rejects from the Seven Dwarves I had called them when I first learned their names. Blade and the Roach had groupies on each arm. Jimendan had only one, but she was a knockout. And there were several more trailing us with the bodyguards, presumably awaiting their turn.

Jorandel took me straight to his room when we

reached the suite. When he had closed the door behind us I said, "Jorie," and didn't know how to continue.

He didn't give me a chance. He pulled me onto the bed and into his embrace, not roughly but with such fierce and tender need that I responded without thinking, without hesitation, with love. It was like the first time again, slow and sweet and attentive, only this time there was no uncertainty, no unfamiliarity, no hesitation. The lean pressures of his body were as much a part of me as my own hungry responses. His eyes were as vividly blue as the tropical sea outside, and deep enough to drown in. And his sweet, slow smile was a promise he knew very well how to keep.

Afterward, lying naked in his arms with my legs tangled in his, my head resting on his chest, and the strong beat of his heart against my ear, I knew I'd just made telling him more difficult than ever. And I knew I still had to tell him. And I knew how it would end.

He brushed his fingers through my hair, cupped his hand under my chin, and gently lifted my head till he could see my face. "What is it, cousin?" he said, those blue eyes studying my face. "You've been quiet since dinner. Are you angry with me about the window?"

I closed my eyes briefly. "That's none of my business, is it?" I said, and shifted, getting an elbow under me for support. "But . . . we need to talk."

He studied me with a curious expression, half frown, half grin. "This sounds serious, cousin."

"It is," I said.

"I hate when things get serious."

The only thing to do with that was ignore it. "Jorandel, I'm not really Candy's cousin."

"I know," he said, expressionless.

I was so set on getting said what I had to say, I didn't really hear him. "In fact, I never met her before the day I joined you in San Francisco."

"I know," he said, and this time I heard him.

"You know?"

"I wondered when you would tell me." He untangled his body from mine in one swift, graceful movement and sat on the edge of the bed, his back to me. "You're a private eye. I saw your license." The dazed and sweaty comfort we'd been sharing was gone for good.

"Investigator," I said automatically, while the meaning of his words slowly sank in. "You saw my license? You mean it was you? You came in my room and searched my things?"

"I like to know who is traveling with us." He turned to look at me, his eyes unreadable. "I knew you were not what you said you were."

"Candy's cousin? I don't see why I couldn't have been," I said, offended.

"You weren't here to loose her from us," he said. "And you weren't here to get close to the elfrock stars." There was a surprisingly bitter hint of self-mockery in that. "You made no deception of that: you didn't even like us. But you stayed. Even when the Roach fed you a mickey. I wanted to know why."

I sat up too, and numbly began to put on my clothes again, piece by scattered piece. "You knew all along. And you never said anything." I sounded stunned. The sudden transition from the lazy afterglow of lovemaking to this thinly veiled hostility had caught me by surprise.

"I was waiting for you to tell me." He spoke as to a stranger, his voice level and utterly emotionless.

We were strangers, really. I said, "Why?" and my own voice was nearly as devoid of emotion as his.

He shrugged. "Why did you not?"

"I'm telling you now."

"Yes." He picked up his robe and put it on. "Why?"

"Because I found out what Candy hired me to find out."

"The great detective," he said.

"Not so great, lately, I guess." If I were any good at what I did, surely I'd have been prepared for this. I had known him well enough to see the end coming, but I hadn't been prepared. When it came, it was another of his bewildering games, and I didn't know the rules. "Jorandel, what's this about? Why are you so hostile all of a sudden? If you've known all along I was a detective, what's changed now?"

He turned his face toward me, and his eyes were cold, exactly the blue of deep ice where it meets the sea. "It is between us now," he said, as if that were an answer. "What did Candy hire you to learn?"

"She thought someone meant to kill you. She wanted me to find out who." Something flickered in his eyes when I said that. Some strong emotion, but it was buried in the depths of ice and I couldn't guess what it was. It didn't matter. The bond between us had acquired the weight of chains. "I found out," I said wearily.

"Did you?" He rose suddenly and walked to the window, his back to me. "And who, in your belief, wishes to kill me?" The waiting stillness of his posture belied the mockery in his tone. He was frightened of something. Of what I had learned?

"Your brother," I said, watching him.

That was so far from whatever he expected that it startled a little hiccup of laughter from him, but he didn't turn around. "My brother? You believe that *Jimendan* wishes to kill me?"

"Yes." I told him all of it, as briefly as I could, more out of a sense of duty to Candy than because I imagined that any mere facts would alter his obvious determination to disbelieve. He listened with still and careful attention, politely, as to the ramblings of the dangerously insane. When I was finished he waited for a long moment, still with his back to me, before he asked whether I was finished. His voice gave nothing away. I said, "Yes. I'm sorry, Jorie, it's the only thing that makes sense. It must be Jim."

One moment he was utterly motionless, apparently relaxed, hands clasped behind his back, as he had been all the while I was talking. In the next he was transformed into a raging lunatic, hurling himself across the room at me with hands outstretched, his face a mask of fury. I moved fast, but not quite fast enough. I managed to avoid the direct collision he wanted, but I didn't quite get out of the way. One of his flailing hands caught me, clawlike. With the easy grace of an athlete he used that to catch his balance and slam me so hard against the wall that I saw stars.

I also saw his free hand uplifted, a white-knuckled fist leveled at my face. I was too stunned to dodge or fight back, and I knew there wasn't a damn thing I could say to stop him, so I did the only thing left open to me: I stared him straight in the eye with the coldest, most contemptuous expression I could muster.

It shouldn't have worked. If he was as angry as he appeared, he shouldn't even have noticed. But he noticed. He froze. For a long moment we stood like that, I with my back pressed hard against the wall where he had thrust me and was still holding me, and he with his fist drawn back ready to strike. His expression didn't change, but a light went out of his eyes. He lowered his fist and carefully withdrew his other hand from my shoulder. I waited, watching him steadily. After a long moment he said in a curiously flat, lifeless voice, "Get out."

I went. I had to step sideways to get past him, and I hesitated to turn my back on him. But he stayed where he was, facing the wall, while I left the room. I could feel the tension like an electric current flowing through that intangible bond between us, and I knew he felt it too. But it was a strangely dull thing, distant and damaged. I closed the door gently behind me.

There were two loose groupies in the common room, and one bodyguard. I was glad there were no musicians present. It would have made the long walk from his room to mine even longer. When I got there, I didn't take time for a shower, though I did comb my hair and change quickly into more comfortable clothes. It wasn't clear whether his instruction to "get out" meant I was to leave only his room or the entire Cold Iron entourage, but the latter seemed wisest at this point. It wasn't even as difficult as I had thought it would be. He'd made it damn near easy.

I'd already packed most of my clothes that afternoon, in expectation of being sent away. I tossed in my bathroom things and my crumpled concert costume, made a last quick check of the room to be sure I'd got everything, and closed the little travel bag Candy had bought for me.

Nothing had changed in the common room. I looked around one last time at the litter of guitars and thought of the Jorandel I had come to love, the troubled genius whose music stirred my soul. I had always known he was a sociopath, and yet I must have imagined I was immune to his fits of violence, or why would it stun me so to learn that I was not?

But I hadn't imagined that. On the morning after the first night we slept together, I had been ready and damn near willing to die at his hand. I remembered the sense of acquiescence to his power when he grasped my hair and pulled my head back that morning, and it was as though I recalled a tale told me by a stranger. How could I have felt like that? How could I have so submerged my soul in him that I hadn't even the sense to survive?

It didn't matter. Whatever spell he'd cast, whatever sleepwalking madness I'd suffered, I was awake now. I hefted my bag and left the suite with exactly the sense of controlled haste and subdued panic with which one emerges from a darkened alleyway in the dead of night. There might be dangers yet ahead of me, but the worst were those I was leaving behind.

When I got downstairs to the lobby I considered asking for a room, and realized I wanted to go home. I wanted it the way a child wants things, desperately, anxiously, instantly. Armed with quarters obtained with some argument from the supercilious desk clerk, I installed myself at a public telephone to talk to airlines. It was an unlikely hour to do business, and at the best of times airlines are not big on granting instant gratification, but I found a flight with space available and just enough time to get to the airport to catch it.

I thought I would sleep on the plane, and so did the in-flight crew. We were given hard little pillows, miniature blankets, and dim lighting. The plane was half empty, so I had three full seats to myself on which to stretch out in something close enough to comfort that tired as I was, I certainly should have been able to sleep. But I couldn't relax. No matter how diligently I concentrated on all the mind-blanking relaxation tricks I knew, images of Jorandel intruded. I kept thinking of that last scene with him, inventing better ways I could have reacted, things I could have said—and, more than anything, wondering exactly what had happened there.

What had provoked his hostility, even before I told him my theory about Jim?

And what sudden, unexpected fit of sanity had finally freed me of my self-destructive fascination with his dark and compelling personality? It wasn't a case of love disillusioned and destroyed by an episode of brutality. I wasn't disillusioned; I'd known his caprice and his capacity for violence. And I loved him still. All that showy little scene had done was to awaken some core of self-respect in me, which said that love or no love, I would not be abused.

I don't know when, in the course of that thought, I realized the importance of that word, "showy." What he had done was entirely for show. An act: a final performance for me. Why? To get rid of me? But that was unnecessary, and he knew it. If he wanted rid of me, he had only to tell me to go. As indeed, in the end, he had. Why, then? What purpose did he serve by feigning a degree of anger he didn't feel, by threatening me? Was it only another of his interminable games? Just curiosity, wondering how far I would let him push me, and how I would react when I'd been pushed too far? Or had he been hiding some other emotion under the feigned rage? But I couldn't imagine what emotion he would be at such pains to conceal.

The thought crossed my mind that it might have been another attempt on his part to "help" me, as by writing "Papa's Little Girl" to jog my memory: perhaps he knew I needed to find the strength and the self-respect to reject him, to refuse to be further abused, to walk away. But I knew I was only making that up because I wanted to believe in his basic goodwill. It was as much an illusion as anything I had ever believed about him.

And it really didn't matter, in any case. There was nothing I could do about what had happened, nothing I could change even if I wanted to. Nor was I sure I would change anything if I could. I was best off away from him, away from the whole Cold Iron lifestyle. I had solved the case. I had done all I could to prevent another murder. If there were any chance of proving Jimendan had already done murder, and of bringing him to justice, there might have been some sense in staying with them. But if he had, even the police would be hard put to prove it. I hadn't a hope.

I did not feel I'd earned Candy's money, but neither did I quite see to whom I could return what was left of it. I supposed her parents were her rightful heirs, but she wouldn't have wanted them to have it. It was a problem to resolve later: perhaps I would donate it to some charitable cause she might approve, to help abused or homeless children or something of the sort. Shannon would doubtless have something to say about it. For now I was more concerned with getting home to her, to apologize for past idiocies and enjoy what was left of the Christmas season.

I'd given her no warning I was coming. There hadn't been time, and anyway she deserved a pleasant surprise from me for a change. I was too tired to fuss with buses or BART, so I splurged on a taxi and went directly from the airport to the office, comfortably absorbing the familiar sights of the Bay Area on the way: streets, stores, buildings, bridges, all safe and secret in the eternal winter rain. It was a long way from the tropical paradise I'd explored with Jorandel. In Honolulu people were even now basking on beaches in brilliant sun. Here they huddled under umbrellas, and the sun was at best a bright spot in the grim winter sky.

The sodden Christmas decorations on Berkeley's lampposts didn't bother me a bit. In front of our office building, a hundred years old and still standing after two good-sized earthquakes, I paid the taxi driver with the last of my cash and hurried inside, out of the rain. The corridors smelled of wood polish and wet overcoats. I didn't wait for the antique elevator with its ancient and surly operator. It was quicker to take the stairs. They creaked under my feet. At the top of the last flight I adjusted my shoulder bag and started down the long corridor to our office.

Moonshadows wake the dancing land
The stars have stung the laughing man
My footsteps echo on the sea
Somebody save me . . .

Jorandel's voice, with Cold Iron backing him. I thought it was my imagination. The weary mind plays unfriendly tricks sometimes. But it didn't go away: it got louder, the nearer I got to our office. I paused, one hand on the corridor wall, blinded by memories. Of all the things that might have greeted me on my return to Berkeley, this was the last thing I had expected. It was only Shannon playing the *Midnight Son* album on the office blood box, but . . .

I didn't know she had the album. I hadn't thought of hearing it again, now that I'd left them. Christmas trees and decorations I could handle. Jorandel's voice on a pair of six-inch speakers . . . I should have foreseen that, but I hadn't. I wasn't ready. I hadn't had time to build any barriers between that music and my soul.

Someone came out of an office behind me. I took my hand off the wall, squared my shoulders, and kept walking. Whoever it was, he probably didn't even glance my way, but I wasn't going to be seen having a fit of the vapors in a public corridor. Jorandel's voice out of six-inch speakers was something I was going to have to get used to pretty damn quickly, since the *Midnight Son* album was at the top of the charts. I was likely to hear a lot of it before something else displaced it. When you have to do something, there's no time like the present to start.

Shannon was at her desk by the window with a cup of hot coffee cradled between her hands. The Christmas tree was in the opposite corner, so she could stare at it without turning around. The office wasn't very big, and the Christmas tree was. If I sat at my desk, facing hers, I was likely to get stabbed in the back by plastic icicles or aluminum stars. When I came in, Shannon glanced up with a frown that became a smile when she saw me, then went serious again when she saw me looking at the tree.

I put my bag down on the couch by the door. "It's pretty," I said, nodding toward the tree.

She smiled almost shyly. "Thanks. You really like it?" she said, amazed.

"I'll get used to it," I said. The Cold Iron song ended and an announcer began to proclaim the wonders of a household cleaning product. "Oh, it's the radio," I said stupidly. "I thought you'd gone out and bought a Cold Iron CD."

"Was that Cold Iron?" she said. "You're supposed to be with them, aren't you? Or did you find your murderer?"

"I found him," I said. "For all the good it'll do."

"What's that mean?" She didn't wait for me to answer. "You want some coffee? I just made it. You look tired as hell. Have you been up all night, or what?"

"More like and what," I said.

She sorted that out. "Oh." Grinning, she went to get me a cup of coffee. "Sit down," she said. "Jeez, Rosie, I've missed you."

The radio was informing me that the weather continued cold and rainy. I knew that already. I closed my eyes, listening to Shannon fuss with the coffeepot. She always had trouble getting it off its stand without knocking the top loose and getting wet grounds all over the floor. She was the most elegant woman I had ever met, her every movement perfect unstudied grace, and yet she couldn't operate the simplest household appliances without disaster.

It was, however, always graceful disaster. She was inept, but never clumsy. If I dropped a basket of coffee grounds I'd be all over the room trying to catch it, burning my fingers, splashing wet grounds on everything in sight before the basket finally hit the floor. If Shannon did it she would either catch it in midair with no wasted movement and a minimum of spill, or she would step gracefully out of its way and calmly set about cleaning up the mess after it landed. You had to know her a long time before you even noticed how inept she was, because she was so damned self-assured you almost assumed hers was the customary way of doing things. "Of course I spill my coffee grounds on the floor. Don't you?"

"What are you laughing about?" she asked.

I had closed my eyes and hadn't seen her come back. "Oh, thanks," I said, taking the proffered cup of coffee. "Jeez, I need this. You don't know how hard it is to get decent coffee in foreign parts like southern California and Hawaii."

"I wondered where you'd been," she said. "Having a glorious Hawaiian holiday, is it? While I slave away in the icy Bay Area rain?"

"Just so," I said. "Glorious Hawaiian holiday. Complete with sociopaths, drug abuse, and the odd murder between luaus. You don't know what you've been missing."

"I begin to guess," she said. "Poor Rosie. You wanta go home and sleep it off before you make your report?"

I only half heard her. The radio had segued from weather to news while she was getting my coffee. Most of it was things I didn't want to know: a small war here, a famine there; the sort of thing you have to learn to ignore because you can't fix it and you want to. But it didn't stop there. "The music world today mourns the loss of the Jorandel—" I stopped breathing. I think my heart stopped beating. ". . . of the elfrock group Cold Iron, who died early this morning . . ."

Breath and heartbeat began again, both of them in overdrive. There was a curious, high-C ringing in my ears. I thought stupidly, "Why is he saying Jorandel, not Jimendan?" If Jim had carried out his plan to murder Jorie and take his place, the announcer shouldn't know it was Jorandel who died.

". . . of a fall from the window of his hotel room in Honolulu, where Cold Iron was to have performed for two more nights before going on to . . ."

Oh. Jim hadn't done it. Jorie had miscalculated, as I had always been afraid he would. He had stepped out a window once too often, without first being sure that there was someone present who would and could stop him in time. I thought of the dizzying distance from that hotel window to the ground below, and I put my coffee cup down very carefully on the china blue Formica table in front of me. My hand shook so badly that I spilled almost as much of it as I saved. He'd have gone face-first with never a glance back for his expected rescue. And when it hadn't come, he'd have had the whole way down to know what he'd done, to watch the ground rush up toward him. . . .

Somebody save me . . .

I said, "Excuse me," very politely, and stood up. The

world tilted and I had trouble getting out of the office door without falling. Shannon steadied me: no questions, no superficial utterances, just a calm and supportive arm around my shoulders to keep me on my feet. I could see his smile, that impish upturning of the corners of his perfect Cupid's bow mouth, and the demon of laughter in his summer eyes. Had he dared to laugh at Death, when he found it at last? Had he gone down into that final darkness willingly? Or had he struggled, when it was too late, against gravity, against the unresisting moments rushing past him, against the inexorable, endless night? He was afraid of the dark.

Somebody save me . . .

The bathroom was not far down the corridor from our office, but even so, I barely made it in time. Shannon put up the seat for me and held my hair out of my face and offered me a glass of water to rinse the taste from my mouth when I stopped heaving, and she did it all without hesitation and without question, with no indication that my behavior was in any way odd. *I always throw up when I hear of a death on the news. Don't you?*

We'd been together a long time. And while our work ranged mostly from dull to boring, with about as much danger involved as that inherent in the average typing job, it did get interesting once in a while. When the daily routine can include laying down your life for the other guy and knowing she'll do the same for you, an inevitable intimacy develops, whether you'd be friends otherwise or not. If you would be, that intimacy enhances it. With us, it amounted to a friendship and affection deeper than in the average blood relationship.

She never did ask any questions. She knew I would talk when I could. And I did, in fits and starts, while she locked up the office and drove me home. I told her all of it: the music, the love, the sex, the drugs. The psychotic episodes. The playful afternoon of temples and beaches on Oahu. I told her about Cold Iron, about the Roach and Blade and Killer, about Vyla and Candy, about the luau and the concerts. I told her about my father, about Christmas, about "Janie's Got A Gun" and "Papa's Little Girl," and how Candy had helped me through the recognition of my past that Jorandel had forced on me.

And I told her about the drug overdoses and the windows.

I doubt I was exactly coherent, but she let me ramble and pieced it together as best she could, held my hand as long as I needed it, and left me alone when I needed to be alone. She was, I admit, a little hesitant about that last. But that was only because in my place she'd have had as desperate a need for companionship as I had for solitude. It's often difficult to give someone you love something that you know in his place you'd hate. But she did it, after I'd sworn half a dozen times that I'd call if I needed her.

But I was too exhausted to need anything but sleep. I stood for a long while after she'd left, listening to the silence of my little cottage on McGee Street, watching the interminable winter rain outside the windows. It was an arduous task to walk from the front door, where I'd said good-bye to her, to the shadowed comfort of my bedroom at the other end of the house. I'd talked out the worst of the horror, but none of the grief. There would be no escape from that but time. I was numb with it, dizzy, sick. *Somebody save me.* My eyes burned with unshed tears, my head ached, my bones were made of lead. I lay down in the close and lonely silence, closed my eyes on all the burdened memories, and slept.

21

Watery afternoon sunlight filtered through my bedroom curtains when I woke, and the room was swimming with dusty shadows. After only a week of my absence, the house had acquired the feel of a place no one lived in. But it was my house, and I had a strong nesting instinct. It was good to be home after too many hotel rooms in unfamiliar cities.

At the back of my mind I had that feeling of dread you have when you wake knowing that something bad has happened, but you don't yet remember what, and I started searching for it the way a child picks at a scabbed knee, fascinated by the raw skin underneath and frightened of hitting a spot that really hurts. For a long moment I lay drowsily watching dust motes sift through the air while my sleep-dazed brain fumbled with elusive memory.

It came back in a rush, with a sinking sense of horror and despair so violent I thought for a moment I was going to be sick again. Jorandel was dead. Jorandel, fey and beautiful boy-faced horror, fallen angel, sociopath, my love. Jorandel was dead.

It was one thing to be apart from him by choice, knowing he was making brilliant music—or unpleasant scenes—somewhere else in the world. It was quite another to know that he was not somewhere else in the world. That he was dead. That his musical genius and his slow, sweet smile alike were gone forever. I hadn't expected to see him again, but to know that I never could, that he was not there to be seen, left a lacuna in the universe that nothing else could fill.

Odd that I had to be told of it on the radio. I would have thought I'd feel his death, a sudden aching void within me when he died as though a part of me had died with him. I had felt it when he began to fail the night he nearly died of a drug overdose. It had been as though a light within me flickered and went out.

I had felt nothing like that this morning. When he died, I must still have been on the plane coming home, and the only thing that had disturbed me then was memories. Whatever had bound us, it must have been weaker than I thought, or perhaps have been broken when I left him. No hint of loss had traveled the invisible lines of force I had imagined between us, and nothing told me when they snapped, as they must have done, when he died. No lights went out.

Perhaps they were already out. Perhaps they went out when I walked away. I wondered only briefly whether things would have been different if I'd stayed. It didn't matter. I hadn't stayed, and he very possibly wouldn't have let me stay. Anyway it was done now. He was gone. I couldn't bring him back by agonizing over responsibility. He'd have jumped whether I was there or not. I was no more responsible for his life than he was for mine. We must each bear the burden of our own oppressive needs; and bear, too, the responsibility for finding a way to lighten the load when it threatens to overwhelm us. He chose his way. Now I must choose mine.

I wouldn't choose a window. I wouldn't choose death in any form. I would learn to live with his, and carry on. The first step was to get out of bed, so I did it. When in doubt, do whatever comes next, and try not to think beyond it. I showered, put on clothes that were not trendy, built a pot of coffee, and returned to the bedroom to unpack my travel bag.

The first thing I found under the dirty clothes and bathroom things I had tossed carelessly on top was Candy's Diskman and a collection of Cold Iron CDs. Jorandel's picture was on the cover of the *Midnight Son* album. Those impossibly blue eyes smiled their secret smile at the world like someone who would never die. The CDs fell out of my hands and I sat down. It was sheer good fortune that I landed on the edge of the bed instead of the floor.

Emerson had packed Candy's belongings. I had wondered what he would do with them. At some point after I had packed my bag he must have put these things of hers in it. Perhaps as a memento of her friendship. Or as a joke: elfrock for the lover of Mozart.

Or for the lover of Jorandel. *Somebody save me.*

I picked up the *Midnight Son* CD again and looked at it. That sweet, boyish face looked back at me, absurdly beautiful, deceptively innocent, forever frozen in a look of impish and oddly seductive amusement. For one brief moment I hated Emerson with all the fierce and broken fury of heart-shattering loss. But it was only a frantic effort to stave off grief, and I couldn't sustain it. I knew he must have intended only a careless gift. There would have been no malice in the gesture. He might even have meant it as a kindness. At worst it was a subtle reminder that he thought I ought to leave them, for my own good.

If that was what he wanted, he had it now. I'd left them. And Jorandel had left the world. I gathered up the CDs with trembling fingers, carried them across the room to the wastebasket, and dropped them in. And without a second's hesitation I bent to retrieve them, blinking back tears. They were all I had left of him or of Candy, all I would ever have. It might have been wise to discard them, but you just can't go around being wise all the time. It hurts too much.

I was still standing there with my hands full of CDs, unable to decide what to do with them, when Shannon walked in. She must have used her key instead of ringing the bell in order not to wake me if I were still asleep. When she paused in the bedroom doorway, I just looked at her. I don't know what my expression was like, but she stared at me and said in shocked concern, "Jesus, Rosie!"

I said, "I found these CDs." My voice sounded odd.

"I see that." She crossed the room to take them from me. "I'll put them away." She said it kindly, and very firmly. "Have you eaten?"

I watched her make room for the CDs in a bureau drawer and close them in. "No." At her glance I said defensively, "I made coffee."

"Good. We'll have some." She guided me out of the

bedroom with great solicitude, as if I were about a hundred years old.

I felt about a hundred years old. My body moved with the stiff and awkward caution of the extremely aged or infirm. I said querulously, "I can walk by myself, you know," and she let go of my arm, but she kept hovering all the way to the kitchen as though she feared I would fall and break my hip or something.

When she had me safely installed at the kitchen table, she poured me a cup of coffee without spilling the grounds on the floor and sat down opposite me to watch me drink it. "We'll go out to eat," she announced firmly. She was no more enthusiastic about cooking than I was. "You need to eat something."

"I'm not arguing," I said.

"Oh," she said. "Right." She got up and poured herself a cup of coffee, spilled the grounds on the floor, and silently cleaned them up before bringing her cup to the table to sit again. "Do you want to talk about it?"

"No."

"Should I?"

"Only if you want to."

"I called Hilly." She waited for a reaction, but I couldn't find one, so I just looked at her. After a moment she looked away from me, admired her perfectly shaped and painted nails for a pensive moment, and finally said, "They're calling it suicide."

I shrugged. "I suppose it was."

She nodded. "The tour's canceled, of course. But Hilly says the others are already arranging for studio time as soon as they get back to the mainland. With a new producer. I forget the name."

"Quick work," I said sourly. "I suppose it's important to get it out while he's still news. Free press, you know. Sensational suicides must help sell records."

"They do, I suppose," she said.

"And a new producer, already. I guess they can do that. Veladora's contract was with Jorandel, and they kept saying the only way he could get out of it was to die." My voice cracked. I shut up.

"Yes." She tapped one fingernail gently against the Formica top of my venerable kitchen table, watching her coffee with contemplative expectation. "Hilly said that, too."

I shrugged. "It wasn't exactly a secret."

"Let's go to dinner," she said abruptly.

I looked at her. She was gazing abstractedly out the window at the scotch broom, blackberry brambles, and weeds in my backyard. "What else did Hilly say?"

She shrugged elaborately. "Nothing much you hadn't already told me."

"What, for instance?"

She regarded the end of a strand of her dark, silky hair. "He mentioned how hard it was to tell the two of them apart. Jimendan and Jorandel. Most people couldn't, he said."

"That wasn't a secret, either."

"No."

"They did it onstage, for Christ sake," I said. "Jeez. I told you about it. I mean, that was the whole point. Jimendan could pass for Jorandel once he'd got rid of everybody who could tell them apart."

"I think we should go to dinner," she said, rising.

"Just a damn minute." I stood up, too. I'm not sure why. "What are you getting at?"

"Food," she said.

"I mean about Jim and Jorie," I said.

"I know." Her tone was deeply sympathetic.

"Well?" I said, staring at her.

"Well, he isn't passing for Jorandel," she said simply.

It took me a moment. When I understood what she was getting at I sat down again, too suddenly. I said, "No. Oh, no," in a hollow, frightened voice, and she sat down next to me.

"It's just an idea," she said, putting a reassuring hand on mine. "It could be wrong. Maybe they were with people who could tell them apart when it happened. Hilly didn't know the details yet."

"I don't believe it," I said.

"That Hilly didn't know the details?"

"Damn it," I said.

"Look, I didn't mean to mention it. I probably shouldn't have. There's nothing to prove anything either way. There's nothing we can do, at least not till we get the details. Hilly's gonna call me back. Rosie, I'm sorry. I should've kept my big mouth shut till I knew more. Don't worry about it, okay? We don't know anything yet."

"We know it fits." I tried to lift my coffee, and my hands were shaking so much I spilled it. I looked at the spreading stain on the defiantly untrendy winter clothes I'd selected, and said unhappily, "It fits better than my stupid theory. I just didn't see it."

"You couldn't," she said. "You loved him."

"Yes." I was still studying the stain on my dress. "I'll have to change. Before we go to dinner." I got up and had to catch the back of my chair for support. "Damn it," I said. "I think I'm gonna be sick again."

"You can't: you haven't eaten anything," she said.

That didn't stop me. Shannon kept reminding me throughout that it was just a theory; we didn't know anything yet. And I kept thinking how odd it had seemed that I needed a radio report to inform me of Jorandel's death. "I guess throwing up is better than throwing furniture," I said when I could speak again. "Jim and Jorie always threw furniture whenever anything upset them." I laughed suddenly at the memory. "Once Jorie threw a whole huge room-service feast all over the common room." Amusement died. "I forget just why."

"I'm sorry, Rosie."

I shrugged. "I'd like to think I'd have figured it out eventually, anyway."

"We don't know yet," she said again.

We went to the bedroom to find clothes I hadn't spilled coffee on. "There was a kind of bond between us," I said. "Jorie and me. I don't know how it happened. Or what it was, exactly. Just—a connection. I could feel all the time where he was, without looking."

"Handy, if he was likely to throw furniture at you," she said wryly.

"He never did, you know." I put on a fresh flannel shirt, but my trembling fingers wouldn't do up the buttons. She pulled me toward her to do them for me. "He did threaten to hit me once," I said in a fit of honesty.

"Last night. Or this morning. When I told him I thought Jim wanted to kill him."

"Think you could eat now?" she said when my shirt was buttoned.

"I don't know. I don't care. Yes, I s'pose I should."

"Good. Come on."

"I've always wondered what was so damn compelling about sociopaths," I said. "What women saw in Jim Morrison, for instance."

She looked at me. "And?"

"And I still don't know," I said wearily.

"So we know you're human, anyway." She led me out the door and down the slope to the street where her car was parked. "What do you want? Chinese? Thai? Indian? Italian?"

"I don't care." I let her put me in the car and close the door behind me as though I were an invalid, and watched while she walked around the hood to get in on her side. "When's Hilly going to call back?"

"When he knows something."

"He must've given you an idea when that would be."

She started the car and peered through the wet windshield. "Tonight, tomorrow, maybe next week. He really didn't know."

"I need to *know,*" I said.

She looked at me. "You need to stop thinking about it. You need to concentrate on eating your dinner like a good little girl. Come on, Rosie, this isn't like you. Where's the dauntless detective I know and love?"

"Dauntlessly detecting a major flaw in her logic," I said, but I grinned. "Okay. Dinner. How 'bout haole food?"

"What food?"

"That's a word I learned from Killer," I said. "I think it means Caucasian. He used it about what we call little old lady food."

"Sandwiches on white bread, dignified hamburgers, cole slaw, American fries?"

"Exactly."

She pulled the car away from the curb. "Okay. Now tell me about Killer. He sounds interesting."

It was a convenient change of subject, or at least a

sufficient bending of subject that it got my mind off Jorandel. I told her about Killer, about his mother, about Maunalani, about the luau. And about the music at the luau, but that led back to Jorandel and I faltered, thinking bleakly that everything seemed to lead back to the music, and consequently to Jorandel, whose magic kindled it. It was brilliant music, stunning in its clarity, frolicsome, enchanting, passionate . . . but was it worth the sacrifices that had been made for it?

No music was worth three lives. "The night Jim was hurt," I said, "Jorie threw a fit about it. And he kept saying, over and over, 'nothing else matters.' I didn't know what he meant, then."

"Maybe you still don't," she said.

"Maybe."

She found a parking place near enough the restaurant that even though the rain had begun again we didn't get totally soaked on our way in. When we were seated, had studied the menu, and placed our order, I drew a deep breath and said resolutely, "Tell me what's been going on while I was gone. Any new cases?"

"No, and the old one's finished. I got photos of the guy getting out of his wheelchair to open a recalcitrant gate."

"Was it much trouble to make the gate recalcitrant?"

"Not really. I just replaced the spring with one a little stronger. He couldn't get leverage, the way the gate was positioned." She grinned suddenly. "And I found out why the client didn't trust you. You reminded her of her sister, who once stole a boyfriend from her."

"Jeez. I wouldn't want a boyfriend of hers."

"I didn't think it would be politic to point that out."

"Did she pay you?"

"With expectable reluctance."

"Since your photos saved her several hundred thousand dollars, you wouldn't think she'd begrudge you a couple thousand to get it."

"She told me how little film costs."

"Did you ask her why she hadn't done the photographing herself, if she was so concerned about costs?"

"No, I told her we had an agreement. I didn't feel the need to justify our rates. I just wanted them paid."

"You're so good at that," I said.

"At what?" She looked wary.

"I don't know. Self-assurance, I guess. I'd be justifying myself all over the place, and all you do is tell the broad to honor her agreement."

"That's not self-assurance, it's plain laziness. It's too much trouble to be always trying to win people's good will when they'd sooner think they've been cheated."

The waitress brought our food and we lapsed into silence, concentrating on the serious task of eating. I was monstrously hungry, and even the occasional accidental thought of Jorandel didn't hinder my effort to alleviate that. I was finally regaining my balance, adjusting to the hard knowledge, not new but newly confirmed, that things weren't always what I wanted them to be or even what they seemed.

The "little old lady food" helped as much mentally as physically. I had a club sandwich, cole slaw, and a cherry coke. Nothing could have been less exotic. I needed the prosaic, the ordinary, the mundane, as much as I needed nourishment. Perhaps more. I had not even realized how much my association with Cold Iron had altered my personality until I began to come out of it over that very mundane meal.

Mind you, it still hurt to think of Jorandel. Lost love always hurts. So does growing up. "Whenever you learn something, it seems at first as though you've lost something." George Bernard Shaw said that. He knew what he was talking about. Even without the deaths it would have hurt to leave Cold Iron, but it was the wisest move I'd made in my life. I didn't belong in that world. I hadn't been strong enough to withstand its lethal attractions. I'd learned a lot about myself while I was with them, and I knew that as a result I would be able to survive worse situations in the future, but first I needed time in the security of my own world to incorporate the lessons into my life.

It was dark by the time we left the restaurant. The rain had ended, the skies had cleared, and there were bright stars winking at us through city lights and smog. All the stores were open late for the Christmas shoppers who thronged the sidewalk with their arms full of packages and their visions, presumably, full of sugarplums. Bright rectangles of yellow lights from tinseled windows reflected cheerily in broad puddles on the street. Christmas trees blinked colored lights behind panes of water-streaked, heat-misted plate glass. A somber young man passed us, lugging a huge shopping bag from the top of which peeked the head of an enormous teddy bear. Children wandered by in small, excited clutters, sucking sticky candy canes and giggling. A herd of teenagers stalked resolutely into a housewares store, intent on philanthropy.

"I don't think it will ever be my favorite season," I said, "but it is interesting."

"Thus spake the staid anthropologist," said Shannon, "of quaint and curious native rites."

"Shut up and drive me home," I said, and she did.

When we got there she showed an inclination to leave me to my own devices, which was only civil in view of my known fondness for solitude. But I didn't feel like being alone just then. I invited her in, and she agreed with an alacrity that betrayed how reluctant she had really been to desert me before she was quite sure I was okay. While I reheated the leftover coffee we discussed world news, local politics, recent cases, and the Posthorn Serenade CD I had left on the office bloodbox when I joined Cold Iron. She wasn't a Mozart fan, but she'd listened to that CD and liked it.

From there the conversation segued naturally into general music appreciation, and that inevitably led to elfrock music and Cold Iron. She looked stricken about that, but I said, "I guess it's inescapable. Everything seems to lead back to their music in the end. Maybe it's a law of thermodynamics or something. Like, 'Everything takes longer and costs more.' It's okay: I'm feeling much sturdier about it now."

"That isn't a law of thermodynamics," she said.

"What? That I'm feeling sturdier?"

"Everything takes longer and costs more."

"I know it does, but why do you mention it?"

"Oh, God," she said. "I guess you are feeling sturdier."

"Sorry. Sometimes you feed me straight lines."

"You wouldn't think so if you knew how to think straight yourself."

"Touché." I grinned at her.

"Welcome home," she said, laughing with pure affection that went straight to my heart. It was one of those moments that, in a painful and perilous universe, are worth living for.

"Thanks."

The phone rang before either of us could say more. I answered it, and Hilly's voice said gruffly, "Rosie? You okay, kid?"

"I'm okay, Hilly." I carried the phone back into the kitchen and poured myself a fresh cup of coffee.

"I did admonish you," he said. "But would you listen? Never mind, I know how it is with nubile young women and glamorous male elfrock stars." He spoke pompously, as always, and as always I couldn't tell how much of it was tongue-in-cheek, how much quite seriously meant. "And observe how it concludes, I ask you. Debacle, disaster, mischance. I am perusing my thesaurus. Pocket edition," he said quite seriously. "Catastrophe, disorder, ruination. My dear, are you sure you are quite all right?"

"I'm just fine, Hilly."

"It is a great solace to me to hear you say it," he said. "Is Shannon there?"

"Yes. Did you want to speak to her?"

"No."

I had moved to hand her the receiver. At that, I put it back to my ear. "Oh."

"We have conversed," he announced. "It is your dulcet tones I require to audit now. I assume the information she requested was meant, in fact, for your shell-like ears as well?"

"You don't have to go all delicate about it, Hilly. She asked about Jorandel's suicide. And yes, I want to hear what you've got."

"I have gleaned information from diverse sources in Honolulu. None of it conclusive."

"Were there any witnesses?"

"Oh, my, yes. Several individuals, in fact."

Obviously I was going to have to pry it out of him a phrase at a time. He had moods like that. "Who?"

"There were numerous observers outside the edifice. He screamed, don't you see," he said apologetically. "Before he bounced."

My fingers tightened painfully on the receiver. "Bounced?" I said, trying not to think about the scream.

"Repeatedly, on the way down," he said. "The edges of balconies protruded."

"I see." And I did see, all too graphically. My imagination has always been painfully vivid.

"And there was the iron-rail fencing, where he landed," he said. "Spiked."

"Oh, God." Cold iron. I could see that, too.

"You're sure you're quite all right? Should you really be taking this information? Perhaps I should give it to Shannon, after all."

"No." My voice cracked.

"I begin to feel uneasy."

"I'm fine, Hilly," I said again. "Just tell me the rest of it. Did anyone actually see him jump? Not just the fall, but the jump?"

"From the exterior, there were no reliable witnesses," he said. "But within the suite two spectators observed the incident, his sibling and his bodyguard."

"Frank?"

"That was the name," he said, pleased. "Frank Cowper. According to the police report, Cowper arrived either during the actual leap or at least before egress was achieved. It was protracted, you understand, by Jimendan's effort to thwart it. He was, in fact, injured in the proceeding."

"Jim was?"

"Yes. Abrasions to the arms and a pulled shoulder muscle. Quite what you might anticipate, in the circumstance. Nothing peculiar in that."

"No," I said. "No one else was present?"

"Other than the brother and Frank Cowper, no one."

"Frank says he saw it happen?"

"He observed the egress," said Hilly. "It appeared to him that Jimendan was attempting to avert his brother's precipitous descent. As this was not, apparently, a unique occurrence, Jorandel having attempted such descents before, Cowper had some sagacity in preclusion and leapt to Jimendan's support, but too late. He was, opportunely, able to thwart Jimendan's endeavor to emulate his brother's act."

"Are you saying Jimendan tried to jump, too?"

"Precisely. No doubt it seemed the thing to do at the time," he said blandly. "One can see the fascination, of course. The free-falling body plummeting through moist tropical breezes toward the inevitable tryst with mortality below. Exhilarating, I have no doubt. And naturally there were extenuating considerations. It must, I should think, be disconcerting to so closely observe one's brother's demise." When I didn't respond, he added, "Particularly when he screams."

"Yes, about that, Hilly," I said.

"Interesting you should notice that," he said. "The police found it worthy of consideration. Suicides, it seems, do not routinely vocalize on the way down."

"Some of them must," I said unsteadily.

"To be sure," he agreed. "Trauma at recognition of the terminal character of the deed. Regret, perhaps. Yes, indeed. Some of them scream."

I was silent for a moment. He didn't volunteer anything further. I said at last, reluctantly, "Hilly, you knew them. You knew everything about them. Do you think it was suicide?"

"You appear to hold some distinct alternative in mind. What would it be? Defenestration?"

"Defeneh-who?"

"Stration," he said. "A tossing out through a window. As in the hypothesis that Jimendan propelled his sibling rather than, as he would have us believe, attempting to recover him. That Jimendan, to put it another way, killed Jorandel."

"That is one possibility," I said unhappily.

"So it is," he said.

"You mean you think it's possible?"

"Assuredly it is possible. Anything is possible."

"But do you think that's what happened?"

"If one omits the other possibility . . . maybe."

"What other possibility?" I think I hoped he would come up with something I hadn't. But he didn't.

"That Jorandel killed Jimendan," he said.

There it was, in plain English right out in the open in front of God and everybody. Somehow, stated in Hilly's voice, it acquired the incontrovertible ring of truth. "But that's silly," I said desperately. "It's Jorandel who's dead."

"Is it?"

He asked it so kindly and so regretfully and with such evident willingness to believe whatever answer I gave him that I could not respond with a lie. Not even one I'd been trying all evening to believe. "No," I said miserably. "No, I don't think it is."

22

Unsettling as it was to know he was getting away with murder, we still would have left it alone if Jorandel had let us. I lay awake for a long time that night, and for the next few nights, going over what we knew again and again, looking for an angle of attack from which we could go after him with a reasonable hope of getting him convicted. There was none. At least, none that I could find. And each time I came to that conclusion I started over again, determined to find something, some starting place, some possibility of catching him out.

I doubt I'd have worked that hard at finding a way through the defenses of the average murderer; like most people in and out of my profession I place some reliance on the police. I tend to figure that if they can't do a job, and nobody's paying me enough to do better, I probably can't. There are some things a private investigator can do better than police, if only because we don't have their work load or budget constraints. But catching murderers is only occasionally, not generally, one of the jobs for which greater funding and undivided attention is much help. In this case I didn't see how either would do much good.

It wasn't a conclusion that pleased me. That I had fallen in love with a murderer, and slept with him even as he was planning further murders, was not a comfortable thought. I even spent some time trying to convince myself I was wrong about the whole thing. But there was no getting around it. It was certainly Jimendan who stayed up late with Candy the night she died, but it was probably Jorandel who was seen taking to her room the soda that killed her. Jorandel did give Andy the drugs that killed him. Jorandel wanted out of the contract he had signed with Veladora, and as I had been told over and over again, the only way out of it was to die. "Jorandel" died. Apparently that satisfied the terms of the contract, at least as long as Veladora didn't see "Jim" and recognize Jorie.

The survivor had bangs, but no one seemed to know whether his late brother had also. If he hadn't, that would prove it was Jorandel, so I'd set Hilly to find out; but if he had, it did not prove anything. It's a very simple matter to cut bangs.

If Jorandel had killed his brother, he had everything in his favor and a damn good chance of getting away with it. We might be able to prove that he was Jorandel. In fact I'd be surprised if the other band members didn't figure that out fairly soon themselves, if they hadn't already. But proof he was Jorandel wasn't proof he'd killed Jimendan. I knew he must have, but as far as I could see I hadn't a hope in hell of proving it.

I had asked Hilly to suggest, or have someone suggest, to the Honolulu police that it might be Jimendan and not Jorandel who died. But even if they followed it up, nothing would come of it. Those mis-fingerprinted drivers' licenses were too damned official. All Jorandel had to do was produce Jimendan's and his own fingerprints, and he was home free. All the suspicions in the world were meaningless beside that. Even elves who recognized him probably couldn't sway human law, though that at least would put him back in Veladora's power and negate his gain.

The brothers' history was useless, legally. Who could prove it had really always been Jorandel who tried to jump, before? Jimendan had been as much given to fits of irrationality as Jorandel, and to imitating Jorandel. And even if it had always been Jorandel who jumped before, what was to stop Jimendan from trying it once and succeeding where Jorandel had failed? Frank was apparently the closest thing there was to an eyewitness to the actual murder, and either he hadn't arrived in time to see what happened or he wasn't admitting he had. Either way, that blew the only possible evidence.

I was pissed enough to want to go after him anyway, but I wasn't dumb enough to do it. Besides, a lot of the anger was at myself. How could I have been so damned blind? If I had recognized what he was doing as soon as I had all the relevant information, Candy and Jimendan might be alive today. If I hadn't been so caught up in my own neuroses that I couldn't think straight, I might have stopped him.

But "might have" isn't "could have," and in any event I didn't. It wasn't any more use to agonize over past idiocies than it was to perpetrate more by spending time and money on a murder I knew I couldn't prove. Eventually I came to the same bitter conclusion Shannon and I had agreed on in the first place: leave it alone. Forget it. Walk away.

I threw myself into the partnership work, which meant repossessing cars for the Bank of America. I drove all over northern California looking for listed vehicles, occasionally finding one and driving it home. The errant owners usually didn't even hide the damn things. It was mostly a matter of finding the address and picking up the car. Once in a while it got interesting; I'd had run-ins with irate owners and their dogs, over the years. But the main thing I ran into this time was a conviction that it was a lousy way to make a living, particularly at the Christmas season when there's supposed to be all this giving and there I was taking.

The consolation was that most of the owners involved really weren't downtrodden workers who couldn't afford to make their payments. They were doctors and lawyers and contractors who either bought a car beyond even their ample means just for the status of driving it, or who had taken it into their heads for one reason or another that they "shouldn't have to pay" what they agreed to pay. I don't have a lot of sympathy with selective stupidity. Not even when I've recently suffered a massive case of it myself.

Christmas itself approached inexorably, and while I still couldn't take the innocent pleasure Shannon did in the season, I found it much less oppressive than in the past. In some ways it was even amusing. She talked me into a Christmas tree for my home and spent hours after work with me, haunting discount stores choosing lights and decorations for it. We had a little two-person party, the week before Christmas, putting the damn thing up in a little red-and-green metal stand, stringing lights, and hanging decorations, with much eggnog and popcorn and a judicious dose of Christmas carols from her CD selection on the office bloodbox brought home for the occasion. It was fun.

Cleanup the next day was less fun. There were needles and bits of tinsel everywhere, a stained spot on the carpet where the tree stand had failed to stand under the burden of an unbalanced tree (we finally had to lean it in a corner), and Shannon had spilled the unpopped popcorn all over the kitchen and cleaned up only the kernels that fell in plain sight. Housework is not my forte. I vacuumed the middle of everything and decided that tinsel, needles, and popcorn kernels in the corners wouldn't hurt anyone. I spent some time staring at the stain on the carpet, and seriously considered soaking the rest of the carpet to match, but decided it wasn't worth the trouble. Then I went out for breakfast. Cooking isn't my forte, either.

Berkeley is a great place for people who don't cook. There's food everywhere, in every price range, and if you know where to look, you can get wonderful stuff for not much money. I got an almond croissant as big as the average house cat and roughly half a gallon of hot black espresso and carried them gingerly, under an umbrella, through the steady drizzling rain to the office. I meant to enjoy them in glorious solitude while I waited for Shannon to show up with the new list of cars from Bank of America.

It was late in the morning and the corridors were empty, all the secretaries already slaving over hot computers, and their bosses either meeting with clients or not yet arrived for the day. Our office was on the west side of the building, where we got no morning sunlight but, on reasonably clear days, a fine view of San Francisco across the bay. Since weather clear enough to see as far as the bay was a good deal more common than mornings when it wasn't raining and the fog lifted early enough to let the sun shine, we got the better deal.

But the office was gloomy in the mornings without the lights on. So gloomy that you couldn't see anything, not even shadowy shapes, through the frosted glass in the door. And I wasn't particularly on my guard; Bank of America was currently our only client, and people just don't go for revenge against the detectives who repossess their cars, at least not once the repossession is complete. If they catch you in the act, certainly, but not after. The only intruders we had to worry about were the common or garden variety sleazeballs any city dweller has to be on guard against, and they are usually easy to spot. I'd have noticed if the door were jimmied or if someone had been lurking in the corridor shadows. But the shadows were empty and the door was quite properly locked. I went in, flipped on the light, and was halfway to my desk before I realized I wasn't alone.

I also wasn't carrying my .38, or any other weapon worth mentioning. An almond croissant as big as a house cat still doesn't have claws. The espresso, however, was hot. I'd mapped out my moves before I really saw my assailants. There were two of them, both large and clean and tidy in a jock sort of way; like out-of-work football players, in T-shirts, blue jeans, sneakers. One of them wore wire-rimmed glasses. That was the one with the gun. He was backup, obviously, for the one with the knife. They wanted to do it quietly if they could.

Instinct said go for the knife, not only because it would be first but because it is, for some reason, a much more daunting weapon. The guy with the gun could kill me in a fraction of a second. The knife would take longer. Maybe that's why it's scarier. Reason, however, said get rid of the gun, so I threw the espresso in his face. Which left me with one oversize croissant and a half-furled umbrella with which to fend off the knife. Absurdly, I hurled the croissant. Even more absurdly, the knife ducked. Well, hell, in the heat of the moment he can't have realized it was only a croissant.

I made it to the door before he recovered. He caught up with me in two quick steps, but I got the umbrella between us and that startled him, too. The thing was, the gun wouldn't be put out of service long by espresso—it wasn't all that hot—and I wanted out of his sight before he decided it was time to give up on silence. I slashed the umbrella at the knife's face and he grabbed it with his free hand, lunging at me with the other while I reached behind me for the doorknob. I found it, yanked the door open, and the knife blade collided solidly with the wood about two inches from my retreating arm.

But not solidly enough. It didn't stick. And he was damned fast. I didn't see what he did, but I felt it, the fiery shock of sliced flesh and the ugly grating of sharp steel against bone. Then I was out the door and running. The neighboring office was only a few steps down the corridor. For a second I hesitated, not wanting to lead the bad guys into someone else's unprotected nest. But the gun still hadn't fired, and the knife wasn't even chasing me. Maybe I'd just disturbed them at a burglary and they'd reacted to the shock, as armed burglars will, with violence. Maybe, given half a chance, they would just leave.

My left arm was dripping blood all over the floor. I opened my neighbor's office door, stepped quickly through it and to one side just in case, and told the startled receptionist to dial 911. He took one look at my arm and did as he was told. I looked at it too, and wished I hadn't. The muscle of my forearm was slit almost from wrist to elbow, neat as a butcher's cut, with white bone showing. I would be lucky if no tendons were damaged. I cradled the elbow in my other hand, dripping blood all over the front of my shirt, and said stupidly, "I'm sorry, Peter. I seem to be bleeding on your boss's carpet."

He looked up from the phone. "Is the perpetrator still on the premises?" he said.

I stared dully. "What?"

"The perpetrator," he said. "They want to know is he still on the premises. It was an assault, wasn't it?"

"Oh. I think so. I mean, yes it was, and I think they're still here. Tell 'em there's one with a gun, too." I leaned against the wall while Peter relayed the information to 911. The room was a little unsteady. Noisy, too, with an odd roaring sound I couldn't identify. And the air seemed sparkly.

"Here, sit down," said Peter, materializing at my side. "No, don't worry about the blood. We're insured."

"Against blood?" I said.

He smiled. "Don't argue, just sit down before you fall down." I sat down and he reached for my arm. "Let me see." In his spare time he was a scoutmaster and presumably well versed in first aid. I let him see. "Not pretty," he said, "but I think you'll live." He produced a white hand towel as if by magic and wrapped it tightly around my arm.

"Where did you get that?" I said dazedly. "Do you keep hand towels in your desk?" It seemed important at the time, I'm not sure why.

"As a matter of fact, I do," he said. "I don't like the paper towels in the john. Can you hold this up a little higher? It'll help stop the bleeding. And press here." He placed my hand to his satisfaction on the towel around my arm and indicated by example how hard to press where. "How do you feel?"

"Like I've been knifed," I said.

He smiled again, though he looked a little white around the gills. "I meant in general. Dizziness? Roaring in the ears? Light show?"

"All of the above."

He nodded. "Means you've lost some blood."

"I knew that already."

"Call it a reality check," he said. "Now we know the blood isn't a mutual hallucination."

"Oh, good." I closed my eyes. "Peter?"

"Yeah?"

"Thanks."

"No problem."

Things got a little hazy after that. There were seemingly dozens of police, paramedics, and questions. Somewhere in the middle of it all my partner arrived and followed my spoor to Peter's office. As soon as I knew she was there I gave up all pretense of consciousness. She would take care of everything. From then on I performed the few actions required of me in a daze, responded to questions without the smallest concern for coherence, responded negatively when asked whether I had any allergies, and subsided gratefully into a comforting fog of painkillers.

At the hospital they stitched my arm back together, told me how lucky I was that no tendons were irreparably damaged, wrapped me from wrist to elbow in soft, protective gauze, and released me to Shannon's custody. The police took a description of my assailants to go with the fingerprints they'd lifted from the office, told Shannon to let them know whether anything was missing, and departed.

Shannon wanted to take me home. "Forget that," I said. "We'll go to the office."

"You're not fit to work."

"I'm full of painkillers and happy as a clam. And I want to know what all this is in aid of."

"If there's evidence, the police will have found it."

"They don't know what to look for."

"Do we?"

"Yes," I said. "Better than they do, anyway."

"What will it be?"

"What will what be?"

"What we look for."

"Evidence," I said smugly.

"Ah," she said, and drove me to the office.

There was still blood on the corridor floor. I averted my eyes. "The door was locked," I said.

"They were inside?" she said. "With the door locked?" She studied the lock. "I can't tell it's been tampered with."

"We'll change it," I said. "They have a key."

"How do you know?"

"They were inside," I said. "With the door locked."

"Ah," she said again.

"That means you think I'm leaping to conclusions, right?"

"Could have been magic," she said. "Where would they get a key?"

"From the building manager," I said. "It wouldn't be hard: violence or money either one should work pretty well."

"I hope it was violence."

"Yes," I said. "But I don't suppose it was." She unlocked the door and we went in. Everything seemed to be in perfect order, or as close to it as it ever was. There was fingerprinting dust on every smooth surface, though they'd made a cursory attempt to clean it up. Aside from that everything looked exactly as it had when we left work yesterday.

"Nothing," said Shannon.

"We're not through yet." I sat at my desk and surveyed the room. "The typewriter's still here. The blood-box is in my car: I forgot to bring it up this morning. And that accounts for our valuables."

"Such as they are." Sitting at her desk, she pulled open the pencil drawer and said, "They didn't take my Snickers bar, either."

"That's nice." Absently I pulled open a couple of my drawers, though I knew there was nothing in any of them that anyone would go to the trouble of stealing. I was right, too. But there was something in one of them that someone had gone to the trouble of bringing. A small brown glass bottle with a black plastic cap. I lifted it gingerly to get it in the light. It was full of white powder. "Damn," I said.

"What?" she said, glancing up. "What is it?"

I took the cap off, tipped a few grains onto the palm of my hand, wet a fingertip, and put them in my mouth. "Soda."

She stared. "But why?"

I put the cap back on and dropped the bottle on my desk. It rolled against the stapler and lay still. "I don't know," I said. "Maybe in case the gun and the knife failed. It wouldn't do him any good to get me busted, so I don't suppose it's that kind of plant. My guess is he figured I couldn't resist it."

"Jorandel?"

"Who else?"

"But—Jeez, Rosie! Would he think you're dumb enough to take a drug you don't even know where it came from?"

I shrugged. "Probably."

"Get rid of it," she said in sudden revulsion. "Dump it. Throw away the bottle."

"Yes," I said, making no move to do it.

"I'll do it," she said.

"Two sets of intruders is too much to believe in."

She paused with the bottle in her hand, looking at me. "You mean if there were two sets of intruders, somebody else brought this, and the guys who attacked you didn't come from Jorandel?"

"Wishful thinking." I looked down at the sling protecting my injured arm. "Damn him. This isn't just insulting, it's downright sloppy, *and* unnecessary. What threat was I to him, anyway? So I could tell him from Jimendan. So what? Damn it, why didn't he think it through? He's smarter than this. Or he was."

"I expect fratricide could muddle your thinking." She took the bottle to the window, dumped the contents into the drizzly wind, and closed the window. "I'm gonna take this to the dumpster," she said. "I don't want it around."

"You think he's flipped?"

"Rosie, he was always flipped. I'll be right back."

I stared at raindrops racing each other down the windowpane. He was always psychotic. He wasn't stupid, not when I knew him. When Shannon came back I said, "I'll have to go after him."

"We," she said.

"What?"

"We'll have to go after him."

"It's Christmas," I said. "You were looking forward to spending it with your boyfriend. I may not be back in time, and I'm sure not waiting till after."

"No, I don't think we should," she said. "Bob'll understand."

"In his place I don't know that I would."

"That's just one of many reasons you're not my boyfriend."

"Shann, I can handle this. You don't have to go with."

"I know it," she said. "But I'm pissed. People have to know they can't go gunning for my partner and expect to get away with it." She sat at her desk and looked at me. "Any ideas where we start?"

"I guess the first thing is just to get to him. That's the quickest way I can see to make sure we're right and he is Jorandel, not Jimendan."

"How does one go about dropping in on an elfrock star?"

It could have been a problem if I hadn't known Vyla. Her card was still in my purse. I called her home number in California and got her on the first try. That was the easy part. Telling her what I wanted was harder. It would have been simple enough just to tell her I wanted to know how to get in touch with Jorandel or Killer, but it didn't feel right not to tell her what it was about, since one way or another Killer was mixed up in it. And that wasn't something I wanted to explain on the phone. In the end I made an appointment to have lunch with her the next day.

We took Shannon's car; I wasn't fit to drive. She made a quick call to her boyfriend while I packed, and just as she'd predicted, he made no problems. I guess he knew what he was getting into when he started dating her. We should all be so lucky. I called Hilly while she packed. He expressed expectable concern and insisted we stay with him while we were in L.A. He had room enough; the main dwelling on his estate was so large you could get lost for days just trying to get from a guest room to the dining room in time for dinner. We'd stayed there before. It was a long way from anywhere, but everything in L.A. is a long way from anywhere. L.A. is a long way from anywhere. I thanked him, rang off, and we set out.

The rain ended when we crossed the hills into the inland valley. It was replaced by tule fog so thick we nearly missed the turnoff to I-5. The world was a wet gray tunnel most of the way to Buttonwillow. It was a long day of difficult driving for Shannon and difficult introspection for me. I still wanted to believe I hadn't slept with a murderer. More than that, I wanted to believe I didn't love a murderer. But anyone will commit murder, given sufficient provocation—at least that's what they say. I'd just fallen in love with someone whose sufficient-provocation level was low.

Shannon said, "Maybe it's not so much that it's low: maybe it's just that you don't really understand it. I mean, you keep saying what a genius he is, how important the music is to him. And the freedom to make the music he wants. Artists have done worse than murder for the sake of their art before this. I guess to them the freedom to create is as important as breathing is to us. You'd kill to keep breathing, wouldn't you?"

"Yes, I expect I would." The windshield wipers whisk-thumped across the moisture-beaded windscreen. "But I don't think I'd kill you."

She glanced at me, a knowing grin. "If it were the only way to keep breathing, you might."

I thought about it. "I don't think so. But I guess I can't know unless it happens. Which let's hope it doesn't."

"I don't think it was easy for him," she said. "From what you tell me, he's been through hell, looking for a way out even while he was setting it up. I think he must've hoped until the very end that some alternative would come up. And who knows, maybe at the last minute he really did think better of what he was doing and try to save Jimendan."

"He didn't try to save Andy. Or Candy. And if he did try, he still didn't save Jim."

"I'm just trying to say maybe he's not quite as ruthless as you're thinking."

"Maybe he has some redeeming qualities? I know he has. But not redeeming enough."

She hesitated. "You're convinced it was Jorandel?"

"Oh, God," I said.

"I mean, because maybe you're harsher on him than you would be if you didn't love him."

"Maybe. But I didn't manufacture the evidence."

"But that's just it. There isn't any hard evidence. Only circumstantial at best, and for reliability that's right on a level with eyewitness accounts: low."

"The idea is to remember to look for somebody else it could fit as well. I've looked."

"Let's go over it again," she said. "We haven't anything better to do for the next five or six hours, and who knows, maybe we'll come up with something."

"If there were anything to come up with, I'd have done it sometime in the last five or six days."

"Maybe not. Maybe you're too close to the problem."

"Okay. Jeez. Okay." We went over it again. What the hell, she was right about circumstantial evidence. But it kept coming out the same way. There was no way to know who Candy had overheard, so that was out. The guys who mugged me in L.A. knew who I really was and what I did for a living, which pointed to Jorandel, since he was the only one besides Candy who knew that about me.

"Not," said Shannon. "You said Emerson had checked up on you. And Candy might have told the Roach."

"Oh, sure. After telling me he'd kill her if he knew she sold her earring."

"Okay, but she could have told someone. So could Emerson or Jorandel, for that matter."

She was just as unhelpful about Jorandel falling downstairs. Nobody had an alibi: anyone could have pushed him. When I asked why anyone would, since by now it seemed unlikely that anyone had ever meant to kill Jorandel and in any case that would have been a clumsy way of doing it, she said it was no clumsier than a window, could have been a case of mistaken identity, and that motive wasn't nearly as important as opportunity.

"What about Jim getting beat up to match him? You think it was a coincidence that his injuries were just the same?"

"Not impossible," she said. "Not likely, either, I admit. But I like your idea that Jim did it or had it done to himself."

"Oh, right, he was planning an altruistic suicide, making it easy for Jorie to take his place to get out of the contract, right?"

"Anything's possible," she said imperturbably. "The point is, all the band members were present in the suite when he was injured?"

"Yes. And besides, you didn't see Jorie's eyes. I'd swear he was responsible. He was for sure guilty."

"But as you said, maybe only because he should've protected his baby brother."

"Anyway, they were all there. So that doesn't prove anything. Any of them could've hired someone."

"Okay, now the murders. Who else could've given Andy those drugs?"

"Nobody: I saw Jorie do it."

"You saw him give Andy a package. Maybe it was the drugs. Even if it was—where'd he get them?"

"I don't know. I asked him once, but of course he didn't tell me. You know, that's something, too. That morning when I asked him about the drugs. He read me a temperance lecture. I never thought about it till now, but maybe he was trying to warn me off Candy's soda because he knew damn well it would kill me. As it killed her."

"You mean because he knew it was too strong, or contained something it shouldn't?"

"Exactly. It was the morning before she died. If he hadn't already brought her the bottle that killed her, he was about to."

"Or Jimendan was."

"Yes, okay, it could've been Jim."

"And either of them could have done it in all innocence, not knowing it was lethal."

"Do you believe in Santa Claus, too?"

"Yes, certainly," she said without hesitation. "Now, about this batch of drugs Jorandel gave Andy. You said there was some reason to believe it wasn't the same batch that Jorandel overdosed on? Because if it was, that would surely point to Jorandel's innocence."

"He didn't give me a straight answer about that. But, hell, overdosing was just a fact of life to them. It doesn't prove anything."

"So that brings us back to the window. And we don't know a damn thing about the window. Jorandel could've pushed Jimendan. Jimendan could've tried to push Jorandel and got pushed by accident. Jorandel could've been trying to jump and Jimendan trying to save him. Or the other way around. There's no telling."

"Which leaves us right where we were. With no reliable evidence you have to go on theory, and the only theory that really fits everything is that Jorie did it all."

"No. That's just the only theory we've come up with that fits everything. There could be others."

"You keep disagreeing with me," I said, irritated.

"Only because you're wrong," she said. "Look, I'll admit it's probable Jorandel did it. But it remains important to keep an open mind."

"Jorie's the only one with a motive."

"Oh, don't be daft," she said. "You don't know their motives. You're judging him because you know him to be psychotic. But all those other elves, no matter how well behaved they might have been while you were with them, are almost by definition sociopaths; they're elves. 'Fallen angels too bad to save, too good to be lost, who have every charm but conscience.' Isn't that what the books say elves *are*? A sociopath is a person without conscience. And a person without conscience, no matter how well behaved most of the time, is very likely cruel sometimes, if only by accident. Look, just as an example: you said the Roach is a moral retard. We know he dosed you with something foul just for the hell of it. Honestly, admit it: he could have done any of the rest of this, too, couldn't he? And he'd be a better fit as villain than Jorandel is."

"No motive," I said.

"As far as we know," she corrected.

"Right, okay," I said crossly. "So as far as you're concerned the whole thing could be an accident, right? And nobody's guilty. Or anybody might be. So why are we going after Jorie?"

"Because he's the likeliest suspect," she said. "All I'm trying to say is that we should keep our minds open, and our eyes. If evidence turns up that says it wasn't Jorandel, let's be ready to see it. The idea is to solve the case, not to get revenge. Right?"

"Do you really think it wasn't Jorie?"

She kept her eyes on the road and didn't answer for several long moments. "Okay. That theory fits best. Except for one thing, Rosie." She glanced at me. "One very important thing that I know you're overlooking because you're too close to it."

"Oh?" My voice was brittle. "And what might that be, pray tell?"

"You don't fall in love easy, and you don't fall for losers." With a wry grin she said, "Psychotics maybe. But you're levelheaded. Objective. Love doesn't blind you to a person's flaws. And you didn't see Jorandel as a murderer, not the whole time you were with him."

"There was a lot I didn't see," I said. "I wasn't exactly at my best."

"You may've been drunk, and stoned, and troubled," she said. "But you were still you. Look, gut-level honestly, do you really believe he's a murderer, even now?"

"Gut-level," I said, "No. But nothing else fits. Don't do me any favors, Shann. I've been over this a million times in my mind, and I can't find another solution, and I don't think you can either. Believe me, I'm open to one if it turns up. I hope to hell it does. But now you answer one. Gut-level honestly, do you really believe he's *not* a murderer?"

"No," she said. It didn't matter that she qualified it with, "But I don't know him." The fact was that at this point I was pretty sure I didn't know him, either.

23

The tule fog lifted before the Grapevine, thank goodness, and the rest of the trip to Hilly's place was a swift rush through the gathering gloom of a clear winter evening. Driving etiquette on southern California freeways is very different from that in northern California. The speed limits are adhered to even less rigidly, and the lane speed differences are negligible. Slower traffic does tend to keep right. Everybody else vies for position in all the other lanes rather as if each driver regarded all other vehicles as moving obstacles. Feelings tend to run high, slights real and imagined are responded to with everything from finger gestures to gunshots, and I'm always relieved to see my exit approaching.

Shannon was pretty tired by then, and devoted all of her attention to driving. I had napped on the way down while she coped with tule fog and traffic, so I was more awake, but not a lot fresher. Shock, the aftereffects of painkillers, and the throbbing pain that increased as they wore off were having their effect. My protestations to the contrary, I really couldn't have done this without Shannon. No way could I have made that grueling drive alone. I began to regret having undertaken it in company. My home and my own warm bed looked more attractive the farther we got from them.

When we arrived at last, Hilly took one look at us and sent us to our rooms with promises of dinner in bed. "We will converse in the morning," he announced portentously. "It can wait." He rang a bell and a frail, bent, elderly gentleman with a bald, freckled head and an ingratiating smile promptly appeared from a nearby doorway. "Igor," said Hilly, "will convey your luggage." To Igor he added, "The lilac and lavender rooms, Igor."

Hilly was a tall, plump, sturdy man with mounds of curly brown hair and a neatly trimmed beard, whose rosy good health made Igor look even more decrepit. It seemed absurd for such a vigorous man to order such a delicate one to menial labor.

But Igor bobbed and nodded, smiling incessantly, and wrested our overnight bags from us with fierce resolution against which it would clearly have been useless to protest had we tried. When he had them safely in his grip, he said, "This way," in a piercing voice as unsteady as his gnarled and bony limbs, and set off down the corridor at a brisk if uneven gallop.

"See that they are comfortable, Igor," Hilly called after him. To us he added, with a brief unreadable smile, "Go, before he eludes you."

We went. Once out of Hilly's sight Igor's pace slowed, but not by much. Obviously he wasn't as feeble as he appeared; it was all I could do to keep up with him. I was too dazed to take in much of the passing scenery beyond a general impression of opulence; my arm ached and I wanted a nap. Several corridor-miles later, or so it seemed, Igor halted abruptly at a door exactly like all the other doors we'd passed, opened it, thrust Shannon's bag inside, and said, "Lilac room." Opening the door next to it, he thrust my bag inside, said, "Lavender room," and nodded several times in confirmation of this information. Then, glancing at us sharply, he demanded, "What else?"

"Thanks, nothing, I guess." Shannon sounded as dazed as I felt. Igor nodded abruptly and dashed away. Shannon and I looked at each other without expression, looked through the open doors to our rooms, and burst out laughing. "Well," she said. "Visiting Hilly is always an adventure."

"I've had enough adventures for one day," I said sourly.

But my room was gorgeous, with ankle-deep carpeting, old masters on the walls, bowls of fresh-cut lavender filling the air with its heady perfume, and most important, a bed. I didn't bother to unpack. I should perhaps have showered in the adjoining oak-and-tile bathroom, but I didn't. I sprawled on the bed and was asleep within minutes.

When dinner was brought, I woke long enough to eat it—succulent prime rib, asparagus in a delicate cheese sauce, baked potatoes with mounds of sour cream, and a tall gin collins (Hilly knew my preferences)—and to take a soothing shower afterward. That was an awkward procedure with only one functioning arm, but I managed. Afterward I meant to get together with Shannon to plan tomorrow's activities, but instead I fell asleep again and didn't wake till morning.

Sunlight slanted golden through the east window beside my bed when a slender brunette brought me breakfast and informed me that Hilly would meet me and my partner for coffee on the east terrace in one hour. It was a royal summons, but one I had no objection to obeying. My arm was stiff and tender but slightly less painful today, and some twelve hours' sleep had left me well rested and alert, ready to tackle anything. Even Jorandel. I ate hurriedly, got dressed, and set out in search of my partner and the east terrace.

Igor was waiting in the corridor to lead us to the east terrace, and I doubt we could have found it without him. Hilly was ensconced in a white wicker chair in the warm winter sunlight with a broad glass table before him laden with heavy bowls of ripe fruit, a silver coffeepot, and fine china cups. A silent old woman who might have been Igor's wife poured coffee for us and, at a gesture from Hilly, disappeared into the house.

The terrace was a broad swath of cool gray marble with an intricately carved ebony balustrade. Hilly's estate sprawled beyond it in well-irrigated emerald acres down velvet hillsides, long-shadowed in the morning sun, and Hilly observed it with the air of a benevolent despot surveying his domain. He was never one for polite social noises. One wasn't required to ask after his health, and he didn't ask after ours. When we were seated he produced a batch of papers from a portable file by his chair and launched without preamble into the matter at hand. "The deceased sibling," he announced, "wore bangs. When you were with them, Jorandel did not, is that correct?" He lifted his eyebrows at me expectantly.

"No, he didn't," I said. "In fact he made a point of it, when people mistook them for each other. He'd point out that Jimendan did. And that Jimendan wore more bracelets, and weighed a little more than he did, and all the other differences between them that were easiest to change." Which was something I hadn't really thought about at the time, and had thought about too much in the last few days.

Hilly nodded. "It is possible to tell whether hair has been recently trimmed. Had there been no bangs, of course, we would apprehend that the deceased was Jorandel. Since there were, a determination as to their date of origin might be helpful. I have set that in motion. If they were cut within a day or two of the death, of course, we learn nothing, since bangs do require the occasional trimming. But if they had not been cut for some time, that will establish that the deceased was Jimendan." He looked up from his papers again, a steady glance at each of us to be sure we were following his reasoning.

"Is there really any doubt?" asked Shannon.

"Not in the view of the police," said Hilly. "The fingerprints of the deceased match those on Jorandel's driver's license, which satisfies them that he is Jorandel." He looked at me. "According to your intelligence, however, I believe that is, in fact, conclusive indication that he was not Jorandel, but Jimendan?"

"According to Candy," I said. "But I don't know how reliable her information was."

"I think we can take it that in this instance, at least, it was wholly reliable," he said, leaning back in his chair and looking infinitely pleased with himself. "My own sources attest that it was common knowledge among a certain set of young male students at their high school when Jimendan acquired Jorandel's license for him."

"Hilly," I said, "you're amazing. How the hell did you find that out?"

"It was nothing," he said, sipping his coffee with a satisfied air. He put the cup down, leaned back again, patted his protruding stomach contentedly, and said with a sudden, impish grin, "Muffin attended the same high school. Further, she dated one of the young men in question." He sighed lugubriously. "Like most feats of prestidigitation, you see, my methods seem deflatingly unsophisticated once exposed."

"So why check the age of the bangs?" asked Shannon.

"The brothers might have been perpetrating a hoax among their friends," he said reproachfully.

"You're right," she said. "The hair should be checked. But I think it's safe to assume, in the meantime, that the survivor is Jorandel. So then the question becomes, did he kill his brother or did he just take advantage of his brother's death? And if the latter, then who did kill his brother? Or was it suicide?"

"If it was suicide," I said, "why did somebody send those jocks after me yesterday? Not to mention the soda they left behind."

"It would seem imperative to Jorandel," said Hilly, "that his masquerade remain undisclosed, whether or not it was preceded by fratricide."

"Okay," I said, frustrated. "So we're right back where we started before we left Berkeley."

"Well, not quite," said Shannon, grinning. "Not by some five hundred miles we're not."

"You know what I mean, damn it."

"Yes." She broke a group of grapes from a cluster in one of the bowls on the table and popped one thoughtfully into her mouth. "Well, somebody did send those guys. I don't like that. I resent it. We have to do something about it. Of course, if we'd had any sense we'd have made some effort to track them down in the Bay Area. But we didn't, so I guess we're just going on the assumption that they did come from Jorandel, or from someone in Cold Iron. That being the case, we're in a better position to do something about it here than when we were five hundred miles from them."

"But what, exactly, do you intend to do?" asked Hilly.

"I don't know," she said. "I guess that depends in part on what we're doing it *about.* I mean, are we concentrating here on murder, or assault? Or both? Or what?" She looked at me expectantly. So did Hilly.

I waved my good arm in an expansive gesture of exasperation. "Come on, guys," I said. "Why look at me?"

"It's been your case from the beginning," said Shannon.

"Since when does that make me an expert? Besides, you know what I think."

"That Jorandel killed Jimendan, Jimendan's bodyguard, and Candy," said Shannon. "The question remains, since we haven't, so far, come up with evidence of murder. Do we look for it, or concentrate on the assault, or what?"

I scowled at her.

"You are at a loss," announced Hilly, "due to the paucity of evidence."

I admitted it.

"Then I suggest you pursue all possibilities without prejudice," he said.

"Okay, fine," I said. "I still don't know what we're going to do. I mean, we have a lunch date with Vyla, and I think she can get us to Cold Iron, so we can find out for sure whether it's Jorandel who's still with them. But then what? Do we confront Jorie and hope he confesses, or what? I mean, this is stupid. We both overreacted to my getting knifed, and we didn't stop to think. Before that happened, we were going to leave it alone because we knew damn well we couldn't prove anything. Well, what's really changed?"

"You were knifed," said Hilly.

"Something we should've investigated in the Bay Area, not here," I said.

"True, perhaps," he said. "But you are here. That being the case, you may as well verify Jorandel's identity if you can, as a preliminary step."

"A preliminary step to what?" I said sourly.

"To further investigation," he said.

"It's pointless," I said. "We know he's Jorandel."

"We *think* he's Jorandel," Shannon corrected. "Once we've confirmed it, we could do a little stirring of the hornets' nest. Make sure the other Cold Iron members know what he's doing, for instance. As you describe them, I guess Blade and the Roach might be content to ignore a murder or two, but the idea might at least make them nervous. And I don't think Killer would like it at all. Let's just get it in the open and see what happens."

"Stirring hornets' nests," said Hilly, "can be hazardous to one's health."

Shannon shrugged. "You got a better idea?"

"No," he said sadly.

"Then, let's do it," she said.

For lack of anything better, we chose to regard that as a plan. First we went over the whole damn thing again with Hilly, looking for a better angle of attack. But as before we came up empty, so when we set out for lunch with Vyla it was with the sole intention of getting to Cold Iron to identify Jorandel and see what we could stir up from there.

After coffee with Hilly on his east terrace, lunch with Vyla could hardly have seemed other than mundane. There were no ancient retainers lurking in wait to perform minor services at the smallest signal, but only ordinary harried waiters and waitresses, ignoring our needs. Vyla herself, sleek and elegant as always, seemed physically more exotic on the mainland, against a backdrop of dry valley farmers and storekeepers, than she had in Hawaii, against that backdrop of tropical luxury and long-limbed, suntanned beach bunnies. But she was the same practical, unflappable woman who had befriended me when I had such great need of a practical, unflappable woman friend.

The news that it might be Jorandel who'd survived didn't disturb her as much as I had feared it might. She nodded, her dark face serious and intent, a spiral of glistening black hair shading one uncharacteristically solemn eye. "I wondered," she said. "Killer says they don't see much of him now. He comes to the studio when they're all through for the night, records his vocals, and leaves again before they show up for the next session. When he has something he wants to tell them, he leaves a message on tape. And when he's not at the studio, he stays home. Nobody but Frank ever sees him."

"I s'pose Jimendan might act that way, if it *were* Jimendan," said Shannon. "Upset about his brother's death, and all."

Vyla nodded. "That's what Killer said. But I can tell he's uneasy. He feels there's something wrong. He doesn't say anything, but I can hear it in what he doesn't say."

"The thing is," I said, "I think I was wrong all along.

It wasn't Jim who was planning Jorie's death. It was the other way around."

"Yes," said Vyla. "I see that now." She paused, reflecting. "And when I go back over all that you told me before . . . it does fit." She looked at me, her expression full of sympathy. "What are you going to do now?"

"I want to get to him," I said. "I want to see him, to make sure I'm right. And then I don't know. See if the other band members have guessed, I suppose. If not, see how they react when they do know. See how he reacts."

"Stir the hornets' nest," said Shannon.

Glancing at my bandaged arm, Vyla said with a hint of the irrepressible merriment I had come to associate with her, "Just be careful you don't get stung."

"I know," I said. "But I don't see what else we can do at this point. We were going to just leave it alone, but if he won't leave us alone . . ."

"You know," she said thoughtfully, "it could just as easily be one of the others. Blade, or the Roach."

"Not Blade," I said. "He's just a fixture. There isn't room in his head for anything but sex, drugs, and elf-rock. And as for the Roach—" I shrugged. "I'd far rather it were he, because I knew from the start that he was, as Jorie says, a moral retard; and it would mean I wasn't as wrong about Jorie as I think I was. But where's the motive?"

"Same as for Jorandel?" she asked.

"To get Jorie out of his contract? I don't know. I guess I can see the Roach imagining he was performing a kindness by killing a few people to get Jorie what he wanted. But I'd swear Jorie knew what was going on. The night Jim was injured, and he kept saying 'nothing else matters'— What could he have meant but the music, and that Jim had to look just like him if the murder and masquerade were to work?"

"He could have meant just the masquerade, couldn't he?" asked Shannon. "They, or he, could have been planning some switch we don't even know about, that had nothing to do with Jorandel's contract, or Jimendan's murder, or any of this."

"Yes, okay, he could have been," I said. "But usually the obvious is a better guess. Anyway, what's it matter?

It has to have been one of them who killed Jim, right? So let's stir hornets and see which one tries to sting. We'll just keep an open mind and be ready for anybody."

"I can put you in touch with Killer, of course," said Vyla. "And I'm sure he'll help you however he can. But since Jimendan or Jorandel, whichever it is, is keeping himself apart from the band, what will you do if Killer can't get you to see him?"

"We'll think of something."

She drew out one of her business cards and scrawled on the back of it. "I'll give you Killer's address and phone," she said. "Let me know if there's anything else I can do to help." She paused in her writing to look up. "And you come back and tell me all about it when it's over, will you?" she said, and made a wry gesture. "I'll be dying of curiosity, and Killer doesn't always think to let his parents know what's going on. He was a better correspondent in the old days, before the band made it. Then he'd phone or write every time he needed money, which was often, and we could pry a little news out of him. Now we hire a clipping service, and it's not uncommon for that to be the way we find out about little things like world tours."

"But you've spoken with him recently?" said Shannon.

Vyla nodded. "He's worried." She finished writing, capped her pen, and handed me the card. "Not that he's said so, but he's called a couple of times since they got back to the mainland, and I know that's one of the reasons." She looked at me again. "He'll be glad to see you," she said.

I thought she meant he'd be glad to know I was looking into the deaths. "When I was with them before, I was so muddled I could have *watched* a murder and not known what I was seeing. In fact, in Andy's case, that's pretty much what happened. I just hope this time I'm able to see what I'm looking at."

"So do I," she said, eyes dancing. I wondered what the hell was so funny, but for some reason I felt too shy to ask.

We left Vyla at the restaurant, sipping a cup of thick,

dark coffee and looking thoughtful. Shannon was quiet for a while after we got back into the car. When she finally spoke, it was only to ask what I wanted to do next. "Back to Hilly's?" she said. "Or you wanta call this Killer?"

"Let's find a phone and call him, anyway," I said. "If he's home, and agrees to see us, we can go there. If not, we can go back to Hilly's." I looked at her. "You're brooding about something. What is it?"

"Nothing," she said. "Or maybe everything. I guess I wonder if we're on a wild-goose chase. But what the hell, in a way you can say we've got a client for it, since we're using Candy's money."

"I hate to use her money to catch Jorie, when she meant it to save him," I said. "It feels like I'm betraying her."

Shannon, always eminently practical about money, said shortly, "She doesn't care what you do with it now."

"I know," I said. "I still don't like it."

"Then hope you're wrong about Jorandel."

"I do hope that."

"As long as we're considering alternatives," she said, "you keep leaving out Killer."

"He didn't do it." I thought about it. "Is that what you've been brooding about?"

"I like Vyla," she said, as if in answer.

"Me, too," I said. "Don't worry. The one thing I do know in all of this is that Killer isn't a killer. He's the only one I'm that sure of, but I am sure. When you meet him, you'll see."

"You can't always tell by looking."

"No, you can't," I said. "Look, there's a phone." She parked, we counted coins, and I called Killer.

He answered on the first ring. I'd forgotten the sweet sound of his voice. "I just talked to Ma," he said. "She told me you'd call. You comin over?"

"If we're welcome," I said.

"We?"

"Me and my partner. Did Vyla tell you why we wanted to get in touch with you?"

"Yeah." The single word sounded oddly deflated, as though he had hoped we had some other, more important reason to want to see him. But I decided it must only be that it was nearly as painful to him as it had been to me at first, to think of Jorie as a murderer. Whatever their other flaws, and whatever their personal disagreements, all the members of the band were fiercely loyal to Jorandel and his music. His song "Brothers" with its flowery phrases about blood brotherhood was a dramatic but surprisingly accurate reflection of their devotion to him and, through him, to each other. In a very real sense he was their focus in life as in music, and even Killer might be hard put to condemn him, even for murder.

I knew he would face what had to be faced. He gave us directions to his house, which turned out to be in one of those narrow, wooded canyons that are right in the middle of some of the most heavily populated areas around Hollywood and yet seem so countrified and so far from the bustle and crowds of the city. He lived deep in a grove of eucalyptus, in a beautiful structure of polished wood and stained glass and natural stone that seemed to incorporate the pillars of early afternoon sun filtered through tall resinous trees as part of its design.

"Not the sort of place I imagined for an elfrock star," said Shannon, parking her little Toyota at the edge of a drive lined with weedy geraniums in full bloom. "Though I guess really it is perfect for an elf, isn't it?" Moist air laden with forest and flower scents wafted through the open car windows. The worn stone stairs to the wide redwood porch that surrounded the house were lined with terra cotta pots filled with herbs: trailing mints, bushing rosemary, tall gray sage, soft Greek oregano tumbling over the edges of its pot, and others I didn't recognize.

"It suits Killer," I said.

She switched off the engine, still staring at the house. "My God," she said, "is that him?"

I glanced up. He was standing by the porch rail in a shaft of golden sun, a big dark bulk of a man with that tumble of glistening ebony curls concealing his face as always. He had on only a pair of worn and faded blue jeans, torn at the knees and riding low on his hips, no shirt, no shoes, and none of the baubles and bangles they all wore in public; no bracelets or necklaces, not even an ornate belt buckle or, as far as I could see, earrings or finger rings. Just Killer, half naked, primitive, and beautiful, like his house. "Yes," I said, surprised at the warm glow I felt at the sight of him. "That's Killer."

"Aptly named," she said, and I remembered abruptly how he had looked to me when we met: a mountain of muscle padded with baby fat, his broad face unreadable behind the mare's nest of black hair, the sort of halfling whose presence in a bar makes you decide to try the one down the street instead, unless you're in the mood for a fight.

"Not really," I said, grinning, and struggled impatiently with my seat belt.

Shannon silently unfastened it for me and returned her steady gaze to Killer. "You go first," she said firmly.

I was already half out of the car, waving my good arm in delighted greeting, then awkwardly lowering it again when my left arm in its sling wouldn't work well enough even to push the car door shut behind me. Having got it closed at last, I hurried between the car and the geraniums to the stairs and took them in a rush, only peripherally aware of Shannon following more sedately behind me. The mingled scents of mint and rosemary followed me as I brushed past their pots.

He didn't move till I paused on the top step next to him. He wasn't even drumming unconsciously on the rail before him. I stared up into the mass of hair that hid his face, suddenly uncertain. The corners of his mouth twitched as he turned toward me then, his shoulders glistening golden in the light. He tilted his head just enough to let one dark eye show. It was dancing with merriment, very like his mother's. For a moment I thought he was going to put his arm around me in that soothing big-brother way he had, unthinkingly affectionate; and I thought that if he did, somehow everything in the world would be all right.

Then he looked past me at Shannon as she came up the last few steps behind me. His hair swung down again to conceal everything but the unexpressive curve of his lips and the elegant pointed tips of his ears. Almost imperceptibly he braced himself, suddenly wary, like an animal at bay. With an odd surge of protective affection I thought, Why, he's shy! Aloud I said, "Killer, this is my partner, Shannon Arthur." He stuck out one massive hand to her for shaking. Her touch seemed to reassure him; he relaxed and mumbled a greeting, and then without a word he put his free arm around me in exactly the unthinkingly affectionate gesture I had imagined and guided us into the house.

24

His house was even more beautiful inside than out. The room we entered was huge and filled with light that streamed in through a dozen windows of clear and stained and prismed glass, splashing the floors and walls with radiance. There were deep area rugs in fascinating textures of natural fibers, afloat on broad expanses of hardwood floor polished to such brilliance it seemed to glow. The furniture was of rough-hewn wood and rich woven fabrics in subdued colors, the tabletops thick, shining, amber glass, the walls a soft gold, almost white, except where the prismed light painted them with rainbows.

In one corner under a huge plate-glass window through which he could watch a panoramic view of the valley while he played stood a complete drum kit, its metal bits gleaming in the sun. Beside it, sedate and stately and highly polished, a grand piano faced the window and the drums. An acoustic guitar had been leaned casually against the piano bench as though he had only just put it down when we arrived.

Once inside, Killer took his arm from my shoulder and stepped awkwardly away from me, looking at the room as though it were as unfamiliar to him as to us. An enormous black tomcat prowled in through the door behind us, found a patch of sun on a deep golden rug, and sprawled in it, blinking lazily up at us, his eyes brilliant topaz in the light. "That's Vicious," said Killer.

"What, the cat?" asked Shannon, eyeing it uneasily.

"Yeah." In this room his gentle voice seemed less at odds with his appearance than it had against the backdrop of groupie-littered hotel rooms. Surrounded by the warm honey-gold of sun on polished wood, he seemed not so much savage as primitive, all gold and brown himself like a fading sepia photograph, oddly diminished by the transience of history and hopes and happiness. "You like sit," he said in the three-note singsong of the islands that made it sound more like a statement than a question, and his lips twitched in the hint of a smile. "I mean, would you like to sit down?" He enunciated carefully, but there was still a hint of the islands in the cadence of the words.

"Thanks." Shannon chose a chair from which she could keep an eye on the cat.

Killer's lips twitched again. "It's only his name," he said. "He's a sweetheart, really." He scooped the cat up and it dangled bonelessly against his ribs, purring audibly. Its topaz eyes narrowed to slits of blissful satisfaction. "You want a beer or something?"

"No, thanks." I sat in a chair next to Shannon's, absently cradling my left elbow in my other hand. I had thought Killer's attention was wholly on the cat, but when I glanced up, I caught the gleam of dark eyes watching me from behind that veil of hair. Suddenly self-conscious, I released my protective grip on my injured arm and smiled nervously. "So tell me about the recording," I said. "How's it going?"

He poured the cat onto the floor and fell into a chair facing ours. "It's okay." When he leaned his head back, his hair parted just enough to show his nose and part of one eye as well as the tips of his ears. It should have looked silly, but it didn't. "It's Jorandel," he said abruptly.

"What is?" said Shannon.

"At the sessions," he said.

Confused, she said, "But Vyla said you never see him."

"Yeah." He looked at her through his hair, moving only his eyes. "He tapes stuff when we're *pau.* Finished for the night. He comes in and tapes his tracks and whatever he wants us to work on. Makes suggestions." His hands moved, unconsciously drumming on the arms of his chair. "And it's his music. Not Jimendan's."

"How can you tell?" she asked.

He looked at me helplessly. I told her, "You just can,"

and realized that wasn't very helpful. "It's like, I don't know, handwriting or something. If it's his, it's his." I looked at Killer. "Do the others know?"

"Dunno." He stood up suddenly and paced across the room, moving from sun to shadow to sun again, his back to us. At the nearest window he paused and stood with his face to the glass, but I had the feeling he wasn't seeing whatever was on the other side. "You think Jorie killed Jim." It was a statement, not a question, but I answered it anyway.

"I think he was planning it the whole time I was with Cold Iron." I told him why.

He nodded slowly, turning to face us. "Fits," he said. "But it could fit other ways, too. You could fit it around the Roach, or me, or anybody. One of the roadies, maybe. Or it could still be accidents and coincidences. You got no proof of anything."

"No, and I don't see how we'll get any. Which is why we were going to leave it alone, till this happened." I gestured with my injured arm.

Sudden stillness. "Ma said somebody knifed you." I could just see the glitter of his eyes behind the hair. "You think Jorandel ordered it?"

"I can't think who else," I said. "They left behind a bottle of soda. I figured the idea was, if they missed, maybe I'd use it to kill myself for them. Seems like it's quite a pattern for the people around Jorandel to OD"

He moved back to the chair and flopped into it, drumming the arms. "People around me, too," he said. "People around any of us."

"But Jorandel's the only one with a motive to go after me."

"Because you can tell them apart."

"Yeah." I hesitated. "Though it's not like him to be so damned stupid. I mean, he could've realized there was nothing I could do, so I'd stay out of it as long as he left me alone."

He nodded. "He's different. Jim's death—" He broke off, at a loss for words. "Changed him," he said finally, helplessly.

"If he'd try to kill Rosie because she could tell them

apart, what about you?" asked Shannon. "Aren't you in danger now, too?"

"Nah. He'd think I'd go along with it, you know? For the music. For—" He hesitated. "You know the song 'Brothers'?"

"Rosie showed me it," she said.

"For that," he said, relieved not to have to explain.

"Loyalty?" she said.

"Yeah." His voice was muffled; the subject clearly embarrassed him.

"To the music, to him, to what?" said Shannon. "My God, what kind of loyalty would make you ignore murder?"

"Brotherhood," I said, to rescue him. She glanced at me, started to say something more, and subsided. Killer drummed the arms of his chair. After a moment I said, "When did you realize he was Jorandel, not Jim? What gave him away? Just the music?"

"Little things," he said, thinking about it. "At first I just believed what they said, but—the music, the things he says, way he moves when we do see him, and—there's Frank, too, yeah?"

"What about Frank?" said Shannon.

"He don't treat him like he was Jim," said Killer.

"In what way?" she asked.

He turned his head toward her, tilting it so his hair fully concealed his face. "Hey, you know, him and Jorie, they're best friends, eh?" he said. His hands paused in their ceaseless drumming. "He was always good to Jim since Andy died, but, you know, he was just doin it for Jorie, mostly. How he treats him now—they're best friends."

"So Frank knows," said Shannon.

"Sure, he knows. How could he not know?" said Killer.

"Same way anybody else could not know, I guess," said Shannon. "I mean, I gather a number of people don't know. Including the other guys in the band."

"Oh, Blade and the Roach," he said. "Well. I dunno about the Roach, but Blade don't know nothin'. He's so stoned, he don't know who he is half the time."

"You think maybe the Roach knows?" I asked.

"Hard to tell," he said. "Don't s'pose he'd say."

"For that matter, you haven't said, have you?" said Shannon. "I mean, to them?"

"Nah." He stopped drumming again. "Well, hey. I thought he was just takin advantage, you know? Jim's dead, and Jorie needs outta Veladora's contract, so why not be Jim?" He shook his head slightly. "Cold, yeah? From our way of lookin. But Truebloods think differently. And what would Jim care, really? He's dead." He leaned back, his hands limp on the arms of the chair. "But I didn't know Jorie killed him."

"We don't know that now," Shannon said fairly.

"Seems pretty damn likely," I said.

"Ma said what you wanted to do," said Killer, "you wanta see him. I can take you to the studio tonight, but dunno Jorandel'll show up. Usually he don't. Plus, if he does, then what?"

"The whole thing's a wild-goose chase," Shannon said, suddenly weary. "We went off half cocked when Rosie got knifed, and came chasing down here after Jorandel even though we knew we didn't have a damn thing on him. Now that we're here there's really nothing useful we can do. So we figured we'd just stir things up and see what happened."

Killer said quite seriously, "In a nice British mystery, the murderer would confess and then politely take poison in the library."

Shannon was startled into a very inelegant guffaw. Killer grinned irrepressibly. It was a nice moment, but I couldn't forget it was Jorandel we were talking about. My own grin was probably a trifle forced. I had come chasing after a murderer in a fit of vengeful rage. But if I caught a murderer, it would be my own sweet boy-faced lover.

Of course he wasn't sweet, he wasn't my lover, and that boy face hid the mind of a psychotic monster. Somewhere in the past few days I had finally lost the last illusions I had clung to, and had stopped making excuses for him. But I had not lost the bond that tied me to him, invisibly and ineradicably, so that whatever I thought of him he was still a part of me, and whatever he did to me he did to a part of himself. It was no protection: if he killed his brother, he would not hesitate to kill me. It was only a burden, the last dark remnant of an attachment I could neither endure nor end, but only, desperately, defy.

Killer was watching me, and for once much of his face was visible, but I could not read his expression. His eyes were so dark they seemed almost black, swimming with shadows and yet translucent, glinting with light. He seemed about to impart some universal truth or perhaps some terrible news: but all he said, in his sweet and gentle voice, was, "You sure you don't want a beer?"

The trip to the studio that night was a silent one. We had gone back to Hilly's to regroup and collect a few essentials, like for instance a borrowed .38—"just in case," as Hilly put it. "It's untraceable," he said, "so if you're obligated to use it, just discard it prudently, and don't worry." I slipped it in my shoulder bag and hoped I wouldn't have to use it. It might have been more logical for Shannon to carry it, since she had two good arms, but she didn't much like guns and anyway it wouldn't fit in her purse. When she did carry a handgun it was always some useless little toy that wouldn't make her slender handbags bulge.

Hilly gave us dinner and tried to give us bodyguards to take along with us, but we talked him out of that. "Even if he does show up," I said, "it's not likely that he'll attack us himself, right in front of God and everybody. The whole point as far as he's concerned is to pretend he's not a murderer."

"But he is psychotic," said Hilly.

"If he throws a fit we can't handle any other way, we have your .38," I said. "We won't need more than that."

"I hope you're right," he said.

We met Killer at his house, since it was between Hilly's and the studio, and rode the rest of the way in his car. I expected a swift and noisy little sports car of some costly variety, but he drove a stately vintage Ford pickup, robin's-egg blue with gleaming chrome work and supple leather upholstery. The engine was clearly not of the same era as the body. It wasn't noisy, and it wasn't little, but it was swift. He maneuvered the freeways with native expertise. I'm usually uncomfortable being driven instead of driving, but with him at the wheel I experienced not a moment's unease. At least, not about the trip itself. But I was uneasy about its goal.

I suppose we all were. For Killer to spend the time in silence was perfectly expectable, but at no point did he do any absentminded drumming, on the steering wheel or on anything else, not even when we were stopped at traffic lights, and that was a sure sign of tension with him. And for Shannon to spend that length of time in total silence was nearly unprecedented. But she spoke only once, when we were about halfway there, and then only to ask him to turn on the radio.

He did it. They were playing Poison's "Something to Believe In" and I nearly asked him to turn it off again. I like Poison well enough, particularly the sexy front man and the knockout drumming, but parts of that song hit just too damn close to home. The lyrics were just what Jim might have written for Andy. And now Jim was dead as well.

I didn't have to say anything. That verse bothered Killer as well. He punched a button to change the station and got something by Distance that positively sparkled with joyous musical clarity. I don't think elfrock music was what Shannon had in mind when she asked for the radio, but she accepted it with good grace even when the Distance song was over and the station played some other groups that were, perhaps, more difficult for the uninitiated to appreciate. It was a magic metal station. Not everyone is comfortable with Trolls, Cereal Killer, Demondance, and the like. Most of them, in fact, were more raucously grim than I really liked, but at the time it seemed preferable to silence.

I hadn't asked Hilly what he'd done to get Jorandel to the studio, but whatever it was, it worked. When we pulled up outside the building Killer nodded toward a sleek little black sports car of the costly variety I'd expected him to own, and said, "that's Jorie's."

"He's here?" asked Shannon, startled.

"Looks like," said Killer.

"Well, that's what we wanted." I sounded a good deal more confident than I felt. Stirring hornets' nests had seemed a good idea in the abstract, but now it seemed a lot more like bearding the lion in its den. I've always wondered why the hell anyone would try to put a beard on a dangerous wild beast he could just as easily leave alone.

I knew him the moment I saw him. There was no confusion, no hesitation, not even a fractional second of doubt. He was dressed like Jim, he wore bangs, he had even gained weight or achieved an illusion of it to soften the knuckly image, but he was Jorandel. We came into the studio, I saw him in the recording room through the glass, and it was as though an electric current passed between us. He felt it, too. He was bent over a guitar, working out some swift fingering that sounded very like Jim's work and yet clearer, sweeter, more poignant. He couldn't have heard us come in, and he was turned away so not even the movement of our arrival should have caught his eye. But the shock that made me catch my breath at the sight of him brought his gaze up to meet mine. For one long, frozen instant the two of us were held like that, pinioned by whatever force it was that bound us beyond emotion, beyond need, beyond desire.

His mouth formed a word, maybe my name, but no sound came out. When he moved, it was as in a dream, slowly, almost woodenly, without taking his gaze from mine. He put the guitar down and crossed the room unsteadily, opened a door, and we were not ten feet from each other, with nothing between us but the past. He said expressionlessly, "cousin," as if acknowledging my existence. His gaze moved past me to Shannon, and I saw his appreciation of her appearance and, more than that, his automatic acceptance of her as his by right. The elfrock star's casual arrogance, unconscious and unquestioned. Had I foreseen it, I would have expected to be, if not jealous, at least annoyed. I was neither. I was bound to him, but I realized in that moment that although I cared very much about him, I did not, in any real sense, care for him. Not anymore.

It was very freeing. I said, "Jorandel," acknowledging him as coolly as he had acknowledged me, and his gaze returned to me, steady and level, but dazed by drugs. He was dressed as Jim had always dressed, in too much glitter and too many scarves, playing up the magic-metal elfrock-star image even when the only audience he expected to impress was his band. In that costume, and with tousled bangs cut a little long and unevenly, to look as though they were old and in need of a trim, he looked so like his brother that it no longer seemed surprising that he could fool nearly anyone, perhaps even the band.

His gaze traveled downward, to the sling that held my bandaged arm. "What happened to you?" he asked.

"I think you know," I said. His gaze met mine again, wide and innocent. For the first time I became aware of Blade and the Roach beyond him, staring at us through the glass, Blade dazed and smiling as always, and the Roach serious and intense. I wasn't sure they could hear us, but I hoped so. "You should have left it alone, Jorandel," I said. "If you had, I'd have left you alone."

He shook his head. "Cousin, I'm afraid I fail to take your meaning." And, as an afterthought, "And I am not Jorandel, I'm Jim." He smiled, that dauntingly sweet boy smile, angelic and beautiful. "I believed you could tell us apart."

"I can, Jorie." Someone moved behind Blade and the Roach, and I looked through the glass in sudden, unaccountable dread, but it was only Frank doing something with the equipment in the shadows. I nodded toward him. "You may have fooled the others," I said, "but not Frank. He knows who you are." Jorie shrugged, that angelic smile still pulling at his lips, but I hardly noticed: Frank had looked up when I spoke, his face a sudden mask of murderous fury. That established that they could hear us in there. But what had I said to enrage the usually placid Frank?

"You have no weapons against me," Jorandel was saying softly, his eyes dangerous. "It's you against us, cousin. We will deny it if you make these claims publicly. My band will stand by me."

I glanced through the glass again. Blade, the Roach, and Frank had come together, listening, watching, and I could see the determination in their faces. Even Blade, a little bewildered, a lot stoned, his vacuous smile as cheerful as always in that pale, saturnine face, looked braced for battle, though he clearly didn't understand what was at issue. "They'll stand by you for the masquerade," I said, "but for murder?" I stared at them through the glass. "Is murder okay with you guys? You go along with that?"

"What murder?" Jorandel sounded confused, but he looked sly and, oddly, frightened. Without waiting for me to respond, he said, "Killer, you brought these humans here. Remove them."

"No," said Killer, quite simply. We had moved apart when we entered, Killer going automatically nearer the recording room door than we did before he stopped, remembering our purpose, and threw himself into an available chair. He sat now with his feet on a packing crate, looking utterly relaxed. But he wasn't drumming. There was a coiled-steel tension in the way he sprawled, apparently careless, his hands clasped behind his head.

Jorandel changed his tactics at once and without hesitation, like a blind man encountering a brick wall and resolutely feeling his way around it. "You failed to introduce us, cousin," he said, producing a leering smile for Shannon. To her he said, with sweet, sly innocence, "Will you have us one at a time, honey, or all at once?"

"I wouldn't have you if my life depended on it, Jorandel," she said, just as sweetly.

"You keep calling me that," he said plaintively. "Jorandel's dead." Something dark and ugly shadowed his expression briefly and was gone. Sudden unexpected tears welled in his eyes and spilled, unheeded, down his cheeks. "I couldn't stop him." His voice was a thin, complaining wail, helpless and very young. "I couldn't hold him."

"Don't try that on me, Jorandel," I said, repelled. "Jim never tried your window trick."

"No," he said wonderingly, "he never did. I thought it would be a problem."

"Wasn't it?" I said.

White-faced, he shook his head, a small boy frightened by fortune. "No. All my concern was for nothing, in the end," he said, gazing at me with puzzled eyes. "I had spent so much time and effort on it. Planning the switch, I mean. It wasn't easy, but I had to do it, for the music."

"I know," I said gently. "I saw how hard it was for you." Behind him through the glass I could see Frank and the others watching, listening. Blade looked bewildered, the Roach grim, and Frank as placid as ever, all signs of anger gone now that Jorie had started talking. I prayed they would stay where they were, silent, separate, till he was finished.

"It was hard," said Jorandel. "I didn't like to hurt him." He paused and looked, frowning, around the room. "Where is he? He should be here."

It wasn't an act. He was more stoned than I'd guessed. He was looking for Jimendan. This was too awful, too pathetic, the monstrous psychotic elf diminished to a fool. I couldn't speak. I couldn't tell him. I could feel his pain, feel the blinding agony of his loss and his confusion, and I couldn't name it, couldn't force him to know what he'd done.

Shannon did it for me. "He went out the window, Jorandel," she said. "How did you get him to do that?"

"Oh," he said, and his knees wobbled. "Oh, yes." He put one hand out blindly for support, found the back of a chair, and lowered himself onto its arm. And quite suddenly he was in control again, slyly aware of the situation, watching, calculating, judging. "Cousin," he said, as if just noticing me. "Your arrival was a pleasant surprise. I wasn't expecting you. Jorie was upset when you left, you know. First urchin died; and then, just like that, you abandoned him. It was a lot to take. He was fond of both of you. I'm not sure that isn't why he—"

"Cut it out, Jorandel," I said. My tone was sharper than I meant it to be; he had shaken me.

That sly smile again. "Are you feeling guilty, cousin?"

"No." My tone was too sharp again. "Jorandel, damn it!"

His smile broadened. Jimendan's smile, sly and cruel. "Then why are you trying so hard to convince yourself I'm my poor, dead brother?"

"I know you're Jorandel." I didn't sound certain.

"Face it, cousin," he said, sliding easily out of his habit of slightly formal wording and into the crude street-speak Jimendan had sometimes affected. "Jorandel pulled the window trick one time too many. Maybe because you dumped him."

"I didn't dump him. He kicked me out." I heard what I'd said and swallowed hard. "Damn you."

"It doesn't matter which he is, Rosie," said Shannon. "Either way, he killed his brother."

He looked at her, his eyes huge and brilliant in his translucent face, the skin around them smudged with shadows like bruises. "I tried to save him," he protested.

"You were planning it the whole time I was with you," I said. "You got rid of Andy because he could tell you apart. And Candy for the same reason. And after you fell downstairs you had Jim beat up so his bruises would match yours. And when you got back to the mainland you tried to have me killed. That was stupid, Jorandel. I couldn't prove anything. I was ready to leave it alone."

He was staring at me oddly, his brief distress forgotten. "Is that what happened to you?" he asked. "Someone tried to kill you?" He glanced inadvertently over his shoulder through the glass.

I looked, too. Frank, Blade, and the Roach were still there, unmoving, just as they had been the last time I looked. I turned back to Jorandel, puzzled. "You know that," I said. "You sent them."

He shook his head. "No," he said. "Cousin, you know I could never do that. It would be like killing a part of myself."

"No harder than killing your brother, surely?"

He shrugged. "No," he said, his voice wryly amused. "But I couldn't do that, either."

"Come on, Jorandel. They left a bottle of soda for me. Are you telling me you didn't send that?"

"Soda?" he said, puzzled.

"Soda, Jorandel. Like what killed Candy."

"Damn it!" He surged to his feet, his face a mask of fury, and I thought he was going to attack me. But he turned toward the glass between us and the recording room, abruptly and absurdly impotent, shoulders hunched defensively, like a battered child. Again, I followed his gaze. Blade and the Roach were as they had been, but Frank had moved away from them. He had his back to the wall, his hands very casually in his jacket pockets. I am suspicious of hands in pockets. It was all I could do not to reach for Hilly's loaner .38, just in case.

"You need help, Jimmy?" Frank's voice was clear and cool through whatever speakers linked us to the recording room, and as casual as his relaxed pose against the wall. "Want me to get rid of them?"

"No," said Jorandel, shaking his head, subdued and polite again. "No, thanks, Frank."

Seeing him like this, broken and beaten and utterly defenseless, tore at my heart. "You really didn't know somebody came after me, did you?"

He looked at me, visibly gathering his resources. "I don't believe it now," he said. "I think you should leave, cousin. We have work to do here." His voice was brittle, and there was in his eyes that same look of fear that had been there when I first asked whether the others would stand by him even for murder. It was not fear of being found out, it was fear of finding out.

I stared through the glass at the others. Blade smiled vacuously out at me, his pale eyes puzzled. The Roach bent tensely to put down the guitar he held. Frank rested placidly against the wall, separate, patient, silent. And I finally realized the truth. "Oh, Jorandel," I said. "You didn't do it, did you?"

"What?" said Shannon. "Rosie, what—"

I ignored her. I had to get through to Jorandel while his defenses were down. "When did you start planning it?" I asked. "Did you think Andy's death was an accident? Is that what put the idea in your mind? But what about Candy? You didn't think that was a lucky accident, too, did you?"

His expression took on the look of a dull child clinging to the one thing he understood. "I liked Candy," he said stubbornly.

"I know you did," I said. "You gave her a pair of very expensive earrings. You must have liked her a lot."

"I did," he said simply.

"But like a sister, is that it? You loved her, but you weren't in love with her?"

"Yeah, I guess," he said, losing interest.

"Her death wasn't an accident," I said. "Any more

than Andy's was. Or Jimendan's. They were all killed, Jorie. For you. To get you out of Veladora's contract."

"Fuck off," he said.

"I won't, Jorie. You have to face this. You planned Jim's death, because you wanted out of that contract so badly, but when it came right down to it you just couldn't do it, could you?"

"No," he said. "I didn't do it. I didn't kill him. I was thinking, how will I get him in a window? And when I saw him in the window—Mab's grace, I could not kill my brother." He had sat down again, properly in the chair this time instead of on its arm, and now he hugged himself and rocked back and forth like a disturbed child, his eyes tormented. "I tried to stop him," he said, his voice very small and frail.

"I know you did," I said. "What made him go in the window, Jorie?"

"He was stoned," he said. "Never had I seen him so stoned before. And what he said—Oh, Earth defend me—he said he did it to be more like me." He looked up at me, his eyes wide and frightened. "You know how he *would* try to look like me, and sound like me, and be like me."

"I know," I said gently. "I heard Frank coaching him, once." I smiled faintly at the memory. "He was trying to learn to say 'fuck off' just the way you do."

Jorandel smiled, too, but only with his lips. His eyes were clouded with pain. "Yes," he said. "Just so."

"You got your drugs from Frank, didn't you?" I said.

He looked up, startled. "Cousin, what can that matter now?"

"He got drugs for all of you, didn't he?"

Jorandel shrugged.

"The drugs that killed Andy? The drugs you OD'd on? The soda that killed Candy?"

He closed his eyes. "Fuck off," he said.

"The drugs that put Jim in the window, maybe?"

He jerked as though I had struck him, but all he said was, "Fuck off."

"That's enough," said Frank. His voice startled me. I glanced up, but he wasn't where I looked for him, against the wall in the recording room. He was at the door, pulling it open, coming to us. "Get out," he told me, and knelt at Jorandel's side. "It's okay," he said gently. "It's okay."

"It's not okay," I said. "He'll put up with a lot from you. Especially to get out of that contract. He might even accept Andy's murder, and Candy's. But not Jimendan's, Frank. You went too far when you killed Jorie's brother."

25

Jorandel tried not to believe it, even then. He shook his head in adamant denial and said, "No," but his voice broke and his eyes were terrible.

"Jorie," said Frank. "Jorie, it's a lie. You know it's a lie. You were there. You saw." They had both forgotten us. They were alone in the room, best friends crouched together in the dark and lonely confines of betrayal.

"I nearly saved him," Jorandel said slowly, reluctantly. "With your smallest aid I *could* have saved him. But you hindered me."

"I was trying to help," Frank said desperately. "Jorie, please—"

"Fuck off." Jorandel's voice was soft, expressionless.

Killer had straightened, taking his hands from behind his head and putting his feet on the floor, but he made no other move. In the recording room the Roach, grim-faced and intent, headed for the door between us; and Blade, clearly bewildered, followed. Behind me Shannon put a steadying hand on my arm.

"Jorandel, I was trying to help," Frank repeated.

"Fuck off." His voice was still flat, indifferent, but his eyes, gazing steadily at the floor between them, were cold.

"You needed out of the contract," said Frank. "Listen, Andy's death was an accident. Honest to God, Jorandel. But I saw you planning, after that. Jim's accident, the injuries to match yours—I was proud of you for that, Jorandel."

"Fuck off."

Frank might not have heard him. "But I knew you couldn't go through with it. When I saw how much it hurt you to hurt him, I knew you couldn't do it."

Jorandel lifted his eyes, bruised and lifeless, to meet Frank's pleading gaze. "The soda you gave me for Candy," he said, prompting.

"I had to kill her, Jorie," he said anxiously. "You know she wouldn't've gone along with it. She wasn't one of us. She couldn't be trusted."

Jorandel nodded heavily. "Rosie could not be trusted, either," he said.

"Of course not," said Frank, encouraged. "It wasn't safe to leave her alive."

Jorandel lifted his white, set face to Frank. "And Jimendan?" he said. "What did you do to my brother?" The Roach was at the door, pulling it open, but neither of them noticed him.

Frank seemed to feel he was convincing Jorandel of the necessity of what he'd done. "I gave him a little stardust," he said. "A little prompting. He always wanted to be more like you, Jorie. And you were always going for a window. He watched you often enough. I only suggested it, Jorie. I didn't have to *do* anything."

The Roach let Blade through the door and closed it softly behind them. They were within a few paces of Frank and Jorandel, and they stayed there, watching. Even Blade seemed to understand, at last, what was being said. His perpetual smile had faded, and his eyes were shocked.

"You did something when I tried to stop him," said Jorandel, his voice as lifeless as his eyes. "You pushed."

"Don't you see, Jorie?" said Frank, pleading. "It was the only way out of that Faerie-damned contract. You said it a million times: the only way out of it was to die. But it wouldn't work if you died, so he had to. You see that, Jorie, don't you? I couldn't let you stop him. I knew you didn't really want to, that you'd be grateful to me when it was all over. You knew he had to die."

Killer and the Roach knew Jorandel very well indeed. Better, it seemed, than Frank did. They both moved at once, but Jorandel was a Trueblood elf pushed past endurance. He was faster. He had Frank up against the wall in a stranglehold before anyone could stop him. "You son of a human," he said. His voice still soft and expressionless, but it takes very little expression in a

Trueblood's voice to make "human" a truly vile imprecation. "You Sword-forsaken—"

"Jorandel," said Killer.

"Fuck off," said Jorandel. He banged Frank's head viciously against the wall. "You killed my brother." He cursed again, still in that flat and lifeless voice that was somehow so much more frightening than open rage would have been. "When I would have saved him, you hindered me."

"Jorie, I had to." Frank's voice was hoarse, straining against Jorandel's savage grip on his throat. But although he was easily half again Jorandel's size and probably could have swatted him away with one casual blow, he made no real effort to free himself. "You know I had to," he said almost patiently. "It was the only way out of the contract."

"Fuck the contract." Jorandel slammed his head against the wall again. "Fuck you. Fuck everything. Oh, Mab's grace, how has my music led us so astray?" He let go of Frank abruptly and turned away, his face a taut white mask of agony. Killer took one step toward him and paused, clearly at a loss.

Frank put his hands in his pockets, feigning easy relaxation, even managing a frayed smile. "Jorie," he said cautiously.

"You were my friend," said Jorandel. There was no anger in his voice or in his face, only shock and wonder.

"Jorie, that's why I did it."

Nobody saw it coming. Nobody moved but Jorandel, and he moved so swiftly and so suddenly that he had Frank down before Frank knew what hit him. Elves are too capricious to be easily overwhelmed by strong emotion; but once aroused, even a Trueblood whose only magic is in his music can be a formidable foe. Despite their comparative sizes, Frank was helpless against Jorandel. He couldn't land a blow. Jorandel was too swift, too savage, too feral in his fury to be dealt with by ordinary means.

Frank would, if forced, resort to extraordinary means. And Jorandel was forcing him. It must have been like fighting a wild animal. There was no way Frank could stop him, short of killing him. Hilly's .38 was useless for this, and so was an arm in a sling. Without really thinking what I was doing, I dropped my shoulder bag and pulled the restrictive sling off my arm before I dived into the fray to try to extricate Jorandel before Frank thought to use the handgun I was almost certain he had in one of his pockets. I've done dumber things, but not by much. If Frank couldn't handle him, I've no idea why I thought I could.

I don't know whether Killer was trying to save Jorandel or me. Maybe both of us. He landed next to me, on top of Jorandel, and we both tried to tug him off Frank. But he had his thumbs dug into Frank's eyes and he wasn't letting go. He didn't even seem to notice us.

I don't suppose I was much help, really. But Killer was big enough and strong enough that, given a moment, he could have got Jorandel up. Only he wasn't given a moment. Frank had remembered the gun in his pocket. With Jorandel's thumbs digging into his eyes, he didn't even take time to pull it out of his pocket. He just fired.

Jorandel crumpled. So did Killer. At that range, one bullet had gone right through Jorandel to hit Killer as well. I was left clinging in helpless shock to the two of them while Frank hauled himself up to sit against the wall, rubbing his eyes with the backs of his hands, in one of which he still held the automatic he'd shot them with.

"Drop it, Frank," said Shannon. She had got Hilly's .38 out of my forgotten shoulder bag and leveled it at him, her arms braced on the back of a chair.

It was the best she could do in the circumstance. If she hadn't tried to get the drop on him, he might just have shot us all. But it wasn't good enough. He froze for a fraction of a second, opened one eye to study her, said, "Okay, don't shoot," in a startled voice, and then in as swift and practiced a gesture as any movie villain that ever lived, he leveled his weapon straight at my face. "Standoff," he said, smiling with satisfaction. "This thing has a very light pull. You can kill me, but your partner will die with me."

She glanced at me helplessly, uncertain. "Do what you have to," I said, not really caring at that moment what choice she made. Killer had landed with his head in my lap. His hair had fallen back to expose his pale, still face. I couldn't tell whether he was breathing. Forgetting Frank, I put a hand on his chest and my own heart lifted at the feel of the slow, steady beat of his.

I didn't have to touch Jorandel to know that somehow, somehow, he was still alive. He lay curled on his stomach with one arm outflung, his face turned away from me, hidden from me beneath the wild tangle of his hair. That light inside me that was his life was flickering, dimming, but incredibly it had not yet gone out.

"Put the gun on the floor and slide it over here," said Frank, "and nobody'll get hurt."

"People are already hurt," said Shannon.

"The gun," he said.

She stared for one long second at that automatic leveled at my face, and I wished with sudden and vicious recklessness that she would shoot him and have done with it. But I really knew just as well as she did that she couldn't take that sort of chance with my life. It was the only sensible thing to do: once she surrendered the .38, there would be nothing to stop him from killing us all. But she couldn't do it. She lowered the .38, hesitated, then bent to put it on the floor, straightened again, and gently kicked it across the room toward him.

It ended within inches of Jorandel's outflung fingers. I wondered briefly whether that was intentional, but probably not. She must have thought he was dead. And anyway, that frail spark of life he clung to just wasn't enough. To make use of the .38, he would have to be conscious, aware, and have the strength to act. That was too much to hope for.

"Okay," said Frank. "Okay." He kept the automatic leveled at me, considering his options. If he'd had any sense he'd have shot me straightaway, the moment the .38 left Shannon's hands. His one small hope of getting away with this was to kill us all. But I guess he hadn't figured it out yet. He gestured at Shannon. "Get over there with the guys," he said, glancing toward Blade and the Roach. I had forgotten about them. They were still standing in the doorway, Blade looking the soberest I'd ever seen him, and the Roach as taut as strung wire.

"Frank," said Blade.

"Shut up," said Frank. To Shannon he added impatiently, "Move." And, turning back to me, he gestured again. "You, too. Get over there." He hauled himself awkwardly to his feet without reaching for the .38. "Move."

I lowered Killer's head gently to the floor, using only my right arm; the left wouldn't work. During the struggle with Jorandel I had apparently torn the stitches and blood seeped through the bandages, dripping down my fingers. Oddly, it didn't hurt much, but I made a fuss over it anyway, playing for time. Not that time would do us much good. If I did what Frank told me, I couldn't think of any reason he wouldn't kill us all. If I tackled him, he would certainly kill me, but would it give the others a chance?

Not unless they moved faster than they were likely to. Besides, I just hadn't that kind of fatal courage. I wrestled my arm back into its sling, clambered unsteadily to my feet, and went where he told me. I had often wondered why people lined up so willingly for mass murderers to kill them. Now I understood. The one who resists might save the others, but that's a big maybe. It would be hard enough to throw away your life on a certainty. I couldn't do it on a chance. I kept thinking that as long as I was alive, there was a chance I'd stay alive. That must be what victims always think.

It's faulty reasoning. I should have tackled the son of a bitch. By the time I'd joined the rest of the group, he'd made up his mind. I hadn't even fully turned to face him again when he fired the first shot and Blade went down.

"God *damn* it!" I whirled to face him, and so caught his second shot in the arm instead of the heart. It felt like a baseball bat. I fell back against the Roach, who automatically caught me and held me up. I thought afterward that I must have seemed a very convenient shield, but perhaps I wronged him. Maybe he really meant to help me. Maybe somewhere under that amoral, arrogant exterior there lurked some remnant of Trueblood honor. Anything's possible.

The third shot came so close on the heels of the one that hit me, I barely perceived it as a separate event. Somehow I got my feet under me and turned to Shannon, because I knew it hadn't hit me or the Roach. It hadn't hit her, either. I turned drunkenly back to Frank. He was leaning against the wall, the automatic dangling loosely from numb fingers as his knees slowly buckled and he slid to the floor. The room reeled and I clutched at the Roach's arm to steady myself. Frank had left a trail of blood on the wall behind him. The third shot had somehow, ridiculously, hit not one of us, but him.

And then I saw Jorandel. He held Hilly's .38, forgotten, in one hand. The third shot had come from that, not from Frank's weapon. But he had not fired in anger. It had been the only way to stop Frank and save the rest of us, so he had done it. But not willingly. Whatever bond existed between Jorandel and me, the one between him and Frank was infinitely deeper, stronger, unalterable even in this extremity. Past actions were irrelevant. Since Jim died, Frank had been the only friend Jorandel really had, the only person he could trust and talk to, the only one with whom he could safely lower his guard and be himself.

And Jorandel had been Frank's whole life, his justification for existence. In a very real sense, in shooting each other they had shot themselves. They stared at each other like frightened children, dazed and bewildered. Jorandel sighed; a long, wavering breath fraught with determination and despair. Then he lurched awkwardly onto his hands and knees to crawl toward Frank with agonizing deliberation, puppet-stiff, his feline grace reduced to fumbling resolution. His face was translucent white, so pale it seemed to shimmer from behind the veil of tangled hair that fell over it as he dragged himself, bleeding and broken, across the floor.

He remembered the .38 and hurled it aside, but the gesture was feeble and it cost him his precarious balance. The arm that supported him slipped and he just caught himself before his face hit the floor. He couldn't keep himself from falling sideways, but he kept his head up and he never took his gaze from Frank.

Frowning in concentration, Frank lifted one slack and wavering hand to reach for him. Jorandel hauled himself forward on his elbows, legs dragging, grunting with effort, and not one of us made any move to help or to stop him. It must not have taken as long as it seems in memory, but that awful tableau held us frozen till Jorandel's strength gave out and he collapsed, just out of reach of Frank's extended arm.

Frank tried to move, to cover that last distance between them, but he lost his balance and his strength, too, gave out. He fell forward, one arm outstretched. Their hands just touched, but neither elf nor human knew it.

It seemed to me that all the light went out of the universe when Jorandel died. There was a sudden, aching emptiness within me that howled of darkness where there had been stars. His death was a door closed on wonder. Those summer-sky eyes would never smile again. That voice, so pure and clear and compelling, would never lift again in song. The music was gone, dead with him, the ghost of it trapped immutable on audio recordings but the life and the light gone out of it forever.

The thing that had bound us was nothing more or less than a sparkling lilt of melody, stilled as his voice was stilled. After all the wild chances he had taken, the calculated risks and the half-curious, half-fearful glances at death, he had found it in the most ordinary of places, through friendship and misguided trust and unintentional betrayal. Now whatever he sought, whatever he found, was beyond a boundary I could not cross. It didn't even hurt as much as I had thought it would. It was only agony, bewildering and blind.

Shannon knelt beside Blade, and I wanted to go to Killer; but in that lowering and star-shot darkness I could not seem to find my way. I felt the Roach's arms tighten about me and I wanted to tell him to let me go; but when I opened my mouth, all that came out was a weak and windy whimper like the mewling cry of some small and damaged animal; and then the darkness drew me in.

26

"Oh, Ma," said Killer, his voice impatient and embarrassed, stretching "Ma" to three syllables at least.

"Don't you 'oh, Ma' me, young man," Vyla said fiercely. "You sit right back down and tell me what you want so that I can get it for you."

"Ma," he said patiently. "I gotta go pee, okay?"

"Oh," she said, mollified. "I guess I can't do that for you."

"No," he said, grinning. His progress toward the bathroom was slow and careful, and he used the backs of chairs and whatever else was handy for support on the way, but he made it safely out of the room on his own. Vicious paced sedately behind him, his tail forming a sleek black question mark in the air.

When they were out of sight Vyla turned to me, her dark almond eyes full of laughter. "I guess maybe I'm a little overprotective," she said.

"Maybe a little." I smiled lazily at her over my homemade, alcohol-free eggnog. "But I think he likes it."

She gave a little choking gurgle of laughter. "Well, if he doesn't, he's stuck with it anyway." She held up a glittering blown-glass star. "Where do you think this one should go?"

There was an enormous Christmas tree in the corner beside the piano, where the drum kit had been. Vyla had put the drums in storage. "You can't use them now, anyway," she had told Killer yesterday when we brought him home from the hospital. "And that's the best corner for the Christmas tree."

"What Christmas tree?" he'd demanded. "I don't have a Christmas tree."

"Tomorrow is Christmas Eve," she'd said severely,

"And you will have a Christmas tree. Your father's bringing it when he comes to pick me up tonight."

His father, an elf-heavy halfling who ought by rights to have been awkward and sneeringly out of place in Christmas festivities, but wasn't, duly arrived lugging a tree it would have taken two or three human men to carry. We had already met in the hospital, so I wasn't as surprised as I might have been by either his smiles or his silence. He spoke even less frequently than Killer did, but he was as comfortable to be with as Vyla was.

With a minimum of fuss and a maximum of efficiency, he had set up the tree in a red-and-green metal stand a good four times the size of the one Shannon had produced for my tree, watered it, surveyed the result, and with one unobtrusive gesture and a whispered word lent it a magical glamor that made it, lopsided and twin-tipped as it was, the most beautiful Christmas tree I could imagine. Then he smiled almost shyly and said with unexpected deference, "Humans do the same thing better, but it takes them longer."

I said inadequately, "It's wonderful."

He nodded. "As I understand it," he said, "that is their purpose." It was more words at one time than I had previously heard from him, and I wasn't surprised at his prompt escape afterward for home.

Today when Vyla came over she had brought the box of decorations about which she was now happily demanding my advice. From no Christmas trees most years, I'd gone to being intimately involved with three Christmas trees this year—one in the office, one in my home, and now one in Killer's home—and I was actually beginning to enjoy them. "That branch right there, where it'll catch the sun," I said, pointing.

She hung the star from the branch and stood back to admire it. "Is this really all right with you?" she asked.

"Yeah, why, doesn't it look good from there?"

She looked confused for a moment and then emitted another giggle of laughter. "No, I don't mean the star, I mean the whole tree. And Christmas Eve, and the presents, and everything." She looked at me. "You're kind of stuck here till Shannon can come back for you." Shannon had gone home days ago, when she knew I was all right, to spend Christmas with her boyfriend. I had not wanted to go till I knew Killer was going to be all right, too. "And I know you still have a little trouble with Christmas," said Vyla.

"Less every minute," I said, watching Killer come back into the room. "Don't worry, it's good for me. Regard it as therapy." He paused just inside the doorway, leaning heavily on the back of a chair, and looked at us. "You okay?" I said.

"Don't you start," he said, releasing the chair and moving toward the next available handhold. "I'm okay."

"You need some more eggnog, honey?" said Vyla.

"Jeez," said Killer. "Yeah, okay, Ma. Make some popcorn while you're at it, why doncha. Keep you off the streets."

"Okay, but then you have to help Rosie decide where to put the Christmas decorations."

"In the box would be good," he said.

"Killer," she said repressively.

"Okay, okay," he said.

"Sit down," she said. "Rosie can unpack them and hold them up, and the two of you can decide where they go."

"Ma, I'll sit down when I get to my chair, okay? Go away," he said.

"Okay," she said, grinning.

I looked at the box of Christmas decorations. "You don't have to do that," he said.

"I'm beginning to like it." I went to the box and sat on the floor beside it. "But I'll be slow unwrapping them, one-handed." Frank's bullet had hit the arm that was already injured, so I wasn't totally disabled, but with two injuries that arm really was useless.

"I'll help you." He lowered himself carefully to the floor beside me, shifted, and reached in his back pocket. "I forgot," he said. "I've been sitting on your present." He grinned and held out an audio CD. "Pa brought it over yesterday."

It was a Cold Iron album. The cover was a photo of Jorandel and Jimendan in twin mode so effective I couldn't tell which was which. The title was *Posthumous*.

"This is the album you were working on? When—when everything happened?"

"Yeah. We had enough tracks to print. Not what Jorandel woulda wanted, 'cause he wasn't satisfied with a lot of them. But hey, it's out in time for Christmas." He tried to produce a smile, but it didn't really work.

I put it down and looked away, out the window. The eucalyptus outside dripped with rain. "How is that possible? I mean, how could it be produced so fast?"

He shrugged. "Veladora." Vicious stalked into the room and stood looking at us, tail waving. "It's his, you know," he said, holding out a hand to the cat. "He wanted it out while the scandal's fresh." Vicious tiptoed suspiciously around a threatening rug on his way to touch his nose delicately to Killer's fingers.

"What do you mean, it's his?"

"It was Jorandel, not Jimendan, on that album. And Veladora owned Jorie." Killer withdrew his hand, and Vicious followed it into his lap with a proprietary air and a brisk flick of his tail.

"So he didn't really get out of his contract, after all." I picked up the CD again and looked at it. "Poor Jorandel. He'd hate that."

"Yeah. Good thing he don't know." He thought about it, absently rubbing Vicious under the chin. "It's good for the Roach and me, I guess. Getting it out early will help sales. And he has to honor our contracts with Jorandel."

"What will you do now?"

"Dunno. Nothin, till I'm fit to play again." He put his free hand over his bandaged side in an unthinkingly protective gesture. "After that, I guess find another band, maybe. Or do session work for a while. I'm awful tired of touring." He looked at the CD in my hands. "You wanta hear that?"

"Dunno." I looked at him. "Is it any good?"

"Some of it." He lifted his head to look at me through his hair. "What you gonna do now?"

"Same thing I've always done," I said, surprised. "Nothing's changed, for me."

He looked at Vicious. "Seems like a lot's changed."

"Nothing as major as losing everybody in your band

except the Roach. I've still got my partner, my job, everything I had before."

"Except Jorandel."

"I never had Jorandel." I thought about it, looking at the CD I'd put on the floor beside me. "I didn't really even want Jorandel. There's no room in my life for an elfrock star. Besides, I told you once I'm not attracted to psychos."

"You were attracted to him," he said stubbornly.

It was a question, even though it didn't end with a question mark. It was a question I didn't want to answer. I suppose that's why I tried. "Yes, I was attracted to him," I said. "And repelled by him. I loved him. And I hated myself for it. You asked once if he'd hurt me, and I said not yet. I knew he would. But he also helped me begin to heal a hurt so old and so deep I couldn't have lived with it much longer and stayed sane." I had been sitting with one knee drawn up against my chest. Sighing, I put my chin on it, staring at the floor. "I don't know how to say what I felt about him. I don't know if I *know* how I felt about him."

I looked up, but he just looked back at me, waiting. All I could do was struggle with more words. "When he died, a light went out, like the sun going down. It left an empty place. No pain after the first shock. No nothing. Just me, stumbling around alone in the dark, you know? And then I saw that I wasn't alone, and I began to realize it wasn't the dark that blinded me, it was the light I'd been standing in. Like stepping out of sunlight into a shaded room, and when your eyes adjust you can see just fine. Better, maybe, because the sunlight washed out all the colors."

I picked up the CD jewel box and looked at it, studying the twinned elves with their sultry blue eyes. "I'm not glad he died," I said. "In fact, in an odd way I miss him, and I'll certainly miss his music. But I'm damned glad I'm free of him." Epitaph for a sociopath.

"Popcorn," said Vyla, entering the room with a laden tray. "And fresh eggnog. Killer, you shouldn't be sitting on the floor. And look, you haven't put up a single decoration. What have you been doing all this time?" Her teasing smile said pretty clearly what her guess was.

"Ma," Killer said repressively.

"Yes, dear?"

He changed his tactics. "I don't want eggnog," he said. "I want a beer."

"Oh, honey, do you really think you should?"

"Ma."

"Okay, okay, I'll get you a beer," she said.

We all had beer, and much tree decorating, and later much planning of tomorrow's activities. Vyla had vetoed Killer's idea that we should go to her house for a traditional Christmas dinner. She didn't want him traveling so far, so soon after getting out of the hospital. Instead, she would bring the traditional Christmas dinner to us. I was included as comfortably as though I had always belonged with them. Decisions had to be made about cooking and gift opening and a myriad of details I would never have imagined much less considered. By the time she left, she had half a dozen lists of things to do, things to bring, last-minute purchases to make, and even a list or two of lists to keep them organized.

I had talked her into taking me shopping the day before, so I was ready with hastily purchased gifts for each of them. She had talked me into playing Santa Claus, and smuggled bundles of packages and stocking stuffers into Killer's house for me to put under the tree tonight after he'd gone to bed. We hung the stockings on the grand piano for lack of a fireplace, tucking their pin loops, stretched over clothespins to keep them from slipping, under the lid and closing it firmly over them. It was all very festive and silly, and I found myself looking forward to stuffing oranges in stocking toes and spreading Vyla's beautifully wrapped "Santa" packages under the tree for Killer.

But when I crept out in the dead of night with my injured arm precariously balancing the bags of fruit and nuts and candy and gift-wrapped boxes that loaded down my good arm, I found he had been there before me. There were matching envelopes sticking out of the tops of our stockings.

I thought I should ignore them. He had to have known I would see them, but maybe he expected me to pretend I didn't until tomorrow, since tonight I was supposed to be Santa Claus. I put down my load and distributed the packages under the tree, startled to see that several were addressed to me. I had expected a duty package or two from Killer's parents, with impersonal all-purpose female gifts like scented soap and colorful scarves, but I hadn't expected "Santa" to bring me anything.

I was as absurdly thrilled as a child. I shook them and eyed their size and weighed them and finally, reluctantly, arranged them under the tree with Killer's, to wait for morning. Gathering the fruit and nuts and candy and the tiny packages that went with them, I carried it all to the piano and sorted things into piles for stuffing into stockings. The top two lines of the note on the envelope in mine was in Killer's childish scrawl. They said, "Rosie, Since I won't be here to . . ."

I turned resolutely to his stocking, aware of an unexpected sense of desolation. So he was going somewhere. Big deal, so was I: day after tomorrow I'd be going home. There'd never been any question of anything else. I tried to put an orange in the bottom of his stocking, but there was no way I could do it without first removing the envelope in the top. It was an airline ticket. I swallowed a lump in my throat and put the ticket aside. But my pleasure in the task was gone.

I'd been thinking of him as a big brother, a safe and undemanding friend, a brief certainty in a world full of enduring uncertainties. After Shannon came to take me home, I would almost certainly never see him again, and it hadn't occurred to me to question that. I was independent, self-reliant, content with my own company, and I had just escaped a very unhealthy relationship by the skin of my teeth. I wasn't looking for another, no matter how much healthier it might be. So why did I care where he went, or when, or even with whom if it came to that? What could it possibly matter?

I had to take the envelope out of my stocking to put in the stuffers. He must have known I would have to. Was I really supposed to avert my eyes from that note and not read it till morning?

I am amused to admit that I tried. I put it aside unread and mechanically filled my stocking with the things I'd piled up to put in it. But when I picked up the envelope to put it back in, I didn't avert my eyes.

"Rosie, Since I won't be here to keep an eye on you while your arm heals, and since you can't work anyway at least till it's out of the sling, and since worry about you will almost certainly delay my own healing, will you please take pity on a poor crippled halfling and come keep him company at Maunalani for a while?" The envelope contained a round-trip airline ticket to Hawaii.

I thought irrelevantly how much better his written English was than his spoken English, and I wondered exactly what he was offering or asking, and I wished I had thought to bring some Kleenex with me. But how could I have known I would need it? I could hardly have expected to cry over Christmas stockings.

He cleared his throat to let me know he was there. I blinked several times and swallowed hard before I turned around to face him. He was standing in the doorway, one hand on the frame for support, and his hair was tucked behind his pointy ears so that, even in the dim and colorful light cast by the Christmas tree, which was all I'd turned on, I could see all of his face at once. It was broad and beautiful and very worried.

For a long moment neither of us spoke. He looked at the envelope in my hands, lifted his gaze to my face, and the worry lines deepened between his brows. "I didn't mean to make you cry," he said.

"I'm not crying," I said. I gestured helplessly with the airline ticket. "It's just that . . . I don't know," I said desperately. "I don't know what you want. I don't know what I want. I don't *know*!"

He was at my side in an instant, his arms around me, and a kiss pressed comfortingly against the top of my head. "Hey," he said. "Hey."

"If you're asking," I said, and swallowed hard, and tried again. "There's no room in my life for an elfrock star."

He chuckled. "I ain't an elfrock star. I'm just a drummer without a band."

"But you'll be an elfrock star again," I said. "And besides, I'm not sure there's room for anybody in my life. Oh, Killer, damn it, I'm confused."

"I know," he said. "Slow down. You don't have to decide the rest of your life tonight. You don't even have to decide whether to go to Maunalani. Hey." He pulled away just enough to look down at my face. "We're friends, yeah?"

"Yeah," I said cautiously.

"Okay," he said. "Hey. That's a good start. We could be friends for the rest of our lives, yeah?"

"Yeah, if we work at it," I said.

"Then let's work at it," he said, his dark eyes sparkling with laughter and affection. "And then we'll have the rest of our lives to decide whether we wanta be more than friends. So you won't have to decide the whole thing tonight."

"Oh," I said gratefully. "Do you have to be so damn sensible?"